SANDBOX WARS

APACHE SNOW SERIES
BOOK THREE

WILLIAM L. CASSELMAN

ALASKA DREAMS PUBLISHING

SANDBOX WARS
Book Three of The Apache Series
©2022 By William Casselman

Production Design and Cover Art ©2022 by Alaska Dreams Publishing

Published by Alaska Dreams Publishing
www.alaskadp.com
1st Paperback Print Edition October 2022
PAPERBACK PRINT ISBN: 978-1-956303-16-2
1st Hardcover Print Edition October 2022
HARDCOVER PRINT ISBN: 978-1-956303-17-9
E-Book version available.
Visit http://www.alaskadp.com for links.

DEDICATION

To my understanding wife, and all my children and grandchildren. To my sons who have served in Iraq or Afghanistan. They all came home alive, for which Mona and I praise our Lord Jesus Christ.
To our men and women in uniform who have served in these Sandbox Wars.
To my three buddies I served with in Vietnam: Mike Kimbrel, Frank P. Demario, and Chuck Dudley.
To our fallen troops and all those who have served in our Armed Forces. America should be very proud of its servicemen and women. With a special honor to those who came home in flag-draped coffins. They are all heroes.

CONTENTS

AUTHOR'S NOTE

Military operations come under classifications from General to Classified, then Secret, and upgraded to Top Secret, which could be followed by another word or words behind it, such as, "Top Secret Omega" or other designation for a particular operation.

As I am not authorized to use the titles of real-life operations, the names I have created are fictitious military operations. 'Security Option C-1' carries a fictional Top-Secret rating with an added C classification.

PROLOGUE

SERGEANT AUDIE MURPHY, on his third combat tour in Afghanistan, is often kidded about his father naming him after the famous movie star and Medal of Honor recipient. He leads a patrol of eleven men, all members of the California Army National Guard. Initially, Murphy joined the Guard to assist with statewide emergencies. Since then, he's received two Purple Hearts for wounds from previous tours to Afghanistan and three Army Commendation Medals for gallant actions.

A Christian since age 14, Murphy prays he completes this tour without another wound and that all his men return alive. During eleven patrols in the last 40 days, they had not engaged the Taliban or other insurgents. However, Sgt. Murphy feels a bit nervous and double-checks his squad's equipment and weapons before departure. Their assignment is a foot patrol through a small nameless village located just outside the City of Kabul approximately 12 miles from Bagram Air Force Base, a joint military command used by the Air Force, Army, Marines, and the Afghan military.

Late in the evening, Murphy's squad is dropped off to begin the patrol. Their transportation will return for them in three hours. Getting his men into line formation, they step out and enter the hamlet. The area is quiet, with very few lights on. Murphy knows these people are primarily peddlers and goat herders. Mornings come early, and there is little nightlife in such villages. The platoon commander had advised Murphy, "This is *simply* a security patrol to let the villagers know that Uncle Sam is concerned with their welfare."

After passing through the village, the squad splits into two smaller groups to check goat pens and several small barns on the way to the pick-up point. The latest intelligence has reported Taliban activity east of the village, but Command believes insurgents are attempting to recruit new members from among these villagers. They are halfway through the village and so far, the streets and alleys are quiet.

Murphy feels the most challenging part about going into populated areas is not knowing who the enemy is. The Taliban wear no uniform. Unless a man is carrying an AK-47 or flashing a long sword, he could easily be posing as a peddler or a goat herder. Murphy notices that his recently assigned Afghan interpreter has suddenly disappeared. He turns to his corporal, "Where's our Terp?"

The corporal glances about for the man. "He was just with us—"

"I don't like this; it's too damn quiet." Murphy is about to gesture to his RTO (radio-telephone-operator) to contact Command when all hell breaks loose. Coming from several locations, multiple automatic weapons open fire on Murphy's squad, and three men go down. "Return fire! Return fire!" He yells and again tries to get his RTO's attention, knowing they need assistance, then sees his RTO go down under a barrage of AK-47 fire. Shot three times, once in the head, the RTO lies dead, his radio rendered useless by gunfire.

Using hand signals, Murphy orders his point man up the next alley, hoping to escape this ambush. The man acknowledges the signal, takes three steps into the alley, and drops as two bullets enter his chest. The dark night is lit with flashes of automatic weapons fire. The Taliban have brought not only AK-47s but three small pick-ups, each mounted with a Russian .51 caliber heavy machine gun.

"We've been led into a trap," Murphy says to his corporal. "We've got to find cover!"

The squad returns fire with M-4s, targeting flashes from the enemy's rifles. In the darkness, they can't see anything but weapons fire, but they must keep moving as their own M-4 bursts become enemy targets.

The Taliban occupy three tiny clay houses, and Murphy's only option is to withdraw his men toward the stone well located in the village center. His hope of using it as cover is shattered when three Taliban open fire from the shelter of the stones. Another .51 caliber machine gun opens fire, and Murphy realizes whoever set up this ambush did an excellent job; all the escape points were useless.

Unable to find adequate cover in time, two more squad members are shot down. The medic crawls forward to reach them until his body is riddled by a Russian-heavy machine gun. Now, the only hope lies in someone hearing this heavy concentration of weapons fire and reporting it to the authorities. When Command cannot raise them on the radio, they will send a backup force to investigate. *I sure hope it's a Cobra gunship; otherwise, we're toast!*

Their transport isn't due for another 45 minutes, and any help from Bagram will take at least that unless it's a gunship. He takes a quick count of his squad; only five men are capable of fighting, and he doesn't believe they can last much longer. Seeing a small, darkened building nearby, Murphy signals his remaining squad members to head for it. "Take cover in there—move it! Get goin' or die where you are!" Even as he speaks, another man falls.

Fortunately, the building is an empty shell. Within its protective walls, he quickly counts and is relieved to find no more losses. *I've lost six men.* Two seriously wounded men have been dragged in. Murphy is now sure their recently assigned Afghan interpreter has led them into this trap. He knew such treachery had happened many times since the war began in 2002. *I hope I survive to get my hands around that man's throat!*

The Taliban close in on their building, to finish off the trapped Americans. Heavy machine guns shoot holes through the clay walls. Stone fragments become shrapnel inflicting numerous minor wounds as the building is shot to pieces. With so many weapons in use, the noise inside the building sounds like a giant buzz-saw. Murphy is wounded in his right arm but continues firing with his left hand while encouraging his men. Between shooting through a doorway and two narrow windows, the men stay glued to the floor. A squad member screams as a bullet tears into his upper left thigh. Bleeding profusely, another soldier crawls to him, pulls out a battlefield dressing, and wraps the wound. A second bullet passes through Murphy's left shin and into the hip of a wounded soldier beside him. Another is shot in the shoulder. Ignoring his own wounds, Murphy drags the young private closer to him and sees the bullet has gone through. Semi-conscious, with his eyes tightly closed from the severe pain, the wounded man clutches his M-4. Murphy applies a battlefield dressing to the man's injury, then wraps a second dressing around his own leg before cinching his belt tight around his leg to slow the bleeding. Dropping back, Murphy orders his corporal to count survivors.

"Sarge," the corporal shouts, "Four men still alive including us! But we're all shot to hell! What are we going to do?" Only the corporal and himself are capable of returning fire. Murphy has a choice to make; either go down shooting or take a chance on surrendering. He knew the Taliban sometimes used American prisoners to trade for Taliban prisoners. He also knows they cut the bodies of dead Americans to pieces with their swords and then leave them for the birds to prey upon. If a helicopter gunship is on the way, the Taliban will likely grab their few prisoners and run to hide in caves in the nearby hills.

"Stop shooting... stop shooting! We're giving up!" He looks to his corporal, "We've got no other choice! They caught us flat-footed and without help, we're done for. Lay your weapons down and ready your-selves for what might lie ahead. At least we might be alive to go home —someday."

The corporal doesn't argue. He knows they can't make a run for it, not while surrounded by those heavy weapons. They begin shouting, "We give up...We surrender! Stop shooting! We give up!"

The shooting stops. A group of Taliban rush into the building and immediately begin kicking, stomping, and slapping the survivors. With such brutal abuse, Murphy is rendered unconscious.

Three weeks later, Sgt Murphy and two survivors appear in the news. At home in America, Murphy's father watches in silence, tears running down his cheeks, as his son is publicly executed. His head is cut off by a man dressed entirely in black, his facial features hidden. The corporal is executed in the same way.

The other ten American bodies are found two days after the ambush, burned in a large funeral pyre, along with some Afghan locals. The Americans are later identified by DNA in Germany, and their remains flown back to the USA.

1

JUST ANOTHER TOUR IN THE SANDBOX

THE SOUND of children's voices brought Bill out of sleep and his senses were assailed by the aroma of bacon and fresh coffee. He pushed the covers away and slipped out of bed. Floorboards creaked as he walked to the bathroom and the hot water pipe clattered when he turned on the sink faucet to wash the sleep from his eyes. *Home,* he thought, *be it ever so humble, there's no place like home.* And humble this certainly was. The typical military officer's two-story three-bedroom duplex came with a single-car garage, a tiny yard and more than a few 'fix-it' projects to keep Bill busy when he wasn't on duty. The refrigerator was noisy; the appliances were pre-Vietnam, water pipes leaked in several places and there were large rust stains in the tub. *Home is where the heart is.* In a few short days, he would be leaving his heart behind and didn't know if he would ever return.

Kitty Warrens had let her husband sleep in, knowing they only had two days before he and Bravo Company boarded a plane for the long flight to Bagram Air Force Base in Afghanistan. This would be Bill's third combat tour since they got married not long after he graduated from West Point twelve years before. He had only been home six months from his last tour there and they'd been told they would have at least a year stateside before their next deployment, but things changed. Rumor had it that insurgents were giving the Afghan forces a hard time. American reinforcements were required.

Ten-year-old Billy and seven-year-old Helen burst into the kitchen ahead of their father. "They make more noise than a herd of camels in a sandstorm!" Bill said as he kissed Kitty and slid onto a chair. Billy laughed at his father's silly remark spewing milk and nearly spilling the whole glass.

"Daddy said we could have a picnic at the park today, mama." Helen beamed.

"And tonight, we're going to a movie." Bill reached out to tug one of her glossy pigtails. *God! I'm going to miss these gems! Why do we have to go to war, Lord? This day belongs to my family. Tomorrow belongs to the country.*

The next day, Bill had a meeting at 1600 hours with his Colonel. This last-minute troop review for his company would concern his problem troops, the few men who would not be going overseas with the company. Bill disliked leaving anyone behind, but he didn't need to take trouble with him. Although he didn't always agree with this, he didn't want problem troops in combat. He had learned the hard way they could fail to do their job, which could lead to the death or wounding of others. There were 144 men in his company, men he was responsible for, lives he valued.

Bill stood 6'4" and with Airborne training, he maintained a 190-pound muscular physique. No six-pack abs, his stomach was tight from all the running in training, often with a 90-pound pack on his back. Bill could still run out front with the young kids who would often bait him on with "C'mon, Old Man, try to keep up, we got a stretcher handy if you need it." At 35, he looked forward to retirement in maybe four years—unless he made Major, which would justify reenlistment. Academy graduates, known as the "Ring-Knocker" Society, due to the enormous Academy rings they wear, often obtained quick promotions and better assignments. Many would someday reach the senior ranks if they kept their noses clean.

Kitty shaved his head bald weekly; his blue eyes were radiant, clear, and piercing. Combat scars couldn't be seen unless he took his shirt off... shrapnel wounds in his right shoulder from his tour in Iraq, and chest wounds from an AK-47 on his second tour in Afghanistan. He had spent six months in the hospital leaving Kitty to raise the youngsters. Young Bill was born while he was in Iraq.

The hospital staff had talked about a Medical Discharge because he wasn't expected to recover 100 percent use of his body. Bill ignored them. From day one, after his release from the hospital, he pushed himself with exercises, working his way up to putting in ten-hour days, six days a week. His family was there to help him from that first climb up the stairs to his bedroom. Upon their return home from leave, his men were on hand to help. They exercised with him, lifted weights, and ran with him, which did not go unnoticed by upper staff. It was evident that Bill was extremely well-liked by his men.

When he felt ready to take the Soldier's Physical, he passed with 100 percent. The doctors attempted to stop him from taking the Airborne Qualification Test but again, he passed. He made five jumps—three during daylight and two at night. But he wasn't done. He wanted to be HALO (high altitude, low opening) qualified. The Colonel waved it down to two qualifying jumps; a dozen of his men jumped with him; the rest waited at ground zero.

A week later, Bill was called into his Colonel's office, "Be seated, Captain." The room was quiet as a Sergeant Major presented both men with cups of boiling hot black coffee. The Colonel drank it, and he expected his men to do the same when on duty. Bill let the coffee cool for a moment to keep from burning his lips.

"I asked you here, Captain because I personally wanted to congratulate you on the job you've accomplished in coming back from such a serious wound. I know they talked about a Medical Discharge with a 70 percent rating, but I was planning to fight for a full 100 percent. I watched you train, sometimes 12 hours a day toward the end, with two or three of your squad helping, I knew you were on the road back. But honestly, I never expected you to pass the Airborne exams, and then you did HALO on top of that. Shows what living a healthy life brings to the table for us God-fearing men." The Colonel paused. "Captain, would you like a well-deserved job here at Regiment? We can always use men like you to help in our training program. You've got two combat tours behind you, two Purple Hearts, and a few medals for Valor. I'm not making fun of your record, Captain. I see you as a soldier's soldier. Your whole company loves you."

"Colonel, the goal I had in mind from day one when all I wanted was to lay down and whimper, was to get my Company back. I know we're going back over. Those big thinkers in DC have gotten their feet stuck in the mud. They've made too many promises. We either kick the Taliban's butt or leave and let them have it." Bill took a sip of coffee, "Maybe anyone who desires to be in national politics should have to serve in the military for two years and officers should serve as enlisted personnel to get a feel for enlisted life, to better understand their personal needs, better training and a pay raise for a better standard of living. Nearly a third of my troops work second jobs to keep their families fed and in decent clothes. The national guardsmen sent to Afghanistan never signed up for that when they joined the guard."

"All good points, Captain. Many of our young officers tend to forget what a young troop endures as a family man."

"Yes, sir. I learned some things from my men in Iraq. I sat down with them one night, took my shiny gold bar off because I wanted them to be frank with me. I didn't grow up with money, but the academy, sir—well, sir, it made me feel like an officer and a gentleman. I made it to West Point because of my dad. I haven't forgotten the days when he was homeless, passed out drunk in some downtown alley. Mom did her best for us, but we were poor. She couldn't afford the junior college I attended for a short time. I knew the military would be part of my future when I saw my dad's pride receiving his medal, the tears in his eyes. Because of him, I'm a West Point Graduate and a Company Commander—all because of what he did in 1969. I am proud of him; he will always be my hero." Bill stopped; his eyes started to water. His dad had died shortly after the Medal of Honor was awarded to him by the Vice President in the VA hospital. Lost paperwork had prevented proper procedures for his father's award, but when it turned up, Bill Junior's life was changed.

"Captain, one on one, I agree with you. I owe this Eagle to the men and women who have served with me—men like yourself." The Colonel stopped for a moment, recalling an old memory, and then continued, "Did I ever tell you that I was a bright and shiny second lieutenant when I was shipped off to Kuwait, 24 hours before Desert Storm began?"

Bill had heard the story a couple of times, but he shook his head and replied, "No, sir. I know you've served four combat tours—"

"Yup, the third day in, my life was saved by an old Senior Master Sergeant, who took a bullet in the arm that would've hit me about where you got yours had he not shoved me aside. Maybe that's why I like to keep these old fart NCOs around my office. I remember my days at West Point, but it didn't do so well preparing us for war in the Middle East. The Vietnam Veterans had already retired from teaching and the NCOs that remained rarely talked to us. As a platoon commander, I remember asking my regiment's Command Master Sergeant what the Vietnam War was all about. He laughed at me... then got serious, 'We rarely bothered getting to know junior officer's names in Nam. They wore those stinkin' gold bars into combat like a trophy, giving snipers something to aim at. We'd tell them repeatedly to take the bars off, but very few did. The college kids would spring up and gallantly lead their troops right into a jungle ambush.' He told me it happened until they finally began teaching better battle tactics for junior officers back here in the states. It took some time and some hard-nosed veterans to get this man's army ready to fight these desert wars. I'll be thrilled when this Afghanistan War is over. We've been there too long; spilling good American blood on that wasteland; it's time to bring our people home."

"I was lucky, sir, I had top NCOs, and once they knew I was willing to listen to them, they taught me how to fight a war in the desert."

The Colonel nodded in agreement, "It's been nice talking with you, Captain, but I'd better let you go. As of 0800 hours tomorrow, you are back as Company Commander. Please give my apologies to your lovely wife. I suspect she was hoping for a stateside office job; you're right, another tour is coming up. So, get your men into condition, 'ready to chew nails' as my first Top Sergeant used to say. Spend a lot of time at that firing range. We have plenty of munitions here and not so much over there, so turn them into either a Daniel Boone or Davy Crockett able to take a man's eye out at 100-yards. You have a few new guys coming in. I'm keeping my fingers crossed I can get your company up to full strength before you leave."

Bill stood abruptly to attention and saluted his commander. The

Colonel nodded, rose to his feet, and returned Bill's salute just as smartly.

"Thank you, Colonel, you've just made it Christmas again, at least for me. But Kitty... her father was a career soldier, and she married a soldier."

"You're a lucky man, Bill; that is genuinely a great wife you have. You have no idea how many officer's wives come here to cry on my shoulder because of domestic problems." He shook his head and waved the matter off. "Get your orders from my Sergeant Major. Can you believe it? He's about to retire and wants one more combat tour. He wants to go with you on this next one, but I doubt he could keep up with your kids." The Old Man grinned at Bill, "When he retires, there'll be a parade with the whole regiment. I'll give one of my speeches, add some unclassified history, pin the Legion of Merit Medal on him, and that's it. He goes home a civilian, but I'll always remember him as a damn good fighting man."

"Well, Colonel, the flowing tears will probably make the field appear as if we'd been soaked in a rainstorm."

The Colonel nodded and waved Bill out the door. "Get out... I got business to do."

"Yes, Colonel. I'm gone."

A minute later, Bill quietly knocked on the Chief's door and walked inside. "Sergeant Major, it's doubtful I'll be here when they retire you. So, for my own knowledge, just how many years is it?" Bill asked.

"Well, sir, counting National Guard Time, I've got some 42 years in this man's army."

"Wow! That's a lot of GI chow, Chief. How many jumps have you made? I see two combat stars on those jump wings."

"Including back when I was a Green Beret under President Reagan when we jumped into those, 'No one needs to know about this place,' zones... I've got 44 combat jumps and 17 HALO drops in combat. But, Captain, it's been a great life for the wife and me. We've got five children, 16 grandchildren, and our first great-grandchild is due in four months. Right after we move west to Arizona, we're becoming full-time RV people."

"Have you found a replacement yet, someone the Colonel can see?" Bill asked.

"Are you kidding, Captain? I've already put together a shortlist with six Senior Sergeant Majors who have had prior assignments to Airborne. All of them said they wouldn't mind some cushy office time under a full Colonel."

"But he hasn't looked at it yet?" Bill asked.

"Nope. I think he's waiting until after I leave, but that's a bit late. I need time to show the man his job, and it'll take time to get orders cut. The Colonel was supposed to choose a new aide, and for a while, I thought he was looking at you. So, I guess I have another talk with him about it. His wife usually calls four times a day, nothing important... she wonders how he's doing. Is he walking too much or drinking too much of his iron coffee? That kind of thing."

"Sarge, you give me a lot to look forward to if I was to ever become a regimental commander.

The Chief grinned and replied, "I just feel it's better you know this now, so it doesn't come as a big surprise later.

2

BACK AT THE HOUSE

Kitty was not looking forward to Bill's deployment. She and the children would remain in base housing while he was overseas. However, she was hoping to spend a couple of weeks with her family in Washington State and a few days with her mother-in-law in California. Bill had suggested that she bring his mother back to help with the children, but also because he knew that each time he went on tour, it was hard for both her and his mother. Kitty hadn't solved the room shortage, yet, but it would give her an excuse to redecorate.

Wherever they lived, she allowed Bill one wall to display his military honors. Here, it was the light green wall that supported the stairs. Bill had hung his father's Medal of Honor certificate and Bronze Star and Purple Heart citations. He had told Kitty that he was proud of the Purple Hearts that some vets often referred to as the "forgot to duck" medal. There was a service photo taken after his old man had graduated from Airborne Training beside an almost identical photo of Bill and two photos of their wedding which because of Kitty's Japanese heritage, had been a combination Buddhist/Christian ceremony.

Bill Jr. and Kitty met at a Japanese Cultural Affair in Los Angeles. After completing his Airborne training, he was home on leave. After two hours of visiting historic and modern Japanese art, he was about to leave the museum when Bill backed into a young woman. Her beauty stunned him. His first impression was that she was Oriental; her eyes were slightly round, her skin a beach tan, her glossy black hair hung long and loose about her shoulders like a cape, and she was dressed in a traditional Japanese kimono. Her eyes, bluer than hazel—not at all an Oriental feature, nor were her high cheekbones. She was an exquisite combination of two nationalities.

"Do you speak English?" Bill asked after he got his West Point cool under control.

She looked up into his eyes, about nine inches above her own, and replied, "Yes... and Spanish, French, German, and some local street Mex as well as Japanese. I was born here in the U.S.A. I'm an interpreter here at the museum."

Bill managed to convince her into joining him for a late dinner and a few more dates. A month and a half after they met, they were engaged and married a few months afterward. He was assigned to the 101st Airborne at Fort Benning, Georgia where they found a shabby apartment on the third floor of a pre-WWII hotel turned apartment building, but Kitty made it livable in no time. Tensions in the Middle East took Bill to Iraq for his first combat assignment within months of their arrival. Kitty discovered that she was pregnant soon after he left which made the separation more difficult and started a tradition of nightly notes that became frequent letters between them. She poured her heart into them, and he tried not to relate to many battle details.

Bill left in command of a 32-man platoon, part of a two-platoon company that would see heavy losses before returning home. By the time the tour ended, Bill was one of 107 survivors from a company of 144. Many of his troops were wounded, but too many flag-covered caskets returned on large transports. Bill had had more than one close call. Two months after he arrived, he had been too close to a detonating explosive device. The explosion knocked him off his feet and showered him with dirt, dust, and debris. His left shirt sleeve was in shreds and his left arm was scraped from shoulder to hand and his left thigh was scraped and bruised. It burned when the nurse in the hospital cleaned his scrapes and applied medicated ointment. They cautioned him to take care of it every day to ensure no infection settled in before it healed. Other than that, he was stiff and sore for a few days. Four months later, a bullet grazed his upper right arm, another minor wound that healed in a matter of days. Barely a month later, he was driving a jeep when a truck passed him and hit a mine several hundred yards ahead and a chunk of flying metal hit the front of his jeep leaving a huge dent.

Barely two weeks later, Bill was severely wounded by flying shrapnel during a skirmish. He refused to leave the battle scene, ordering the medic to do the best he could to sew up the wounds in his right shoulder and bandage them tightly. By the time he finally left the field, his wound was infected, and he was running a 102-degree fever. He went to the hospital convinced that he was attending the theater in New York and demanded the best box seat and when the doctor came in, Bill thought he was Ricky Gervais. It took some work for the 'comedian and his assistants' to talk Bill into joining them on stage and he laughed as he helped them adjust the 'spaceship breathing device' over his face. He spent the next three days in the ICU sleeping peacefully with the help of sedatives while strong antibiotics battled the infection. Only when the infection was under control, did they allow him to wake up. His men took turns at his bedside until he awoke, confused and disoriented. "The fight's over, man, we're all back at base, safe and sound, so pay attention to the doc and come back to the playpen. We all wanna hear more stories about that fishing boat in the desert and the sand cloud fish you caught! That was a doozy of a state you were in by the time we got you back here!" They laughed.

The nurses laughed when he asked them about it. "Oh, don't pay attention to them. They're just jealous cause you been getting better food in a cool room!"

"Can I go back, now?" Bill asked seriously.

"Ask Ricky when he comes in!" They said over their shoulder as they whisked out of his room. Though Bill asked after Ricky many times, the man never came around and it wasn't until after he was released that he learned who Ricky was.

Back in the war. On patrol, he spent many long cold nights with his men, snuggled up together without fires, shivering through the icy early morning frosts. During the surprisingly chilly winter nights, he learned a lot about them and how they ended up in Iraq. Airborne was strictly a volunteer service; some had just gone with the flow, and it put them in the air, others chose it for adventure, and a few wanted to live on the edge experiencing the thrill of free-fall as they plummeted out of the sky. He listened without comment, part of a group he could never be part of. It had always been that way; officers were part of another world to the enlisted men. On one level he could relate to them, but officer's school put a barrier between them. However, the battlefield often leveled the playing field and barriers could be set aside.

As the days passed, he gained strength and his thoughts turned to home and Kitty and the son he had not yet seen. On his return home, Bill was promoted to First Lieutenant. His priority was to move Kitty from the apartment building now scheduled for demolition. They found a small two-bedroom apartment above an old drugstore on the south side of Columbus. With troop buildup, housing was still sparse on the base and although new housing had been completed, old units were demolished to make room for new and he was still too low on the list to be eligible for one of these. After the move, but before they were settled in, he took leave so they could visit his mother and her parents before events took him out of the country again.

Deployment orders came down just after little Billy turned two. This time Bill was sent to Afghanistan. Once again, two companies of troops, over 250 men, lifted off the tarmac at Fort Benning. During the long flight to Bagram, Bill immersed himself in memories of the precious time at home with his family. *Would he see them again?* He glanced around at the other men and one or two met his eye. Somehow, they each knew what the other was thinking. *Will you make it through this? Will I make it home again? Will I come home a whole man or an invalid my loved ones will have to care for til the end? What lies ahead for us?*

Hell waited for them. Upon landing, they were held on board as flag-draped caskets were loaded onto a transport next to them. It was a sobering scene for those new to this war zone, a stark reminder of the thoughts of home that had plagued them on the way over. Blistering heat and high humidity were almost stifling as they deplaned at Bagram and joined the lines of personnel processing in. And there was little relief from it in the tiny, cramped room he was assigned to, temporarily they told him. It was noon when they landed, five hours later before he completed processing in, only to be sent to a briefing that lasted another two hours and another before he was deposited at quarters. He dropped his bags, turned up the ac unit, and went in search of food only to find snacks and lukewarm sodas in vending machines. He was tired and hungry, and he missed Kitty and little Billy and home, and he was to report at 0700 to begin orientation. *This is what it means to 'hit the ground running,'* he thought as he returned to his room.

Bill crawled out of bed at 0500 to take a shower with tepid water. In the mirror, as he shaved, he saw a man whose pale blue, red-rimmed eyes looked out from deep dark circles. His skin was tanned from hours in the southern sun, but the man looked exhausted. *Jet lag,* Bill thought. *How long will it last? Maybe getting some food will help.*

Forty-five minutes later, Bill sat in the cafeteria looking at a plate of eggs, toast, and sausage, a cup of coffee, and a glass of orange juice. He ate slowly, savoring the taste of the food even though it was Army chow. The only thing he'd had since leaving home was an army field meal, two cups of warm, wickedly strong coffee, two bottles of water almost as warm as the coffee, a package of crackers and cheese, and another of mixed nuts on the plane and a soft Milky Way and a bottle of ice-cold root beer from the vending machine last night.

The orientation room was packed with new arrivals ten minutes before seven. A large screen was pulled down on the low dais in the front of the room, four chairs were lined up on the left side of it and a lectern was near the center. Bill sat with his squad leaders on the far-left side of the room near a long table set against the wall. At precisely 0700, a major stepped to the lectern and tipped a mic to speak. "Welcome to Afghanistan and Bagram Air Force Base. I am Major Leland Huxley. I know all of you are anxious to get out and do some sunbathing on the sand, but before you venture out there, there are some things you need to know generally about living in the desert. This is not like the desert back home, let me assure you. For the next two days, we are going to talk about the hazards of the desert. Spiders, snakes, scorpions, and soldiers —know your enemy—be aware of your surroundings. How to identify those that can and will kill you. We're going to talk about health, the importance of water, and personal hygiene. What can make you very ill or cause life-threatening illness. Pay attention, listen carefully; your life and your health depend on it."

Bill only lasted halfway through this tour. After being shot while stumbling into an ambush, he was medivaced out by helicopter and flown to Bagram. Stabilized, Bill was flown back to the states via Germany. It was a couple of months until he was back to full-duty status.

BACK IN THE HERE AND NOW

Bill had told her that unless Command dropped them smack in the middle of Iran, Afghanistan would be their destination. He preferred working with the hill people of that land to going back to the Iraqis. He had seen a lot of corruption in both the military and civilian ranks in Iraq. Bill also enjoyed working with the Kurds, surprised to find that most were Christians.

Captain William Warrens started his company off with a five-mile run in full combat gear, weapons, and 60-pound combat packs that were weighed by the platoon's training NCO to ensure everyone had the same weight. Rocks were used for weight the first day; but on the third day, it would be an entire combat issue that included MREs and extra water, bringing these packs to more than 90-pounds. On the day of deployment, the company would be issued a personal load of ammo for their M-4s or shotguns and side-arms. The Heavy-weapons squads would have most of their equipment onboard the aircraft, all boxed up, with large crates of explosive ordinance in metal containers strapped to the floor between the troops. Grenades and B-40 light-anti tank weapons and other personal ordinance would be issued after arrival in Bagram.

THE TRACK

Bill knew the men of B Company were in good shape, but he wanted them to see that the group's old geezers were ready to cut the mustard. So, he had the NCOs run with their squads while the senior NCOs and young officers ran with him. They ran on a cross-country two-mile grass track, which had been used since Airborne troops first prepared for Vietnam. The Colonel had once suggested Airborne troops be sent to North

Texas to train for the Sandbox Wars, but the official response advised him the costs involved would not allow for such training expenses. Bill never understood how the military believed the thick woods of Fort Benning could be compared with Iraq or Afghanistan, but he was only a 1st Lieutenant and young officers were not supposed to question such things.

Kitty awakened him at 4:00 a.m., knowing he'd oversleep. She pushed him out of bed, then rolled back over to fall back asleep. She had done her wife's duty and was none too happy to see her husband shipping off to fight again. Kitty loved him dearly, but she was upset he was returning to Afghanistan. She had prayed he would take the nice comfortable job he was offered at headquarters, but Bill had opted to return to combat duty.

Forty-five minutes later, Bill had B Company lined up by platoon and was letting them relax and finish their stretches. The skies were reasonably clear, with no wind, and the air was cool this morning.

While in the hospital this last time, Bill had realized the military was not holding on to their finest combat doctors—those who had gained experience in combat wound surgery. After a tour or two of duty in a combat zone, many left the military for civilian practice. The war had transformed many of them into exceptional surgeons. Doctors learned a lot removing shrapnel and bullets from the torn bodies of soldiers, civilians, and the enemy at an FOB (Forward Operations Base). Bullets were hard on the human body as they blasted through and sometimes stuck in an organ or a bone. Shrapnel was often worse, as tiny bits of metal slashed a body up and transformed big pieces into small pieces as they ripped through bones and larger body parts. This is what field doctors, nurses, medics, and corpsmen had to deal with. Corpsmen were Navy personnel and often assigned to the Marines. Unlike other Navy personnel, who fought Marines in bars, Navy corpsmen were highly regarded by Marines as a fellow platoon member.

Bill shook those memories out of his mind and checked in with Chief Sergeant Major Henry 'Hank' Leroy Johnson to ensure all was in readiness for the run. A fortunate Company Commander, Bill was the only platoon in the regiment to have such an experienced Chief Sergeant Major assigned to him at the company level. Most NCOs of this senior rank worked for a Regiment or above. While Bill was proud to have him, he still wasn't sure why he was privileged to have such an experienced NCO under him.

On morning runs, Bill allowed the men to wear sweats under their fatigues to help them stay warm. He didn't want anyone becoming ill this close to deployment. They began the run with four men to a line; Chief Johnson was positioned off Bill's right shoulder. Though he was 56 years old, Bill knew Johnson would never falter in a five-mile run. He was in top shape and preparing to leave on what Bill thought was his fourth deployment. The Chief's salt and pepper hair was cut short, his hazel gray eyes surrounded by an outpouring of wrinkles, and his first age spots, which made some men look like they had a case of measles, had only recently appeared. He was ready for the morning run; fueled with a desire to show these young sprouts he could still keep up with them.

During one combat tour, Chief was shot in the back by friendly fire when a soldier forgot to put his rifle on safe. Because of this, he remained attentive to ensure this didn't happen again. Later, for his battlefield actions, he was awarded the Bronze Star for Valor and an Army Commendation Medal. He had also earned three Purple Hearts and had made three HALO jumps into Iraq which gave him battle stars for his jump wings. Now he was really looking forward to retiring and planning to open a bar with another retiree.

Running beside Bill was the Company's senior Radio Telephone Officer, or RTO. Staff Sergeant Jimmy Olson, a 27-year-old redhead of Irish stock, liked being an RTO. In this way, he usually knew what was happening. Olson had told Bill that his dad was a fan of the original black & white *Superman* comics. When he saw Olson in a colored comic book, he knew what he'd name his first son, though the boy's mother put up quite the objection. This would be Olson's second tour in Afghanistan; during his first tour, he completed three HALO jumps and earned two Army Commendation Medals and a Purple Heart. He was waiting for the final okay on a Bronze Star for Valor. A burning helicopter had crashed near his position, and he rushed in to pull two soldiers to safety despite sustaining facial burns and second and third-degree burns to his back and legs.

Running at the front of the company were Bill's top people; Sergeant

First Class Louis Paul Roman, a prideful, 36-year-old dark-skinned Italian. He was the Company's senior Medic who supervised the other medics.

The company's platoon leaders were Sergeant Major (E-7) John Hallsworth McCullough—a robust, verbal Scotsman who would lead 1st Platoon until a new officer arrived to become platoon commander. 2nd Lieutenant Dave Thomas Parker, Second Platoon Commander and a graduate of Reserve Officer Training Corps (ROTC) at Arizona State University, Tempe. Third Platoon was under the firm hand of 25-year-old 1st Lieutenant Douglas Keith Graham. B Company's Heavy Weapon Platoon was in the temporary command of Sergeant First Class James T. Averell from Casper, Wyoming. SFC Averell had been awarded both a Silver Star and a Bronze Star for Valor during his first tour in Iraq. In a deployment to Afghanistan, he was awarded two Bronze Stars for Valor and a fourth Purple Heart. His chest of personal award ribbons included four Army Commendation Medals for distinguishing himself in combat. The men he led saw him as the real deal in the area of soldiering.

Bill thought Averell a true hero, but stateside, he was a bit of a problem child. Lately, he was becoming a full-blown alcoholic which many of his friends believed was due to extreme Post Traumatic Stress Disorder, though officially, he had not been diagnosed. B Company's enlisted personnel could read him well enough. They knew he was trying to hang on for his 20-year retirement. It angered him to contemplate leaving the service on a Medical Discharge.

Sadly, Bill knew far too many of his experienced troops were in the first stages of PTSD, or worse. Still, when deployed and away from the booze, Averell quickly proved himself to be the best Heavy Weapons man in the Division.

The Heavy Weapons boys handled the M-60s, three vehicle-mounted, and three M-60s for ground action. Their work tools consisted of mobile and stationary 60-mm and 81-mm mortars, along with a dozen B-40 grenade launchers. Usually, the company used Humvees to move around the desert for quick reaction response, but Bill was expecting heavier armor. There was talk of being assigned Strykers and possibly Bradley Fighting Machines once they arrived in Afghanistan.

BACK TO THE RUN

Four miles into the run at a medium pace, B Company was still together; not one soldier had dropped out. Bill decided to press them for the last mile; hoping none of the men would twist an ankle, get a hernia, have a heart attack, or worse—drop dead. He had briefed his squad leaders to expect this move at the four-mile mark, so when he pulled the whistle out of his pocket, the Chief shook his head in dismay. Twice he blew the whistle, and to his surprise, the men were ready, giving a thunderous, "Airborne—All the Way!"

Bill left the grass trail and stepped onto the high school quarter-mile track. He ran down the straight-away at a brisk pace, not quite a run, but close to it. All his men, including the Chief, stayed with him in tight formation. When they finished the fourth lap around the school's football field, not a single man had dropped out.

Per the Chief's stopwatch, a relic from his days with the high school football team, the Company finished, in rank, the last mile in five minutes 43-seconds. That time spread through the ranks rapidly, as smiles popped out, back slaps could be heard, and squad leaders went around shaking the hands of the men they led.

"This has to be some kind of a record, Chief," Bill said.

"Are you kidding? Who else would be evil enough to put his troops through a dead run on the fifth mile? I'm still waiting for the medic's report. Then I'm walking into the bushes and puking my guts out. You can tell the troops I'm relieving my bladder, but it's the other organs that are revolting now."

"Move out, Chief; I'll handle the medics." He turned to yell to the troops, "Men, I am really proud of you. You did that last mile in under six minutes… and with heavy packs! But now I want you to walk it off, don't sit down. Drop your packs and stretch it out. If you need to upchuck, head over there to the side." Bill pointed south of where the Chief had wandered off too.

"We'll spend 10 minutes cooling down and get together for a talk. If I see one weapon lying on the ground, that whole squad will run an additional mile; you all know the rules. I don't want to start getting sloppy now. Sloppiness can mean death in our business, and I hate writing those letters home to your parents. Be nice to go through this coming deployment without having to write a single letter. Okay, walk it off."

SFC Roman took the platoon medic's reports and wrote them down on a small-lined pad he kept in his lower left side pants pocket. Finished, Roman walked up to Bill, saluted, and delivered his report. "We did extremely well, Captain. Two men with dry heaves, but they'll be fine by the time we're ready to leave. I suggested they take it slow going back. One man is limping slightly, so when he cools down, I'll run him over to the hospital for an X-ray to ensure he hasn't got a stress fracture or worse. A couple more with upset stomachs were fine once they got rid of breakfast. Their medic told them not to eat before the run, but there are always a few who just won't listen."

Chief walked up, "Do you mean me, Sergeant?"

"Of course not, Chief," Roman replied. "I know you've been in the Army long enough to know better than to stop at a certain doughnut shop and load yourself down with cream-filled glazed doughnuts and a large coffee."

"Were you following me, Roman?"

"No, Chief, I simply happened to be two cars behind you in the take-out line. But I saved my doughnuts for later. You appear to have eaten some of yours."

"No privacy, just no privacy in this man's Army." Chief walked off, rubbing his tummy in hopes it would settle down. He knew Roman was right and what troubled him was why he bought the damn doughnuts in the first place. He didn't like doughnuts. It was a sudden urge, and now he was paying for it... Dearly.

Bill had to force himself to keep a straight face; he didn't want to add to the Chief's embarrassment.

THE END OF RUN CHAT

Squad Leaders got word from their platoon leaders as the men gathered into a loose company formation and stood at ease. No one smoked and there was no talking.

"All right, men—can you all hear me?" Bill said in a raised voice.

"Yes, sir," was shouted numerous troops while others waved their hands to acknowledge him.

"I'll make my part of this short, and then you can hit the showers. You know the drill, if this is your first deployment, you need to listen to your squad leaders, some of them are combat veterans." Bill stopped to look around, gazing into the faces that encircled him. "I won't lie to you; most of you know I never have, so know this... This deployment isn't going to be a walk in the park. The only men you can fully trust are these men right here around you. Squad leaders, talk with your new guys about the rules of engagement. I want prisoners whenever possible, though not at the risk of losing one of you. Remember our 'Terps'... that's interpreters for you beginners... are foreigners you'll meet when we get over there. For the most part, they're good guys... treat them well. You might try to learn the local language from them. However, some Terps have burned some of our troops in the past. Investigations have shown some allied with an insurgent faction. We'll have to see who we get and look into their history before we get too trusting."

Bill held his M-4 high over his head, "This is your little sister... treat her as if she was. Protect her, be tender with her and when you need to, kill with her. Do not drop her, do not let any foreigner get his hands on her. If you do, I'll send you back to the FOB to clean latrines and work in the chow hall, and anything else I can think up."

He un-holstered his Baretta 9mm and lifted it. "I carry the Baretta 9mm, mainly because I like the feel of it. I have carried a Colt .45. Personally, I did not like the weight when loaded or the feel. When departing the FOB, the magazine in my pistol has only 12 rounds so I don't jam it with 14 or 15 rounds. I chamber the first round after I go through the gate. I prefer the new 9mm Hydro-Shockers Hollow Points. Incredible stopping power, but they are not issued, you have to purchase them yourself, but it is worth the expense. Both of my other magazines are loaded the same way. If any of you wish to carry similar ammo, you will not have a problem with this command. But no, I repeat, no homemade specials. All ammo will be company manufactured. In my first tour, I noticed our 9mm ball ammo wouldn't always do the job. These will."

Bill holstered his pistol and raised his 12-inch K-bar Knife, which had a black-wooden handle and a blade sharp enough to shave with. "Your knives are your fallback weapon, and therefore you have been trained in its use. I carry three knives of various lengths when going into combat, and each one has its uses. Bayonets are not mandatory in my company. In my opinion, bayonets tend to mess with our rifle's sight picture and increase the barrel's weight. I'll leave that up to you. I have a four-inch boot knife, remember to use the sheath. I've seen some troops get their ankles cut up from forgetting to use a sheath... which is just plain stupid. Many veterans strap the sheath to the outside of their boot... Enough on knives." Bill didn't mention the third knife, a dagger with a three-inch blade in a sheath taped to his left forearm. He only carried this in combat as a backup weapon.

"Spend this last night with your family, or the last beer or whatever at the club. Curfew is midnight—after that, you are a no show and that means you're AWOL. Married troops will be home by midnight, but I doubt that will be a problem... Just don't strain any muscles." He watched as smiles appeared on numerous faces. "If you're single, avoid the hookers off base. You come down with a dose of the clap, and you'll not only be unhappy but in a world of hurt with me. Remember, you're government property, so take care of yourselves. You can ask some of the old guys what venereal disease can do to a person's body. Enough said on that! This Company will form at 0530 hours with everything you are taking on this trip in your pack or your duffle bag. There will be no suit-cases or fanny packs. Strictly military. Families may come to the flight line to say goodbye at the fence, but time will be tight, so do not abuse the privilege.

Do not even think about carrying a loaded firearm aboard the airplane. If you see someone with a loaded weapon, notify your squad leader who will pass it on to his platoon leader. Someone will take them off the plane to unload their firearm, and then they can ride outside on the wing for good measure. So, make it easy on everyone, do not load your firearms. Everyone got that? If we crash in some desert, then we'll haul out the ammo. If we crash in the ocean, all bets are off."

He didn't continue until he received a good number of, "Yes, sir!"

"There is plenty of ammo in Afghanistan. If you want a particular load for your M-4, you can buy it through Blackwater Security. But it had better be American-made, or it will jam your weapon. Be careful hanging around those dudes; you might end up under the worrisome eyes of Army Intel or CID.

We will have chow for the single men at 0600 hours; married men should have already eaten. Take it easy on the chow, we have a long flight ahead of us, and we don't need a lot of air-sick troops making it rough for all of us. There will be MREs on board with extra snacks for the long flight, and you can thank the Chief for that."

"Thank you, Chief!" The shouts went out loudly and with enthusiasm.

"Squad leaders, you'll inspect your men's equipment between 0630 hours and 0800 hours. The last goodbyes for family men will be from 0800 to 0810. Form up by 0812. Platoon Leaders assign single troops to help carry the Heavy Weapons equipment onboard. I'll do a final inspection, and hopefully, we will board at 0830. Our plane is expected to roll out at 0900 hours—if they have all the rubber bands wound up.

"For the next 12, possibly 13, months, the Sandbox is going to be your home. Before we leave, I've invited a very old friend of mine out here, who was impressed with you men and today's run. He remarked favorably on how you held formation that last mile. In a minute, I'll introduce you to Pastor Joshua Sanders, a Vietnam Veteran and a dear friend to my father. He spends most of his time working at the VA Hospital in Los Angeles... And as we used to say, he's been off to see the elephant. If you have any questions about that saying, see me later. This is Pastor Joshua Sanders."

Once a viral young man, Joshua had been instrumental in finding William Warrens Senior's missing Medal of Honor paperwork. For a time, he jumped between pastoring a large Southern California Church and tag-teaming with Doctor Scott Ahern in Los Angeles. Then he left his pulpit behind to work full-time with veterans, primarily PTSD patients, using the Lord as a new approach to healing. Struggling against non-believing doctors and scientists, they proved this spiritual healing with an unprecedented number of patients now living everyday lives.

Joshua looked out over the troops and was reminded of the day 47 years earlier when he and his men had gathered for a photo before loading their own aircraft. *We were so young, ready to take on anything and anyone... Nearly a third of us never came back.*

"Pastor... Pastor Sanders," Bill touched his shoulder lightly.

"Sorry, Bill, all these fine men had me going down memory lane." Joshua smiled and then addressed the troops. "As your good Captain said, I spend a lot of my time helping men like yourselves and men and ladies who came before you at the VA Hospital in Los Angeles. I was pastoring a church when the Lord told me I was needed full-time at the VA. I was blessed to have a fine assistant pastor to take over for me, and he's doing a dynamite job.

I am a Vietnam Veteran, and I work alongside Dr. Scott Ahern, a former Medic and now a regular Medical Doctor, though he specializes in the brain. There's a more technical name for it, but that's what he does. We work together, using medicine and faith to help our people.

While working with your Captain's father, former 1st Lieutenant William Warrens Senior, Scott and I stumbled upon a terrible mistake. A gallant man was wounded three times while saving the lives of four of his men during the Battle for Hamburger Hill in Vietnam's infamous A Shau Valley. Under constant enemy fire, he refused to leave his men behind. His paperwork was lost or misplaced, and people back at headquarters thought he'd been killed. Things were somewhat different back then, military-wise and politically. Many people back home were tired of hearing about Vietnam and the men and women who had served there. If you've studied the history of your division, you know the hill was called Hamburger Hill because it took 11 days to make it to the top and drive the enemy off. Some of you may have read the book or seen the movie. As with anything else, they didn't give the 70 men who died there and the 440 wounded men much justice... this was the bloodiest event in their lives. It took them a long time to deal with it.

The thought that he had killed those four men haunted Bill Senior. That led to a severe case of PTSD and a long stint of alcoholism. Eventually, it took his life. Your captain grew up with that. William Warrens Senior became Bill's anchor, he grew up learning about PTSD. So, if you have any problems over there, you're fortunate to have such a man leading you. With the Lord's help, we were able to get three of the four men to the Medal of Honor ceremony at William's hospital bed. The Vice President of the United States was there to present Bill senior with the Medal. Nearly everyone in attendance had tears of joy in their eyes. It may have been oh so late in coming, but it still accomplished a lot. I remarried William and Loretta in his hospital room. Bill later attended West Point, where he finished toward the top of his class.

Okay, that moment in history is over... When you leave, I'll hand out my card and give a few extras to your Captain. If things get tight over there, drop me a line or when you can, give me a call. Sometimes I cannot talk very long if I'm in a group, but I'll call back. We can write if you prefer, but I want you to know that I'm here for you. If you process out when you get home and want to visit LA, give one of our groups a try. We'll find you a spot... we never turn anyone away.

Before you leave, I'd like to pray for you; I take in all faiths. I've learned teachings from an elderly Jewish Rabbi, talked with Mormon Bishops to make sure I have their teaching's down right and half a dozen other religions. This year I'm studying Hindi to help the Hindu Americans serving our country. I've even spent a few months with an Imam to know something about the Koran and their faith. Believe me, there are times I'm not sure which deity I'm teaching about; it gets a little more confusing the older I get. You see, this may confuse you right now, but working with PTSD patients, I'm looking first at the man and his illness, not his faith. Of course, if you ask me about my walk with Jesus, I'm prepared to witness to you. Now let me pray...." Joshua prayed silently, and they all heard him say, "Amen." He continued in Jewish and finally stopped with a prayer of Islam. Bill had told him there were six Muslim soldiers in his Company, and Joshua wanted to bless all of them.

When Pastor finished, Bill let out a loud, "All right, Troopers, the trucks are in the parking lot! Be nice to the drivers; they're just working a job, too. Don't leave any trash in the bed, or you'll pay for it on the plane. Plenty of room for calisthenics. Now move out!"

"Do you need a ride, Captain?" Chief hollered.

"No! I'm riding with Pastor. I'll see you at headquarters at 1630 hours."

"Yes, sir!"

They sat in Bill's classic 1957 Chevrolet two-door Nomad wagon, also known as the 'Surfer's Wagon'. Bill and his dad had rebuilt it, and he received many admiring looks as they headed home for a brief meet with Kitty. Because of the kids, Kitty had a second car for family outings.

3

TIMES UP!

THE DEPARTURE DATE was on a Saturday which allowed school aged kids to be at the airfield to see their fathers off for Afghanistan. Nearly a whole platoon of Military Policemen was assigned to ensure none of the civilians, including wives and children, ran through the gates for a last-minute hug and kiss from husbands and dads. Even with warnings, several spouses tried to shove their way through. Though the MPs attempted to be as gentle as possible for these emotional women, they had to keep them on the other side of the fence. Tempers flared from both sides as several heart-rendering scenes played out.

MPs were trained to be on the lookout for crazies and fanatics; both homegrown and those who made it into the US illegally while often posing as threatened migrants. These people would give up their lives to blow up a couple of C-5a aircraft loaded with munitions and some 400 troops. MPs were under orders to challenge once, and if the subject did not cease an advance toward the aircraft, deadly force was authorized. There would be no warning shots, a miss might bounce off the tarmac or the parked aircraft and hit the troops or the women and children. MPs were not trained to shoot to wound in such situations.

Younger MPs had received lectures from veteran MPs who had come back from the Sandbox, having survived bombings by women and children. They talked about the mistakes made on the perimeter or on patrol. The first mistake was thinking enemy terrorists were not up to the American soldier's high standards. Early on, they had been taught that the Afghan Taliban was an ignorant savage who usually lived in caves. But the truth was, this land in the Middle East belonged to the Taliban. They were tough well-trained fighters, intelligent, and though many of them did live in caves, it was to escape first the Russian and then US airstrikes.

Green Beret veterans compared the Taliban to the Apache and Comanche warriors of the Old West. Many US historians believe the only way American Troops could defeat these desert Indian tribes was through an excessively high number of troops. Historical records show the first use of biological warfare occurred in the late 1800s. The US Army knowingly left smallpox-infected blankets to be found by the Indians. This nearly destroyed the Blackfeet Nation. The army used starvation by killing off the Indians' main food supply, the buffalo. Another method was turning tribe against tribe, making allies out of Indian groups who supported the US Soldier. Similar actions were being used against the Taliban in Afghanistan.

CALL TO FORMATION

Bravo and Delta Companies hurried to form up by platoon. Several hundred soldiers lined up and prepared to board with their weapons. Heavier weapons, munitions, ammo crates, and rations were already loaded by forklifts. Once the troops were lined up, Captain Bill Warrens called Bravo Company to attention.

"Men, I know this is hard on your wives and children, but once aboard this flying 'Pig,' you can call them on your phones until we leave US air space. The plane's crew will notify you when we enter communications blackout. Make sure you say nothing over the phone concerning this trip, the enemy is always listening. In World War II, the saying was 'loose lips sink ships,' and that is still true today. Do not take any photos while aboard this aircraft. You may not use your private computers while this plane is in flight, as it might interfere with the aircraft's onboard computers and navigational aids. This mainly concerns internet use—

you may still play offline computer games. Our crew chiefs have my full backing, so do not give them any back talk, just comply, or your squad is down on the deck for 100 push-ups when we land." Bill left Bravo Company at attention while Delta Company formed up and their Company Commander began pre-boarding information regarding the use of electronics on their assigned C-5a.

Bill nodded at Chief Johnson, and the old sergeant shouted, "You will load by platoon, only one jump seat per troop. No one moves upstairs until a seating arrangement is figured out for the second floor's big seats. I'm sure you've all been briefed on the C5a Galaxy and its 1970s airline-style seats in the upper deck. Store your gear under your seat, but hang your rifles on the red rigging straps behind each of the jump seats... Again, those weapons will not have magazines in them. If I find any, that's another 100 push-ups for you and your whole squad. All trash will come off with you in Afghanistan; they'll have a dumpster by the ramp for you to throw it in. If the Air Force gets mad at us, they're liable to fly us home in some old C-47 dual prop job, which may or not make it back across the Atlantic Ocean. If that happens, we'll have to finish this trip in 30-man survival rafts. And seriously, gentlemen, your officers, and senior NCOs would be in a real foul mood if that were to occur. You'd be better off swimming with the sharks."

Bill let that settle in and then he took over, "Smoking will be allowed once we reach cruising altitude, and the Crew Chief notifies us that it's safe to smoke. Field strip your butts and use the cans attached to the walls for your ashes. And ashes only, because this is a two-day trip, I don't want to see butts overflowing those cans... There will be no smoking during our two refueling stints with an Air Force KC-135 out of Germany. This includes e-cigarettes and pipes. Just so we all agree, I care less what your home state says about laws governing the use of Mari-juana—You are all under the Uniform Code of Military Justice for this entire tour, 24 hours a day, seven days a week. If you want to risk a pleasant high, be prepared for me to shove my boot up your backside and send you to the brig. Remember, there's a lot of hashish, heroin, and pot over there, and the Taliban often adds poison to their drugs as a way of taking out their enemy. Poppy fields and pot plants are routinely sprayed with poison, so be smart and remember that. Illegal drugs shipped into military operational areas from Europe are also suspect. Think about that before you get high. Just for your education, you can blame our CIA and Green Berets for first using this method in Vietnam. When the Taliban was more or less on our side fighting the Russians, we taught them how to use poisonous chemicals. Now they're using it against us.

For those of you who might not be aware, we provided the Taliban with other weapons to fight the Russians, including shoulder-fired missiles—Stingers! As in surface-to-air missiles. We even gave them our new Stingers, which they now use to down our aircraft. Some might say it's a case of turn-around is fair play, but it is ironic. The United States has done this since the Revolution. We trained both Germany and Japan, who made war against us in World War II. We have also trained Iranians and other middle east countries who now make war against us."

Bill glanced over his company to ensure he had everyone's attention and continued, "All right, we'll talk more during the flight. One final item on my agenda—There will be no fights, no arguments, and if they do develop, you'll find yourself secured to the plane's rear ramp. From there, you can listen to the plane's engines and feel the ice developing along your backside. I do hope I'm getting my point across. You're American soldiers, every one of you a finely trained fighting man, and not a bunch of crazed tourists off to see some vacation paradise. These Air Force crews believe we're a bunch of misbehaved clowns, cannon fodder. If you troops don't understand that remark, talk to your squad leader. Please show them your professional side."

His old eyes held a piercing look of warning as Chief Johnson studied the men, then looked over at his captain. Bill nodded, and the Chief shouted, "Prepare to load the aircraft!" Waves erupted from the mass of family members as hundreds of kisses were blown toward the departing soldiers. "Watch your spacing, no hurrying—We'd look pretty foolish if one of you clowns trip and roll down the ramp taking out half a dozen highly trained killing machines."

Bill stood back and watched as B Company loaded. He was impressed with his troops' ability to stay in an orderly line while glancing to the side for one last look at their families and loved ones. The last troop disappeared into the deep belly of two of the world's largest aircraft. For the moment, it was warm, but once in the air, the onboard temperature would steadily drop until the troops felt they were sitting in an air-conditioned room.

One of the nicknames for the C-5a Aircraft was 'Baby Huey', a 1960s cartoon character: a giant goose baby with super strength. Bill thought the name was quite applicable, as this was one colossal aircraft. He always found it amazing that it was capable of flight.

Bill asked the Navigator how long the flight was and was told approximately 21 hours and 14 minutes unless they picked up a tailwind which would reduce that. "Captain, we won't make a straight shot in. We'll be moving about a bit to make our rendezvous with the refueling tankers."

After the aircraft hit its cruising altitude, 1st platoon of B Company was allowed to climb the stairs to sit in the comfortable seats. Each platoon would be given five hours of comfort and hopefully a nap. On the last night with families, many of the men didn't get much sleep. Some serious partying had occurred among the single troops. Of those staying awake, several men became involved in poker games, spread out on green Army blankets in a cleared spot. Others played chess, checkers, or card games, and a few read magazines or books. Noise was kept to a low roar to allow the others quiet time to sleep.

There was no established chow time, but each troop was issued four MRE meals for the flight. Each squad leader brought two large plastic quart-sized containers of either creamy or chunky peanut butter, with two large boxes of Ritz or another type of crackers. Every man carried his own supply of pogey bait. So, nobody would go hungry during the flight to Afghanistan, which took one worry off Bill's shoulders. Each man also carried three full canteens and there was extra drinking water onboard.

The Chief approached Bill and suggested, "Captain, when you're ready, I think we should check the troops, loosen up a few tight bolts and worried minds with a slap on a back or two."

Bill replied in a hoarse whisper, "I'm sure you're right, Chief. Some of these new men are headed off for their first hunt, and they began the journey by flying in the largest plane the U.S. owns. One that weighs so much, there is no way it should stay up in the skies. Makes one think. I sit here surrounded by these well-trained men and realize some got their anxiety button pushed the moment this big bird took off.

"This is a real test on the ol' 1500 hundred questions psychological test for each man—am I brave or just stupid? Will I stand and do my job or weep like a child when those first shots ring out? Am I a trained killer, or maybe just a psychopath who hasn't been caught yet? Will I, the all-American boy, pull that trigger to defend my country? Will I be able to turn it off when I go back home?' Some can, others... we know they'll have problems, and that answer still seems to elude us. We don't want robots, but it's hard to transform an all-American boy into a combat soldier."

"Right you are, Captain," Chief said and added, "How many of these troops will come home on their own two feet, only to be diagnosed later with PTSD? Some 35 percent of combat troops will display some level of PTSD. These are the things I think about when I see those young eyes looking up at me and how different they will be when we head home. It's almost always the same. Whether they're wounded or not, far too many of them come home with a trunk filled with bad memories from what happened to them or what they caused to happen."

"Chief, I noticed it after my first tour in Iraq. We saw a lot of war that year and lost too many good troops. I also noticed how many of them had changed during that time. Far too many of 'em came home, bringing the war with them. It can cost them marriages, rifts between families, and turned some into drug users or alcoholics. Some end up in prison. I was one of the fortunate ones. I grew up seeing what Vietnam had done to my dad, and I was raised in a Christian home. Oh, I still ended up in need of counseling, but Kitty was there with me, learning how to help me. Now, I try to help our men."

"Captain, I understand what you're saying; you're not the first Christian I've been assigned to. But I think you're the first one who believes in what the Good Book says seven days a week. Far too many 'good Christians' spout off about the Lord's mighty work one day out of seven; the other six days, many of them are hypocrites. We have a young lieutenant who says he's a Christian and hates to have the Lord's name taken in vain. A married man, he's been having an affair with a married woman for some time. That's what I mean, sir, if you go by that book, then you've got to live by that book—otherwise, in my way of thinking, you're just another hypocrite."

"Chief, I really try not to judge my fellow man. I leave that to our Lord. He will offer a far harsher judgment than I could ever place on a sinner's life. Yet, at the same time, I must be able to command these men and that involves making judgments. I spend a lot of time in prayer over this issue."

"Then, sir, what about war and the killing of men in Afghanistan or Iraq?"

Bill nodded in understanding and looked at his hands before he replied, "Chief, these hands have dealt out a lot of death with the weapons we've been provided. I'll admit, because I've seen it in your eyes, too, that at the end of the day, or the moment we've walked back into our FOB and put our weapons on safe, I silently talk to God. Before I close my eyes to catch 40 winks, I ask the Lord Jesus to forgive me for those times I might have been wrong in what I've done. I question whether it was my stupidity or failure to listen to my NCOs that got my men killed or wounded. This is all I can do, Chief. I can repent, ask forgiveness, and then carry on. I have to leave the rest to the Big Guy up there to handle—he's the one with the big shoulders and is all-knowing."

"Well, Boss, let's see what you and I can tell these new troops. I see a couple of them already experiencing the initial shakes. There are a few who fear they might embarrass themselves on that first mission. In any event, it's time for some words of guidance from veterans."

Bill grinned, "Then, let's do it, Chief—Gives me a chance to get to know my men better while you climb upstairs and check on the poker players and ensure those men are comfortable up there. If you notice any tension in the game or games, warn them to knock it off or put a quick end to it. I'd hate to embarrass ourselves in front of the Air Force."

"Yes, sir."

Bill walked up the narrow walk space between the legs and knees of B Company, keeping his voice low while stopping to chat with each of the soldiers. The conversations between soldier and company commander were masked by the moderate roar projected into the aircraft by its massive jet engines.

For such a long flight, the C-5a carried a second flight crew, who would take over the controls at mid-flight. Crews were members of the

U.S. Air National Guard on their 22nd flight into Afghanistan over the last 10 months. In the meantime, the reserve crew would be resting in the aircraft's crew quarters, located right behind the cockpit.

Bill had allowed the platoon leaders to open ammo crates for Baretta 9mm and Colt 45 Pistols. Ammo came in cardboard boxes, or in pre-loaded magazines. Given the okay, they would begin loading six magazines per man. In Afghanistan, the men would carry one magazine in their pistol and two on their canteen belts. A round was not chambered until they were outside the base gate. Three additional magazines were carried inside either pocket spaces sewn into the protective Kevlar combat vest or in packs. Pre-loaded magazines would have to be unloaded to ensure all the rounds were loaded correctly. In the past, pre-loaded magazines had been found tampered with. By the time they finished this flight, twenty-two M-4 magazines, and nine pistol magazines were discovered with faulty loads. Bill always wondered if this was a mechanical malfunction or sabotage.

Company snipers would be issued Barret 50-caliber Rifles and ammo in Afghanistan. All heavy weapons would be issued the day after arrival, along with the company's vehicles and assigned Interpreters. For troops carrying 12-gauge shotguns, ammo would be issued when the Heavy Weapons Platoons were given the okay to unpack their crates. A lot of soldiers in Afghanistan carried 30-round magazines in their M-4s. Because the magazines were curved, they were called 'banana clips.' They were first used in the M-16 in Vietnam.

Before leaving the U.S., the men sat through numerous lectures dealing with social diseases, something a troop could catch if not extremely careful. Another gave advice about making attempts to chat with Afghan women. Too many bad situations had developed between soldiers and local women since American troops arrived in the Sandbox. Problems quickly led to an attack by family members swinging a sword or firing guns to protect the honor of a daughter, sister, or family friend. Soldiers were told to never instigate any action with a foreign woman, for the father, husband, or brothers would likely accuse them of dishonoring her and their family. After killing you, they might also kill her for having possibly caused the problem. Family honor was a big thing for the Afghan people.

The troops were told that most prostitutes were Muslim and could be affiliated with the Taliban. They were reminded to keep their mouths shut and report any suspected grilling by a stranger or even an interpreter to their squad leaders.

When Bill was an assistant platoon leader in Iraq, as a 2nd Lieutenant, he was responsible for 32 troops. Two of his men got into trouble with a couple of local young women because of their zest for companionship. Despite the fact that neither of the young women spoke English and their faces were covered with ornate scarves, the two soldiers thought they had found true love. But what they had found were two sisters 13 and 15 years of age. The soldiers were chased back to the FOB by a mob of 21 sword and club-swinging men and older boys. The mob was held back by Army MPs and five local policemen. The interpreter at the gate quickly found out that the soldiers had dishonored the young girls by daring to hold their hands in public. The father demanded that the soldiers die, and his daughters would also die for dishonoring the family.

Bill and his two men stood before the Company Commander for a 25-minute grilling before the call came down summoning them to the Post Commander. There, a balding and aged full-bird Infantry Colonel, an officer who had no love for Airborne heroes, had harsh words with them. During that meeting, the girl's father, two older brothers, and their Imam (a Muslim Pastor), were present. Bill and his two offenders were berated by the Base's Chief Command Sergeant Major and interpreted by two allied Interpreters. One, Kurdish and one Indian, who together spoke several Middle Eastern dialects.

The Army paid the father $1,000 and provided him with 20 goats. Both men were confined to the base for their own protection and assigned kitchen duties until the Regiment was shipped back home. Bill noticed a 55 percent upsurge in attacks on the Regiment's patrols over their last three months on station. He mentioned it to his Company Commander, who had already noted it. Bill was informed both girls were executed in Honor Killings for offending the family's honor. Since then, Bill was a matter-of-fact lecturer when warning his men about Middle East customs and traditions.

BACK TO THE WARNINGS

Bill shared this story with his men during their training. He also related that the young soldiers suffered meltdowns after hearing about the girls' deaths. He urged the men to stay in groups of four when leaving the post or FOB (Forward Observation Base) when off-duty. "A vast majority of the children in Afghanistan find it a challenge to steal off a millionaire American soldier. Most locals believe all Americans are millionaires and can afford to be separated from their watches, rifles, boots, bracelets, and rings. This way of thinking began in World War One and possibly even before that. In World War Two, Arabs entered the battlefields as the fires still blazed from combat and stripped bodies of anything valuable—German, Italian, Russian, British, or American. They loaded their prizes on goat carts or the backs of camels to haul back to a temporary camp, and for the next week or so, they felt wealthy.

The metal, including rifle barrels and parts from damaged firearms, was usually melted down for different needs. Clothes torn off bodies were used to make other clothes, robes, rugs, and tapestries. Workable guns became trade material or went into a tribe's personal armory. Jewelry was a hot trading commodity; rare gems were pulled out of rings and bands melted down to make other jewelry. Their beautiful woven rugs were well-known throughout most of the world, but few realized where the raw material and multi-colored threads came from. One of the hardest things to sell or trade is the military boot, mainly because most of the locals prefer to keep them for their own use. In Afghanistan, the great sandy deserts eventually became hard rock and hillsides of stone and mountain peaks where such boots come in handy. From what Bill learned, the locals value their boots over the old Russian ones.

Bill advised his men to keep their stuff locked up, or they would lose it. "My dad used to tell me about the mama-sans they hired as maids in Vietnam. Though most were honest and hardworking, there were those who were thieves and spies. So, be careful, vigilant, and don't talk about our operations where any foreigners might be listening."

A good officer, Bill went out of his way to get to know every soldier in his command; where they were from, if they were married or single, and this drew him closer to his troops. He was well respected by his men because they knew he really cared about them, and it helped that he was a veteran of two combat tours.

Bill continued to make the rounds aboard the C-5a, going up one side of the jump seats and down the next row while the Chief was upstairs. Per the Chief's wristwatch, the men had another 41 minutes, and then it would be time to bring up the 2nd Platoon for five hours of stretching out, sleeping, and playing games. Chief glanced about the room, "This is your 40-minute warning—40 minutes before you rotate with 2nd platoon."

When the five hours were up, the men of the 2nd platoon were advised to stand by while the 1st platoon came down. Upstairs, most of the men quickly planted themselves into cushioned airline-style seats. A few were quickly asleep and snoring while the card players were getting briefed on the poker game's point system by SFC Roman. He turned the running of the game over to Staff Sergeant Jimmy Olson. Somehow, the monitor of one game became the official referee for the 2nd floor. He was brought in when arguments developed which kept the Chief from being called; both sides undoubtedly knew that would end up involving calisthenics for everyone.

Five hours later, 3rd Platoon filed in, with 1st Lt. Graham, the platoon commander ordering SSgt. Cecil Watson Jr., the platoon medic to take over upstairs from SSgt. Jimmy Olson. The men liked their medic; he was experienced and took good care of them. He earned a Purple Heart after he was shot in the back, carrying a wounded troop out of an ambush, and saving his life. They thought he deserved a medal of valor for his actions, but a second Commendation Medal seemed to satisfy him. "Saving men is what we medics do, what we're trained for." But he never had to buy a beer if a member of Third Platoon was around.

It was nearing time for a flight crew change. The second crew would be awakened, with time to chow down and wash up before taking over. The first Crew would have a small meal before they washed up and put clean sheets on the bunks to crash for the remainder of the flight. Only the first crew's Flight Captain would be awakened if there was trouble. He would decide if other crew members were needed to assist in such an event.

Bill went up to the cockpit to introduce himself after the first crew left the flight deck. He enjoyed seeing out the front windows and talking with the flight crew.

ARRIVAL—IT'S ABOUT TIME!

From other operations, Bill knew a "Follow Me" truck would be standing by to escort their aircraft to its assigned parking spot. Those two words were painted on a large board with rotating police lights to ensure they were visible on a busy tarmac. He looked over at the Chief, "Army headquarters was supposed to have called ahead to request buses for 400 combat troops and nine deuces to haul our packs, ammo, heavy weapons, and other gear. When this beast gets stopped, make sure there's a line of army vehicles following us."

"Yes, sir. Do you want me to find a payphone if there's no sign of 'Welcome to Bagram' out there'?"

"Nope. We'll just fire off our mortars and announce our presence. I'm sure we can find a Taliban target out there somewhere."

"Not good, Captain. You shouldn't be making waves your first day in Dodge City. Take some time to get to know the Earp Brothers, then we'll go blow up a couple of ranches."

"We've both seen too many westerns, Chief."

"This desert country, sir. It brings it out in me. I was a big John Wayne fan."

"So, was my dad, but he strongly disliked 'The Green Beret'. He thought John Wayne was too old and too fat to play a Green Beret officer."

"sir, that almost sacrilege! The Duke—well, he was too fat at that point. I'd have to agree with your dad on that one."

The aircraft finally came to a jarring halt and the bird's crew chief addressed the soldiers, "That's it, you can unbuckle and go kiss the tarmac outside for surviving yet one more flight in an Air Force aircraft. We use the cheapest parts but have the best mechanics to keep these beasts in the air."

Several troops rallied, shot him a closed fist salute, and yelled, "Airborne!", while the others began putting on their gear. They had all taken off their Kevlar body armor; canteen belts were attached to black combat suspenders which most troops used to hold extra fighting knives, such as a 12-inch K-Bar Bowie, or a quick grab pistol clip, rifle magazines, and first aid trauma bandage. Suspenders made it easier to carry two canteens, extra ammo, a bayonet, and a few grenades when they went into the field.

A soldier's pack held two extra full canteens, four to six grenades, extra ammo magazines, and possibly a First Aid kit. Their gear also included a rain poncho and a camouflage poncho liner rolled up or tightly folded, a canvas bag that held the man's pogey bait, possibly a deck of cards and field rations, and sometimes a Bible along with other pieces of equipment the job may require. Normally, packs weighed around 60 to 70 pounds. With three days of meals added and other needed items, it could quickly go up to 90 pounds or more and for extended missions, it could go up to 120 pounds.

Chief hustled past everyone, telling them to stand by, as he made his way to the back door of the aircraft. But the Air Force surprised him by opening the front door first, across from where Bill Warrens Jr. stood relacing his left boot. Surprised by the change in air pressure, he turned around as the big door slowly opened and saw an Air Force Lieutenant standing atop a mobile stairwell.

"Who's in Command, sir?" The Air Force Lieutenant asked.

"I am Lieutenant, for these men. The pilots are in the cockpit. I sure hope you have a parade of buses and trucks out there waiting for me."

"Not yet, Captain. We had to first make sure you and your men were on board.

The Lieutenant saw the look of concern on Captain Warrens's face and added, "I apologize, Captain, but since the last terrorist bombing, things have gotten really tight around this part of the world. Your vehicles are waiting for my signal to approach."

"That's Okay, Lieutenant." He turned looking for the Chief. "Chief where are our travel orders? We need one to unload this aircraft and allow the carpool to pick us up. They're down at Base Ops."

"I've got everything in our folder, sir, just give me a moment." Chief made his way back up front, issuing orders for no one to exit the plane or give Air Force Security Police any trouble.

"Listen up! First Squad of First Platoon goes into the first bus, then the second. Overflow will need to go into the next bus. I do not want any rivalry going on that would put B or D Companies in a bad light with our new commanders. Be prepared; we could end up spending a few hours out here on the airfield while we get everything worked out. "Make sure you have everything you came on board with. Heavy Weapons Platoon standby to unload specialty items. No one will leave here until the trucks are loaded with our munitions and weapons. We are in no hurry here. I do not want a crate of grenades, a claymore, or a single mortar round dropped. Let's be smart. Pick up your trash and take it with you. Anything else, Captain?"

"Select four armed veterans to guard the Heavy Weapons as they are off-loaded to the trucks. They will ride with those trucks. I do not plan on losing anyone or anything on our first day to a Taliban suicide squad. Grab some veteran troops to guard the buses as we load, no new guys. I don't want some nervous new guy shooting a local out of fear he's a possible Taliban."

"Affirmative, sir."

The Air Force Lieutenant finished talking to Base Operations on his hand radio. "They're moving, Captain; should be here in five or six minutes. I've assigned six men from the Security Forces as convoy escorts. Three pick-ups, each armed with 240Bs and M-4s, and two men will escort your heavy munitions to the Army side of the base to be secured per your requirements in your assigned Conex storage containers."

"We appreciate your assistance, Lieutenant. I understand you are only adhering to security requirements. We'll assist you in any way we can," Bill Warrens said to the young Air Force officer.

"I appreciate that, sir. Oh, sir, here's the first of your buses."

A Ford F-350 4x4 led the first bus. A mount welded to a heavy-duty roll-bar on the back of the truck cab supported a 240B machine gun for the Security Force gunner. Bill remembered when the Air Force called them Security Policemen, and before that, Air Police; now they were Security Forces. It made him wonder why the Air Force kept changing names. The Army had called their MPs military policemen since the first world war.

While the driver remained in the running vehicle, the security officer jumped down with his M-4 at the ready. They were here in the event the Taliban had infiltrated the base to use a suicide bomber to take out the soldiers on board the C-5a or a load of troops in one of the buses. Bill appreciated the added security.

The Security Forces had an established kill zone around the aircraft. This number grew with the second C-5a coming to a stop some 100 yards down the tarmac. No one was allowed within 1,000 feet of the C-5a. If the subject failed to halt, they would be shot when they passed inside the 1,000-foot mark. No one would approach them until Explosive Ordinance Disposal personnel were on the scene to check for explosives. Since the war began in Afghanistan, the military had lost over 100 aircraft to Taliban suicide bombers, rockets, and mortars. Those numbers had dropped since security procedures had tightened on base.

The second Security Forces alert truck arrived with the last of the buses, the third SP truck would drive behind the munition's trucks. A person's vision was limited when riding in the truck cab, which was why the gunner remained in the truck bed. A security strap kept him from falling out during any tight turns the driver might be forced to make.

The Security Force lieutenant asked Bill if this was his first visit to Bagram.

"No, my first tour was in Iraq. My second was here—but it's been enlarged by the look of things. A lot more aircraft—the place looks pretty busy. I've got men with me on their fourth and fifth tours. This is our second decade in this war, and I hope this is my last trip.

"Just like Vietnam. We can't win here because we didn't come to conquer the land and its people like we did in World War Two. We're here helping one government hold on against another with the same religion and the same background, and again, we're backing the rich. That's what happened in Vietnam, the first modern war we lost."

The young Lieutenant nodded and replied, "I'm a bit of a history nut, sir. It was my major in college. That and archeology. That's one of the reasons I'm here, but I've yet to get off base to see any ancient ruins. They have a museum in the city I'd like to see. According to Afghanistan's history, Alexander the Great built a city here. Sadly, most of the ruins ended up buried under our tarmac here. Such a tragic loss. There are many men and some women here who know this is the wrong place for us to be. We're trying to stop massive arterial bleeding wounds with miniature band-aids and not much more than a rubber band to hold things together."

"You have women SPs or SFs over here in the combat zone? That surprises me." Bill said. He had no idea the Air Force was sending female SFs over here. He would soon learn that the Army was also sending female MPs and Security troops into Iraq and Afghanistan with some going on patrol. He hadn't seen any females being assigned to the 101st Airborne; he figured the Colonel would probably retire when that occurred. Of course, there were times Bill thought Kitty could qualify for Airborne. Not that he would ever allow it. When it came to combat, he preferred his wife at home watching over the kids, but he had admitted to being a bit of a dinosaur about it.

"The real problem lies in letting the women off base—They take a lot of verbal abuse from the Muslim men, even from our so-called allied troops. They can only go off base in groups of four or more with no weapons. They're ordered not to become involved in any confrontation with the locals. Our men are ordered to help them to depart the scene. I suspect that if our women were allowed, they could handle themselves quite proficiently."

"So, basically, they are confined on base, spending extra for the Indian beads and pelts they could've bought off-base for a pittance."

"That's about it. We've had far too many of our ladies hurt physically and suffering emotional abuse. These female SFs are a pretty tough lot. Before I got here, two of our base ladies were molested by a gang of Muslims and left unconscious 100 yards from the Main Gate in the middle of the night. From what I learned, both women were infected with multiple social diseases. The mental abuse has left them with severe PTSD. Both were retired on disability. "As officers, we fear a religious war if it happens again. The first time, everyone was stunned and that helped control the situation. If it happens again, 1,000 US troops could be downtown killing every Muslim man over 14 years of age until Bagram was laid waste too. If that were to happen, within days, that massacre would become a new poster child for every terrorist group in the world."

"Then why did the Air Force and the Army, send females over here? It doesn't make any sense to me."

"sir, things have changed. Federal courts have allowed our women a lot of liberties they've been fighting for. We have women fighter pilots and helicopter pilots; only the Green Beret, and Airborne Special Forces Units remain male only. That damn movie, 'G.I. Jane' didn't help matters. But that's going to change, too. For the first year, men will die for being too overprotective. Or, in some cases, going to jail for sexual harassment and possibly killed due to some lover's triangle. The Air Force and probably your Army push sexual awareness training."

"Lieutenant, I hope I have my Colonel's Eagle and drawing retirement pay before we see women in the Airborne. Besides, I doubt my wife would ever understand me having to shower with naked women. Nope, no siree, it would never fly."

"I understand, sir. I think my mother would march right into that shower room, grab me by one ear and march me right out for another one of her famous lectures on 'How to Treat a Lady Properly Until She Proves She's Not a Lady.' Mom was a real hard nose when it came to that."

"Sounds like my mother," Bill said.

Chief came to the bottom of the mobile stairs and shouted, "sir, are you going with the first bus?"

"I'll be right down, Chief." He yelled tossing him a wave as he turned again to face the Lieutenant. "I had planned on staying until our munitions were unloaded, but I can see you're running a pretty good operation here. You know where we're at, so come pay us a visit. After that, only the Good Lord knows where we'll be, but Command will always know. Maybe, if we find things quiet out there, you might want to come out on a five-day patrol and see how the other half lives. You can tell your Colonel you'd like to get a better view of the country terrain out there."

"Thank you, Captain, I'd like that. The only combat I see is when the Taliban sends a few rockets or mortars our way. Spending a week with the Airborne might be something to tell my kids about someday."

"Well, take care," Bill shook hands with the officer and joined the Chief.

4

A NEW HOME

"CHIEF, I think you would've made a real fine train conductor—looks like we're ready to go."

The Chief grinned, "I'm in a hurry to see what kind of housing we get stuck with this time. Knowing the Air Force, they'll probably put us under a bunch of leaky Boy Scout tents, surrounded by rusty barbed wire within shelling range of Kabul. Make it easy for the Taliban to keep us up at night with rocket and mortar fire." The Army bus driver chuckled, and the Chief lashed out harshly, "What are you laughing about Private First Class... Owenby?"

"Easy, Chief, you're tired from a long flight, with too little sleep... You've got steel barbs sticking out. Your remark was a bit humorous," Bill said in a low voice that only the Chief could hear.

"Yes, sir—You're right." Chief drew closer to the nervous driver, "So, Private First Class Owenby, why did my remark strike you as being funny?" The Chief's harshness had dropped considerably.

"Chief, I apologize for laughing; it's just that here on Post, we live in some of the safest buildings in this theater. You'll all be living in metal conex containers with a maximum of four men to a box. The conex units were used to bring supplies over here and then converted into barracks, sort of. Huge Hesco Barriers surround the containers. In other words, more or less a wall that's made up of huge cement blocks—seven feet wide by seven feet long and seven feet tall. Enclosure walls, known as T-Walls, are 12 to 14 feet high in various widths, about ten inches thick and made of concrete and steel. Rebar loops on top make them easier to offload from flatbeds. Everything is constructed to minimize the amount of damage a mortar or rocket will do when the Taliban hit us. We sleep pretty safe and a whole lot better than in trenches and fox holes."

"What happened to all the old-World War II style barracks they used to have here?" Chief asked.

"Torn down... most of them. Those old buildings didn't handle the weather or the occasional sandstorms and wood rots over time. Some of those barracks were over 12 years old and didn't offer a lot of protection from enemy mortar fire."

"Thank you, Owenby. That all sounds great. Disregard my earlier tone; been a long flight."

"How far to our new home?" Bill asked.

Owenby smiled, "sir, ever since the Air Force took to calling their main drag 'Disney Lane'—mostly because of all the colorful signs and strange business names, we've taken to calling our enclosure the Castle of Doom as we're only missing a drawbridge. Anti-Disney people prefer to call it 'Slumville.' Unknown cartoonists express themselves by adding graffiti to the inside barrier walls. The last unit who lived in your place left it up, and some of it is rather objectionable—if you get my meaning."

Bill turned to the Chief, "Better plan on getting several gallons of paint and some paint rollers."

"Yes, sir," Chief replied.

They drove in silence until PFC Owenby pulled off the main road and onto a well-paved lane that went for another 60 yards to a massive fortification.

"Damn! This place reminds me of pictures I've seen of the old Yuma Territorial Prison in Arizona!" Chief exclaimed.

Bill added, "It may look ugly, but those walls are for our protection." He looked to Chief and whispered, "They make me think of the Walls of Jericho from the Bible. I only hope the Taliban don't have any marching bands to bring these walls down."

"They're all Muslims, Captain. I really doubt that routine would work out for them as well as it did for Joshua and his Israelites," Chief replied.

As they drove through the double-wide gate, Bill saw rows of Conex containers. He suspected the structure's walls would provide adequate protection for his men from enemy shrapnel outside a direct hit. At the airfield, he had been told that this enclosure could house 576 troops - well over their number. Each conex came with two sets of metal bunk beds, the same type the military had been using since World War II.

Owenby stopped his bus in front of Bill's new headquarters, a structure with three flag poles in front. Made of four Conex containers set side by side with doorways cut in walls to make Company Headquarters four units wide. Radio equipment had been installed the previous day. Army MPs were posted at the front gate and a two-man mobile MP patrol worked outside the wall for added security. Bill would assign another MP to remain on guard outside Company Headquarters and a roving two-man walking patrol from his own command to cover the compound. In his last two tours, he had learned the hard way not to put too much trust in his allies, not so much for being terrorists, but for merely being thieves. Every week, Bill received reports of jewelry, money, equipment, food, and even uniforms stolen from his men. He doubted anything had changed since his last visit to Afghanistan. Bill knew most of these locals were well below the poverty line. As in previous wars, most third-world people believed all Americans to be wealthy.

During his last tour, Army CID and MPs had busted one large theft ring involving Afghan soldiers. They had worked in connection with some of the women who worked as housekeepers and did the men's laundry. These locals worked for an off-base businessman known to have ties to the Taliban who was later killed in a shoot-out with Afghan Federal Police and U.S Army CID Agents. Three men who were taken prisoner provided information on how they had delivered valuables to several Kabul addresses. When Afghan Forces went to these locations, they found no one but did recover everything from U.S. camouflage uniforms to a box filled with jewelry items, some with US servicemen's names etched in.

"Where's the chow hall and showers, Owenby?" Bill asked.

"That's part of the bad news, Captain. More than eight Army units share one chow hall, and there are only three shower units between us. Both are some distance away. You can either call for buses at chow time or have them scheduled."

"What sort of distances are you talking about?" Bill asked.

"The closest shower facility is a mile or so down the main road. Our chow hall is two miles further on the same road. Good grub, though. You should find the chow hall's hours of operation posted inside your head-quarters along with the list of phone numbers. There used to be phone books, but they kept getting stolen, so phone lists were taped to the office walls. Everything, from the Army and Air Force Exchange phone numbers, pizza callouts, plus some of the local businesses and, of course, base transportation. There is a civilian taxi service, but we never use them—too risky. Most of these people don't have driver's licenses."

"What time does evening chow begin?" Bill asked.

"16:30 hours until 1900 hours, sir."

Bill pointed to the south, "In that direction, correct?"

"Yes, sir."

"Alright then, I guess you'd better return to the airfield and see who else needs a ride to our new desert home."

"Thank you, sir, and welcome to Bagram, Captain."

Bill's senior NCOs were forming up their platoons as the men unloaded from the buses. He knew that the Chief would take charge and give Bill a chance to look over his new headquarters.

Once they were formed up the Chief addressed the troops, "You will be dismissed in a moment to find your new home but understand this, platoon officers and squad NCOs will assign you to your new lodgings. Squads and platoons will stay together because I'm not going to be running all over when I need to find someone. Get unpacked, and then listen up for what comes next. No one leaves this compound until all duties are completed. The Captain doesn't want any biased housing taking place here. We are all Airborne, so behave like it. Our color is Army green and for the next twelve to thirteen months, get used to it. We all represent the United States here, not just a white, black, brown, or red privileged society. So, behave or plan on feeling my boot up your butt! You are all part of this new volunteer Army. So get busy and, for the moment, try to ignore the artwork on those walls. I'm sure there will be a painting party in the next couple of days. Places like this are unofficially known as the Slums, and you can probably see why. Just think of it as home for the next year and keep the racy posters to a minimum. This is still Army barracks, no matter what else this looks like. Command doesn't want some Congresswoman coming to inspect the troops, being embarrassed by some naked pin-up—you understand me?"

"Yes, Chief!" Was shouted back in response by the men of B Company.

Bill's new headquarters building shared doorways leading to Officer Housing on one side and NCO Housing on the other. There were two beds in the radio room where the Senior RTO would work when in camp. Several mementos from previous occupants had been left behind, including a kill list, clearly left as a way of daring Bill's unit to better it. Bill ripped it off the wall—he didn't play that game. To him, killing the enemy was a solemn thing and not one to be taken lightly.

A black Taliban flag was tacked to a wall among an assortment of Taliban head scarfs. Several Taliban knives adorned the walls and a few more were stacked on a shelf. Bill shook his head when he found several human skulls on a shelf which he ordered to be buried in a single hole outside the enclosure. He ripped the Taliban flag and head scarves off the wall and ordered them burned. He felt such adornment on the walls honored the Taliban, and it surprised him the previous commander had felt so different.

Bill had the only Conex with a single metal bed. While inspecting his room, he discovered a poisonous snake curled behind a metal wall locker. The room appeared to be booby-trapped and not by departing American soldiers. He suspected some insurgent had been in this compound and sent a warning to all his men to be on guard.

Whistles were blown, and the Chief had the whole company formed up again, standing in front of their new headquarters. He held up the headless serpent for all to see. "I want every single foot of these build-ings thoroughly searched for booby-traps, biological and technical— snakes can be anywhere, even hanging from the ceiling or inside a locker. Look for grenade and claymore traps. Be especially wary when searching the latrines because these snakes are attracted by moisture. As you veterans know, these vile things could be just about anywhere, even down inside the outhouse hole. One sure way to handle the problem is to pour a cup of gas down the hole and throw in a lighted match. But be sure to stand back because the rising fumes could ignite and possibly blow your eyebrows off. I do not want anyone hurt, so if you see anything that might be a bomb, send a runner here so we can get EOD (explosive ordinance disposal) out here right away. We'll let the experts defuse bombs, but we have to handle the snakes and whatever else has been so kindly left for us.

New troops do not trust any locals working in this compound from the lady doing your laundry to the boy shinning your boots. Each one could be a thief or a Taliban. Treat them respectfully, pay what you owe them, but never trust one. It's safer that way. We've lost some good men who got too friendly and trusting with these people. To an Afghan Muslim, those of you who are of the Christian faith is the enemy, no matter if you're an ally to the Afghan Army. Most of the Taliban feel that almost all Americans are Christians. Remember, for the Taliban Muslims, killing an American soldier, especially a Christian, is a surefire way to get into their heaven. This is no reflection on those of you who happen to be of the Muslim faith. You've been born and raised in America, where we believe in our Constitutional right to believe what we want. Over here, they look at it a bit differently." Chief dismissed the troops to search the compound.

An hour later, Chief came into Bill's new office, saluted, and prepared to report his findings. Bill addressed him in a casual tone, "Chief, let's get one thing straight between us... Whenever it is just the two of us, you have open door liberties, which means no saluting. But if anyone else is in here, we're all military, okay? My name is Bill, but if that's pushing the liberties too far, I understand."

"It may take some time to break old habits, sir. As to the security checks, you were right on the money. We found 17 more snakes, two booby traps going to hidden claymores buried under floors, and one wired to the back of an outhouse. The weight of anyone sitting down would have tugged on a wire, detonating the device. There would've been nothing left of the latrine, the GI, and any other troops standing within 20 feet of the explosion. We were lucky; no one had gone to the chow hall yet and suffered a bad case of the runs."

"How about our new vehicles, were they inspected?"

"In process right now, Captain. You can't believe how many of our brave shooters are afraid of snakes. After what was found in these units, I put men on the vehicles, but most of the rigs have been inspected, and all was in order."

"Chief, keep this between us, but I'm sort of leery of those slimy things myself. I'm okay with rattlers; they're not so slimy. I've been on a couple of rattlesnake hunts in the desert—they usually set off a warning, but not these desert vipers. Once the men have finished unpacking, form them up and march them down to the chow hall. We all need to stretch our muscles after the ride in that oversized Lego toy. We'll let the base know that the Army Airborne has arrived."

Bill reviewed their assigned vehicle list, which provided B Company with a dozen 'Deuces' - two-and-a-half-ton open bed trucks. Most with benches on each side of the truck bed and wooden rails. They were also issued a dozen Humvees and five Strykers, but most of these vehicles would need some tinkering from the engine sounds. They also ended up with four Vietnam-era M1-A1 Jeeps, each set up to hold a 240B machine gun.

An hour later, Bill called for the Chief, and when he showed up, asked, "Has our interpreter arrived yet?" Bill was standing outside the front door to the radio room. " And is he possibly Kurdish?"

"Sir, we have two interpreters; one is Kurdish, and a Christian. The other is from India—a Hindi, and he happens to be a language professor. We're lucky though, the two are good friends who've worked together for some time assisting the U.S. Their backgrounds have been thoroughly searched by CID, and they appear to be the real deal."

"Great, because my Afghan is terrible, except for a few commands. I'll have to bone up before we move into the field."

Chief looked down at his notepad, "The Kurdish Terp is a Mr. Hanci Nabbia, and the guy from India, who looks like my junior college dean, is Mr. Janke Dharkasee."

"I hope to have them doing language classes with our men. One of the first mistakes we made in coming over here early on was not understanding the local dialects. Got the U.S. into some serious trouble because of language and religious protocol differences.

PATROL WORK AND TRAINING

Bill Warrens had his fleet of vehicles tuned up, refueled, and the Humvees on standby alert. Several of them were armed with 240B machine guns with ammo secured in one of the vehicle's 500-round steel ammo carriers. Squad leaders inspected all vehicles daily. After finding the snakes and explosives, Bill had decided that security squads would each pull a 12-hour shift while on base in conjunction with the MPs assigned to this enclosure.

The Army deuce-and-a-half was considered a poor vehicle to transport men on Afghan Roads because of the potential for ambushes in narrow desert ravines in the hills. But all too often, there were not enough Strikers and Humvees available, and the old trucks had to be used. Keeping all of these vehicles running was a 24-hour job for the base mechanics, as the desert and dirt roads could be challenging.

Soldiers were put to work adding to the enclosure's defensive positions. The Chief acquired an Army earthmover from the engineers for a few days. A qualified driver piled dirt up while soldiers filled hundreds of sandbags. Some sandbags were placed on open truck beds as additional protection for troops.

When a convoy left Bagram and Bill's unit was called to escort it, he sent one fire team ahead by at least 1000-yards, either a Stryker or an armored Humvee. This team included a sniper whose job was to clear the road of anything that might be a possible IED, a roadside bomb. When the patrol dismounted for short durations, the 240B shooter and rifleman stayed on watch. The driver manned communications and stood ready to 'haul butt' if they came under fire or needed to support a patrol.

For a week, each of the teams was assigned to various duties and practiced each of them repeatedly until they had it down pat, even in the dark. Specific squads were chosen for special assignments that might be called for in their first three weeks as the troops acclimated to the desert heat. The troops were told it was called 'Climatizing'.

For the first few days, B Company demonstrated incredible feats avoiding being run down by over-excited Afghan drivers on the main road, many of whom had no formal driver training or understanding of road signs.

Americans often lost their temper which resulted in more than one significant argument between civilians and soldiers. When it was between two or three quarreling Americans under Bill's command, the affair was usually moved away from the officers and held outside the enclosure. An NCO would be on scene to observe the festivities and ensure the men kept it to the Marcus of Queensbury rulebook.

Bill reminded his troops, "Just remember, the guy you pick a fight with today may be the one covering your ass out there in Indian country tomorrow."

From his last two tours to the Sandbox, Bill knew how merciless the heat here was, and it was often what led to a scuffle. He did his best to cover these incidents within the company by assigning extra duties to the troublemakers.

During the last day of training, the unit's serious assignments began to arrive. During his next company formation, Bill addressed his troops, "You've all worked very hard since our arrival, and I'm proud of you. But our traveling orders have come down, and it's time for us to enter into this war. This afternoon and tonight, go over all your gear one more time. Tomorrow morning you'll receive your daily routine duties, and you'll have a couple of days to acclimate. After that, we'll be traveling through Indian country. Squad leaders, check your men and their equipment. Make sure each man is ready for combat, and all weapons are ready—this is a combat post, and we could come under fire at any time. Platoon leaders will meet in my office at 2100 hours. Any questions?" No hands raised; Bill knew his men were ready to go.

"Get it done, people. You're dismissed!"

IT'S TIME

An MP escort vehicle sat ready, and MPs watched as the famous 101st Airborne readied themselves for departure. When the order was given, B Company began climbing into vehicles. 1st Platoon led, protected by two armored Humvees. The Company's Heavy Weapons Platoon followed them in line, trailed by the other two platoons.

Kabul and Bagram were surrounded by mountainous terrain, giving the new recruits a hint of what lay ahead. Before long, they would imagine Taliban insurgents behind every rock or stone pile. Eventually, some would suspect every Afghan they saw in the desert as a possible insurgent. Bill could still recall his first encounters in Iraq and how sweaty his hands became as he gripped his rifle. He knew from his own experiences how fear, stress, and quick constant head movements would lead to some nasty headaches. All part of being a babe in the woods.

Three hours into the drive, the lead Deuce ran over an IED, which disabled the truck and wounded the driver and two soldiers. These would be the first three Purple Hearts for the unit. Squads were sent out to clear the area of a potential ambush, but nothing was found. Bill reported the incident to higher command and requested a medivac helicopter for the wounded men, none of whom had life-threatening injuries.

Safety protocol required the Medical Rescue Helicopter to fly over the scene at 1,000 feet to see if it drew enemy fire. If not, it circled at 500 feet for one final check before landing. Bill knew there was always the fear that local Taliban units might possess Stinger Missiles and heavy machine guns, which could quickly bring down a helicopter. The Taliban had shown no respect for the large red crosses painted on these birds using it instead as a major target. The helicopter landed within a short walk from the damaged truck, unloading two additional medics to help the wounded men. Two stretchers took up all the room inside the helicopter, so the third stretcher was attached to the pilot's left side skid. The flight back to Bagram would only take 20 minutes. When the chopper lifted off, B Company's medics returned to their unit.

When Bill got word of the injuries, he became angry. He had not wanted this to happen on their first day out and so close to Bagram, knowing it would rattle his new guys. He sent word over the radio to ensure his wounded men were taken directly to the Army-Air Force Hospital on Bagram, then told the Chief, "At least our guys will get the best of care there—that hospital is as good as any stateside, and they're used to combat injuries."

Chief replied, "I'll have the squad leaders give their newbies a good morale booster. At least no one was killed."

A subdued silence fell over the convoy as it approached the next Afghan community. The last time Bill was near here, he was being airlifted to the Bagram hospital, where he had spent 11 plus hours in surgery. After he was stabilized, he was loaded aboard a C-141 Starlifter and flown to Germany where he spent two weeks in an Air Force hospital before being flown stateside for additional surgeries. He had seen Kabul before he was shot but didn't think too much of it. However, he did like the towering Afghan Mountains and thought he would like to return someday after peace had come to the land.

The desert was hot, with temperatures staying close to 120 degrees Fahrenheit. Most of the locals looked upon them with scorn; after 15 years of warfare, many were weary of all the bloodshed. Many wished the Americans and their allies would just go home and leave Afghanistan to the Afghan people. The passing American troops gave them someone to focus their anger against, and a lot of them shook their heads or waved a fist as the soldiers drove by.

"Who are the Terps riding with?" Bill asked the Chief.

Chief pulled out his notepad and turned a couple of pages to find the right one. He always kept one of these small notebooks handy and could quickly fill out three dozen or more of them by the end of the tour. "They're riding with 2nd Platoon. You need them?"

"No, just want to know where they are in case I need them. Next time we stop, let them know I'm interested in knowing what those civilians were shouting at us. I know they want us to leave Afghanistan, but I'm curious as to what else they're saying."

Chief nodded; he had come to like and respect this young Captain, and he trusted him. In his lengthy career, he had been supervised by many young officers, but he had come to respect the ones who had come from West Point.

Bill looked at the Chief and grinned; he liked working with such a seasoned veteran. He knew the Chief was recently divorced and had two sons in college, one in Pre-Law and the other in Pre-Med. The Chief had spoken of them often; when they had inquired about what their dad did overseas, he tossed them a collection of his notepads and told them to read. As a result, the boys decided not to join the military—the one thing he had promised his ex-wife. They still saw each other, but she just couldn't live with him. These wars and middle-of-the-night rapid deployment missions had cost them their marriage and a daughter who had died from a drug overdose while he was overseas. Black Operations prevented him from going home for the funeral. After that, his wife asked for a divorce and moved out.

"You find anything else about our Terps?" Bill asked, trying to be heard over the sounds of the Humvee.

"Hanci Nabbia's been working with us for over six years, about when Iran began killing the Kurdish people. My notes say he is a Holy Man, a pastor, and refuses to carry a weapon. Nothing but good reports on him. He worked well with the Green Beret for two years, but sort of went berserk when he lost his youngest son to the Taliban. That has all been confirmed."

After four days in the field, they returned to base, their first mission a bust, with no enemy contact. First missions were not intended to be long, but rather an introduction to the field. Having three wounded right off did not help ease tension among the troops.

The next day, Bill and Chief spent a couple of hours in the hospital talking with two of their wounded. One man had three shrapnel pieces in his left arm; luckily, five more had lodged in his Kevlar vest. He had cuts to his neck and lower jaw and had nearly lost his left ear. He had recovered well following surgery and was already in good shape when Bill and the Chief showed up. This young man was sincerely touched by this officer's visit, and Bill knew it, which made the drive over all the more worthwhile.

The second man had shrapnel wounds to his face, which would require additional surgeries stateside, but his vision appeared unimpaired. Two shrapnel pieces had entered his left side damaging some vital organs, but after eight hours of surgery, he was recovering nicely.

Chief was told that they might have lost at least two of the three men without the helicopter. Looking down at these wounded soldiers, he hoped this would be his last tour of duty overseas; it was time to seriously think about retirement. His back hurt, which no one knew about, and he was tired of losing fine young men in a war no one really cared about anymore.

"Gentlemen, we have to leave now, but I'll try to get back to see you before you leave. I can promise you, from my own experience, the plane you fly back home in is a special trip in every way to the one you made three weeks ago. The staff onboard treats each of you as a certified hero, and they should. I know Johnson saved some lives by keeping that truck from rolling over, and with his extensive injuries, that wasn't easy. So please remember him in your prayers. Thank you, you served your unit proudly. I'm not going to say that I'm sorry to see you go home. If, after you've healed up and wish to return, see the Colonel and let him know I'll want you back." Bill shook their hands very carefully and then he and the Chief departed.

Before Chief closed the door to leave, he smiled at the two men. "Never look down on the Purple Heart you'll soon be awarded, you've shed blood for your country. Some famous Americans have been awarded the Purple Heart, but John Wayne was not one of them. He never wore this uniform in real life, so be proud of your service, gentlemen."

Driving down Disney Lane, Bill asked Chief if he needed to stop anywhere, but the Chief shook his head. "Then, Chief, you can guard this fine vehicle while I go inside. I need to resupply my pogey bait bag and check out a few prices. I got birthdays, holidays, and an anniversary ahead of me. Kitty would never forgive me for forgetting gifts. I'd probably get coal in my Christmas stocking when she sends it over."

"You go inside, sir—I'm going to drive over to that pizza joint and get me a couple giant pizzas for our company staff. First Purple Hearts always need a bit of a cheer-up, and since no alcoholic beverages are allowed, I guess Pizza will have to do."

"You know they make their pizza with goat milk, right? Or yak milk?"

"Sure, but it should help cover all those other strange tastes. Then I'm going to bet on how many of the men get the Taliban runs."

"Oh, that's nasty," Bill said.

"Yeah, but they'll stop thinking about those Purple Hearts."

Bill laughed as he turned the vehicle over to the Chief and walked into the lovely air-conditioned Base Exchange. Though officially called a base exchange, the army referred to it as a post exchange. The store was used by all the military services and American and EU (European Union) Civilians assigned here. The size of this place simply amazed Bill. *This has gotta be the most extensive military exchange in the world, or close to it. I wonder if they have a new car lot inside here. I see a bank, and there's an American restaurant and a kiddie land. Kitty would go crazy in here and to think we're fighting a war 20 miles from here. Weird! Man, a 60-inch TV with all the trimmings.* Bill only hoped Chief didn't mind waiting for a bit; he wanted to check the DVD prices; if they were low enough, he might send a couple dozen home. He never got past the pogey bait station. An MP Sergeant came in looking around, spotted the Screaming Eagle patch, and figured he had the correct officer.

"Captain Warrens, do you have a Chief Master Sergeant Johnson in your Company—Bravo Company, I believe?"

"Yes, he's my senior company NCO—has something happened to him?"

"Sir, will you follow me outside? We are detaining the Chief, without apprehension, due to his rank, but we do need to release him to you."

"I understand, Sergeant; I'll take him back to our enclosure, but what happened? He went over to get two pizzas for his staff."

"Yes, he did, but an argument developed between your Chief and the owner of the Pizza joint. The owner, who most of us do not trust or like, accused your Chief of not paying full price. What it comes down to, sir, is the owner put olives on both Pizzas, and the Chief says he would never order them and wasn't going to pay for them. The shouting began in two languages, maybe a third, and that's when I arrived with my Corporal. Your Chief treated us with total respect, but I could not convince him to pay for the olives. He told me you were over here when I mentioned that I might have to place him under apprehension. I tried to convince the owner to remove the olives and place them on another order, but he said he could not do that. His pride was hurt, and when it comes to injured pride, these men are like Italians. I have an Italian for a father-in-law, I know."

"So, how much extra are we looking at, Sergeant?"

"I believe the total price is $5.00, sir. Sort of ridiculous for putting a mark on this man's career."

"Will you hold on to him a bit longer while I go in to take care of the problem?"

"Yes, sir."

When they came up to the Chief, Bill warned him, "You mind your manners, Chief. This Sergeant is doing his best to keep a stupid blemish off your record. Five dollars—I'm even mad at you."

Bill walked over to the Pizza Joint and went inside. He exhaled to flush his anger, then approached the owner and identified himself. He offered to shake hands and after some initial reluctance, the man responded with a surprisingly firm handshake.

"Sir, I would like to offer you my entire unit's apology for my Chief's actions and the embarrassment he caused you in front of your customers. I understand he owes you $5.00 for the olives, but I would like to pay you $50 for this incident and ask that you accept it. If you do, I do not need a receipt, but I ask that you step outside so the MPs can see the matter has been taken care of. Does this satisfy you, sir?"

"Of course, Captain, and thank you."

They walked outside and shook hands, but only after Bill pulled his wallet out, removed a $50 bill, and handed it to him. Both MPs sighed in relief, but the Chief was not happy. "You should watch that man, Sergeant. I suspect he's got a couple of women working in there to worm info out of the flyboys." He was suspicious when he noticed no young Afghan women or men were working in the place.

"I believe the CID is considering that issue, but we're not part of that operation. Most of us refuse to go there; we get our Pizza at the Post Exchange. You can get them frozen or have them warmed while you wait."

"I guess I'm just pissed off. At the hospital, we were saying goodbye to three brand-new Purple Heart cases that got blown up today by an IED. The patrol was ten, maybe twelve miles outside of here. I really hate those IEDs, but I guess the Taliban says the same thing about our Claymores."

Bill got back into the vehicle then climbed back out to thank the MP Sergeant and shake his hand. "You did a favor for us, and we repay favors, so I'll get back to you." Bill handed his Officer's card to the man and had Chief write down the man's military information, so he could find him."

Driving down the road, Bill said to Chief, "Get your notepad and write the following." When the Chief was ready, Bill continued, "IOU to Captain Warrens for $50.00."

"$50 bucks! For what? The olives cost only $5."

"It was 50 dollars to calm down a foreign pizza maker who felt embarrassed by your actions and having the MPs called in. The Sergeant didn't want a blemish on your record for such a stupid event. The MPs didn't know what set you off, but now they do. It was three Purple Hearts in a supposedly cleared area. I saw the tears in your eyes. You've seen too many young boys shed blood for a government that doesn't seem to care. Me, too. When this tour is over, you should retire and enjoy your sons and hopefully some grandchildren—maybe your wife will even take you back if you leave the service. You'll have 32 years in when we get home, and I'm fully expecting you to pull the pin and start enjoying life. If you promise to do that, you can tear up that IOU." Bill grinned, and after a moment, Chief tore up the IOU and began to laugh. They were in good humor for the rest of the ride.

Back at headquarters, Chief told Bill he would write a letter to his wife to test the waters and explain what he felt at the hospital. He'd tell her that this was his last tour, and he would retire once they got home. He hoped she would re-marry him as he had never stopped being in love with her. "I'll probably be the oldest GI to ever get a 'Dear John' in this Theater of Operation."

"Chief, she hasn't remarried, she probably doesn't date, and she hasn't turned transgender or Lesbo. She's also been attending church. Everyone would know if she had a new man. Christians often make the best busybodies—that's how the pastors learn what's really going on in their churches—by listening to the womenfolk."

"I sure hope so, Captain, or I might forget to yell duck the next time a bullet is coming your way."

"You wouldn't do that, Chief. You love my family almost as much as your own. I can even call Kitty and put her to work singing your praises."

"Just wait until I get the Dear John. Maybe—she might not be willing to trust me."

"Start praying, Chief Command Sergeant Major. It got me healed and back into the Screaming Eagles."

"I've considered that, Boss. I know I'll need some real protection in this land. Like all lifers, I feel our politicians don't care very much for our survival. All this giving weapon packages to our enemy doesn't make any sense. I'd better hand off these pizzas before the mice smell the food. Jimmy Olson is the largest mouse in camp; I'm beginning to think he might have a worm or two in him."

When they returned to the enclosure, Bill checked for messages and had a few words with his fellow officers in B Company. Shortly afterward, he ordered B Company to form up in the large training yard at the far end of the enclosure. Bill had a Humvee parked beside him and was using its P.A. System so everyone could hear him. The Chief ordered the men to come to attention, then turned around to face Captain Warrens. "sir, the Company is formed!"

"At ease!" Bill bellowed into the microphone as the system squealed. He repeated himself; the men relaxed, letting rifles slip from their shoulders to rest at their side.

"We took three wounded on our first movement, but thankfully, no KIA. We were lucky, and though wounded severely, the driver kept the truck on the road. It could've been much worse. So, now the bubble is broken, our first Purple Hearts have been awarded—or they will be. I don't know about you, but I always tense up out in the field until we take our first hits. I expect to see two of them back here in four months or less, but it's going to be a lot tougher on the man who took the brunt of the explosion. The Kevlar saved their lives, so make sure you wear your chest and back armor when leaving our enclosure for any reason. You never know when rockets or mortars will rain down on us. When we go out to the field, you will wear all your body armor, which means elbow and knee pads. I don't care how hot you are; you'll be ready for IEDs and ambushes. You will wear shirts. I don't need any soldier hospitalized for second or third-degree sunburns. Legally, you can be court-martialed for that under 'Damage to Government Property.' But I'll probably have you doing 200 push-ups for the Chief." Bill glanced over at the Chief, who held his hard look on the men standing out in front of him.

"Second: The Pizza Joint on Disney Lane, the one with the big colorful plastic pizza disc on top, is henceforth off-limits by my order. The Chief and I had a problem with the owner, a person of Middle East heritage, causing the MPs to be called in. The problem was rectified, but I learned that CID is observing this location as a possible, and I mean just possible, spy joint. They have hired European women to work there in a suspected attempt to gather information from base personnel and horny jet jockeys. I do not want you in there. The pizzas are made with goat's milk, and the meats come from old sheep and donkeys. Diseases could be passed on because the post has no health inspector for private businesses—at least I never heard of one."

Bill looked over where SSgt. Jimmy Olson stood close by with the company's radio field pack and saw the sour expression on his face as he rubbed his stomach. Olsen had already consumed a pizza or two from the place and was concerned.

"So, the joint is off-limits; don't mess with the CID or violate my orders. You can still get Pizza at the Exchange, and I think you can probably buy an RV there if you wanted to." Bill clicked off the microphone and looked to the Chief. "You got anything, Chief?"

"Can I have the mike, sir?"

"Sure, here." Bill handed him the microphone.

"I want to remind you of tomorrow's short patrol which will involve only 3rd platoon. Squad leaders will meet with me tonight at 2100 hours to go over our Operational Plans." He turned to Bill, "That's it for me, Captain."

"Dismiss them when you're ready, Chief."

"Can do, Captain."

Bill nodded and walked back to headquarters. He had three letters to write for the men who were wounded. After talking to the troops in the truck who were unhurt, he had decided to nominate the truck driver for an Army Accommodation Medal. Bill knew the man wouldn't remember what he had done after being hit with that kind of explosion.

5

GETTING INTO THE SWING OF THINGS

THE NEXT PATROL went off without a hitch, no contact. The new guys relaxed when they climbed into hot showers after returning. The edge was partly off but not nearly enough for them to behave stupidly. A rock could still hide an insurgent, but not every stone had a snake behind it. They were still learning to keep their eyes open and what to look for. This was real, and many of them felt ready, or at least Bill hoped so. The worst part of his job was writing and mailing letters home for deceased or wounded soldiers' parents or wives.

When D Company sent out its third patrol, they began taking fire from two snipers on opposite sides of the road in an outlying village. Fire teams quickly dismounted from vehicles and began moving forward to take out the snipers. At the same time, a heavy concentration of machine-gun fire worked to dislodge the suspected Taliban. With quick action on the men's part and following the orders of the young non-commissioned officers leading them, they took one of the snipers alive. The second died from a grenade blast, and two AK-47s were seized.

Bill had been told that Afghan Security and Intelligence had attempted to place one of their men into a Taliban Group, but it had proved unproductive. Only one man had survived this scheme in the last two years. The other agents were found in the passes with their throats cut. A new man was overdue contacting his Afghan handler who believed he was dead. Oddly enough, these soldier-spies were devout Muslims, but hadn't held with the Taliban's fanatical beliefs.

For the rest of the patrol, things had remained quiet. The unit had drawn their first blood without the need for a single casket. Both of Bill's last two tours had taken a U.S. KIA on their first two patrols. In two days, they would leave for their first long patrol with soldiers anxious to get into battle.

The next day was a day off to allow the troops to prepare for the long trek ahead. "Chief, will you read me the latest weather report?" Bill asked. They were alone, standing outside Headquarters.

Chief pulled his notepad out of his left breast pocket and began to read out loud, "Yes, sir. Weather Department at Division Headquarters reports temperatures could go as high as 123 degrees Fahrenheit between 1200 to 1530 hours. It's expected to be a clear night with a one-eighth moon with nighttime temperatures in the low 80s. Same weather is estimated for the next three to five days."

"Chief, can you imagine getting a heatwave report like that on the west coast, maybe off Oregon?"

"Nope, I can imagine the fishermen would be seeing a lot of dead fish floating to the surface if those temperatures hit the Pacific west coast. They'd probably be thinking it's the end of the world. I once read about a bad heatwave hitting the upper Mojave Desert back in 1975. I lived in the L.A. area back then. My old man was fighting with the VA over getting fitted with a new leg. His legs only lasted a year or so before something happened to them. Anyhow, Edwards Air Force Base recorded 133 degrees for two whole days. The Base Commander ordered everyone off the flight line because the men and women working on aircraft left rubber boot sole prints on the aircraft and hot tarmac. They could work in the hangers, I guess, but the Sheriff's Department and Highway Patrol were swamped with calls, helping people whose vehicles had just sort of melted down. Rather than opening the windows, they opted to run with the air conditioners on full and finally overpowered the vehicle's electrical system. Back then, base housing only had massive water coolers on the roofs. So, I guess there were a good number of hospital cases from overheating."

"Would you have taken that station wagon of yours up there?"

Bill shook his head, "Nope. I value my 'Nomad' too highly—and as for tomorrow, I'll have you stay with 1st Platoon, while I move between 2nd and 3rd. We'll keep our Heavy Weapons people spread out among the convoy, ready to deploy at any sign of trouble."

"Captain, as I understand orders, while we're out on patrol, D Company's 1st Platoon will be on standby for the next 24 hours. They'll respond to our location if we come under heavy fire and need an assist. That leaves their 2nd Platoon to reinforce base perimeter security if the base should come under attack. Unless D Company's 3rd Platoon is needed elsewhere, those troops will also remain on standby, along with their Heavy Weapons platoon."

"That was sure a mouthful, but that sounds about right. So, old man, do you happen to recall where we're headed tomorrow?"

"Captain, I may be retiring soon, but I am not senile yet—tomorrow morning at 0700 hours, we'll be departing this vacation paradise for a seven day patrol into the outlying desert in hopes of engaging this elusive enemy.

"So tonight, it's equipment checks and letter writing. I've sent the word down that I expect to see a letter from every man, even if they have to write to one of their buddies back in the states."

SECURITY OPTION C-1

Things remained quiet until 19:47 hours that night when a loud voice came over the radio going to both B and D Companies. Senior Medic SFC Roman was at headquarters playing cards with the regular RTO, Sergeant First Class Jimmy Olson. Jimmy had forgotten he had turned the radio's volume up, following the MP's hourly check-in, because the man's voice could barely be heard.

Roman advised Olson to re-check the radio's batteries, as Olsen replied over the radio, "This is Luke George... Three... Go ahead."

Olsen and Roman had no trouble hearing the voice coming in from Division Headquarters with the volume boosted. Olson noted the time and date in his radio log and waited as the radio message was repeated. The Chief had stepped into the radio room and asked, "What's up?"

"Big stuff, Boss—we've been ordered into a Security Option C-1, and I just confirmed that. All Air Force Security Forces and Army Military Police Commanders are ordered to report to Division Headquarters ASAP, along with all Marine and Army unit commanders. All military pilots are to report to their assigned locations as directed under Security Option C-1. The base is being sealed—all personnel will have to come through Main Gate to be properly identified. People who enter elsewhere will be apprehended, and deadly force is authorized if they fail to stop. Otherwise, we're to follow procedures as directed for Option C-1." Roman read his scribble, which only he could.

Chief turned to a PFC often used as one of the runners, "You, run, do not walk, and locate Captain Warrens—probably in his room. If you don't find him there, check the latrines and then report back here. When you contact him, advise the Captain that we are under Security Option C-1 alert. Move it!"

Within four minutes, Bill was inside Headquarters, receiving SFC Roman's radio message. "Chief, do you know where Lt. Rayson is?" Bill asked. Rayson was acting D Company Commander while D Company's former commander who had suffered an injury in training, was in the hospital recovering.

"No, sir, the runner I sent over to D Company has not returned yet."

Bill turned to SFC Jimmy Olson, "Make radio contact with Lt. Rayson if you can and advise him to report here ASAP."

"You got it, Captain." Jimmy turned back to his radio and made the call.

Bill turned to Roman, "Sergeant, prepare your medical supplies for multiple injuries and ensure all our medics have what they need. Then check with D Company to see if they need anything. We are all part of the 101st, and we will work together for whatever this is all about." Shaking his head in wonder, Bill looked over at Chief, "When the Lieutenant gets here, you will standby here while the Lieutenant and I go over to Division Headquarters—okay?"

"Sir, should I begin issuing extra ammo?"

"No, I don't think so. Not yet anyway. I'll give you a call if the situation calls for it."

"Where's our book for base Security Options?" Chief asked.

Bill shook his head, "Chief, I'm betting they haven't had time to deliver the plans to us. That's probably why we're being brought in."

Chief agreed with Bill and issued an order to another runner, "Spread the word through the company that we are on alert status; the whole base is being sealed. Anyone outside the enclosure is to be contacted to return here immediately. At some point, I'm sure all civilian cell phones will be turned off for security."

"On my way, Chief!"

"Gentlemen, I'm going to head over to Division as soon as Lt. Rayson arrives. I want Company B Personnel in full battle gear. For right now, until I know more, they're to have field packs on their bunks, loaded with three MREs and full canteens ready to go in the event we're ordered off base. Put First Platoon on combat alert status, standing by out front. Also, reinforce our security contingent here with a squad from the 2nd Platoon. Everyone else is on stand-by until I know more. No one leaves this enclosure until I return, or you hear different orders from Division."

Lt Rayson arrived, a bit out of breath, having made a fast run from the chow hall.

"Lt. Rayson, sorry to interrupt your dinner, but we're due at Division Headquarters."

"Yes, sir." Rayson released a weary breath, wiped the sweat off his face, and turned to the Chief, "Chief, do you happen to know what this Security Option Charlie-One is?"

"That seems to be part of the problem, Lt.—division hasn't sent us our Official War Guidelines for the Bagram area. So, as ranking officers, you've both been called to Division to be briefed."

Bill replied, "Honestly, I think we're being sent out to either make contact with the enemy or to reinforce the perimeter for a possible ground assault. But we'll know soon enough."

"Gentlemen, your ride awaits you," Chief said as he pointed toward the doorway.

Bill was surprised to see an MP Humvee waiting for them armed with a mounted 240B, an MP gunner in the back. Behind it was a B Company Humvee with a .50 caliber heavy machine gun on top. With the driver and gunner were three extra soldiers inside the Humvee. Bill turned around to face everyone, "I'll be back as soon as possible. Who knows, this may be one of those crazy Air Force exercises they often pull —but I'll find out." Bill dropped down into the front passenger seat and belted himself in as Lt. Rayson jumped into the back seat. They drove off, and upon reaching the base roadway, quickly accelerated.

The MP was making the trip to Division Headquarters at all possible speed. Bill had to admit the young man knew how to drive, missing most of the worst ruts in the roadway. At one point, he raced around a convoy of mixed donkeys and camels without frightening a single animal. Though he got the attention of an Afghan truck driver coming at them from the opposite direction.

"How much longer, Sergeant?" Bill asked his driver.

"One minute at best speed, sir—or two minutes to get you there safely."

"I'll let you decide, but I have been in-country before, seen the sites and the $20 tour. No girls or booze this time, all work."

"I got you, Captain." He grinned back and sped ahead.

Bill liked all the MPs assigned to their enclosure, and so did his men. There wasn't a stupid or lazy one in the whole bunch, which meant they wouldn't be falling asleep on their guard positions like a new guy might.

Bill never liked going to Division Headquarters. His Captain's bar meant very little in a place where the low rank was often a major, and a Two-Star General commanded everyone. This was an Army Infantry General; Bill knew very little about him. His Colonel, his regimental commander, had given him little information about the man.

"What do you think of the Old Man?" Bill asked his driver.

"The General? I've never met him, Captain, I've only heard positive things. He worked hard to obtain his first star. Grunt work all the way. Served in Vietnam as a Lieutenant, went to Iraq as a Major, and came home a Lt. Colonel, with plenty of medals. Received a Purple Heart and Bronze Star for saving his commander's life. I believe he did another tour in Iraq; I think this is his fourth tour in the Sandbox. He spent several years back in the states in the Infantry Training Command—that's all I've got for you. Oh, I heard one Warrant Officer refer to him as a soldier's general. I think it was a compliment."

"So much information makes you a pretty fair cab driver, Sergeant.

Next time I'll ask you for a list of the best tourist spots this place has to offer."

"Well, sir, we are arriving at Division Headquarters; please adjust your seats and serving trays for landing." He pulled up in front of the front doors to Division Headquarters. Four MPs were on guard duty and two others were running a belt of ammo into two 240B machine guns in place behind sandbag bunkers.

"Where are you going to be, Sergeant? I'm not sure how long this is going to take."

"Sir, I'll be parked right across the road with those other drivers." He pointed, and Bill looked over and spotted seven other Army MPs and three Air Force SFs with one Navy Shore Patrol driver and four armed Marines.

"Your I.D. Captain." An MP Staff Sergeant asked with his left hand held out as he stood beside Bill's side of the vehicle.

"Sure, Sergeant." Bill pulled his wallet out and presented his Military I.D. Card, and it was compared to a list of names on a sheet of paper.

"I'm not showing your name, sir."

"Check the second page and look under Commanding Officer of B Company, 101st Airborne. This is Lt. Rayson, who commands D Company."

"Oh, here it is, sir." He handed the card back and added, "My apologies, Captain."

"That's okay, Sergeant. I would prefer a careful man over a careless one."

"Thank you, Captain," He gestured over his right shoulder, "Head down the center hallway until you find a young female lieutenant. She'll take care of you and direct you to the right office."

Bill and Lt. Rayson walked down the center hallway until they came to a desk where the Lieutenant was waiting for him. "Captain Warrens and Lt. Rayson—these folders are for you. This informs you all about Security Option C1, which was supposed to have been provided to you the day you processed in. As usual, someone in Intelligence—I won't tell you that Captain's name—only I'm the one who received the butt-chewing only my father could've gotten away with when I was too little to strike back. But we did fail in not getting this to you earlier, and I am sorry."

"Well, I have it now, and all is forgiven."

"Thank you, sir."

"Where do we go from here?"

"Follow me, Gentlemen." She guided them down the narrow hallway until they reached a large briefing room where the General conducted group meetings. As the lieutenant opened the door, she stepped aside to allow Bill and Lt. Rayson through. "Captain Warrens and Lt. Rayson of the 101st Airborne," she announced as they entered.

Both officers stood to attention and held it. They knew most General officers disliked having to salute each arriving officer. The General gave Bill and Lt. Rayson a good once over before he waved them to empty chairs near the front of the room.

"Lieutenant, is this everyone?"

"Yes, General."

"Then Post the room; what I have to say is Top Secret Security Option C-1."

"Yes, General, the room is now posted." She closed the door behind her and gestured for two Army MPs who had been standing at ease down another hallway to take over security. "This room is posted Top Secret Security Option C-1. No one but myself may enter. If someone else is with me, and I do not advise you immediately with the words Security Option C-1 you will assume I am under duress. You are to shoot the person or persons with me, even if you must wound or kill me in doing so. They might be carrying a bomb. If for some reason a person leaves, they may only return alone and give you those code words, 'Security Option C-1.' You got all that, Sergeant?"

"Yes, Ma'am."

"You may frisk them if you do not recognize them. No cases, bags, or bombs are allowed inside during this meeting which should last no longer than six hours. During that time, I should always be available at the other end of the hall. If I must leave my desk, I will inform you. If you need a latrine break, notify me, and I will be down here to take over your position one at a time. Remember, you come back with company, be prepared for what happens. Know that I am an expert shot—when I'm not shaking." She smiled at both of them, but they remained straight-faced. "If it appears this meeting will go over six hours, I will make sure you are relieved, and we will also relieve you one at a time for chow and a smoke break. Do you understand your orders?"

They both replied, "Yes, Ma'am."

"Stay awake; you just never know when or if the General will look out here to see if you know how to do this right. He's Old Army.

The General spent the better part of an hour explaining to the Marine Colonel where he needed to position his units around Bagram. He was to work in conjunction with an Army Infantry Colonel, who was given the task to protect both the outer perimeter and an inner perimeter around crucial locations. "Once the order is given, our pilots will be airborne preparing to drop ordinance on those locations as directed. Our main priority is the defense of this base and protecting all civilian and military personnel residing or working here." This was all covered in the first hour, before Bill and Lt. Rayson's arrival, and now it was just outlined for their benefit.

"Captain Warrens and Lt. Rayson, as I understand it, you have two fully manned Airborne Companies—Bravo and Delta Companies, of the 101st Airborne. Is this correct?"

"Yes, sir," Bill replied as Lt. Rayson simply bobbed his head up and down. He was very much in awe of the Major General who commanded Bagram.

"Captain, how many troops can you put into the field, and what kind of vehicles do you have currently?"

"Sir, combined, we can put roughly 400 troops into the field, with each company carrying three platoons and a fully manned heavy weapons platoon. Our heavy weapons consist of .50 caliber and M-60 machine guns, plus numerous 240s. We have 60mm, and 81 mm mortars. We have no actual field artillery as it is not available to Airborne units. As for vehicles, we have Strykers, Humvees, and Deuces, plus a few older model jeeps. I might add, General, that since our arrival, we've completed three break-in humps for which I am reporting a total of six wounded men: no KIA. We were about to begin our long-range patrols tomorrow. I am happy to report a large number of my men are veterans of either Iraq or Afghanistan. This is my third tour, sir, and my Chief Command Sergeant Major is on his 4th combat tour."

"I'm impressed, Captain, but as for now, you'll disregard your big trucks. Where I am sending you, you'll not be needing them. So, hang around..." He looked around the room. "Any questions?" The meeting continued for another hour, and Bill was encouraged by the questions being asked. The Air Force Commander of the Security Forces seemed to know his stuff; he had 31 canine units to put outside the perimeter. Those units would be working with the Army's 27 dog handlers. Bomb dogs were assigned to the main gate, while all other entry control points were sealed off and covered by Army infantry units.

The General left the senior officers to pick each other's brains as he led Bill and Lt. Rayson to his private back office. Bill listened as the General called the front desk. "I'm in back with Captain Warrens and Lt. Rayson. Release the room, but I want Headquarters to remain at alert. Get a hold of the Colonel who's handling our Transportation Corps; I want him here within five minutes. Then get me whoever's in charge of our Bradleys and Strykers, same five minutes."

"Yes, sir."

The General turned back to Bill and Lt. Rayson, "She'll make a fine General someday, quite a strategist, too—you can both relax, sit down. You've got a lot of work ahead of you."

"Thank you, sir," Bill replied.

"Get out your notepads and start writing." The General waited until they both had pens in hand and paper laid out.

"Captain, I'm giving you ten Bradleys, with trained 25mm gunners and drivers. You'll provide the rest. I know you've trained with Strykers, so I will get you another ten and you can arm them with either .50 calibers or 240B's. You'll load your crews in these vehicles, but put your heavy weapons people into your own vehicles; no sense in mixing up the military hardware when this alert is over with. The reason for this alert is that Intel has informed us that the Taliban have planned on mining the roadway through the Khyber Pass, maybe even blowing the whole shebang up to keep us from using it. You are to take your convoy north on that highway to stop them from achieving this goal. You can use those .25 mm guns to de-mine the roadway... I'll resupply you with ammo every morning. If you are attacked, air support will be available. We have plenty of Navy, Marine, and Air Force flyboys hot and ready for action.

Your second, D Company will handle perimeter defense for your new FOB. Lt. Rayson, you'll be shown where that FOB is to be set up after this meeting. If your two companies cannot handle the pressure the Taliban brings against you, I'll send a force of Marines to help you out. If that happens, you'll probably leave here a second lieutenant for forcing me to bring in Marines to save your bacon. On the other hand, I do not want dead soldiers spread across the desert floor. If you really need assistance, be honest with me about what's going on out there, and I'll send in enough air power to send the Taliban to the Hell they were spawned in."

The General poured himself a cup of coffee before he continued, but he stayed on his feet and walked about the room. "You have the experience, Captain, to know when to turn around and let the flyboys take over. I do not want to lose good men for possession of a dirt road, not when I can demolish the whole area with bombs and artillery. Command frowns on my old style of doing things. It's always surgical strikes, precision bombing, and only a limited amount of damage. If we had done that in Vietnam, we would have lost another 20,000 men. I'll help you with field artillery, but only for that first 18 miles, however, I will do whatever I can in the event you need to rescue downed aircraft in your region.

I want no heroic games out there—you got that, Captain? Before this is over, there will be enough medals for all. I just don't want to send home a lot of flag-covered caskets because some officers decided to do a John Wayne. I've seen your file, Warrens; you've got enough awards already to make major. But I don't need a dead officer, you got me? You stay out of those Bradleys and let your men do their job!"

"Yes, General."

"You'll move out with your first company at the assigned hour. However, D Company cannot depart until my regular troops arrive to take over the defense of your enclosure. I'll hold down your fort with a company of MPs; they'll have their own tents. We always have a problem with ISIS and the Taliban and some downright thievery by locals. No sense having you stolen blind while you're out there defending the Flag." The General stopped when he saw movement outside his door. Two full-bird Colonels appeared at the same time with stiff salutes. "First off, Steve, I want to know why my troops from the 101st Airborne haven't received their Bradleys?"

"General, everyone wants them. There is a limit to their number."

"Of those receiving them, how many are actually used for combat missions?"

"Sir, I would have to check my records. It's in my safe."

The General picked up a file folder and opened it, "Colonel, I can save you the time—there are 205 Bradleys assigned to this Post, and a total of 103 of these are assigned to combat units. You've assigned them to MP units for riot work, which we have never had. You hold a couple of dozen on stand-by for replacement units. The rest simply sit around while my combat units collect wounded using World War Two deuces piled high with sandbags. Now turn around and look at these two commanders. They're new arrivals, and one of them has already suffered a half dozen wounded men. You can tell him it was in the best interests of the Army to haul his men around in trucks when we had available armored vehicles."

The Colonel couldn't look at Bill and Rayson. He simply lowered his gaze and slightly bowed his head.

"Colonel, as of now, you are relieved of duty. Pack your bags and prepare to head home. If you have the guts, go by the hospital and apologize to the last men brought in due to inadequate vehicles before you leave. It's still unknown whether one of these men will survive, but his days with the Army are over. Sadly, the others are looking at four to six months in the hospital and possible medical discharges at hopefully 70% disability or better. They were in sandbagged Deuces; those armored vehicles would sure have come in handy. Goodbye, Colonel. My report will meet you at home—you may now leave."

After the Colonel departed, the second bird Colonel looked at the General with a stern glare.

"What is it, Homer? Was I too hard on him? I know we were all good friends who climbed up the ladder together, all West Point alumni. But what happened to him when the thoughts of making General meant more to him than the life of six enlisted men? Or are you upset that I embarrassed him in front of these two officers?"

The Colonel was silent, but Bill could easily see how uncomfortable the officer was for having this occur in front of a mere captain and a lowly lieutenant.

"Believe me, Homer, this Captain needs far more support than the apology of that Colonel who is responsible in part for those soldiers lying wounded in the hospital. He couldn't even apologize to the captain who commanded them. Nor am I done here, Homer; once things settle back down, I'm going to break my Intelligence Chief down a rank for faulty Intel. I'm waiting to see what I get from this warning which is causing me to shut the base down and alert Washington DC that we have problems here.

Right now, you're on the burner. I need Bradleys armed with 25mm cannons, full ammo, and ten days' worth of supplies. You'll provide the gunner, driver, and anyone else you even suspect those Bradleys need; the captain will provide the troops. That's ten Bradleys four hours from now because the mission leaves at 0600 hours, with 20 of your men. If they're even ten minutes late, you'll be flying home with Steven. I'll let you keep your Eagle, but it's going to be retirement if you fail me."

"You can't do that, General. I was best man at your wedding—hell, I'm your brother-in-law, for God's sake!"

"Homer, look at that Captain. He's part of a proud tradition, Screaming Eagles of the 101st Airborne—Bastogne to Hamburger Hill, they've bled and fought. He leaves in six hours, with or without those Bradleys. Do you understand that Homer?"

Homer nodded and walked over to Captain Warrens, "We'll be there, hell or high water, Captain—and please accept my apology."

"Colonel, I'm just proud to be in the same room with you and the General. You're what I strive to become."

Homer nodded, he felt ashamed as he patted Bill on the left shoulder and then faced the General, came to attention, and saluted, "Hell or high water, General." He didn't wait for a return salute but hustled out of the office.

"That's why I made him my best man and why I wanted him and the other Colonel over here. I guess in the last seven years, something has happened to Steve, once he got his Eagle. No matter, I'm only sorry it did. He was once a fine officer."

"Sir, if I may ask, what will become of him?" Lt. Rayson asked.

"You deserve to know, and except for Homer and I, the only ones who do deserve it. Officers need to learn how their inactions can often result in wounded and dead troops. When that happens, these officers will face charges. If I learn he stopped at the hospital and apologized to those wounded men, I'll probably allow him to retire as a full colonel. But if not, I'll propose he lose his eagle and recommend he be retired as a Major. Had this been a real war, he could've been shipped off to Leavenworth for 20 to 30 years—however, this isn't a real war, nor will the politicians allow it to become one. Still, our men and women are wounded and killed in defense of our national interests."

"General, I will not ask your viewpoint. But as your Captain, and this being my third tour, I wish we could either fight it as an all-out war or fill up our plastic pail, grab our shovel and dump truck toys and leave this sandbox behind."

"Ditto," the General replied. "Get moving, Captain; orders for B Company to depart in six hours will arrive in five hours or less. I presume that will give you enough time?" He turned away but glanced back at Bill over his shoulder and added, "God bless both of you. Oh, Captain, I read about your father—he was a damn good soldier and well deserving of that Medal."

"Thank you, General." Bill came to attention, quickly followed by Lt Rayson, both presenting their best parade ground salutes and receiving the Generals in return.

Outside, two MPs waited with vehicles. "We thought you might be going our way, Captain. We're part of the detail assigned to guard your home front while you're away."

"I'm happy to have all the MPs I can get," Bill replied.

Back at the enclosure, Bill thanked his MP escort, walked into headquarters, and picked up the PA microphone. He called for all officers and senior NCOs of E-6 and above to meet at the training grounds. "Form up on the Chief in five minutes." With this small formation in front of him. Lt. Rayson, who didn't like the idea of being left behind at a new FOB, stood by silently.

Bill began his briefing on the upcoming operation:

"B Company will be used in a clearing operation for a long stretch of highway through the legendary Khyber Pass. We'll begin the operation approximately 42 miles northeast of this position and head southeast until we hit the Khyber Pass. Our job is to first set up our FOB, which will be guarded by D Company.

B Company's chore is two-fold: first, we're being assigned ten new Bradley Fighting Machines armed with 25mm cannons. We will use these Bradleys to de-mine this stretch of highway. Sort of recon by fire, but we'll also have a large EOD unit assigned to us. Several heavy equipment dozers and graders, driven by our Afghan allies, will follow us. However, we might not ever see them as they want the road thoroughly blown before they make their move to reach us.

We are to clear those hills of Taliban. As we move through Khyber Pass, beware these hills are mostly stone and will grow in size until they become mountains and can hide a lot of Taliban. We can call in air cover if we become involved in a major firefight. If the shit flies, we'll call in D Company to rescue us. You should know that these hills have numerous villages, and that means civilians. So, tell your men not to be trigger-happy, but let them know some of these civilians can be allies to the Taliban or similar factions like ISIS. This will not be a walk in the park. Our troops will be locked and loaded once we leave the base perimeter.

If B Company starts yelling for help, D Company will be loaded into Chinooks and respond like the proverbial 7th Cavalry to rescue their butts. Understand, we may be facing both ISIS and Taliban insurgents and possibly even some Pakistan tribesmen as we draw closer to their border.

We'll receive ten additional Strykers because we are leaving our Deuces here. The men will be scattered, so let's make sure to keep all of our radios in good order. We will provide ground support for each Bradley. Squad members will be assigned to each vehicle just as we have done with our Strykers and Humvees. As long as we have them, I want the men riding in them to become acquainted with these machines to include weapons and anything else these crews can teach us. I hope to hold on to these vehicles when this is over, if possible. If there is an attack, I want our people to know what to do if the driver or gunner is wounded or killed. The Bradleys are a gift from the General, and he's sorry it took so long to get them to us. No mistake, we are going to be out there for a while, and this General is sending us out First Class.

If our Intel people are correct, D Company could be joining us within two to three days, and it will be slow going. This is especially true if the bad guys somehow blow the pass and close it down at an elbow point or bring a cliff of big rocks down on the highway. Then we must take the time to blow and clear it, which is another reason why those EOD boys are coming along to help us.

MPs have promised me directly to keep our enclosure safe from thieves. I've had some great talks with these MPs to ensure this. When we get back from this mission and find everything is in order, we'll throw them a barbecue.

Okay, that's the overview, gentlemen. Now I want platoon leaders to get with your squad leaders to decide who rides where and bring me the completed list for B Company's 24 vehicles. Supply everyone with enough ammo, MREs, and water, and check with your medics to see what they may need. D Company, stay around for your Lieutenant, as I am sure he has some additional information for you.

Oh, the last thing, ensure everyone's written a letter home and get it turned in to the Chief before 2200 hours... The old man needs his sleep before we leave tomorrow at 0600 hours."

Bill grinned at the Chief, who refrained from any verbal response.

THE CHAPLAIN

Bill watched as the men dashed off in several directions to prepare for their first major operation. At first glance, they looked like kids running for the toy department in a major retail store. Then he saw the line form at the Chaplain's Tent and knew these men were no longer kids. The Chaplain was busy, praying with the men and helping a few with doubts, encouraging them and blessing his flock of Screaming Eagles.

Chaplain Captain Zachary Taylor the Fifth, known as Zach on poker night, no relation to the old president, was a former pastor of the non-denominational New Hope Church in Salem, Oregon. He had been with the Army for just over two years, and this was his first trip overseas. Zach usually carried a canvas satchel that he kept filled with pocket-sized Bibles and preferred to work with frontline troops. He had volunteered to go out on patrol which his Airborne flock, though that was frowned upon by Bagram's head chaplain.

On Saturdays, he preached for the Jewish troops and a few Seventh Day Adventists. On Sunday, he presided over several different Christian services. He also met with Muslim troops to make sure everyone was well taken care of.

Bill had taken a strong liking to Chaplain Zach, as he liked to be called. Though the Chief felt the good Chaplain was a bit too serious at times in his sermons, he liked the man's sense of humor when he wasn't behind his pulpit.

THE CONVOY ARRIVES

Captain Warrens and Lt. Rayson were inside the enclosure at B Company Headquarters listening to radio activity as the base prepared to shut down, when an Army MP showed up.

"Okay, Private, take a breath and tell us what's going on," Chief said.

PFC Wilson, the MP nodded, "There's a large convoy of vehicles coming this way. Their scout arrived at the front gate. Your Bradleys are arriving on flatbeds, with Strykers, some Humvees, men, and ammo— we just need to know where you want them."

Chief looked to Bill, who ordered, "PFC Wilson, unload the trucks outside the front gate, then move those vehicles assigned to us into the training yard. Any vehicles going to D Company can remain outside the enclosure. There's just no room in here for all that equipment. We'll be right out. I'll get extra security on those vehicles parked outside."

"Yes, sir!" PFC Wilson said and popped a salute before hightailing for the entry gate.

"Chief, I want every single vehicle inspected. Make sure each one is ready for an extended patrol, all fuel tanks topped off and oil checked. I don't want to have to worry about breakdowns on this patrol. Make sure we have enough topped-off water trailers. Inspect each to ensure the water hasn't been contaminated. We don't need a bunch of sick troops out there because someone poisoned our water supplies." Bill ordered.

"Yes, sir," Chief replied and hurried away followed by two of his NCOs and a radioman so he could remain in contact with Bill.

Bill turned and gestured for Lt. Rayson to follow him outside for a quiet chat. "Sam, I know you'd rather be taking the lead on this, but the bad guys could ignore us completely, hoping their IEDs and a few snipers will keep us at bay. If so, you can probably expect your FOB will come under attack by a large ground force. I know this is your first tour, so do not take the Taliban lightly. They may dress funny, sound ignorant, and love their swords and daggers, but they're a well-trained force of desert fighters. This is their land; they grew up in this damn heat and can often fight 24 hours a day for days on end. There's been tribal warfare here since Biblical times. Don't give them an inch and be wary of any surrenders. This is usually a ploy to sucker us in. Their fighters are hardcore Muslims, quite willing to die for their God by killing an infidel. For them, this is a holy war. Don't take any chances. Rely on your veterans—listen to their advice before you make any rash decisions. That's how I learned and how I survived those last two tours.

In many ways, the Taliban and the Viet Cong my dad fought are quite similar. A fanatical VC would run into a buzz saw if he thought he could take out an American soldier. Same thing here. So, don't give them any chance or opportunity to get one over on you. They could be wearing suicide belts or shoulder packs filled with explosives, and we've seen them fake death in hopes of drawing American soldiers closer before setting off a bomb. I lost a couple of men that way during my first tour.

If you're sent out to support us, the safety of your company always comes first. They just may use us to set up a trap for the helicopters bringing you in. Hopefully, I'll be able to notify you of a suspected trap and if I tell you to abort, you'd better boogie on out of there and land elsewhere.

Because of what's happened out here in the past, my men and I have made a pact—we will never surrender. The last man standing is to make sure of that, and you know what that means. We all know what happens to Taliban prisoners, especially for Green Berets, Rangers, and anyone wearing a Screaming Eagles patch. We're prime victims for a public execution. We'd all rather go down fighting than appear on TV as they cut our heads off. Nope, not the way we want to die. That will probably never happen; I just want you to be prepared for a worst-case scenario.

You keep your people alive, and if it looks hopeless for us, call in an airstrike on our position. You got that, Sam? I'm serious—this isn't some tomfoolery crap to play on a young officer on his first combat tour. None of my men wish to be taken alive. No one wants a loved one back home watching the evening news and seeing their loved one being executed. Share this with your platoon leaders."

Bill slapped Samson on his left shoulder in a sign of comradeship, "Okay, enough on that.... Back to the road, the General has two prime concerns, our safety and that of all those villagers living in the mountains. We don't know how many of those people are in league with the Taliban or sympathetic to the Pakistani or even the Russians. Use a lot of caution, even when they act friendly. Many of the things we were taught don't always come into play over here. It's a learning business. Though this is my third tour, I'm still much of a tenderfoot.

Lt. Sam Rayson nodded in understanding, waiting to get his voice back. "Captain, that's some serious shit you're hitting me with—not quite what I expected."

"I got much the same speech when I was over here the last time by my company commander, the kind of thing that's been going on since America started fighting wars." The two men shook hands.

6

HITTING THE ROAD—AGAIN

Seventeen miles from the post's outer perimeter on a public dirt highway, Bill's point Bradley drove over a small anti-personnel mine. Though shaken by the blast, the Bradley's heavy armor prevented anyone inside from being seriously injured. Still, there were a couple of bloody noses and a few bruises. The mine would have killed any man, woman, child, or animal who might have stepped upon it.

The Bradleys' sergeant reminded his people to remain inside the vehicle in case there were other mines in the immediate area. To prove his case, he asked the 240B gunner to fire his weapon around the Bradley as close as possible. Three more anti-personnel mines were detonated, covering the Bradley with sand and shrapnel. The Taliban were getting more imaginative laying mines in hopes of killing the most people, especially those who might have escaped an earlier explosion.

Being on point, this Bradley was at least 100 yards in front of the convoy. The driver began to back up, but Captain Warner ordered him to halt, then contacted the next Bradley and ordered that driver to proceed forward slowly staying in the leader's tracks. "Have your men use small arms fire to check for other mines across the road and stop when you pull up behind that lead unit. I'll have our men begin shooting up the sides of the roadway to ensure we don't leave any mines behind that might harm anyone else. EOD can come out and check the area after we've moved off." He closed the radio call by ordering the rest of the column to hold until the second Bradley made it to the point.

For the next several minutes, the two forward Bradleys sprayed the roadway with a barrage that detonated four more anti-personal mines.

Bill called Chief to his side, "Looks like the Taliban have an insider at Division Headquarters. They knew we were coming; we're going to expend a lot of ammo clearing this roadway, and we haven't even reached the pass. As soon as this area is safe, get the mechanics on that lead vehicle's track. I want to be in Jalalabad before it gets dark. And pass the word, everyone is on high alert—the enemy knows we're coming this way."

The second Bradley began pulling ahead, spraying the roadway with automatic fire and Bill got back on the radio, "Attention all units, in about 100 yards, leave this road to the right, line up and proceed out into the desert. Be watchful of anything that looks suspicious, especially sand mounds on the desert floor. Sing out if you see anything. And to satisfy your curiosity, yes, this road is the only one in this immediate area... Out."

Jimmy Olson was ordered to radio a coded message to HQ regarding a possible leak. A moment later, Bill was back on the radio, "Point Bradley, continue firing 25mm on the roadway, keep extending your range. I'd like to make this roadway safe for civilian traffic. Bradley Two will take out any mines you miss. Bradley Two, as soon as Point clears the highway, move up and continue firing until you reach the spot where Point left the road. Then move into the desert and take up your position at the head of our convoy, with Point Bradley 100 yards in front. Any questions?" There were none.

"Okay, here we go... Out."

The gunner continued firing and set off three more anti-personnel mines. The second stream to the right suddenly set off a long string of seven anti-personnel mines and two larger anti-tank mines, which sent a shock wave back through the lead Bradley. The Taliban had wired them together in hopes of taking out a patrol of soldiers and escort vehicles. In the next 30 minutes, the point Bradley exploded over 40 anti-personnel as well as the two anti-tank mines. The road took on the appearance of an old Hawaiian lava field.

Bill checked with Division Headquarters in Bagram and was soon talking with the General's aide. "Be advised, we have diverted off-road and currently proceeding across the desert parallel to the roadway. The road looks to be nearly impassable to vehicle traffic. Suggest you send out road crews to fill in holes with EOD personnel as escort... Over."

"We will handle it; you are to proceed toward your next objective. We've received word as of 45 minutes ago, that Khyber Pass is open. You are reminded that the southeast end of the pass is within one mile of the Pakistan border. Intel believes there is a chance—I repeat a chance—a large force of Pakistani troops are in that vicinity so be on alert... Over."

"I request you advise D Company placed on 30-minute alert status... Over."

"Will do. Check-in two hours from now... Out!"

Bill looked over at Jimmy Olson, "You know, this adventure is beginning to sound a whole lot more like we're out here testing the waters for sharks. Now we have the Pakistan Army to be worried about. I can understand why the Russians bailed out of this place—it's a wee bit unfriendly."

"Downright hostile if you ask me, Captain," Jimmy replied.

Once the vehicle had gotten back in line and the two lead Bradleys had assumed their positions, the convoy continued at a much slower pace moving across the open desert. Hard-packed sand concealed other dangerous pitfalls, such as sudden drop-offs. Staying parallel with the road, they continued east toward the low mountains that line Khyber Pass. Here the foothills quickly become towering giants of primarily dark gray and black stone.

After an hour of travel, Bill turned to his radioman, "Jimmy, check in with all our units; I want to make sure we haven't lost anyone."

"Yes, sir, doing so right now." Before all the units had checked in, Jimmy stopped and turned to Bill, "sir, our Point Bradley reports taking rifle fire from the hillside to the southeast."

"Any civilians in that area?" Bill asked.

Turning back to the radio, Jimmy repeated the question, and the lead Bradley replied, "Negative, just a couple shooters so far."

"No civilians reported, Captain—just two snipers."

"Advise the two lead Bradleys to light 'em up and then advise all other units to stop in place and await further orders."

Jimmy relayed the captain's order, and within seconds, a heavy concentration of weapons fire was launched against the snipers. Bill patted the driver on the shoulder, "Move us up, Corporal. I need to see what we're facing."

"Yes, sir."

Jimmy notified the convoy that Yankee One was proceeding forward. For security purposes on this mission radio communications identified Company Staff as 'Yankee', the Captain being Yankee One. Chief was Yankee Two, Roman was Yankee Three, and Jimmy Olson was Yankee Four. Bill had designated his platoon leaders as cowboys while in the field. First Platoon Leader for the moment was MSgt John McCullough – or Cowboy One. Second Platoon Leader/Cowboy Two was 2nd Lieutenant Dave Thomas Parker, who was on his first tour. Third Platoon Leader/Cowboy Three was 1st Lt. Douglas K. Graham. This left Heavy Weapons Platoon Leader Sergeant First Class James Averell as Cowboy Four.

The Colonel had promised Bill that he would be sending a couple of young lieutenants his way within the month. The modern all-volunteer army left everyone a bit shorthanded, compared with the days of the draft which provided an abundance of troops.

THE CONVOY IS ON THE MOVE

"Yankee One to Cowboy Three, leave your gunners in place and take three squads over to that rock embankment on your right. I want you and two other squads to move back into those rocks, proceed east and clean out those snipers. If you see anyone with a weapon, they're open game. But prisoners would be preferred—if possible... Over."

"Cowboy Three copy. We will be unloading and on foot in two mikes... Over."

Bill settled the extra set of headphones with attached microphone, over his head. "Yankee One Copies. Attention all units, Cowboy Three will be making their way eastward along those rocks—he's taking three squads, so only shoot when you have positive, I repeat, positive I.D. on those bad guys... Out."

A moment later, Bill issued another set of orders to his radioman, "Jimmy, contact Cowboy Two and have him do the same thing Cowboy Three is doing with three squads. Advise him to move up on the northeast side of those big rocks and proceed south on foot. Notify all units that Cowboy Two is moving up from that direction—advise both Cowboy Two and Three not to shoot across the road unless they are mighty sure their target is unfriendly. We don't want any civilians being accidentally shot. Then bring up the next two Bradleys and advise them to continue blasting that big rocky embankment to the north of our men. I want to make sure we chase off any more scorpions up there before we proceed. I imagine there are more than the two of them up there. A whole Taliban hunting party may have moved in after hearing those explosions and weapons fire."

"Yes, sir!" Jimmy replied and sent out the orders.

After 30 minutes of climbing about the southeast hillside, Lt. Graham and his men suddenly came upon a group of 18 to 20 Taliban taking cover in a deep ravine due east of the column. The terrorists, hoping to avoid the heavy concentration of cannon fire from the Bradleys, were surprised. In a quick firefight, the U.S. troops killed or wounded nearly half of them; the remainder fled into an attached rocky ravine. Another squad, hearing the firefight, moved in and tossed grenades into the narrow ravine. When the smoke cleared, no one was left standing. The Americans moved in to secure weapons and checked for wounded and possible documents.

Cowboy Three notified Yankee Station of the brief firefight. "Yankee Station, Cowboy Three, we are continuing to press in, how far should we go? Over."

Bill spoke into his microphone, "Cowboy Three, I do not want you out of sight of the column; you copy that? You're not mountain goats... Over."

"Boss, it'll take us about ten mikes to get back to where you want us. We sort of got into this rabbit hunting bit, and it's hard to back off... Over."

"Follow my orders, Lieutenant—you could be walking right into a trap... Over."

"I copy, Yankee One, we're heading back. I've got five men delivering kill shots on these KIA, just to make sure they stay that way... Over."

"Good idea, a real morale buster for the Taliban; bring the wounded POWs back with you... Out."

Chief shook his head and grinned as he said to Bill, "Looks like you've created another hard charger in that kid."

"Maybe, but by the sound of things, his men will follow him anywhere. He'll make a good commander if he just remembers he's responsible for the lives of his platoon members. This is his first major action—he'll tune it down soon enough. We all did."

Cowboy Two was experiencing his own difficulties. One of the men fell and broke the bone in his upper thigh. Getting him out on a stretcher opened up a short firefight when three Taliban shooters sprang up from under a large slab of stone to face the two men bringing the injured man back. The first soldier in line took an AK-47 round through his left hip. As he went down, the man carrying the back of the stretcher dropped his end and brought up his M-4, shooting two of the men with nearly half a magazine. The injured soldier screamed as his stretcher dropped to the ground. The lead man, though wounded, brought up his pistol and shot the third Taliban, and almost instantly, gunfire raked the rocks just over the heads of the three Americans. The unwounded troop yelled for help and a second stretcher for his squad leader.

"Hey, Bro, I know it hurts like hell, but you'll be all right, and soon both of you will be headed for a nice cool hospital ward and decent chow."

"Great, my second Purple Heart in this damn war! The wife is never going to let me re-enlist!"

By nightfall, when darkness blanketed the entire valley, B Company had been in four firefights. Five Bravo members had been wounded and were readied for a helicopter medivac. A medic from the 2nd Platoon tended to their medical needs until a Blackhawk landed nearby to transport them to Bagram. The following day, all five were in clean beds waiting for flights to Germany for further medical care. The hospital in Bagram was set up for emergencies and some patient care, but most of the wounded were flown out as the hospital was known to be a terrorist target.

2nd Platoon was temporarily short a medic so Senior Medic Roman left Yankee Station to fill in until a replacement was sent out. The next day, a Black Hawk loaded with supplies and ammo brought the other medic back. Not long after the helicopter landed a sniper started firing at it from the hills.

Captain Bill Warrens had been expecting such an attack. Earlier, he had spoken to Cowboy Two, who was heading out to cut off any fleeing Taliban. Heavy Weapons had been sighted in the sniper's approximate location. Two HE (high explosive) rounds from a 60mm mortar were fired. Seconds later, the rounds landed on the sniper's last reported position. Bill ordered his Bradleys to open up with their 25mm cannons, and after 10 seconds of firing, he had them cease fire so as not to endanger Cowboy Two's men. Hardly a single space on the western side of that natural fortification was missed, with hundreds of bullets ricocheting off the rocks in all directions. Bill knew that any Taliban in this area were hightailing it to escape such firepower or taking cover in caves.

Bill appreciated the heavier 25mm cannons, as they really tore up the countryside with their heavy concentration of fire. Standing with Cowboy One and Cowboy Three, Bill watched as the Blackhawk Helicopter lifted off for the return trip to Bagram. Inside the Bradley assigned to Yankee Station, Jimmy Olson logged the event for the Company records. He radioed Bill and asked if he planned to send someone up into the hills to tabulate the enemy's body count.

Bill looked directly at young Lt. Graham and asked, "Lieutenant, what do you think of going up there for a body count?"

"Captain, I realize how important statistics are for a unit, but we already sustained five wounded troops, and... Well, I wouldn't endanger another man in this company simply to get a mark for another officer's statistical board. My men are too important to me, so I would recommend we pull back and proceed with our mission." This was followed by a few seconds of silence.

Bill nodded, "That's exactly the response I favor from an officer who serves under me, a man who values his men over stats and medals. Those guys should consider themselves damn lucky. Our men have done a great job today, but this mission is long from over. Every man out here is important to this mission's success; make sure they all understand this. Chasing Taliban up through their stomping ground may have to happen, but not today."

As he walked by, Lt. Graham turned to Bill and said, "Thank you, Captain."

"You earned it. Okay, let's get those new supplies and ammo delved out to those who need them and check your men for water. I don't want anyone showing signs of dehydration. It's hot, and we're stuck with it! But no one goes thirsty—you got that?"

"We got it, Captain," Lt. Graham replied.

Bill contacted Roman, "Before we head out, make sure our medics are re-supplied." Then, "Jimmy, same for the RTOs—new batteries all around and check for any needed parts... We'll take advantage of this brief stop."

"You got it, Boss."

"Jimmy, just when did Captain become Boss?" Bill asked.

"You're the top man out here, sir—so, you're Boss."

"Okay, but don't get too comfortable with that. When we get back to base, it's back to sir or Captain... Okay?"

"I understand totally, your honor," Jimmy said and moved out of the way just in time to escape Bill's right boot from connecting with his rear end. Bill really liked this young kid; it made him think what it might have been like to have had a kid brother.

At 2100 hours that night, the troops were still a good several hours away from Jalalabad City, having been delayed by the firefights, but Division understood that. Bill didn't want to run the convoy at night unless he absolutely had to. After a camp was set up and secured, he allowed small cooking fires, but only behind the vehicles to avoid any possible sniper fire. This allowed everyone to cook their own MREs, making the packaged food slightly more appealing. Like the K-rations of World War II and Korea and the C-rations of Vietnam, these MREs were not that appetizing, but they kept a troop from starving.

B Company maintained a high-security level, with four-man patrols on perimeter patrol. The Chief reminded these men, "No sitting, sleeping or talking on guard duty, nothing that might get you killed by a slick

Taliban with one of those real nasty looking swords. Your wives or parents wouldn't appreciate you coming home with your head separated from your body."

Four of the Bradley Fight Machines were kept on alert, each gunner keeping 25mm cannons pointed in one of four directions. They and the driver would be relieved halfway through the watch. The men knew they were to be prepared to jump with the first shot fired. Still, they were to wait until the unit's mortars had fired off yellow parachute flares around the perimeter in hopes of illuminating the enemy.

Bill and the Chief went over security plans multiple times. Without having steady air cover, they agreed this was the best they could do for now. Chief wanted to send out a couple of listening posts (LP), but Bill vetoed the idea; he knew how well the Taliban maneuvered in the dark. He didn't want to wake up in the early morning hours to find four of his men with their throats cut. Chief even volunteered, but Bill said, "No— you are too damn important to me, and I don't want to have to face your kids and tell them how stupidly you died. They'd probably want to clobber me for letting you do it! Besides, Chief, remember officially you're my second in command, and the Number Two man seldom pulls LP duty."

7

THE ATTACK

AT 0302 HOURS, a security patrol reported seeing a possible firelight in the east toward Jalalabad City. A single squad was sent out on foot patrol to reconnoiter for 200 yards. Bill was concerned with the Taliban sneaking up under cover of darkness to probe their defenses and possibly stage an attack. They were under orders not to engage the enemy if sighted, but to return and report their findings to Bill. By 0412 hours, the patrol was back, and the squad leader advised Bill, "sir, Once I cleared those boulders up ahead, I used my binoculars. sir, that roadway up ahead is all ablaze—must be dozens of torches stretched out for a couple hundred yards. We estimated some thirty Taliban in view. Most are heavily armed, and others were placing IEDs in the roadway. Torches were creating a lot of shadows, making the enemy look as if they were dancing about, which made it hard to get exact numbers. So, there could've been more out in the darkness."

Bill couldn't quite understand why they had the roadway all lit up unless it was to help the Taliban mine the road. The enemy had to know where B Company was encamped as light from the fires could carry for miles across the desert floor. "They must think those rocks are blocking out their fires—probably didn't think we'd send out any foot patrols in the dark. But whatever the reason, this is giving us a big break, and I intend to take full advantage of it."

Everyone was placed on full alert; Bill planned to move out with the first glimmer of the rising dawn. But just before daylight, a large force of Taliban initiated an attack on B Company. Though prepared for an attack, B Company was not prepared for what came.

A flight of grenade arrows rained down on B Company's FOB. The Taliban had tied Russian grenades to the arrow shafts and used them as field artillery. B Company hurriedly leaped into their armored vehicles as arrows descended from the heavens. The primed grenades fired from hilltops exploded in the air. As with most grenades, these Russian ones allowed for three to five seconds before exploding. The grenades were not primed until the archer was ready to release the arrow. One man handled the grenade as the second manhandled the bow. Even when a grenade exploded in flight, shrapnel rained down on B Company.

In his first deployment to Afghanistan, Bill learned the Afghan people were fascinated by Hollywood. They especially enjoyed old westerns because the American deserts resembled the Afghan deserts. Shortly after Hollywood came to Afghanistan showing films in big city movie houses, bows and arrows began showing up. The Taliban learned about attaching sticks of dynamite and then grenades to their arrows from the American film industry.

Not everyone got inside vehicles in time; some chose to dive underneath them for protection. Cries rose as those caught in the open were pierced by deadly shrapnel. Some grenades landed atop two Strykers and one of the Bradleys. The armor proved too strong for the older fragmentation grenades. The blasts caused temporary deafness among those inside these vehicles, with several nosebleeds and bruises. Shrapnel ripped into the men who had only managed to kneel behind the vehicles before the barrage began.

"Medic! We need a medic over here!" The call rang out across the encampment.

"I've got three men down—Jackson's dead! We need medics!" An NCO yelled.

The shouts and screams lasted for the best part of twenty minutes, as rattled and wounded troops cried out. B Company, with only five medics, was caught unprepared for the grenade arrows. Bill was silent, angry with himself for being caught like this. But this was his first experience with the Taliban using arrows.

Then came a second and a third frightening warning, "More arrows on the way!" and "Take cover! Grenade arrows in the air!" A couple of frightened PFCs shouted as they pointed to the sky. Men on the outer perimeter posts listened for the faint sound of arrows flying over. But the warnings came only seconds before the explosions.

"Everyone, get under your vehicles and get those helmets on!" Chief hollered out as he darted between vehicles and continued issuing orders. He picked up one wounded soldier and tossed him inside a Stryker that was already overcrowded. "Take care of him!"

This flight of grenades, which had come from further away, began to explode in mid-air, and some of the shrapnel was close enough to strike B Company's encampment. This time, most of the men were ready. Twelve more explosions rent the predawn darkness as grenades exploded in the air, and then it was suddenly quiet.

"Now it's our turn!" Captain Bill Warrens exclaimed from inside one of the Bradleys. He ordered the driver to start the vehicle and move out. Eight soldiers were crammed in the Bradley with him, all members of 1st Platoon. With the help of three other Bradleys, all filled with angry troops, Bill moved his unit to the southeast. While his Bradleys' gunner concentrated cannon fire on the rocks directly ahead, Bill directed his other Bradleys to rain hellfire down on the rocky cliff-sides to the left and right of center.

As the sun rose above the horizon, the Chief sent five Strykers southeast of their position, responding with fire from their .50 caliber and 240B automatic weapons. The explosion of cannon and machine-gun fire was near deafening but far worse for the Taliban. At least the Americans had earplugs in place. 2nd Platoon was sent out by squads on foot, armed with B-40s and SAWS, to cover the roadway and ensure the Taliban couldn't move across it and escape to the hills in the north. The remaining members of B Company held position to defend the encampment and see to the wounded.

It took some doing, but Bill's small unit of Bradleys, unofficially designated Trail-Blazer #1, forged a trail through the rocks. They rounded a massive stone face some 60 feet high or better and stumbled upon the Taliban's parking lot. The Bradley driver quickly counted 18 small Japanese and Russian-made trucks. Some of them were outfitted with captured 240s, a couple of M-60s, and two Russian mounted .51 caliber machine guns. The Taliban guards left behind to defend the vehicles from desert thieves opened fire with AK-47s.

Bill saw what he was facing and shouted to his gunner, "Take out those .51s first! Then the 240s, I do not want a single one of those vehicles leaving here!"

The turret gunner commenced firing, a big smile on his face as he utterly destroyed the trucks with cannon fire. Gas tanks exploded, sending geysers of flame upward 30 to 40 feet and showering burning fuel down on other vehicles, causing them to catch fire.

Bill knew the Taliban could see the fiery explosions and realized they had been put afoot. Their rides were being destroyed in an awesome display of firepower.

The explosions caused nearly 80 shooters to rush over the next hill and right smack into 1st Platoon's new ambush site. They had failed to believe the U.S. Bradley could get around the hills so fast and realized the Americans had found their vehicles. Their escape plan had been canceled and all they could do was continue to flee through the hills to the east.

Bill sent a five-man team forward, each man carrying a claymore mine to be set in one of the narrow trails that wound down the hill. The resulting firefight lasted for nearly an hour. Firepower gave the Americans the edge, and finally, the hillside was silent.

The five Airborne troops who had taken in the claymores were supported by a rifle squad that was ordered to move forward and engage any enemy movement to protect them. Everyone knew how vital prisoners were, but the squad leader didn't want his men taking any chances and told them so. When the shooting ceased, Bill would send his two Terps to interrogate any prisoners.

At 0550 hours, the battle ended as the sun climbed into the sky. A final count showed 63 Taliban killed, and four wounded in custody. The enemy had lost a total of 21 vehicles, three more than earlier counted. A report would later show that two of the three Russian .51 Caliber machine-guns seized were found to be in working order. A number of

U.S. weapons were recovered including one.50 caliber machine-gun, which, though fire damaged, was still operable. There were also two U.S. M-60 machine guns and seven 240B machine guns, but they'd been damaged in the explosions. Serial numbers were recorded, and the damaged firearms photographed before being buried in deep unmarked holes. Computer searches would later show where the American weapons had come from, possibly revealing a black-market supply. B Company had also seized 43 AK-47s, 28 hunting grade longbows, numerous arrows with grenades still attached, 31 World War Two Russian military long rifles with limited ammo, and 64 Russian and American made military style sidearms, revolvers, and semi-automatic pistols.

Looking over the captured weapons, Bill suspected the older Russian firearms had most likely come from troops during its Afghanistan occupation. He hoped to see whether or not the American weapons were captured from Allied forces or possibly bought off the black market. Bill had learned through his Intel sources and the rumor mill that illegal arms dealers, perhaps American or an ally, were providing American weapons to the enemy.

Nine Taliban and two suspected ISIS members had been killed near the section of road being mined. Two Russians and one suspected ISIS officer, discovered in a large cave after sun-up, were taken prisoner and communications equipment, explosives, weapons, and ammo seized. Prisoners were secured in wrist zip-ties, with their hands behind their backs then searched carefully for weapons, and any papers were seized.

Bill was surprised to hear about the prisoners and knew Division would be overjoyed to get their hands on them. Though in uniform, the Russian's clothing displayed no rank or unit patches. They had given their names and the Russian who appeared to be the senior officer demanded to speak to an American officer. He refused to say anything else. Bill took them aside and attempted to treat them as fellow officers. He wanted to keep them away from the Taliban, concerned the insurgents might try to kill them before they could divulge any Taliban secrets to the Americans. Bill had heard about Russian advisors, but these were the first he had come across.

When SFC Roman reported American casualties, everyone quickly sobered up and the celebration came to an abrupt stop. Sixteen men of Bravo Company were wounded, five were listed as KIA. Nine of the wounded needed immediate evacuation. Coded radio messages went to Division Command requesting the medivac and relating news of the prisoners.

Bill looked over the medic stats and shook his head, "Our balloon has popped; we've lost five brothers all at once and have sixteen in need of medical aid." He handed the paperwork to Jimmy. "I want a Chinook in here right away to medivac our wounded. If there's not enough room for our fallen, a second Chinook will be needed. Tell them their LZ will be marked by red smoke flares; fire teams will secure the area." Bill turned to Chief, "Take whoever you need and a couple of the Bradley's and find a suitable area for a helipad—big enough for a Chinook, okay?"

"You got it, Captain." Chief signaled a 2nd Platoon squad, "You men, follow me—bring along a half-dozen red smoke flares to set up an LZ."

Tired, maybe even bone-weary, they responded with their best attempt at enthusiasm, "Airborne, all the way!" The Chief's face broke into a grin. He truly loved these young soldiers and was proud of them for not panicking and running around like chickens with their heads cut off when those grenade arrows had rained down upon them. As with Bill, this was a new experience for the old Chief.

B Company took a 30-minute chow break. SSgt. Jimmy Olson lugged his field radio to where Bill was resting against a tall slab of rock. "Captain, I have Lt. Rayson on the horn; he wants to talk with you."

Bill looked over at Jimmy, "Are we secure?"

"Sure, we're still under 'Top Security' with everything coded but I've got you two on a two-way phone hook-up via satellite. No one will hear you; no one can record you, not even the CIA and those CID bozos—at least, I hope so. No way of telling what new devices those spy people have come up with."

"Jimmy, I'm starting to get a bit worried about you," Bill said as he turned his attention to the satellite radio phone Jimmy held out. "What do you want, Lieutenant? Over." Although on the phone, he handled the communication as if he was on the radio.

"I'm sorry to have to tell you, Captain, but I thought it was better coming from me while you're out there. They lost PFC Rutgar Killian in

Emergency Surgery... Over." Bill had been briefed regarding PFC Killian's actions pulling his wounded teammate out of the fire. A sizable piece of shrapnel had hit his head almost as soon as they reached a safe distance. Bill planned on putting Killian in for a Bronze Star for Valor, but now it would be awarded posthumously.

"Anything else? Over."

"Yes, sir, I was also informed that a Division Colonel is flying out on a Blackhawk about midday with an Apache gunship escort. I imagine he's interested in taking those two Russians and that ISIS guy back with him. Do your Terps speak Russian? Over."

"One does, they apparently understand English but have clammed up. Except for this one ISIS prisoner, we haven't seen any big ISIS involvement yet. Oh, we did find two suspected ISIS troops both KIA. We have their paperwork and I'll turn it over to the Colonel they're sending out. I suspect the Russians are advisers. They look in too good of condition to be old prisoners from the Russian occupation. That whole grenade with the arrows thing was right out of an old western movie. I'm not sure we got all the insurgents. I'm wary of going into that pass and moving so close to Pakistan—no telling what may be waiting for us out there. So, I'm going to request either a satellite look-see or a flyover from Bagram... Over."

"I recommend you let that Colonel know how you feel... Over."

"If I do that, he might replace me with you, and then it would be you facing the Pakistan Army when you come out of that pass. Last I heard, they had both Russian and Chinese tanks... Over."

"Sorry, Captain, your last message was filled with static... Over."

Bill sighed, then laughed before he signed off. He didn't believe the old static story interfering with communications. Young officers grow up quick in combat, or they end up dead. Bill's dad had told him about all the young 2nd lieutenants who had perished in Vietnam; usually, the 90-day wonder fresh out of college.

"You wouldn't leave us, would you, Captain?" Jimmy Olson asked.

"Now, why would I do that, Jimmy? I just got here."

"It's just that Division may want you back there to brief the brass and then—"

"Let's change the subject, Jimmy. Besides, we need to make this camp look suitable for an arriving senior officer. Got it?"

The Chief walked in, "I left it with Sgt. Lewis to handle, knowing you'd want two squads for guard duty. I had our Bradleys use their treads to level the new LZ and put four men on guard at the Taliban auto junk shop in case some snipers try to take potshots at us. Two of our 60mm mortars are sighted in and ready to hit the car lot if needed, and our 81mm mortars are sighted in on those desert flats to the west in the event they have additional trucks and a desire to take out our arriving helicopters. They must know we have that ISIS fella and the two Russians. They might try to take them out before they talk."

"Sounds great, Chief, but we still need to patrol and knock out the next ten-mile stretch to finish clearing that damn Khyber Pass. And, we still have Jalalabad City to check out, and that could be a real nightmare now that everyone in South Central Afghanistan knows we're out here. You'd better plan on sending a couple of Bradleys this afternoon to the southeast for a quick scout, escorted by a pair of strikers packed with troops. The remainder of the convoy will move out once this Colonel departs with our prisoners. We need to find a high spot to place two sniper squads with .50 caliber Barrett Rifles to give us an edge. I'm still not too sure what might be coming down this way from Pakistan, if anything, especially since we may have knocked off their main advance force. We don't need to be careless at this stage. Our opponents bet what they had on a possible winning hand, but we ended up showing four aces—" Bill stopped; a worried look in his eyes, and the Chief noticed it.

"Captain, we just fought a major skirmish and ended up on the winning side. Yeah, we took some serious casualties, but with them having the home-field advantage, we did pretty well. Besides, those two Russians and that ISIS dude, they'll probably be worth their weight in gold. No telling what our Intel boys can get out of them."

"Yeah, you're right. Knowing how our government works, they'll both probably end up owning bars in downtown Los Angeles within the year. That's what happened with some of our Vietnamese turncoats; we made them wealthy entrepreneurs for coming over to our side. I read how a few of them even bought liquor stores—the American dream."

"Yeah, I read about some of that. Democracy does have a dark side to it at times," Chief shook his head and walked off to check on his people. He still remembered reading about a young NCO, drafted in 1968, who went over to the Viet Cong. After giving his life story to some foreign correspondent, the man could never return home to the United States. The Chief suspected the VC probably just did away with him after he lost his value.

NOON

SSgt. Jimmy Olsen completed the 2200 to 0400-hour shift and decided on a two-hour power nap before everyone began moving around. But the Taliban attack changed his schedule. After the Chinook arrived to pick up the casualties and the senior officer hadn't shown up, Jimmy told his RTO relief to wake him up before noon. However, he was jarred awake by Captain Warrens at noon. He looked up into Bill's unsmiling face. "Captain, I told my relief to wake me before 1200 hours—sir."

"Jimmy, I ordered him not to wake you up until I needed you. I want you to be rested and ready when that officer decides to show up so you can take notes."

"I'm surprised, Captain, that we haven't heard anything about our overdue guest."

"Something came up and delayed the Colonel, as things often do for senior officers. I want you to contact Division and see what's up. I'd hate to think the good Colonel's ride ran out of gas or broke down. This damn desert can be a rotten place to find oneself on foot. C'mon, Sergeant, let's go for a walk and stretch our legs. I was told the new LZ wasn't too far." Bill grabbed Jimmy by the hand and helped him to his feet. Jimmy noticed 1st Platoon's RTO was holding down the fort until his return, so he waved thanks as he followed his captain out across the desert, making sure to have his M-4 with him. When they arrived, Bill admired the work the men had accomplished in creating a firm dirt helipad. "They did a great job flattening this area out with those Bradleys."

"sir, I was wondering if I could ask a favor of you?" Jimmy asked, and sort of withdrew, unsure if he had messed this up.

"Jimmy, you've known me long enough, and you've worked very

hard for me, so what's the favor? I doubt I can get a USO troop out here to entertain the troops."

Jimmy smiled at his Captain's humor, as a good NCO is often required. "sir, I wanted to go out with the point unit tomorrow morning. They'll need a good RTO, and company work keeps me out of the line of fire—usually. To be honest with you, sir, when everything started blowing up last night, I got rattled. I just need to prove to myself, that, I'm still worthy of wearing the Eagle patch on my shoulder. Otherwise, I guess I'll put in for the Infantry or go to work in some chow hall."

"Look, Jimmy, everyone got rattled last night, even me—you've jumped out of airplanes—Dang, man, you've got three combat jumps, two of them by HALO insertion. You've got nothing to prove here, Jimmy, nothin' at all."

"Except to myself, Captain. Will you let me be their RTO for tomorrow's mission?"

"I'll let you know, Sergeant." Bill did not say anything more as they walked back to the temporary HQ they had set up behind one of the Bradleys. Bobby Baker was standing by as a runner, and Corporal Wright monitored the radio for Jimmy. When they reached the radio, Bill turned to Jimmy, "Okay, Jimmy, but on one condition—if you get yourself killed, I'll tell your wife you shot yourself as a poor blubbering coward, you understand me, Sergeant?"

"Sir, you'd never do that to me—otherwise, I would've never approached you. But you may tell her I got crushed by an arriving helicopter. She'd probably believe that. Back home, I'm always hurting myself around the house. She thinks I'm accident prone."

"Go get your gear ready and report to MSgt. McCullough, he'll be leading the point element—and you're right, he'll need a good RTO. But you won't be leaving until I get the final okay from this Colonel to proceed with this mission. I still think it stinks!"

"Thank you, Captain, and no matter what happens, a ride across the dunes or wading into a bloodbath, I'd follow you anywhere—sir."

NOTIFICATION

At 1612 hours, Bill received word that the expected Colonel had departed Bagram aboard a Chinook and should be on scene by 1700 hours. Four MPs would be aboard to handle the prisoners. The Chinook was escorted by two Apache helicopter gunships. Bill looked over at Chief, "Apparently, they want to make sure these VIP POWs make it back to Bagram."

"Between you and I, Captain, I suspect the Russian is a major feather in our unit's cap. He's probably a senior officer, possibly a full colonel. As for the other Russian, I believe he's also an officer, much younger and probably just a captain, Captain."

"Thanks, we lowly captains appreciate that comment. I'll have to remind Kitty of that one night when you come over for dinner. You're liable to get stuck with grilled cheese sandwiches. She, after all, does not think I'm lowly, just underpaid."

"I like grilled cheese, but I always burn the toast," Chief replied.

When the Colonel's bird landed, he walked straight up to Bill, who was shocked to see his own Colonel from regimental headquarters back home. Until this moment, Bill hadn't known he was in Afghanistan. He snapped to attention and saluted. The Colonel returned Bill's salute informally then enthusiastically shook his hand. "You and your men did a hell of a job here, Bill. You've really impressed our allies and the Commanding General with last night's affair. Catching those two Russians and that ISIS agent is a real prize for the unit—might even bring in a unit citation for B Company. The men of your company deserve commendation for last night, so send me the paperwork, and I'll see that it gets done. You may not realize it, but you really crippled this area's Taliban. Bagram headquarters is really talkin' it up. The General even spoke to the news people about it this morning, one of the reasons I'm late. He wanted me there representing the 101st Airborne."

"Well, thank you, sir. I'll be sure to pass that down to the men."

"Good. Well, let's find us someplace to have a talk. Afterward, you can introduce me to those two Russians. I'd rather we just buried the ISIS fellow neck-deep in the sand for a few days."

"Jimmy, head back and tell the Chief who our VIP Colonel is. It'll make everyone's day."

"Yes, sir, on my way."

Bill and the Colonel walked a few yards into the desert, staying close to the Chinook to keep out of any sniper fire. Before the two officers could begin talking, the sergeant in charge of the three MPs climbed out of the Chinook and approached them. "sir, do I have your permission to secure the prisoners?"

The Colonel looked to Bill, "Captain, do you have someone who can show this man to your guests?"

"Can do, sir." Bill waved toward the encampment and caught Corporal Baker's eye. "That's Corporal Baker." He told the MP, "He'll take you to the Bradley that's holding our two guests. Oh, the Russians both speak fluent English, so be careful what you say around them. As for the ISIS guy, I have no idea. He wouldn't even give us his name."

"Thank you, Captain—we've been ordered to treat them like special cargo; there's a lot of people back at Division who want to have a word with them."

When the MPs departed, the Colonel faced Bill, and took a more serious tone, "Why don't you start at the beginning, Bill, from the point where you began working the highway."

Bill talked for over forty minutes, stopping only to answer the Colonel's questions, as he wrote notes on a small notepad. He noted the names of those Bill wanted special mention of in the report to the 101st Airborne Commander, a three-star general back in the states. Bill used his own pocket-sized notebook to read off the WIA and KIA names from the firefight. "Did you hear, sir, that the KIA count changed to six. One of my men died in surgery?"

"Yes, I was called this morning by the surgeon in charge. He couldn't stop the bleeding from the head wound."

"That gives us six KIA, and twenty-one wounded. High numbers, and this is our first long range patrol."

"This was a search and destroy mission on a major target in a hostile land. You've put a serious dent into the Taliban's game plan. We're still not too sure what their intentions are for this area. A few people in Intel suspect the Taliban might be negotiating some sort of deal with the Pakistan Government. As you mentioned in one of your reports, Intel also feels there's an ongoing leak at Division Headquarters. That's how the Taliban knew you were coming and set up the ambush in hopes of catching you by surprise. The arrow grenades, that's something new. I'm not surprised; guerrilla tactics always bring new innovations into a war zone. This is an old weapon that's been modernized. But you and your men beat them to the punch, took out a good number of them, their vehicle fleet and weapons, and captured two suspected Russian advisors and the ISIS fellow. In one lightning move, you've set them back a year or two in their terror campaign in this area. However, having said all that, this Pakistan thing still has us concerned. We knew the Russians were advising them but surprised to find them this close to Bagram. We've known for a long time that the Russians and Chinese have been selling weapons to Pakistan in their fight against India and the Taliban's battle with us and Afghan troops."

"Colonel, how far does the General want me to go with this? Do I still drive through these mountain passes until I pop out the other side and say hello to the Pakistan Army? And what happens when I suddenly find myself staring at a whole brigade of Russian or Chinese tanks, crewed by Pakistani? Is Pakistan planning on an invasion of Afghanistan? Is there any real intelligence out there to support this theory?" Bill took a breath, slowly released it, then added, "sir, I'm beginning to wonder if my unit's move to the Afghanistan/Pakistan Border is bait—to see if we're attacked by either Pakistani or another international force. Is it possible someone, maybe the Defense Industry or someone else, wants to blow this up into World War III? A lot of people became millionaires after World War II and then Vietnam. My dad told me that's how LBJ got elected President, with the Defense Industry backing his play to keep us in Vietnam."

The Colonel looked at Bill sternly but didn't reply right away.

"Captain, you and I are military men, both West Point graduates. We don't dabble in politics until we put on that general's star. I'll probably retire long before that, as I have no desire to dance that political two-step. I have two companies here, minus almost a platoon, and a third company in reserve that has been moved to Germany on standby because of this new operation."

"Colonel, if we come under fire by a large force of armor, B Company and possibly D Company could be shot to pieces. Our Bradleys won't fare too well against heavy armor, especially those big Russian jobs. The number of WIA and KIA could be overwhelming if that were to happen. They would try to tell the world, probably with Russia and China's help, that our American unit crossed the line into Pakistan, violating their territory. I have to tell you, Colonel, my men are really concerned about this move so close to the border, and so am I—sir!"

"Captain, you just came off an intense engagement, and you've lost some good men. So, I'm going to forget this conversation. I'm also not going to stand here and try to explain the political picture surrounding this whole affair. Bagram's Commanding General has issued my orders, and now I'm issuing those same orders to you. You will continue on through Khyber Pass and complete your mission. As to your closeness to the border, our satellites show your exact position and that of the Pakistan Army, and you will be kept apprised of this information. Your job, Captain, is to make this road safe and clear of mines. The Taliban do not want us here and hope to control the Khyber Pass, and we cannot allow that to happen."

The Colonel sighed as he glanced about the desert, looking at his troops and their vehicles. He looked into Bill's eyes and added, "Captain, you will engage the Taliban, and you will show these desert rats they do not control this damn pass or this country. D Company will be ordered to rendezvous with you here, so as of now, you are to hold here until they arrive later tonight. They will have the night to rest. As the ranking company commander, you will lead your combined unit through Khyber Pass and finish your mission. If Command sees any movement across the border, you'll be notified of the same immediately. I'll be with the General overseeing this operation, but you are the operational field commander. Do you understand these orders, Captain?" The Colonel's voice was very stern, trying to get across to Bill what the Colonel's mission was all about.

After some hesitation, Bill replied, "sir, I would follow you to hell and back, but I will not take my men on a suicide run or violate their trust in me. I'll obey my orders; if I see any sign of a massive armored force right across the border, I will not engage them or cause such action for them to engage us. The armor I've been given for this assignment has safeguarded my men. Please tell the General how appreciative I am for the

Bradleys. When the Taliban hit us last night with those arrow bombs, those Bradleys saved a lot of lives. But, Colonel, I will not risk the lives of my men by engaging heavy tanks if the Pakistani decide to invade. Hopefully, when we're through Khyber Pass, all I'll find is open desert. If not, I'll be calling for that air support.

I'm proud to be Airborne serving under your command. But, sir, we're over here committing the exact same mistakes we made in Vietnam. For every man we kill, another Afghan family learns to hate us, and raise their children to despise us. In the years we've been here, children have grown up to become young holy warriors for the Taliban or ISIS. I'm not even sure what the Pakistani expect to get out of a war with the Afghans. If what you say is true, putting the Pakistan military inside Khyber Pass is just providing a big shooting gallery for our Air Force. It makes absolutely no sense. Our Air Force hitting their tanks in the pass would be like shooting salmon in a narrow stream. There's no way for an armored unit to escape under a heavy aerial bombardment. We're just fortunate the Taliban doesn't have an Air Force, or we'd be that salmon.

None of this makes sense, except maybe it's just the Taliban doing a little saber rattling to impress Pakistan or another major force like the Russians or the Chinese—maybe all three. But in a border war, Pakistan doesn't have a chance. sir, could this be something the Russians are trying to bring about? Start World War III right here in this damn desert? A revenge thing to get back at everything they lost here? We're over here fighting a 2,000-year-old culture war, and it's time for us to pack up our toys and go home!"

"My, my, that was quite a speech, Captain. Do you have anything to add to it?" the Colonel asked. His face was as rigid as stone.

"Yes, sir. I am the son of an Army Officer who earned the Medal of Honor. I am also a West Point graduate and a Captain in this man's Army. Saying all that, I am... I am at your command, Colonel. I will continue through the Khyber Pass, my scout units will be extended, and I want you to guarantee me that I'll have adequate air cover if I ask for it, sir, and—I request your word on that, Colonel."

The Colonel remained silent for a moment as he digested what Bill had just said to him, "Captain, you have my word. I do not know the extent of what lies ahead, other than it's incredibly vital to clear this pass. In all honesty, it might very well have something to do with this security alert, which, between you and I could involve moving our heavy armor and possibly artillery to the Pakistan Border. Why? I have not been briefed on this as of yet. Perhaps, this is just a show of force to keep the Taliban up in the hills—or a warning in hopes of keeping the Pakistan military from invading Afghanistan.

Look, Bill, our enemy, whoever they might be, knows your unit is heavily protected by our Air Force. From B-1s to B-52s, F-16s, and A-10s. As I said, I have not been briefed on Russian, Chinese, or even Pakistani intentions. However, having said that, I do know the National Security Agency and their satellites are keeping this whole desert under close scrutiny. Maybe your two Russians will provide us with some intel that will help sort this mess out. But Bill, I promise you, if you call in requesting air support, you'll have it, even if I have to fly along with my .45 in some pilot's ear. Okay?"

"Yes, sir! Thank you, Colonel. I'll hold here until Lt. Rayson and D Company arrive. Then we will proceed east and complete our original objective."

"I'll keep you up to date, and I want reports coming in from you every two hours. I'll try to get the General to order up some observation flights to see what's happening on the border before you ever get there. I know about the satellites, but sometimes those space birds miss a few things due to solar flares or whatever. I'll check into those flights as soon as I get back and keep you advised."

"Thank you, sir," Bill replied.

"You hit me pretty hard with this, Bill. It's not quite what I expected. It seems the Point is sending out a higher caliber of officer these days, and I'm glad to see it. Of course, after what you achieved to stay in Airborne, I should've expected this. Our men need to be able to trust their officers. That was one of the hardest lessons we learned in Vietnam. Too many 90-day wonders. Three months and they were lieutenants and platoon commanders. Many of them died in Nam from lack of training and experience, and a lot of good men died with them.

I agree that it wouldn't hurt these young men and women to spend a year or two as an enlistee just to see what it's like. Maybe that will happen one day, but probably not until all the old generals have died off.

It's a good thing we have so many seasoned NCOs out there; many of them would make great officers. Battlefield commissions should become a reality again, especially in our line units.

To tell you the truth, Captain, I've been grooming you to become our general's aide and then, hopefully, a General someday. I saw you had the makings for that when you came back and worked so hard to return to the 101st. But just so you know, you now have a certain General behind you. He likes what he sees in you and has kept an eye on your work. Back there in the office, when he dressed down those two Colonels, he liked what he saw in your eyes and everything he's heard from me and others about your care for your men. You love them, yet you still know you have a job to do, and when things happen, you grieve for every one you lose. That's what makes a good officer, Bill, and you have these qualities.

Even if this General thinks well of you, he still demands that you complete this mission. I don't think he believes Pakistan has the guts to take us on between you and me. But being a General, he has to risk the lives of 400 men to see if they do. He just might be sending out our highly trained Airborne soldiers to become Judas goats to see what the results may be. That's the hard part of command—I'll let the General know you have my complete backing to any decisions you make in the field. That especially means a need for air cover and some sneak peeks at the border by our Intel birds. I'll be speaking with the General when I return with those prisoners.

Make sure all those vehicles you captured are totally destroyed and the bodies burned. I'll send out another Chinook for the captured weapons—uh, minus any ancient souvenirs your men might want to hold onto. What did you do with the damaged weapons?"

"Photographed everything and buried them in a deep hole. I'm hoping the serial numbers from those American weapons might expose some illegal sources."

"Bill, come see me when you get back to Bagram, and we'll talk again. Now, get out of my sight before I forget I'm a nice guy. Been a long time since a junior officer talked to me like that, I guess I was overdue." The Colonel punched Bill in the arm, turned away, and walked toward his helicopter.

Bill saluted the Colonel's back, did an about-face, and jogged back to the camp. He passed MPs escorting the three prisoners to the helicopter. All three were in handcuffs and wearing hoods to prevent them from seeing anything during the flight back to Bagram or during their ride to Division Headquarters. In the intense desert heat, Bill could only imagine how hot it must be under those black hoods.

The Colonel's helicopter was loaded with wounded soldiers. As the Chinook lifted off, the two Apache gunships, which had remained airborne, joined the Chinook. Bill had decided to send the captured weapons still in working condition back by vehicle, with an escort to make sure the firearms arrived without incident.

At Bagram, the prisoners were turned over to U.S. military Intel and CIA Operatives. A party of Russian Diplomatic Officers from Kabul, a civil servant from Pakistan, and an Afghanistan Army Intel officer awaited them outside the General's headquarters apparently alerted to the arrival by an unknown inside source. They all wanted time with the prisoners, however, they were denied visitation. This attention only helped confirm that Bagram Division Headquarters had a leak problem, and the CID was assigned to find it.

Inside a closed security room, the suspected ISIS agent decided to identify himself as a German citizen and demanded to see a German Embassy representative. During their brief stay at B Company's encampment, the two Russians were each found to be in possession of three different passports, which had been sewn into their pant legs, each having a different name. One first tried to say they were Israeli Army Officers being detained for ransom, however, when B Company's resident Jew arrived and hammered out a bit of Israeli history and culture, that gig was up. One passport identified the older man as a Russian Army colonel; the younger man was a Russian Army major. Their military I.D. cards were contained inside their passport, with a small telephone book that could easily fit into a medium-sized palm. All the handwriting was identified as Russian.

Arriving at Bagram, the two Russian officers demanded to see a representative from the Russian Attaché Office in Kabul. Russia no longer operated an Embassy in Afghanistan but did maintain a State Attaché out of the Turkish Embassy. After that, both men remained silent.

BACK WITH B COMPANY

After D Company arrived at the rendezvous point with B Company, the joint unit, under Bill's command, received marching orders over the satellite phone at 2136 hours. Experience had shown that satellite phones provided somewhat safer classified communication than radio. It was believed the Russians listened in on U.S. radio communications. Even on the satellite phones, communications were kept short, and in code. This meant Jimmy Olson spent another 19 minutes decoding messages before giving them to the Chief who, in turn, briefed Bill.

"Captain, B and D Companies are to break camp by 0600 hours... and continue to operate as before the last attack. We are to continue chewing up the highway, clearing all mines. Along the way, we will embrace the enemy at any opportunity. At the end of Khyber Pass, the unit will set up a temporary FOB and hold for 72 hours. We are to report any contact with the enemy. Air cover will be available 24/7. Our orders are to keep the border under observation and to report any sighting of Pakistan military personnel, vehicles, and aircraft. If, after 72 hours, we have not reported any Pakistani activity, we may return to Bagram. Again, air cover will always be available. Upon arrival at Bagram, you will report to Headquarters to debrief Post Intel and Joint Services. 'Get it done, Captain'... that's from the Colonel—sir."

Bill turned to his radioman, "Jimmy, are you sure you decoded this right? This doesn't sound much like Army orders. This sounds more like —never mind." Bill walked away, that same uneasy feeling deep in his gut.

Jimmy looked at the Chief, "Those Pakistani seem to be like the hillbilly cousins to those Palestinians we've all read about. Like the rest of the Muslim fanatics, they seem to want to shove these two countries into a blood feud. Maybe they're hoping to get a chance at drawing blood from Americans and possibly the Israeli. Last I heard, Saudi Arabia, Jordan, Egypt, and some other nations don't want to get blood on their hands for fear of losing our U.S. Dollar. But they might let these two countries go to war just to stir up the Muslim people and show the rest of the world how powerful Allah can be. I'm learning to hate religious wars, past and present. Look what happened to Rome and the Greeks."

Chief looked at the young man, "Jimmy, you're a bit more intelligent than I've given you credit for. I think it's about time you started thinking about taking your exams for E-7. We can always use another Sergeant First Class around here, and you wouldn't be confined to that radio."

"Thanks, Chief; I've been thinking of testing for that, but even as an SFC, do you really think the captain would let me handle a platoon, I mean as head NCO?"

"Look, young-in', I'm already supposed to put you out on a point vehicle due to some bizarre promise the captain made to you. Now I'm thinkin' about putting you upfront with the lead Bradley—I'll even have a couple of words with their gunner, and maybe, he'll let you take hold of that 25mm. Look, Jimmy, you've got to learn never to hope for more excitement in a war zone. Someone's just liable to be listening and will toss your young, eager ass into the mix to either sink or swim."

"But, Chief, we've all listened to your old war stories, over and over. I just want to be able to have a few of my own for when I'm old and gray."

"Old and gray? Why you Jimmy, you're a clown—but a likable one. Maybe you'll get your wish, and if we survive, you can tell the whole world how you once faced down a battalion of Pakistan tanks, if we survive, that is. And again, so you can have those great stories to tell, I'll have the men tie you to the hood of that Bradley, teach you to have a bit more respect for your old and gray senior NCOs."

"Of course, I respect you, Chief. You're the only soldier I know who served with Audie Murphy in WWII, brought all those wounded and frozen Marines out of the Chosen Reservoir, and danced with Raquel Welch when the USO came to Saigon."

The chief's raised eyebrow was Jimmy's signal that it was time to make a break for it. Chief wasn't even alive when Audie Murphy was awarded the Medal of Honor, nor was he old enough to have served in Vietnam. Making any reference to the Marines was a slam to a senior Army NCO. But before he could grab Jimmy, the young redhead cleared the foxhole and ran full bore for the latrine pit.

Chief watched him run and smiled. *Someday, I'll have his two large ears in my hands, and we'll see who's laughing then. But darn, he is the best RTO in the Battalion—he'll make a good SFC.*

New orders rolled up in his left palm, the chief went in search of

Captain Warrens. He found him checking out a report of bullet holes that indicated a shot went through one wall of the Stryker and exited the opposite wall. That shouldn't have happened unless there was a defect in the armor. Bill had heard rumors of some defense contractors trying to save expenses on material. He knew producing inferior armor would save a lot of cash. He was troubled by what he found and photographed the damage. "These holes didn't come from a .51 caliber... More like an AK-47. This shouldn't have happened. We'll file a report on this when we get back to Bagram; hopefully, it's just this one vehicle. Anything manmade can have defects, people make mistakes, and machines we make can make mistakes. My father told me that the M-16 was one of the worst weapons designed for jungle warfare. Thankfully, we have the M-4s, which was a major upgrade."

Bill slapped the side of the Stryker, just above the bullet holes, and turned to the Chief, "Except for our security posts, have B Company fall in between the Bradleys at 1830 hours for a briefing, and include D Company officers. They can brief their own people afterward. Between now and 1830 hours, I want the Strykers carrying .50 calibers. Assign half of them to keep an eye on this hillside to the southeast. The other half is to keep an eye on the road and those hills beyond. They can move a bit faster than the Bradleys, and speed could be an asset if we come up against a major force later."

After a pause, Bill had another thought. "After the briefing, I want two squads and a Bradley to move over to that pile of cars and trucks to cover the troops scouting the area for trails. Maybe they can give us some idea how many Taliban escaped. Make sure our men stay out of those rocks. It's too late in the evening to go climbing around up there. And make sure they keep their eyes open for snipers. Advise the Bradley gunner to stand ready. If any shooting starts, he can engage the enemy position. Choose a platoon leader— your choice but assign one of the young lieutenants to make up a guard duty roster for tonight. Use men from both companies."

"Yes, sir, will do," Chief said and walked away. He had in mind to give the guard duty to 2nd Lieutenant Dave Parker. Any positive mark on his record would help if he hoped to become a Captain someday.

A Second Lieutenant's promotion to First Lieutenant was automatic from 18 months to two years. The rank of Captain could take longer. Chief had recently been advised that he was being considered for Warrant Officer Three, also known as a Chief Warrant Officer. This would be a sizable pay increase and would boost his monthly retirement check when that time came. If this promotion came through, Chief would become the Regimental Chief Warrant Officer at Headquarters and serve directly under the Colonel for all enlisted matters.

8

MOVING ALONG, SINGING A SONG

AT 1830 HOURS, most of B Company was loosely clustered between the armored vehicles; all aware that Bill had sent two squads towards the foothills to look for trails. Bill had decided to send up a five-man sniper team to safeguard the two squads and the Bradley crew was advised to keep an eye on both the sniper team and the two squads. The sun was heading for the western horizon, and Bill wanted his people back inside the perimeter before dark.

The sniper was Corporal Herman Remmel, on his second tour to Afghanistan. During his last tour, he had earned two Bronze Stars for Valor as a sniper; his weapon of choice was a .50 caliber Barrett Rifle. His spotter was PFC Bob Campbell. The other three men included Jimmy Olson, acting as RTO loaded down with his M-4 and a satchel of grenades. All five men had night vision scopes attached to their helmets, and each wore a clean sweat rag wrapped loosely around their necks. With temperatures holding around 120 degrees, the sweat cloth didn't stay clean very long.

Among the men on their first tour, one or two always thought the warnings they received were simply war stories used to frighten the new guys. A medic didn't mess around when he delivered health lectures but one man in every squad usually succumbed to sun exposure and intense heat. The victim often passed out from fever and ended up spending at least a week in the hospital. Dehydration was also a concern, and this was why Bill made sure they had an adequate water supply on this trek. Numerous 500-gallon "water buffalo" trailers were towed by various vehicles.

Since World War II, soldiers had learned from fighting in North Africa and several Pacific jungle islands to Vietnam to pack half a dozen pairs of socks for any operation that might last longer than three days. Without dry socks and foot powder, feet became overly moist and were soon covered in painful blisters, which could quickly transform into an ailment kindly known as Jungle Rot or Trench Foot. This could become a disabling condition and, in some cases, the loss of a foot.

JIMMY OLSON

Jimmy and the two riflemen took up a position on the lip of a cave entrance. No one wanted to go inside because they had left the remains of five deceased Taliban there following two grenade blasts. Their temporary position was about 60 feet above the ambush site. The edge of the cliff was well over 100 feet above the cave entrance, so they did not expect visitors from there. The Taliban's main force had retreated to the cave when their vehicles were destroyed and had run right smack into B Company's ambush.

A two-man sniper position and the three-man listening post were on top of the ridge, maintaining communication between Jimmy and Bill. The second sniper at the Listening Post was armed with an infrared night scope mounted on his 7mm sniper rifle. At the same time, his spotter's helmet was fitted with infrared goggles in addition to a pair of powerful infrared field binoculars hanging from his neck. Together, the two men carried some of the most expensive sniper equipment on the market. Both men and Jimmy were armed with M-4s loaded with 30-round magazines as well as multiple grenades. Being an RTO, Jimmy also carried a sidearm.

So far, they had seen nothing, but this was a post where no one would doze. Falling asleep on such a post was an excellent way to never wake up again. The Taliban were well known for their ability to sneak up on an enemy position and silently slit the throat of a dozing man. They would catch some sleep when the unit moved east later.

Jimmy was restless and knew every sound he heard just had to be a Taliban. But so far, not a single post had reported any movement or sound for most of the night. Then, at 0410 hours, Jimmy's position alerted to movement behind them. They could see nothing with their infrared scopes. "Lima Papa One requests a patrol to check out the car lot. We're unable to see anything, but have continuous noise—sounds like someone might be removing parts from those vehicles we destroyed —it might just be thieves. If you say so, we can move and get a better eye on whoever it is... Over."

Before midnight, Bill had moved the two squads looking for trails and assigned them positions 100 yards directly west of the car lot. After the lot had been burned, the four-man security force had been removed.

"Lima Papa One, move carefully and quietly and keep us advised. Post #Two, maintain position but stay alert. Everyone be sure of your targets. I don't want any friendly fire incidents on my watch." Bill ordered the two rifle squads to remain in position. "All positions, this might be teenage thieves wanting to strip some vehicle parts. Do not fire unless you see weapons. Confirm... Over."

"Post #One confirms we are moving. Confirm Lima Papa is only three of us... Over," Olsen whispered into his radio.

"You are confirmed, just three of you. We will be your eye in the sky. Warning, Lima Papa, do not, I repeat, do not use the same trail the Taliban came down on. They might have set traps—confirm you heard me... Over."

"Lima-Papa confirms. Post #Two is also on the move, but we cannot see the car lot until we go over the next ridgeline. Will report then... Out." Olsen gestured to the point man, giving him the okay to lead out, with Jimmy in the middle.

Bill contacted Post #Two and advised them to hold position. "Keep your eyes open. If those are Taliban, they might try to sneak back over the hillside when the shooting stops. Again, make sure of your targets!" Bill handed the microphone to Roman, "I sure hope it's not a bunch of stupid teenagers. Suppose one of them picks up an axle from a mini-truck or a tie rod. They'd get blown away because the infrared might show it to be a heavy caliber machine gun, or a rocket launcher, or possibly even one of those old Czech long rifles."

A few moments later, Olsen came on the radio, his voice barely a whisper, "Lima Papa One, we have multi-body movements—estimate a dozen unknowns moving through the debris field. Also, picking up engine heat from two vehicles at least a quarter mile to the east, bodies very faint—possibly three. Request you send a team to support Post #Two and an additional team, supported by a Bradley to take out those two trucks... Over."

Roman handed the radio back to Bill, "Lima Papa Two, set up at your best position. A fire team will be in route to support you coming in from the northeast of your position. We will not start up the Bradley until we can take the unknowns by surprise, or the shooting starts. Still possible these could be teenagers salvaging parts to rebuild what they own. We will wait until they fire on us. Confirm... Over."

"Sierra Papa (sniper post) One, confirms. We should be set up in three to four mikes... Over."

"Post #Two now in secondary position; we can see people moving. Too dark to tell who they are. Request flares when Sierra Papa One is in position. Need one; possibly two flares to identify unknowns... Over."

"Yankee One copies. Will send up two flares 10 seconds apart—a red flare followed by a green. The green flare will signal the mortars to light up the area with five white signal flares. If they're Taliban, the shooting will begin, and you may return fire. One Bradley prepared to move out. Confirm... Over."

"Post #One confirms... Over."

"Post #Two confirms... Over."

"Post #Three (the two rifle squads) confirms...Over."

"Be advised, two Strykers will make a quick move across the desert to block escape route from the southeast, two Bradleys will move in from the northwest as soon as the shooting starts to collar these people— repeat, be sure who you're shooting at. Confirm...Over."

"Post #One confirms... Over."

"Post #Two confirms... Over."

"Post #Three confirms... Over."

"Yankee One to Post #Three, hold your position and pick up any runners. I want prisoners, if possible, but do not endanger yourselves. Confirm...Over."

"Post #three confirms... Over."

"Yankee One to all units, radio silence until the first two flares go up. Do not confirm... Out."

Jimmy felt a rush surge through his body, producing a mild case of tremors as he climbed through the rocks. Beneath the light of a partial moon, he moved slowly, crouched down so as not to give his position away. He had to know where to put each step and stay close enough to see the man in front of him. And he had to keep a lookout for snakes, drop-offs, and the enemy. He could hear metal-on-metal sounds ahead as they got closer, and it made him wonder. *Why are these people endangering themselves by making all this noise? Why risk another engagement? Surely they know we're still in the area?*

Jimmy knew he'd have his answer soon enough and wondered how many more good men might die or be shot up out here before his curiosity was satisfied. His hands were gloved; one maintained a firm grip on his M-4 as his other hand guided him over rocks. He often felt he was on the verge of falling forward, but his open hand grabbed a stone to maintain his balance. More than a few times, he checked the satchel hung over his left shoulder to ensure he still had his grenades. He was concerned he might have lost one or two due to his high wire act, but he hadn't.

The suspected scroungers, Bill hoped were just typical Afghan juvenile gang members out to score some plunder were, in fact, Taliban. They also wanted the heavy metals from the vehicle's axles, tie rods, steering columns, and vehicle frames. Some to be used as weapons, others to rebuild disabled vehicles. Out here in the desert, thousands of miles from the closest auto parts factory, these parts were extremely valuable. Taliban fighters were among the destroyed vehicles removing everything they could with only hand tools and muscle. They couldn't use cutting tools or anything that would present a flame or create a sound. This made for a lengthy process, and mistakes were made as tools or parts were dropped on other metal pieces.

Usable parts were cautiously stacked and tied down on a flatbed of one of the vehicles they had brought with them. During the day, the Taliban drove right into Kabul, bringing in debris. Workers, allied to the Taliban, removed the parts to either meltdown or reuse. They converted metal into weapon-sized pieces for their IEDs and shrapnel plates for rockets and mortars. These plates, when exploded, sent out dozens to hundreds of tiny metal pieces. Ball bearings and truck doors became shrapnel. A sheet of one-inch squares held together by thin steel pieces was rolled and placed inside a rocket or a mortar round. Upon impact, these pieces would break apart and become extremely deadly. Russians and the Chinese taught this to the North Vietnamese Army and Viet Cong in their war with the Americans. In Afghanistan, the steel of a wrecked vehicle lived on to kill American troops.

Jimmy could hear people up ahead. From the voices, he knew it was the Taliban. *Well, that shelved that idea. There are some crusty old farts out there giving orders, probably telling them they're making too much noise—too late, Old Man!*

He wanted to call it in, but they were too close. The soldier in front had heard the voices and froze in place. Then, after reaching back to tap Jimmy, they cautiously slouched down until the rock shelf hid the three of them from the car lot. Jimmy reached back to feel for the man behind him, contacted the man's rifle, let go, and found the right kneecap, which was bent forward. Jimmy tapped three times to signal 'hold position'. Everything was done in silence; any movement they made was slow, deliberate. They waited for the first flare and didn't have long to wait.

B Company's Heavy Weapons Platoon, using 60mm Mortars, launched the first parachute flare. It ignited a hundred feet directly above the car lot and produced a surreal red light. The Taliban knew the jig was up; they attempted to shoot the parachute flare out of the sky with a heavy concentration of AK-47 fire.

Then the green flare popped open as the red began to fade. So far, the Taliban had failed to hit either one. As the scene glowed under the green flare, the sky lit up with AK-47 tracer rounds which made the infra-red scopes and goggles useless for a time.

A senior Taliban commander ordered his men to cease fire, advising them that their fire was giving their positions away. Loud and excited voices rang out. Suddenly, the newly arrived vehicles, loaded with car parts, began to break for freedom. However, a Bradleys' concentrated 25mm cannon fire ignited the darkness. It destroyed the trucks, killing both the drivers and passengers. The Bradleys' ground unit moved in and took nine Taliban prisoners who had been hastily throwing metal chunks into truck beds only seconds before.

Two 81mm mortars opened up with illumination flares transforming darkness into daylight which allowed B Company to see several of the Taliban. They had been caught in the open as both Post #One and Post #Two opened up. The Taliban started firing on the Bradley and its ground support and the area quickly became a massive shooting gallery.

Sniper One began taking out targets of opportunity. Simultaneously, the Bradley, having stopped escaping vehicles, moved up the hillside to begin a gradual elimination of the enemy. The 25mm cannon made a frightening whirling sound, like a hundred chain saws supported by a kettle drum. Its firepower produced a blinding light.

Jimmy used the ledge he had hidden behind to brace himself and took aim at the enemy. He saw one man go down, clutching his throat, and for a brief micro-second, it left him with a squeamish feeling. It passed with the subsequent firing of his M-4 and wounded a second Taliban with an upper leg shot.

Post #Two began to move down the hillside, and as ranking man, Jimmy ordered the others to slowly proceed toward the car lot. "Keep it smart, no John Wayne stuff." He advised the captain of their movements by radio.

The steep rocky hills prevented the Strykers from moving in. They took up stationary positions as their squads disembarked to set up a protective half-circle to catch any fleeing Taliban.

Meanwhile, the Bradley's 25mm gunner continued to send out a devastating stream of fire while the driver moved in closer. A Taliban soldier stood up from the middle of the debris field and fired a shoulder-mounted rocket, aimed right for the Bradley. But the gunner was trained for such events and turned a steady run of cannon fire at the incoming weapon. He scored a hit before the rocket could impact the Bradley. Though some of the shrapnel did strike the vehicle and rattle the crew.

Two SAW gunners aimed their weapons, and each man went

through an entire belt of ammo in an attempt to blow up a second Taliban rocket. Meanwhile, an 81mm mortar targeted the Taliban's rocket position. Within seconds, that area of the car lot was covered in a fiery explosion and fell silent.

The last rocket blew up 10 feet from hitting its target, showering shrapnel and debris over most of the Bradley. The gunner, wounded by the blast, would require a medivac back to Bagram. He had received eight shrapnel wounds for which he was later awarded a Purple Heart and an Army Commendation Medal.

But the battle was not over. Jimmy Olson suspected the Taliban might try to hold out until the last man. He inched forward, with one troop staying three feet to his left and a foot behind him to give Jimmy an unrestricted view of the area. With rocks often the size of a house trailer it was challenging. After 10 minutes of crawling and losing sight of the car lot several times, Jimmy discovered a well-used trail that had a branch trail leading toward the lot. Jimmy instructed the man on his left to go up the trail 20 steps, "Look out for mines and tripwires. Keep your head down, and don't fire unless you have to. No sense giving your position away," Jimmy whispered.

He turned to his second man, "I'll head up this hill and see if I can see the car lot—but only 20 steps. You stand fast and cover our backs; we'll meet back here in five minutes." Jimmy was hoping for another illumination flare then realized he would rather have darkness for the moment. The two men moved 20 steps and a bit farther. Jimmy could still only see the shots fired from the two squad positions of Post #Three. The driver and two men had stayed with the unit to provide cover as the wounded gunner was being attended by the medic.

Once the two mortar rounds hit dead center, no one knew how many Taliban were still alive. But Captain Warrens had warned his new guys over and over again, "Until you put one in his head, the Taliban will live to kill you."

Cautiously, Jimmy moved back down the trail to meet his two men, and they proceeded back along Jimmy's path. He had changed his rifle's selector to full-automatic, working on a hunch, then he saw the first burned truck less than 15 feet away. It was the front bumper of an older Ford pick-up truck, with all the chrome removed. He glanced about and thought he saw some movements behind one of the wrecks. But he couldn't fire, not knowing if it was one of his Company guys moving in or a terrorist. He gestured to his men and moved cautiously forward. Jimmy had only gone a short distance when suddenly, a hard blow to the back of his head and shoulders knocked him to the ground, dazing him. The blow severed Jimmy's rifle strap, and his M-4 lay somewhere at his feet. Thankfully, his helmet absorbed most of the blow. The trail was extremely narrow at this spot, and Jimmy had a hard time getting back to his feet to turn around. Rattled from the assault; Jimmy couldn't see who he was facing. The figure was coming at him for a second try. His weapon scraped stone and sent out sparks. *He's got a sword, and he's trying to take my head off!*

The Taliban was armed only with a long sword, held with both hands over his head preparing for another downward stroke. Had the man been armed with a rifle, Jimmy would've been dead. The sword in the hands of an angry man nearly froze Jimmy.

When the man saw that Jimmy's rifle had dropped, he moved in for the kill. With a sudden realization of impending death, Jimmy propelled himself forward. Using his helmeted head as a battering ram, he slammed into the Taliban's chest and barely managing to stay on his own feet, drove the man to the ground. As he fell, the man released his grip on the sword. Jimmy didn't have time to search for it, the man was sitting up, the sword once again held in both hands as he moved to stand. Reacting purely from the desire to survive, Jimmy drew his pistol and fired three shots in quick succession, striking the man in the chest. The sword clattered onto the rocks at his feet. With a quick glance to assure himself that his attacker was no longer a threat, Jimmy picked up the sword and studied it as another mortar flare lit up the area. The blade was over three feet long and resembled a Russian scimitar except the point was weighted down. Jimmy learned later the extra weight at the end of the blade helped with decapitation. The handle was ornate, with golden designs engraved into it. Jimmy, still feeling a bit dizzy, decided to take the sword with him.

The fighting was over, and seven Taliban had surrendered. Though his shoulder and head hurt, Jimmy returned to the FOB and immediately sought out his company commander. "Can I keep the sword, Captain?" He asked as he handed it to Bill, who inspected it carefully.

"Jimmy, did you just come across this in the dirt, or did you find it next to a dead body?"

"No, sir. I sort of won it in a duel. He got in the first hit, dented my helmet up some, and cut through my shirt, but my vest saved my hide. I shot him with my pistol before he could have at me again."

"Give me all the details," Bill ordered and listened as Jimmy told the brief story. "That's quite a story, and I believe every word of it. But it helps to have two troops who witnessed it. This sword is more than just a sword. From what little I know I suspect this is a Chief's sword. I've seen them before. It's pretty old and usually passed down from father to oldest son. You were probably fighting the Chief of this local faction, possibly even their tribe, but this sword is old. The handle needs to be photographed, as well as the blade because of all these engravings. We'll send the photos to a museum in Kabul for identification. Wow, I wouldn't be surprised to hear this sword is over 200 years old. It might've been used against the Russians, probably even the British before that, over the last two centuries. It's quite a treasure. What would you do if the Kabul Museum wants to keep this sword to display—it's their heritage, after all?"

"I'd give it to them, Captain. I won't stand in the way of a country's history and all that heritage stuff. I simply don't want the Taliban or ISS to get their hands on it, or some supply jerk back at Division."

"The General will make sure of that, Jimmy. But do you realize what happened when you defeated that young chief?"

"Except for being alive—no, Captain, I didn't think of it."

"By defeating their leader, you probably caused the Taliban to surrender, and now we have additional intelligence to gather. I'll be recommending you for a decoration. But we won't say anything about the sword until it's been certified. Turn around and let me have a look at your back."

Jimmy's shoulder muscles hurt as he pulled his vest carefully over his head. He winced as a stabbing pain shot down his neck and dropped to his knees as his legs suddenly gave out from under him.

Bill quickly moved in and helped Jimmy lie down on his stomach so he could examine his wound. Using his flashlight, Bill saw all the blood on Jimmy's upper back and lower neck. A wide gash over eight inches long marred the young man's helmet. Jimmy's body relaxed as he slid into dark oblivion. Realizing that the man was unconscious, Bill looked more closely at the wound and saw a small section of Jimmy's spine in the long laceration. "Medic! I need a medic!" He shouted and stood back as the medic went to work on Jimmy.

"Sir, I can bandage him up, but Jimmy needs to be medivac'd to Bagram. He may have sustained nerve damage. I can't believe he made it back here after that attack."

Holding Jimmy's helmet in his hands, Bill knew that without his helmet, that sword would have severed his head in half. He kissed the top of the helmet and added a "Thank you, Lord!" and the government manufacturer for using good old American steel in making these helmets. Bill sent word to the Chief to get a medivac in at first light to take their wounded and arrange transport for the prisoners.

Though Jimmy was still unconscious, the medic advised Bill that his pulse was rapid but strong. The medivac trip back to Bagram was painful for Jimmy and the other wounded troops. At the base hospital, Jimmy was stabilized and then flown to Germany where he would undergo two surgeries. In time, he recovered and returned to B Company. Bill requested that Jimmy be awarded a Purple Heart for this sword wound. He was later awarded a Bronze Star and his third Purple Heart.

The sword was examined and placed in the Afghanistan Central Museum as a historical artifact.

BACK WITH B COMPANY

The Taliban car lot was stripped by Bill's men, and all the usable steel was piled up to keep it from being turned into weapons or spare parts for the Taliban. Division advised Bill that the captured wreckage would either be picked up by Air Force Civil Engineers or buried. Bill imagined the metal would eventually be melted down in Kabul and the steel used for various things, including metal piping, fence railings, and girders for buildings. He hoped so, but Intel suspected some of the legitimate

Afghan companies had ties with the Taliban, which still worried Bill, but it was out of his hands.

B and D Companies were on hold. Information Intel had learned from their prisoners confirmed the Taliban were working with ISIS, their weapons provided by both Russia and China. Bill found it strange that a one-time enemy like Russia, who did serious harm to the Afghan people, could become an ally to the Taliban. *That would be like us becoming allies with the North Koreans and the North Vietnamese. No, thank you!* Division Intel at Bagram had also learned information concerning Russia's plans for Afghanistan and a possible Russian build-up on Afghanistan's northern border.

Bill was not interested in Russia's plan, believing that to be way above his pay grade. His primary focus was on his current mission and the Pakistan Army possibly waiting for them. Reviewing his Khyber Pass maps, he still could not understand why the Pakistan military would want to risk their troops moving across the border and entering Afghanistan through the Pass. It just made no sense to him. *Our only safety for this mission lies in our airpower controlling these skies. If the Pakistani tanks moved into this pass, they'd be wiped out. No, this has got to be some kind of false flag to divert us from what our enemies might actually be planning. Maybe the Russians will attempt to invade from the north to finish what they started and couldn't finish. Our support of the Afghan people helped turn Afghanistan into Russia's Vietnam. So, they left. But now, just maybe they want to come back, and they have our spy guys busy looking to Pakistan instead of to the north. But no one's asking for my opinion.*

That afternoon, B and D companies received orders to move out at 0700 hours the following day. They were to proceed with their mission. Bill awaited the arrival of the Chinooks to dispense of vehicle parts. If extra time was needed, he would have a platoon from D Company remain to guard the Civil Engineers until the job was done. He sent two Bradleys and three Strykers ahead, with two squads from B Company's 1st Platoon to continue blowing up the road and taking care of the anti-personnel mines for the next five miles. He requested air cover, and three Cobra Gunships from Bagram took to the air. The remainder of B Company was on a 50-50 watch. This allowed the men time to chow down, clean weapons, and possibly catch a catnap.

Sergeant First Class Paul Roman took over as the Captain's RTO until Jimmy Olson returned or a replacement was sent out from Bagram. Roman and Bill took a moment to have lunch. Roman opened a package of crackers and spread a thick paste of generic peanut butter over them while Bill mixed fruit with a tin of pound cake he'd been saving. Before they could begin their meal, Bill was advised of three inbound Chinooks, with the lead pilot requesting to know if the area was safe. Assurance was confirmed and Bill set aside his plate and headed for the landing area. Chief joined him, and together they watched as the three helicopters landed close to the used car lot. A squad of men was placed on guard duty for the Chinooks; another stayed with the Civil Engineers while they went to work dismantling vehicles.

The engineers unloaded scrapping equipment - acetylene torches, generators, fuel, high-powered portable steel saws, and nearly a dozen large toolboxes. This was not going to be a two-to-three-day job.

"Chief, I want an M-60 and a rifle squad placed on the far side of those birds. They'll have to dig in and set up sandbags to protect their position. I don't want to give the enemy a chance to take them out. Tonight, we'll add Humvees with some sensors... out to about 100 yards. I want listening posts inside those sensors, on the flats, and up in those rocky hills out in front. I don't want any snipers taking pot shots at our guests. Tell our 60mm mortar crews to sight in on those sensors, but first load up flares. If we get a visit tonight, which I think is possible with these Chinooks sitting here, I want to light up that area. If nothing happens, it's still good training for the men."

"Yes, sir," Chief replied and began to walk away, then stopped and turned back. "sir, do you think they'll let us skip this tour of Khyber Pass? I read all about those British battles in the 1800s and have seen enough old movies about it to make me nervous."

"As much as I hate the thought of going through this pass, Chief, the Khyber is used for more than just a route to Pakistan. There's a lot of innocent people living in those hills up there. Most of these villagers still use camels, sometimes cattle, and a few donkeys to move their wagons. And dirt bikes. The last time I was here, some Afghan bikers were using old Army motorcycles left behind by the British. These people may be poor, but they sure know how to make things last. They need the pass for access to Kabul and the rest of Afghanistan. Many of them have formed alliances with the Taliban, often because they didn't want to see their kids murdered or girls sold into slavery. That's still going on. Without this road, they have to travel the long way around to get to Kabul and other large settlements for trade and jobs. I knew one guy on my last tour who rode his Honda 90 nearly 100 miles each way to work as a typesetter for an Afghan newspaper. Most of the time, his travel time took longer than his work shift, but his family needed the money to survive. A Honda 90 can go a long way on a gallon of gas. I asked him why he didn't just move closer to his job, and he said, 'This is where I was born, met my wife, and raise our children. My whole family is here. In another town, I'd be a stranger.' I couldn't fault him for that."

Chief looked at him for a moment and asked, "If he was a stranger, how'd he get the job in the first place?"

"I asked him that. Education—he'd gone to school and graduated so he could spell without his editor looking over his shoulder all the time. He was hoping to become a reporter eventually, and maybe now he is. Or he's been forced to join the Taliban to save his family. It's a real mess over here—just like Somalia, Vietnam, and all those other third-world countries. Makes me so thankful to have been born in the U.S.A."

"This place never fails to surprise me, Captain. These people remind me of settlers in the 1800s. The Taliban are different. Sort of a combination of our old KKK and Mafia. I know they see themselves as true patriots, heroes of their country—holy warriors for Islam, but they murder their own people. Each country seems to have a name for them, but they're all bloodthirsty fanatics. Then I think about the war in Vietnam and how the VC massacred whole villages—all their own people. Outside of our Indian Wars and Civil War, I don't remember ever reading about Americans massacring fellow Americans to gain freedom and territory, though there was that John Brown character and those southern guerrillas who all but destroyed Lawrence, Kansas."

"That was Colonel Quantrill and his men, Chief. John Brown took out a few other towns, but I can't recall their names. Humanity has been committing murderous atrocities since Cain and Able and it'll continue until the Good Lord returns. Now get to work, no more slacking. I need to have a word with these pilots. I'm sure they're a bit edgy about being stuck in Indian Country and then learning they have to spend a night or two out here. Aviators hate being stuck on the ground when bullets start flying. Report back after you post perimeter guards. If you believe we need other vehicles out there take a Stryker and a Humvee. If the unit needs to retreat to our position, that'll give them more than enough vehicles to haul their butts back here."

"Yes, sir." With that said, the Chief was on his way to carry out his orders. As not to forget anything Bill told him, he wrote his orders in the small wire-bound notebook he always kept handy.

The six Chinook pilots converged on Bill's temporary headquarters, which amounted to a large hole surrounded by a three-foot high wall made of sandbags. When the companies pulled out, many of the full sandbags would be piled on vehicles to be used at the next camp. The lead pilot, Major Jake Askins, shook hands with Bill. "Nice vacation getaway you've got here, Captain. Where's the beach?"

"We got the sand, but no ocean or lakes nearby."

"Where do you want us, Captain?"

"The encampment is right over there. Ask for Sergeant Roman; he'll set you up with a fox hole. And, Major, since you'll be here for a night or two, please tell your men no moving around after dark. We're expecting trouble tonight with those birds parked here. And, sir, we don't salute in the field, too easy for snipers to pick out the officers."

"Thanks for the advice, Captain, and thanks for putting those guards around our birds. I'll sleep better knowing that."

Major Askins recalled his meeting with Bill's Colonel, who briefed him on the assignment to bring out the engineers. "Major, you'll be working with the 101st Airborne, a good bunch of frontline troops commanded by an experienced combat officer—Captain Bill Warrens. Your primary responsibility is to get those engineers out there to salvage every possible scrap of metal from captured Taliban vehicles. We don't want the Taliban to salvage that scrap metal for shrapnel to be used in IEDs and other weapons. Warren's people will handle security; if any problems develop, you can contact me here at Division."

"Sir, is there any real danger of us being attacked out there?"

"Major, I know you've only been here for a month, but this whole damn desert is a war zone. Just remember, when you land out there, you'll be very near the northwestern entrance to the Khyber Pass so avoid flying any closer to the border. No sightseeing, or quite possibly some Pakistani fighter jock will shoot a missile right up your ass. Then we'd have an international incident on our hands."

"No problem, sir. I promised the families of my pilots to bring everyone home alive."

ON THE GROUND FOR A NIGHT OF FROLIC

The crew chief for each bird stayed behind to watch over their aircraft and take care of the few problems reported by the pilots on the way out. With all this sand, there was almost always something malfunctioning.

SFC Roman had a steaming cast-iron coffee pot hanging on a steel rod over a wood fire. At sunset, the fires would be extinguished to prevent the Taliban from using them as a target point. The Americans had learned early that the Taliban had some expert riflemen, most of them trained by the Russians.

The major spoke up, "Captain, I was told to place my men under your command while I was on the ground. My combat experience is minimal. I've only been here a month, and this is our first time staying out overnight."

"I'll tell you what, Major, until nightfall or if any shooting starts, you continue to command your crews and those engineers. I'll handle my men and the defense of this area. It's been quiet this afternoon, but I'm a realist. I expect the Taliban to have reorganized by now. With those Chinooks on the ground, we should expect an attack sometime tonight — probably between midnight and 0400 hours. They love to mess with our sleep. Now, with your permission, I'll explain our defensive position; you may have a couple ideas of your own for me to consider." Bill doubted the major, an aviator, would have any ideas, but he was polite.

It took Bill less than half an hour to show the major the unit's position and explain why it was done this way. By the time they returned, the coffee pot was steaming up a fresh pot of non-military coffee. Bill had made sure they brought a couple of cases of real civilian coffee, a lesson learned from his former company commander. Roman provided large baggies of natural sugar, powdered creamer, and packets of hot chocolate, so the men could make simple mochas. When the Chief joined them, he shook hands with the pilots, and looked over at Roman, who was minding the radio, "Good job with the coffee, but, Roman, you have to be the ugliest barista I've ever seen."

"Chief, if you can talk the captain into hiring a good-looking female barista from back home, I'm game. I think all the men would contribute to cover her pay, combat, overseas deployment, and any insurance she might need if she gets wounded."

"In your dreams, Roman—keep up the good work. Any radio traffic from the road crew?" He checked his wristwatch, "They should be heading back soon. Better give them a call. I want them back here before dark so I can position that Bradley and get all our men fed and ready for tonight."

"Yeah, the back of my neck is already itching, and that's always a bad sign," Roman replied. "Remember what happened before, when I nearly scratched my darn head off? They walloped us!"

"Superstitious bunk, Roman. It's just that we've got those three big birds sitting there. An RPG could easily take out one of those Chinooks. I sure hope those pilots and crews don't plan on sleeping in their birds tonight. We're good, but mistakes are still made, and that desert is wide open."

Before Roman could reply, the company radio came alive, and Roman advised the RTO, "You're coming in five by five... Over." He wrote down their message, surprised by it, and handed it to the Chief who read it and handed it off to Bill. "Looks like the mice are active. They've not engaged —just see a lot of movement up in the hills."

Bill nodded, "Roman, advise them to pull up stakes and return here. I want them back before sunset."

Roman sent the message to the lead vehicle in the pass. Before he could refill his coffee cup, another radio message came in from the group, "We've taken two prisoners. On our way back."

"Two prisoners? That's all he was willing to say. Must be concerned about radio security—just too much technology out there. Maybe we should go back to using tin cans connected by a string like we did in the Boy Scouts," Bill said.

"Unless there's trouble, we'll know all about it soon enough," Chief replied.

Roman patted the Chief's left elbow, "We got word from the Afghan Civil Engineers working the road west of us. They've begun repairing the road, filling in holes we made blowing up IEDs. They've been advised by Division that we'll be holding this position tonight and not to proceed until we move out. So, who's protecting the engineers, sir?"

"Colonel advised me that the Afghan Army has that task, which I'm sure overjoyed those civilian Engineers," Bill answered.

"Chief, an hour before sunset, begin bringing our men back from that far ridge-line. D Company will continue handling the west side of the valley to ensure the Taliban don't try to sneak up on us from behind. If they spot anything unusual or hear something, remind D Company to notify us right away. Once we move out, D Company will follow but remain a mile or so back. The two companies can take turns on point while blowing up the road. A 3rd Platoon squad will stand by. If shooting starts, I want them moving fast to support that team out to the south. We'll position a Stryker to provide cover-fire, and I want the mortar pit on stand-by alert after dark."

"You got it, sir. I just wish the men who gave us these orders were out here with us. It might teach them something. Oh, I'll have the men chow down early and get all the fires doused before the sun hits the horizon. By the way, Roman has the neck itches, if you believe in such a thing."

SFC Roman waved the Chief over to his RTO position and spoke to him in a low tone, "I just received a short, coded message from Staff Sergeant Becker. He won't say much over the radio, but he does say his prisoners are VIPs. Maybe they picked up a couple of Pakistani scouts or more Russians? Could be some pretty National Geographic female reporters over here doing a story."

"You wish, but no sense speculating. I'll let the captain know."

"Thanks, Chief. I dislike giving him only partial information."

"Face it, Roman, you're afraid of the captain and where he might assign you next." Chief shook his head, smiled, and walked back to where Bill stood, grimacing as he chewed on an energy bar.

"Does that bar taste that bad, sir?"

Bill shot the Chief a stern look, looked at his nutrition bar, and shook his head. "It's just all that crap from Division and keeping these birds out here overnight. Like waving a flag and daring the Taliban to attack. I'm still leery of taking our men to the end of Khyber Pass; the Air Force could've handled this job with their drones and satellites without endangering two Airborne companies. Maybe it would be wiser just to leave it mined. Put big warning signs up to tell the locals to stay off the road. As far as we know, the Taliban mined it to stop the Pakistani from coming through the door. Last I heard, those people weren't getting along too well —lots of old wounds from past wars. Maybe the Taliban picked up on something you and I don't know about. Russia might be considering another invasion of Northern Afghanistan and the Taliban are preparing to stop them. It's not like the Taliban and the Afghan Government are talking to one another. Just too many scenarios to process. Gives me a headache and makes me glad I don't work Intel. Too much heartburn in that job."

Chief nodded in agreement, "With all the racket we're sending out from our recent engagement, and all those IEDs exploding on the highway, those Palestinian listening posts on the border have got to know something is happening across the line. But one thing really bothers me, Bill."

"What's that, Chief?"

"Do the locals have an alternate road to reach the border—or their mountain villages?"

"Most likely, look how many trails we've already discovered since we got out here. People have been going through these mountains since Noah's boat unloaded all those animals. There's a lot of open desert out there and scores of trails made by caravans and armies that fought in this region. Things are all screwy over here, and it's only getting worse. I mean, why are we concerned with the Khyber Pass? It's not like we're going to send one of our convoys through there—"

"Oh man, do you think some General at the Pentagon is thinking about invading Pakistan? Could that be what this is all about? Like we need another war over here. Dear God, I sure hope that's not it. I doubt the American public could put up with another war, and Pakistan has so little to offer us, not to mention they have nukes!"

"Chief, I don't see us getting into it with someone who could nuke Bagram and take out Jerusalem."

"You're right, but why does anyone care about this damn Khyber Pass?"

"To be honest with you, I've got no idea. It's way above my pay grade," Bill replied. He finished the last bite of his energy bar and moved closer to the Chief, "Between you and me, I am sincerely hoping and praying this is our last deployment to Afghanistan. 14 years is too long to be involved with this damn war!"

"Sir, I've never heard you talk like this, at least not out in Indian Country. Back home, after a few dozen beers in us, we all tend to exchange views on these sandbox wars. But—well, I'm glad you kept it between us two."

"Don't worry, Chief. you're my sounding board because I trust you. As to my fellow junior officers, especially those on their first tour, they're still gung-ho and hoping for medals to adorn their chests and quick promotions. They seem to forget just how many people can get hurt or killed to fulfill a young lieutenant's wish. I recall some of the talks I had with my dad when I was a kid. He worked under a Colonel in Vietnam who made foolish mistakes to achieve glory and get his first general's star. A lot of good men died on that Apache Snow operation —the Battle for Hamburger Hill—all members of the 101st."

"Glory-seeking heroes. They've cost this nation a lot of lives since our Revolution. Men like Custer, Patton—the list is a long one. Hollywood glorified many of these men, and that's a shame. I'm just glad you're not one, Captain."

"Nope, I've got a family to go home to, and the more live troops I can take home, the better I'll feel about myself." Bill suddenly remembered something his dad had told him during one of their talks. "Chief, do you know what the troops did with a glory-seeking officer, or, just a nasty officer, who didn't know how to lead his men properly?"

"If you're talking about Vietnam, I know they used to *frag* them or at least try to."

"Yeah, my dad said they had this major transfer into the 101st a few months before Hamburger Hill who used to volunteer his men for special duties in hopes he could earn his Lt. Colonel's silver leaf. Well, the troops got really weary of all those special assignments, especially the ones that produced a lot of body bags. So, one night someone dropped a fragmentation grenade through the hooch window right over his bed. The pin was still in, so it didn't explode. They apparently hoped this would get the officer's attention. But it didn't. The major continued until another grenade was dropped in, this time with the pin pulled. Supposedly it bounced off his face, waking him up. He was out the door so fast he didn't even get hit with a single piece of shrapnel."

"Did your dad ever say whether or not they caught the culprit?"

"They didn't, but he did say that officer went back to the states early and transferred out of the 101st for a much safer field. He left before Hamburger Hill took place, missing out on all the medals that were awarded for that 11-day battle."

"From everything I read about that battle, it was one hell of a fight. More than 70 American troops were killed, and over 300 wounded and over 600 enemy killed. I'm glad I was too young for Vietnam, but from everything I've read, I can see why you compare this place to Vietnam. It's understandable. Afghanistan and Iraq are terrible places to wage war. Maybe someday we'll be stuck jumping out of a transport over Iran. But I sure hope not."

"Enough of this, let's go check on the engineers. I'd like to see those helicopters out of here before the Taliban can score with a rocket or some fanatic makes a suicide run at it with a satchel of grenades."

"Yes, sir." Chief shouldered his M-4 and yelled new instructions back to Roman. Roman had two runners available, and the Captain had his handheld radio if he was needed quickly.

THE PRISONERS

Over an hour passed before the advance unit returned. Bill waited in his foxhole for SSgt Becker to show up with his two VIP prisoners. With both Iranian and Russian technology provided to the Taliban, ISIS, and al-Qaeda, Bill and his commanders suspected the Taliban could have communication equipment available, monitoring American transmissions. This is why leadership was being issued via satellite phones.

SSgt Becker's patrol came into view, and a few moments later, Bill learned that they had sustained three wounded troops. A medic was already en route to lend a hand.

When the Bradleys' door opened and the troops climbed out, Bill saw the two prisoners. Hands behind their back, cuffed with zip-ties, they had to be helped out. They wore military fatigue shirts and desert camouflage Boonie hats. One prisoner appeared to be white even though his heavily tanned face was mostly concealed beneath a bushy brown beard. He stood nearly six feet. The second man was very dark-skinned and looked to be middle eastern. His long black beard was braided, his right arm supported in a blood-stained sling, and he walked with a limp. The complexion, uniform, and footwear told Bill the first man was most likely a Russian officer, probably an adviser to the Taliban.

After Becker set the prisoners near the smoldering campfire, he reported to Bill. "Merry Christmas, Captain! We brought you a couple of illegal aliens."

"Any idea what you have here, Becker," Bill asked.

"Captain—we found them in the back of a cave at the end of our patrol area. From what I've learned and documents we've found, which our Interpreter Nabbia was able to help with, this local guy is an Iranian from Tehran. He's tied in with ISIS but gave no name or rank. He tried to make a fight of it, but we did our best to keep him alive. The other is a real Russian Colonel and speaks English but refuses to speak to this lowly enlisted man."

"How much intel did you find with them," Bill asked.

"We loaded down three of our packs, enough to keep our Intel boys back at Bagram busy for days or maybe weeks. They tried to set fire to the paperwork, but we moved in too fast. I think we caught them napping."

"Good job, Becker. How bad is our friendly ISIS commando?"

"Sir, the leg injury is old, but he got the shoulder injury when he jumped me. He came out of the darkness, and knowing we'd want him alive; I turned the long knife he was using to jab him in the shoulder. We bandaged it up; it really wasn't much of a wound. I know he planned a lot worse for me."

"I thought you said he surrendered."

"Eventually, Captain, sir. After he was lying on the ground nursing his wound."

"Any communication equipment or other weapons?"

"There was a large battery-powered radio too big for us to carry, so it was destroyed with grenades. Based on limited knowledge of such things, I suspect it had satellite capability. We took what I guess were their codebooks. We found both Afghan and Russian-made RPGs, some old LAWS, 17 IEDs, which we rendered useless, and three Claymore mines which we brought back for EOD to inspect and get the numbers from. I'm curious about where they came from—guessing black market —and we reappropriated several American M-4s and what ammo we could carry. Oh, I also took a real nice Glock-45 off that Russian; he had it in a shoulder holster but never went for it. I'd sure like to keep the knife that fellow tried to use on me—if I can?"

"The knife is yours but keep it in your pack until we get back to Bagram. The Glock will have to go to Intel to see where it came from. We've all heard about some American weapon companies selling stock to some country that delivers it to Iran and Syria. So, maybe we can help nail those bastards down. What did you do with the other weapons?"

"When the first grenades didn't bring the roof down and didn't destroy the radio, we threw in a few more and that completed the task— the ceiling came down."

"Sergeant Becker, that was an excellent report. I'll make sure your whole patrol gets credit for bringing in these two very interesting prisoners and finding their weapons and communication cache. I'm sure this will help your next promotion and that of your men."

"Thank you, Captain. What's going on with all these Chinooks parked over there?"

"Once I read our new orders, I'll brief all the officers and NCOs at one time."

"Yes, sir."

Bill was about to go meet the new prisoners when he heard the sounds of a large helicopter in the distance to the west. He was surprised to see that it was a CH-54 Sky Crane, the heaviest load helicopter in the military's inventory. Hanging beneath the helicopter on eight-inch-thick steel cables was a Bradley with a large Pearson Snowplow blade attached to the front.

The Chief came up, "Bill, I wasn't aware we had any Sky Cranes in Afghanistan; they must've brought it from Germany. I wonder why we're getting a weird-looking Bradley with a snowplow?"

Bill thought about it for a moment, "Maybe someone at division thinks we're taking too long blowing up the road with cannon fire, so they sent us this beast to get the work done quicker. I'd sure hate to be riding in that thing when it hits a mine."

"Knowing how the big brass thinks, maybe we're doing our job too well, and someone's complained about all the noise we're making, frightening children and animals. If I recall my reading, that blade can go down nearly a foot or more in soft dirt, like a road, push up the mines, or explode them. It could make our travel time a lot faster, but it makes me wonder what those guys use to protect their ears?"

As Bill watched, the Sky Crane lowered its heavy load to the ground. The enormous helicopter was escorted by two Apache gunships. Clouds of dust billowed up from the west, and a moment later, Bill spotted the lead Stryker coming in. Lt Rayson and D Company had finally arrived to join B Company. For the last few days, they had remained a couple of miles behind, holding their back door. Bill had been advised earlier that D Company would be moving up to arrive before nightfall. Setting their vehicles up in a half-circle directly west of B Company, the troops began setting up their night positions.

Lt. Samson Rayson reported to Bill as soon as he arrived, glad to straighten out his legs after their short drive. Bill escorted Rayson over to meet the two new prisoners. Chief went to assist D Company set up for the evening and assign security positions. Though D Company came with a senior NCO, he was only a Sergeant First Class and didn't have the combat experience the Chief had. He gladly listened and accepted advice on what was needed to secure their area for the night.

The Sky Crane dislodged its load and took off to return to Bagram.

Hanci Nabbia, their Kurdish interpreter tried to get the ISIS officer to talk, but the man was calm. His unfriendly facial expression showed his attitude and his lack of appreciation for the Kurdish people. He even spat on Nabbia. Occasionally, he cursed in a language that Nabbia knew was clearly Iranian.

When Bill approached the two prisoners, they stood and faced him. Bill surprised his men when he saluted the Russian Colonel; however, Bill only nodded in the Iranian major's direction. Nabbia had learned the man's rank when he heard the Russian Colonel address him back in the cave.

So, he's not ISIS, but an actual Iranian military officer. Now that's going to really make our Intel people happy. Russian and Iranians working together —bound to make things more interesting back at Division, Bill thought as he ordered, "Remove the Russian's wrist ties and get him some coffee; he's had a bad day." The Colonel smiled and returned Bill's salute, which told Bill the man at least understood English and probably spoke it as well. He gestured for the two prisoners to sit back down on the ground but left the Iranian's hands tied. He asked Nabbia to interpret for him in case the Russian did not understand or pretended not to.

"It's not necessary, Captain; I am quite fluent in your language. I also speak Kurdish, Iranian, Afghan, Turkish, and some Pakistani. A result of my training for this assignment, which I am delighted, is now at an end. You must understand, I've grown quite weary of living in filth and sleeping in these accursed caves."

"If you can answer me, sir, how long have you been in Afghanistan?"

"My Iranian comrade speaks no English but tries not to smile at my answers. He knows he's probably headed for the gallows. Still, he is most likely unaware that I'll be hopefully, turned over to the Russian Embassy, probably back in Washington D.C. after your CIA has had a chance at me. Having said all this, can we have some of that great-smelling coffee? I've drunk enough tea to become an Oriental."

"Of course, Colonel." Bill turned to one of the guards and asked him to bring two cups of coffee, then asked the Colonel to inquire if the Iranian officer would like a cup, but the man shook his head when asked. "I suspect he thinks it's either poisoned or filled with some sort of truth serum."

"Good, then I'll take the second cup," Bill said.

"Sounds fair enough," the Colonel said in an understanding tone. "As to how long I've been in this delightful land, I feel I can answer this question. If you had asked me how long I'd been assigned to this group, that must wait for when your spooks shoot me full of truth sermon. Your CIA operates much as our old KGB did, loving drugs and needles. Though, I do so miss the days of beautiful women and liquor to obtain answers. I'm very fond of the old James Bond movies—quite thrilling. I have been here four years and seven months. I traveled through beautiful Iran and spent several fun-filled nights in Iraq playing poker with members of an American Marine recon unit. I had them convinced I was working for your Blackwater Security Company. Nice young men, it is sad so many of our best boys are first to fall. I have come to detest this country's sweltering summers and snow-bound winters. I have been frostbitten more times than I can count—I hate this place! During my first winter, I was snowed in up in those mountains southeast of here for five long months. I nearly starved to death and suffered frostbite to both my hands and feet and lost a chunk out of my forehead. That's when I began having ill thoughts toward my superiors in Moscow. May I ask, Captain, is this your first or second tour?"

Bill cast a quick glance at the Iranian. "Actually, this is my third tour in this part of the world, one in Iraq." Another sip of coffee and Bill awaited the next question. Angry looks from the ISIS officer did not escape him.

"I've noticed your Airborne patches, so you're one of the famous Screaming Eagles? I've read the history the brave 101st has shown since World War Two. Quite a record, one to be extremely proud of. Can you tell me how many jumps you've made, and are you—what is that word? Oh, yes, are you HALO qualified? We, of course, have something very similar in the Russian Army, an Airborne drill team to put on shows for the public, much as you do in America."

"I've done quite a few jumps; I love the excitement of them. And I try to keep out in front of the young troops, or they'll start thinking I'm getting too old for this shit."

The Colonel laughed, "Believe it or not, Captain, this is the same in every army I've worked with. Even these ISIS and Taliban bloodsuckers," he made sure to smile at the ISIS major, "—have the same problem. To stay ahead of the youth takes a lot of work. But I've found the Taliban to be a most competitive group in this regard. Their old soldiers keep it up until they are either killed or die in their beds. They'll even terminate a senior officer's life if they feel he's getting too old to carry out operations, especially if it will help younger ones move up in seniority. No historical traditions in the Taliban, which is sad."

"I hadn't heard that one, Colonel. I thought all the old Taliban handed their rifles over to the young troops and the old men returned to their herds."

"Oh, some do, but I'd estimate less than half. I've found the Taliban to be one of the more vicious soldiers in this land. I'd compare them with the Zulu warriors of old Africa. The radical Muslims I've seen are all mostly rabid dogs; I wish President Putin would stop dealing with them. To be honest, I was assigned here as a young major and wounded twice. This made it hard for me to return, but I was no longer—sorry, too easy to open up with a fellow soldier; I must maintain a few minor things to give to your CIA in hopes of securing my release. If you look at our history following World War II, most of the men we were forced to deal with on both sides were savages. The Vietnamese, Cambodians, and Laotians. Now it's the Chinese—what more can I say? Before joining the Communist Party —a requirement to make senior rank, I was a member of the Russian Orthodox Church. I have not visited a church since I first arrived on this assignment. But I still pray, silently. If they had discovered I was a Christian, the Taliban would have sent me home in small pieces."

"Colonel, I've enjoyed our talk; hopefully, it will not be our last. It's time to prepare our camp for the night, so I must place you back in restraints. I can't afford to have you escape during the night, so you will be well guarded. I'll make sure you're fed and kept warm; there'll be no fires. They tend to become an easy target for snipers. Maybe we'll get another chance to speak."

"I would like that, Captain. Please take care; these hills are filled with Taliban snipers." He grinned, "To show you evidence of my desire to return to my Mother Russia, I will give you this tidbit—I so enjoy your American dialect—so many words meaning something else. Of all languages, your version of the English language is the hardest to learn— so much slang. However, I did hear several voices speaking of rumors concerning Pakistan. Though I do not believe it, we also picked up rumors on a planned Pakistani invasion. I do hope they prove to be baseless, as that would be tough on all sides."

"Thank you, Colonel. If you need water, coffee, or a latrine break, ask this Corporal here."

Bill nodded to the Corporal, who replied with a quick, "Yes, sir."

"Follow me," Bill said and led the corporal aside for a private chat. "Corporal, our Russian friend seems to be extremely talkative and friendly; be on your guard. This man is a highly trained operative. I want three of you with him at all times. He may try to escape, and he knows this desert better than we do. Got it?"

"Yes, sir, I understand."

Still carrying his sealed orders, Bill sought out the Chief, and the two of them watched as D Company finished unloading gear and setting their area up for the night. Bill heard a song playing low over a radio that one of the troops had. It wasn't much larger than a cell phone, and Bill stopped. He smiled to the Chief, "The wife told me about this tune; she played a bit of it for me the last time we Skyped. I don't remember the title, but I think the artist's name was Arlyne Curiel —yeah, I think that's right. It was a song written for one of our troops, David Anthony Mitts, killed over here in 2004—or was it 2005? Not sure about the year, but the song was written to help the man's mother deal with the loss. I remember all this because one of the lines really choked me up—'Heaven is needing a hero like you.' I think that's right. I asked her to record it and send it to me so I can play it for all the troops."

Chief listened to the tune, and Bill could see the old man was moved by the song, confirmed by his eyes glassing.

"What's up with you two?" 1st Lieutenant Rayson asked as he walked up and handed his pack to one of his PFC runners. "Find out where I'm at for the night and get our Company Headquarters set up."

"Yes, sir," the PFC replied and was on the way to find D Company's head RTO.

"So, what's happening out here, Captain? I don't see any action, just what I picked up from your radio reports. We weren't due to relieve you for several more days."

"I don't know much, Sam, but these are our orders—thought we'd go over them together." Bill knew the young officer preferred to go by Sam, having been kidded most of his life over his full first name—Samson.

"Headquarters probably thought I might open them and blame it on the paper pushers back there. But as you can see, it came to you all sealed up, sir."

"Don't worry about Division; we'll give them plenty of smiles with the two new prisoners my patrol took. One is an Iranian major, who supposedly can't speak American, but be careful talking around him. I'm not too sure about that. He wore some sour looks when the multi-lingual Russian Army Colonel chatted with me. I suspect the Colonel is former Special Forces and working Russian Intelligence, but we had a fascinating conversation."

"How long has he been here, Captain?" Lt. Rayson asked.

"He said several years and I believe him. Our Intel boys will enjoy his sense of humor. He told me that they'd heard rumors about a Pakistani invasion of Afghanistan. I still believe using Khyber Pass would be foolish for any commander to undertake. In the days of mounted cavalry, this would work. But not with tanks that are too susceptible to air attack. As I said, he was quite friendly and even hopes to be turned over to the Russian Embassy in Washington DC."

"Well, should we sit down at your CP, and open those new orders?" Lt. Rayson suggested. "All I was told was to get these to you ASAP, and that meant a real bumpy ride. You guys really chewed up the landscape; we had to take to the desert multiple times... And what's with that big Tonka Toy they airlifted in?"

"That Tonka Toy will help with the demining operation, but it's got to be rough on the operators," Bill replied as he led the way to where SFC Roman was on his butt with a set of headphones on his head covering only one ear. Roman wanted to hear if anything broke loose outside of camp as he kept a close eye on the prisoners. "Did you, by any chance, bring along any extra water trailers? Because we're nearly out of water," Bill said.

Lt. Rayson grinned. "We have several water trailers, but I was told they'd be flying out additional full trailers as we need them."

Both Bill and the Chief nodded approval, and then Bill said, "Let's see what our masters of mayhem have planned for us; I'm feeling a bit anxious just sitting here. Oh, I almost forgot, the Army MPs have been reinforced to ensure our enclosures back at Bagram are not broken into by thieves and scoundrels."

"Hell, it'll be the MPs who probably rip us off," Chief said.

Bill opened the sealed envelope and saw it carried two smaller sealed envelopes; one for B Company and the other for D Company. A single sheet of typing paper was folded and attached to B Company's. Bill opened the folded letter, read it through, smiled widely, and looked directly at Chief.

"What?" The Chief asked. "What do they say I did now?"

Bill stood at attention and popped a crisp salute, holding it until Rayson stood. The Chief slowly got to his feet to return his Captain's gesture.

"Orders—which are apparently locked in our Colonel's office safe, say you've been promoted to Warrant Officer III. Which means I can continue calling you *Chief.*" Bill put his hand out and shook the hand of a shocked Chief Warrant Officer. They all knew this would be a nice pay raise for the Chief and a significant raise in his retirement pay. This new rank also allowed the Chief to enter the Officer's Club and enjoy commissioned officers' services.

"I guess this is why the Colonel gave me these," Rayson reached into his right shirt pocket and withdrew rank pins and two sets of cloth Chief Warrant Officer patches. These were subdued to keep a sniper from seeing his rank status. His Chief Command Sergeant Major stripes, also subdued in black and green would be removed. Both officers pulled their knives and cut the stripes off each arm of the chief's uniform.

SFC Roman had watched the whole affair and appeared with three full paper cups of coffee. "Congratulations, sir."

"Well, thank you, Roman, and thanks for the coffee. I know you'll spread the word around by chow time but remind them that warrant officers only get saluted once a day, and are not required in the field. I would prefer not having some Taliban sniper light up my life before I get the chance to retire." He stood up to knock his cup against Bill and Lt. Rayson's.

"Now, let's see what our orders say," Bill said as he sat back down and opened the envelope. At the same time, Lt. Rayson read his orders, which were an exact copy of Bill's. They both finished about the same time, and Bill asked Rayson, "Did the Colonel say anything that's not written here?"

"Yup, he said the Air Force will be patrolling the Afghan/Pakistan border with aircraft and drones. If the Pakistani cross the border in anything larger than a small patrol, our flyboys will attack. He also reminded me that we have two Navy carriers patrolling the Gulf. Unfortunately, we'll be the first blocking force the enemy encounters. We'll have half a regiment of troops and our armor, plus nearly a full Division on its way to assist us. If they move across the line, they'll face a formidable threat, and they should also know this. He hopes it remains only a rumor. Ironically, his word not mine; it seems we cannot be reinforced right now for fear the Pakistani Army will assume that we're preparing to invade Pakistan. That's why the Colonel feels only our two companies were sent on this mission. We're not quite big enough to be looked upon as an invading army. His last order was to make sure you understand that our combined companies will not cross the border unless ordered by Command."

"Have you been through the Khyber Pass, Lieutenant?" Chief asked.

"No, Chief. This spot is the closest I've ever come to Pakistan, but it sure doesn't look like the Khyber Pass I saw Gary Cooper and Rock Hudson fighting in when they made their movies."

"If I remember right, they filmed those in the hills above Burbank," Chief said with a grin. "I've been through some of the pass a few years back and found it to be extremely ripe for an ambush. There are several villages back in those hills, most probably under the control of the Taliban. If we get word the Pakistani are on the move, we'll have to deal with those Taliban. In a Pakistani invasion, I doubt the Taliban will want to ally themselves with us. Which means we'd be fighting two enemies. If that happened and someone wanted my opinion, I'd leave that damn pass and fall back here to await support. Too easy to get ambushed."

Bill spoke up, "We'll get into that later. Sam, you should use this time to get your men set up for the night. B Company will handle the east part of the circle and D Company the west side. Ensure everyone knows the passwords. I don't want to lose anyone to nervous trigger fingers. We'll have a Commander's Call at 1730 hours for all officers and NCOs E-6 or higher, but get the men fed first. Our first joint patrols will go out at 1900 hours, in time to set up some ambush points. That'll give you time to brief your men. It should be dark by 2030 hours, and by then, we all need to be ready for visitors. Just too many targets out here for the Taliban to resist."

"Bill, the Colonel strongly reminded me that you are in complete charge of this operation—this is your baby! If you're severely wounded or KIA, then I take over, and then it falls upon the Chief. Our beloved Colonel didn't feel our other officers had the Chief's experience; he's third man in the command structure for this operation. And based on his experience, I do not believe any of our young officers would dispute that."

"Sam, the Chief, and I have discussed this quite a bit. I've heard rumors like this before and nothing came of them. We haven't crossed their border, and as we've already said, they'd be pissing in the wind to attack us and use the Pass to invade. Understand, that pass could become a deathtrap for us if the Pakistan Air Force led the invasion. Unless we have air cover near, those Pakistani planes could be overhead before planes from Bagram reached us. I hope our people watching those satellite screens will let us know if their Air Force heads this direction."

"Yes, sir. I'll see you at 1730 hours." Lt. Rayson stood up, threw the remainder of his coffee cup into a nearby fire, and walked off to find D Company. He stopped briefly and turned to look over the Chinooks. He had to agree with Bill; *These birds make a prime target for the Taliban.* He needed to make sure his company was ready by nightfall.

Bill turned to Chief, "You'd better take some men down to help those engineers load whatever when they're ready to go. We may need to launch them in the middle of the night to get them out of here. Send one of our Strykers over to get one of those water trailers from D company. Then get a tarp over all the water trailers—I want them to look like a bunch of sandy boulders. Otherwise, some enemy sniper will go after them and put holes in them. I don't want our men getting thirsty out here. We both know how fast dehydration can become terminal. Oh, and when you're done with those little chores, speak to our vehicle crew leaders and put together a list of vehicle needs. Better to get some needed parts flown in tomorrow than wait for them to break down during our offensive."

"Yes, sir, I'll have Roman send out word to our men about the Commander's Call."

"Thanks, Chief. I forgot about that. By the way, I knew the Colonel put you up for this promotion, but in his note, he said the Division Commander got involved and pushed it through."

"Wow, even the General! Can I keep the letter and the note, sir?"

"Of course," Bill replied, and handed both papers to him.

Chief grinned slightly, then folded the papers and placed them in his shirt pocket.

Bill watched him and thought, *I hope I act the same way when I make Major, but that will be my last promotion. I don't think I'll re-enlist to stay in another hitch in hopes I might make Lieutenant Colonel. I owe it to my family —and I'm learning to really hate this desert!*

Bill carried his orders to Roman to place in the Company Log. "Call Headquarters and confirm we have viewed our new orders. Send it in code."

"Yes, Captain."

"Check all our communication equipment and medic kits. If we need anything, get it ordered, also in code."

"Can do, sir."

"Good, you just might make a good RTO yet." Bill walked away to prepare for Commander's Call. He hoped the Colonel's concern about the Pakistani would come to nothing. The Pakistanis used Russian tanks, possibly some Chinese. In either case, he was pretty sure the Bradleys' 25mm cannons would penetrate their armor easily enough. He wished he had received additional training on confronting heavy armor, which is not something a man needs to know when encountering the Taliban.

Bill remembered reading at West Point that the U.S. Army in Vietnam was trained to fight the Viet Cong and North Vietnamese infantry. Later in the war, several tank battles were fought near the North Vietnamese border, putting U.S. armor against Russian armor. A couple of military historians looked upon it as a mini Battle of the Bulge. One historian commented that the U.S. held the advantage in that the Russian armor was crewed by North Vietnamese troops and not Russians.

Watching his men move about the encampment for a moment, Bill sat down to review his map. He needed a moment to consider what he was going to tell his men. With D Company on the scene, the troops knew this was looking more and more like some heavy action coming their way. More than a dozen of the newer men, not assigned a chore yet, pulled out writing pads and began to write a letter home. They were feeling jumpy and needed something to help calm their nerves. They knew if something big was about to kick off, that they'd probably be the lead force going in. Some were proud of this, others were scared. Still, they would stand when called upon, for they were Airborne—the Screaming Eagles, and they knew that reputation had to be upheld.

9

RUMORS GIVE WAY TO ACTION

"So, that's it, fellows. Our brand-new Chief Warrant Officer will be handing out assignments for both Companies," Bill announced at the Commander's Call.

"In the event, I am severely wounded or dead, Lieutenant Rayson will assume command. If Lieutenant Rayson is unable to command, by order of our regimental commander in Bagram, this unit's command, for this operation, will pass to the Chief. By no means is this a reflection of our other officers, but rather to the Chief's many years of combat experience. In the event the Chief is unable to command, then leadership passes down by rank and seniority. Are there any questions about this?" There were none.

"Make sure you get the word out to your troops. I have no idea how long we'll be in the field. One last thing, troops will wear helmets and vests at all times with weapons in hand or within reach. If I find a rifle sitting alone in a fox hole or in an empty vehicle, that troop is in trouble. We have no idea when and if we might be hit, and I don't want to be writing letters to parents or wives because a soldier thought their helmet or weapon was too cumbersome to carry all the time. That means even trips to the latrine.

I expect Taliban snipers to be moving in on us tonight, so those operating the LPs or other postings better stay awake. I catch one of your men asleep; I'll strip him of one stripe on the spot—with a forthcoming Article 15. Officers found asleep on post will have a report placed in their personnel file, which will likely kill any chance for promotion. We're not playing games out here. I've already written more letters to relatives of our fallen and those wounded in action than I had planned." Bill looked around at his men, expecting some questions. There were none. He announced in a loud voice, "Commander's Call is over. Now get your people ready to fight a war!"

There were the usual talks between NCOs, and off to the side, the officers compared notes. Then they returned to their men to brief them. Bill moved to stand near Roman, grabbed up the still warm pot of coffee, and poured himself a cup. His mouth was dry from talking, and he believed the coffee was better than his canteen's lukewarm water. The caffeine would help him stay alert, as he knew he wouldn't be getting any sleep tonight.

Before Commander's Call, a Blackhawk delivered four MPs, and the two prisoners were flown to Bagram before dark. The Bradley with the heavily armored plow blade was making a dirt road between the Chinooks and the car lot road that would make it easier to carry salvaged parts to the helicopters.

Bill finished his cup of military coffee and looked down at Roman, "This sure isn't Starbucks."

"Yes, sir, I agree, but as soldiers have said in past wars, it's better than no coffee."

"When the Chief shows up, tell him I'm over at the car lot. I've decided that from now on, all mines we find that can be safely removed from the road will be stored outside the camp. I'm thinking they just might come in handy if we find ourselves engaging those Pakistani tanks." Bill reached down, grabbed up his helmet, plopped it down on his head, adjusted his Kevlar vest to a more comfortable position, and grabbed his M-4. He made sure the inserted magazine was fully loaded, and his hand-held radio had a new battery, before checking his satellite phone to ensure it was charged. Satisfied, he headed down the new road that took him to the car lot.

"Where's the Captain?" Chief asked Roman.

"Over by the Chinooks."

"Okay, if anything comes in from home base, send a runner to get one of us. I want to keep the radio traffic down to a minimum and send the word out—use runners. The Pakistani may have Russian equipment that can monitor us."

"I'll take care of it. Where are you going?"

"I'm going to go check on those Bradleys... see if the crews need anything."

Bill located the two men on loan to him from Explosive Ordnance Disposal. He ordered them to lay a row of Claymores south of the listening post set up beyond the three Chinooks. "Claymores will make a nice welcoming gift for any friends who might decide to visit. Advise those aircrews and engineers what you're doing." Bill didn't want to lose a man because he walked in the wrong direction to relieve himself.

"Can do, Captain," the EOD sergeant replied, then asked, "You want us to wire in a few surprises in those holes the engineers plan to bury some of those excess parts in?"

"Unless I get the order, Sergeant, I'll not set any booby traps—too risky; it might be only locals looking for things they can sell or trade. I don't want to kill a bunch of innocents just trying to make a living."

"Okay, Captain, I can see that. But, if there's still enough daylight, I'll have our dozer take care of that second debris hole before knocking off. Our last thing will be to cover those two holes before leaving. We'll move some of the bigger boulders on top, make it difficult for scavengers."

"Thanks, Sergeant." Bill stopped when he saw one of the company runners headed his way. "Seems I'm needed." *Must be important. It has to be to get PFC Donaldson to run like that.*

Breathing hard from his 150-yard dash across the sand, Donaldson stopped abruptly in front of his Company Commander and fought down the desire to salute. "sir, it's the General, sir—on the radio—he wants you right now, sir."

Bill nodded to Donaldson, then began to jog back to their temporary CP. The Chief was already there. Bill looked to Roman, "Are you sure this is the General, Sergeant?"

"It's him, Captain, but he's talking in the clear, no code," Roman replied as he handed the satellite phone to Bill.

"Go ahead, this is Warrens... Over." Bill recognized the General's voice immediately.

"Captain, I'm talking to you in the clear in hopes Pakistani Intelligence picks me up. Rumors are rampant concerning our possible invasion of Pakistan. I am advising you these rumors are false—I repeat, these rumors are false. The United States has no plans to invade Pakistan or any other neighboring neutral country. To show this, your unit will not be reinforced with heavy armor nor artillery. Your current operation on this roadway is to remove or explode mines set in place by the Taliban. This operation will cease as you reach the eastern edge of the Khyber Pass. Secondly, your command will remain at that location until new orders come down. You are to ensure that signs are posted stating that road mines may still exist past your final mine removal point. Make sure these signs are also printed in Afghan. I repeat, there is no invasion planned to invade Pakistan. You are simply in place to assist the Afghanistan Government in re-opening their highway through the Khyber Pass, used by those communities along this road. These mines, put into place by the Taliban, are a danger to the Afghan people and their allies. You may now return to your normal radio frequency... Over."

"Will do, sir... Over," Bill replied. He glanced down at Roman, who nodded in response. The frequency was changed, and Bill listened to his Colonel read off a long string of codes and then sign off.

"Did you get all that, Sergeant Roman?" Bill asked somewhat apprehensive of the communication he had just received. He had never received such a message before in the clear, and from this General, which only made it more confusing. But, after thinking about it, he fully understood what was behind his transmission. *He wants the Pakistani military to know this is not a plan to invade, but only to safeguard this route for all the area's locals. I only hope the Pakistani Army believes it.* Bill waited as Roman decoded the message.

Suddenly, the RTO stabbed his pad with his pencil and blurted out, "I've got it, sir! That strange message from the General sure sounded weird, captain but it was from Headquarters, and so is this code work." Before Roman could tell Bill what the coded message contained, another call came from Division on the primary frequency. This time it was their Colonel, also talking in the clear. Roman handed the microphone back to the captain but listened in case he needed to write something down in the logbook.

"This is Yankee One, go ahead... Over." Bill didn't want his name used over the radio for security reasons.

"Captain, I wanted a word concerning those prisoners. That was a real nice job your men did in taking them both alive. Write up commendations for every member of that patrol, as I'm planning on rewarding them for a job well done. Now write this down; I want the names of those prisoners in your report. This is the phonetic spelling for the Iranian officer, Sierra, Alpha, Mike, Alpha..." and he continued as he identified Samar Masserzibi, followed by the Russian, Vladzki Rubaeish. Bill looked down at Roman to ensure he was recording this information in his logbook. "Until ordered otherwise, I want radio security checks at the top of every hour... Over."

"Yes, sir, can do... Over," Bill replied.

"Do you need anything else out there? Over."

Bill thought about it and replied, "A whole bird full of Big Macs and Whoppers, and some decent civilian coffee. Otherwise, we've got our military needs covered to last a while... Over."

"Okay, stay alert out there... Out."

The Colonel signed off, and Bill handed the microphone back to Roman. He noticed at least half a dozen men listening to his conversation. "I hope you people have something to do; if not, I'm sure I can come up with something." The men quickly moved along.

Bill was talking with Lt. Sam Rayson when his runner appeared with a folded paper. Bill assumed it was the uncoded radio message, and it was. He read it silently, then read it aloud to Sam. "No movement along the Pakistan border observed. Southwest of the Khyber Pass and across the border, the Pakistan Army has 10 older Russian tanks, with the standard accompaniment of infantry. 100 tanks, with infantry, also spotted 100 miles behind the border, possibly conducting maneuvers. A ground force of 50 Taliban were observed moving our way through the Khyber Pass. Expect them around midnight." He balled the paper up and threw it into the fire.

"If the Pakistani are planning to invade, it's at least not soon. But with a force of 100 tanks and infantry, they could still do a lot of harm unless we bomb the pass to block them. That's a fairly small invasion force if that's their plan. Their Intel people know what we have in Afghanistan and what we can bring from Germany if needed. And our aircraft carriers are nearby. No, I think Russia or China, maybe both are just trying to stir the pot."

"They didn't find all this out with drones; they must be using a dedicated satellite to zoom in on our friends across the border," Sam replied.

Bill thought about it for a second and then said, "Sam, I want a squad from D Company, with its platoon leader, to accompany one of my squads up into those hills. My men have been up there before, exploring the rocks, and it's where they located those prisoners. My squad will include a couple of the men who located that cave. I suspect there are some weapons still in there, and these Taliban will try to lay claim to them."

"Captain, I notice these rock formations get larger and higher the closer we move toward the pass. Be easy for the Taliban to snipe down on us from those rocks."

"Yeah, those rocks have a lot of crevices, and caves that provide the only real cover from our aircraft. We took a lot of enemy fire from both sides of the road until we got into the fight at the car lot." Bill caught sight of the Chief. "I'll go brief the Chief and let you pick your men out. We'll meet where that Bradley with the plow blade is setting. All right?"

"Yes, sir." Sam turned to discuss things with his senior NCO, Master Sergeant Victor Charles Georgia. His buddies back home taunted him by calling him VC, which usually got his hackles up.

When he was appraised of the afternoon's mission MSgt Georgia requested to go along, but Sam refused. "Look, Victor, if I go down, you need to fill in as platoon leader as the officers move up."

"Okay, Lieutenant, but our young officers are greener than shit, sir."

"This is how we all learned, Sergeant—being thrown into the lion's den. You make sure Lieutenant Rogerstone has a good NCO with him. But not his senior man—a staff sergeant, preferably one who's on his second or third tour and won't trip over some booby trap."

"No problem, Lieutenant, First Platoon has SSgt Huggels, and this is his third tour. We served together in Iraq, a real good man."

"Sounds great, put your squad together and be ready within the next half hour. The captain wants this patrol out and back before midnight. I'm betting those 50 Taliban will be pestering us before then. Remind the new troops how well those assassins are with knives. I'd call them pig stickers, but that would likely offend someone since Muslims don't touch pigs."

"Yes, sir."

They formed up at the designated Bradley, and Bill began briefing them, "I'm sending each squad out with a member of the team who was involved in finding that cave. Hopefully, they can find it again. The Taliban may have returned, so be ready for an ambush once you enter those rocks. Watch for bobby traps, as they're probably expecting us to return. If you locate the cave without encountering the enemy, photograph everything. This isn't a souvenir hunt, so only bring back what you think our Intel people would find valuable. Again, remember everything in that cave could be bobby trapped. If you see anything that makes you suspicious, and you veterans know what I mean, blow the whole cave up and hustle back here.

Remember, I want both squads back before midnight. You should be able to reach the first cave in under an hour, but you won't have much time to linger. One squad crosses the road here and proceeds south. I've set up a sniper team a mile down the eastern ridge-line road. If someone gets hurt, a couple of squad members will stay, and hopefully, bring him back here; no one gets left behind. The Taliban are moving in a large force estimated at 50, and I don't want you running into them in the dark. We believe they might move against us around midnight, first with probes, supported by snipers. Our sniper team will move back in under cover of darkness unless your squads become engaged. They'll support you with cover fire. The Chief will give you tonight's passwords. Memorize them!

This road has only been demined for the next three miles, so stay off it after that point. I'm sure you can tell where our Bradley stopped killing the earth. If you cross after that point, you do so at your own peril and that of the men with you. I can tell you the number of landmines on this road, both anti-personnel and anti-tank is unbelievable. You've got climbing ropes, so use them. Do not try to climb up and down these rocks barehanded; wear your gloves. Even if you survive the fall, you'll stand a good chance of breaking a leg or an arm, maybe both and you will be in a lot of pain before you find yourself back in a soft hospital bed. Then I am liable to court martial your hide for not using safety lines.

Your officer and senior NCOs are in charge but listen to the veteran squad members who have learned the lay of the land out here. Each of you should carry plenty of ammo and at least three grenades. Leave here with full canteens. If you need time to refill them, hustle over to the water wagon when this briefing is over.

For those of you new to combat—if you have to shoot, go for the body. Make it a kill. Some of these Taliban get stoned on Hashish, and they're hard to bring down. Go for the chest and put at least three taps into any kill—especially the ones charging you with a nasty-looking sword. Take him down fast and hard, or he will reach you before dying. A dead Taliban is one with his head cut off or a round in his forehead; only then is he safe. This is not a night for prisoner taking; this force is probably made up of experienced desert fighters prepared to give up their lives for Allah.

You've been told this before, but it helps to be reminded right before the mission. For this mission only, B Company's squad is Bravo Squad, D Company is Delta Squad; that's how you'll radio in. After dark, maintain radio silence. There will be no fires, so you'll have to huddle together to stay warm. No one sleeps. You can catch up on your sleep later. I'll be sending this Bradley with you to add covering fire, but it will be returning here before nightfall. We can't afford to leave a lone Bradley out there for the Taliban to use their RPGs on. Maintain silence on patrol, especially in the dark. My RTO will monitor the radio through the night in the event you get into trouble. If a firefight breaks out, return fire only when you have a definite target. The Taliban will spot your location by the flash of the bullet leaving the barrel of your M-4, so move after you shoot.

I'm sorry that I've used up some of your daylight, so I won't ask for questions. That's why you have these NCOs. Good luck, God Bless, and let's all come back with a job well done." Bill turned to Rayson and asked if he had anything to add.

"No, sir, I believe you covered it all. Get going, men!"

Bravo Squad headed south until it reached a goat trail and began to climb. Nearly the whole lower range was passable without a treacherous climb, thanks to all the old goat trails. Still, there were a few places where ropes were needed and gaps they had to jump.

Delta Squad crossed the road where the ridge-line was more gradual on their side. On top, they got their first view of just how expansive the range of mountains was. As far as the eye could see, the range was one immense series of towering rocks after another, backed by massive mountains. The new men began to understand why Khyber Pass was so important. The mountains run nearly a hundred miles to the east and almost as far to the west. Until the pass was discovered centuries earlier, this natural barricade had protected this desert country from invaders. This natural fortification made it a far piece of ground to cover, even for a modern-day soldier. Drones and satellite coverage became a significant asset in the war against enemies. It was the observation skills of the ground troops that kept most of them alive.

Bill knew the men couldn't get back before the sun went down, so he had the sniper team prepare to stay the night out. Their spotter had his radio on with messages going through his left earphone. In this way, no one else would hear it and give their position away. The sniper team reached their spot and camouflaged themselves with sand-colored tarps and local shrubbery. One rifleman guarded their position to the south while a second watched their position to the northeast. This left the third troop to keep an eye on all the rocks below them while the sniper and his spotter remained ready to engage an enemy target. The sniper carried an infrared scope for night work; the troops each had infrared goggles attached to their helmets. The team had set up grenade traps to alert them if the Taliban attempted to move on their position. They were advised of the squad working their side of the road but ordered to remain in place and not join them. The patrol was about three-quarters of a mile south of the sniper post.

Once the troops left and night duties were assigned, Bill returned for another cup of scalding coffee. Sam and the Chief joined Bill and Roman to discuss operations, while the other platoon leaders kept a firm hand on their men's coming and goings. Guard posts were relieved with two men at each position. A five-man sniper team was placed on the southwest side of the car lot in the event the Taliban attempted an attack from there. Bill suspected that infiltrators might be hoping to use the remaining car and truck frames for cover. One of the Bradleys was turned around to keep an eye on the northeast, supported by riflemen.

Nearly two-thirds of the force under Bill's command was put on night duty. The other third attempted to get some sleep in order to be prepared to support the others if a fight began. The first-timers would find it difficult to fall asleep. Even the veterans would keep one eye open.

Dinner was the standard serving of MREs. Bill had read that WWI soldiers never had individual meals but had to eat whatever their *cookie* had prepared in the field kitchen. While chowing down, Bill often wondered how many WWI cooks were still listed as MIA for serving inedible dishes and causing many a GI to have the runs.

With the Chinook crews ready for the night and well protected, Bill, Sam, and the Chief inspected the outer security posts. They wanted to ensure the positions out in the sandy plains were dug deep enough for a kneeling soldier to return fire without exposing themselves. With the help of the Bradley plow, this task was completed in record time. The driver, an engineer operator, was presented with a Taliban long rifle as a gift. A Russian SKS was used by the Russian infantry in WWII and afterward by Russian allies. Thousands of these older rifles ended up in the hands of the Taliban following Russia's defeat and withdrawal from Afghanistan. Later, the AK-47 and RPG became the Taliban's primary weapons just as the AK-47 was issued to the North Vietnamese and Viet Cong.

Bill was still unsure how long they'd be out here, but his current position was well protected. At two positions looking out over the plains to the west, he'd positioned several SAW (squad-automatic weapons). To the northeast, one M-60 was in place, supported by numerous 240B machine guns. These posts were backed up by Bradley and Stryker weapons, and airpower could be called in from Bagram. Humvees mounted with M-60 or the newer 240B machine guns, were brought in close, near to Roman and his runners.

"I have to assume—no, I hate using that word—I have to *believe* that at least one surviving Taliban fighter is up in those rocks keeping an eye on our fortifications. He'll climb out after dark to meet an arriving

Taliban force and brief them on our fortifications," Bill said to Sam and the Chief.

"Right," Sam agreed as he turned to Roman, "Sergeant, when you check in with Bagram, request an update on that force of Taliban. See if they've reached our area of the Khyber Pass yet. I'm guessing we have a drone or two up there keeping them and us under observation, at least, I sure hope so."

"Yes, sir," Roman said.

"Going to be a starlit night, Sergeant Roman. You have any idea what time the moon's supposed to appear?" Sam asked.

"No, sir, no idea."

"Thank you, Sergeant." Sam sought out Bill and the Chief and found them talking about fishing and the possibility of taking a fishing trip off Florida when they got home for leave following this deployment. They fell silent when Lt. Rayson appeared.

"Captain, I asked Roman to request an update on that Taliban force we were warned about. He'll request it during the next security check."

"Great idea, but I'm hoping they're still miles away, and they all might fall into a deep chasm," Bill said.

"Roman will send a runner with news if we're out on the perimeter."

"Okay, let's check on the vehicles. I want fire extinguishers removed and placed at least 15 yards away. If an RPG scores a hit, I want undamaged extinguishers to put the fire out and possibly save trapped men. Make sure they are not all stacked together; we don't want a lucky hit to disable our fire defenses. No more than four of those red tanks together and camouflage them with brush."

"I'll handle it right now, sir, "Chief said. Then he was gone, seeing that his Captain had nothing else to say.

"I can see why such a good man was promoted to Chief Warrant Officer," Sam said as he watched the chief walk away.

"He was known as the best NCO in Airborne; last year he was chosen to be Command Sergeant Major of Fort Benning. But he refused; he didn't want to leave the 101st to become an office weenie. So, they made him Command Sergeant Major of the Division—an office weenie. He lasted about two months before all the desk work and pampering of officer brass made him crazy. He asked permission to be returned to the

Regiment. Our Colonel couldn't believe his luck when we got him and when word came down about our deployment, he requested to go with us. Chief wants to remain on combat assignments until he's forced to retire or all the wars end. I think this will be his last conflict. When he retires, we'll be losing a legend."

"Have you ever deployed with him before, sir?"

"Lieutenant, when it's just you and I talking, I told you we can use our first names. The battlefield is different than back home. By the way, I wanted to ask you if that name Samson was a tough one to have growing up?"

"If you mean, was I challenged to fight nearly every other day, yeah, it was a bit tough. I didn't know why the name was so troublesome until I read Samson's story when I was ten years old—about age 15, I stopped losing most of those fights, but I politely refused to join the local gangs. Samson made his mistakes, and in the end, he died for it, but not before making things right with God and saving his people. I saw the Victor Mature movie where he played Samson. There were a lot of holes in it, but that's Hollywood!" Sam turned to look at Bill and asked again, "Have you ever served with him before?"

"I served with him on my first tour. He filled in when one of our Senior NCOs fell ill and had to be hospitalized, then he became our Company's Command Sergeant Major. At the time, I was only a butter bar lieutenant, serving as Assistant Platoon leader. An NCO of such high rank is rarely assigned to a Company, but he really wanted to come back over here. Seems he disliked stateside duty and called in some favors, and I'm glad he did.

When we got to Iraq, I was in awe of him. I felt as if I had both Davy Crockett and Daniel Boone alongside me, and more than once, he kept me from making a bad decision. He ended up saving a lot of lives, and then, when I got wounded, he was the one holding my hand until the medivac loaded me up and flew me out. One of the reasons I wanted him with me—the Chief is my idea of a real soldier."

"What do you think the Colonel will have him doing when we get back home?"

"Sam, I hope he'll have the Chief involved in Regimental Training Courses to prepare our new officers and E-7s to E-9s for duty in places like this. He won't talk about it, but he's served in South America, the Philippines, and North Africa before getting involved in these Sandbox Wars. Another thing he won't admit to is serving with elite groups like Delta and groups from other countries. That man is filled with knowledge, skills, and a vast amount of experience that every man could learn from, so I will do my very best to keep him alive on this deployment. Until he retires, the men need him, and so do I."

"Bill, thank you for telling me this—makes me almost feel like I should be saluting him. Though, it does make me wonder why he never sought a commission, did he ever go to college?"

"He got three years of night school behind him then decided being an E-8 was where he was needed and was stunned when his E-9 came through. Now he's a Chief Warrant Officer, and I saw that surprised look in his eyes again, but then he smiled at finally achieving this goal. He's grateful for all the senior officers who recommended him for this promotion. As you know, most of the Warrant Officers in the Army are aviators, but there are a few who have other roles. I believe he's the only E-9 in our division to instantly become a Chief Warrant Officer. He's very proud of it, but he's not the boastful type. Did you notice how the NCOs congratulated him with simply a handshake? They know what kind of man he is."

Sam nodded, "When I leave this man's army, I'm going into politics and making a stab at becoming a U.S. Senator. My first senate bill will be to get better pay and better housing for our enlisted men and better training schools. The enlisted housing at Fort Benning is an eye sore that causes many family men to live off base in some pretty dreadful and often expensive apartments. Basic pay doesn't cover costs, takes half or more to cover rent, utilities, and food. The rest goes to clothing, car payments, car insurance, and miscellaneous needs. A soldier has a tough time paying for all this. They're broke mid-way through the month, and all too often, borrow money from some loan place or pawn shop to make ends meet. Nearly half of my young guys are working part-time jobs to help their families. But you know all this, I'm just preaching to the choir."

"You're right, Sam; this is not the way our troops should be treated. I'd push for a 40% pay raise and possibly a significant increase in their

HOLA and COLA and basic allowance pay for larger families. These men and women choose to serve their country; they shouldn't have to work a part-time job on the side to make ends meet. Let's check the inner posts again. I don't want to hit the outer posts this late; it could give their locations away if the Taliban has someone nearby."

Sam followed his Captain back to where SFC Roman was handling radio traffic. When he had a chance, Roman glanced up at the captain, "Hourly security checks have been done, and I called into Division to give them your request for aerial surveillance of our area. They told me to expect a reply at 2100 hours."

Bill nodded, "Sounds good. Call all the medics from both companies to report here within the next hour. I want you to inspect med bags to ensure they have everything they need. I want them to check all our men for signs of trench foot. After our last deployment here, we had 13 men with it. Turned out they had rarely changed socks, and several were nearly crippled. One man might have had his toes cut off, but the doctor tried a new medication that healed the infection. If anyone is showing early signs, the medics can treat it. We've got a washing place set up to wash socks and underwear, and we'll continue to provide the same as long as possible. A troop disabled by trench foot is still a casualty."

"How about you, Sergeant? Do I need to have a medic check your feet?" Sam asked.

"Sir, I change my socks every other day, if not before, and when we return to Bagram, I'll throw my old socks away and get new ones from supply," Roman replied.

"Good plan, I do that myself," Sam said.

WEAPONS AND FOOT INSPECTION

The weapons inspection took a bit longer than expected, with several filthy rifle barrels discovered. The foot inspection by the medics found five men with athlete's feet and one case of early trench foot. When the medics finished treating patients, Bill addressed them. "Under the U.S. Uniform Code of Military Justice, each of you could receive an Article 15 for Damaging Government Property—yourselves. What concerns me most is that your medical condition could cause your removal from our ranks, leaving us shorthanded. Does any man standing here not have clean socks?" No one held up his hand. "Then why haven't you been wearing them? Never mind—just get them changed. You're adults now, and I'm not your mother, so act like it! Use the cream and foot powder the medics gave you, keep your feet dry and put clean socks on every day. Wash out your dirty ones, and the sun and this heat will quickly dry them out. If you run out, borrow some and tell your squad leader. I'll see about getting Division to fly out some extra socks on our next supply run." He dismissed them, shaking his head in dismay. "I feel like a parent correcting children instead of an officer addressing troops." Bill sent word through the Chief to all NCOs in both companies to do a better job inspecting their men and equipment. "This is Airborne, not some National Guard outfit!" He looked over at Sam, "How're your feet, Lieutenant?"

"All shriveled up after witnessing the dressing down you gave those medics. But it was necessary. I might have been yelling more, and the men would've forgotten everything I said. You addressed them like a father handling a wayward teenager, and they'll recall it word for word. So, tell me, does this capability come with captain's bars, or was it instilled by your parents?"

"I think it comes when you're placed in charge of a company," Bill replied. "I've already seen a lot of growth in you since we arrived in this country."

"Thank you, Bill, I appreciate that." Sam glanced around at the various positions and added, "This could be a busy night for us."

"I'd estimate we have about 40 minutes until lights out. So, take a walk about, make sure everyone is ready, and remind them we've got sniper teams to the east and two patrols to the southeast and southwest. If anyone needs water, hustle them up. Have everyone get settled in. It's going to be a long night. No moving around once the perimeter positions are in place. I don't want to have anyone moving around until the action begins. The Taliban will have their own snipers up in those rocks by midnight—"

"You got it, Captain," Sam said and was on his way.

What'll I do if we happen to bag a few Pakistani troops tonight? If we're wrong about this, those people across the border could start moving their forward scouts in to size up the area. Of course, bagging a few Pakistani troops could shake Division up. Then they might move some heavy armor and artillery our way. We could also just go home and let Pakistan and Afghanistan work it out. But then, Russia and India would probably jump in. This whole desert would probably be glowing in the dark from nuclear radiation if that happened. Bill shook his head to clear his mind and wandered over to check his vehicle units. He wanted to make sure their weapons had good fields of fire. Bill knew the 25mm Cannons were a fine piece of military hardware. Most often, the Bradleys worked with Army Infantry or supported Marine units, but with the war going into its 14th year, Army Airborne was now getting to play with these Buck Rogers style weapons. *They produce such a volume of fire it looks almost like the gunner is using a laser weapon.*

Adjacent to a nearby Bradley, Bill spotted a pile of disarmed Soviet Anti-Personnel PMN and PMP-6 mines. Next to them was a pile of larger Soviet Anti-Tank TM-46 and 46TM-57 rounds made into IEDs. Bill had ordered that all the disarmed mines be buried, and the men had dug a suitable hole for them. Though they were no longer useful as mines, they could still be used again if the explosive charge was replaced. Had he the time, he would've simply ordered them hauled off and blown up by EOD personnel. But Bill figured leaving the mines at the bottom of a deep hole covered in with sand and rock and then camouflaged, should keep them from being found by the Taliban. *Last I heard, the Taliban didn't have any explosive detection dogs. They'd probably eat them anyway.*

Bill remembered his dad telling him that dog meat was considered quite palatable by the Vietnamese. His dad had sampled it once, only to have his stomach grumble. Of course, his dad had sampled several different local food items while in Nam, except for insects. His dad drew the line there. Thinking about his dad made him grin.

Satisfied with his night perimeter, Bill returned to his foxhole. All the positions were camouflaged, and the fires extinguished. Bill could see the quarter-sized moon rising. He turned to Roman who was finishing off a store-bought protein bar, "Roman, when you make your radio check on the hour, advise all units to go silent. We are now under an Alpha-Alert status." Going silent meant no radio traffic unless it was a real emergency, no weapons fire unless a target was clear, and no moving around. This meant if they had a sudden "mother nature" call, they'd be stuck using the side of their hole. At such times, the troops would use a grenade hole purposely dug in the event a grenade was thrown into their spot. The nearest man would grab and toss the grenade into the deep hole, hoping it would catch most of the exploding shrapnel. Sometimes, it did. Armies around the world had used such holes since World War One.

With the command moved into night operation, the desert went entirely silent. Only the wind made any sound as the troops assumed their best impersonation of being a rock.

Sam, in D Company area, was in his command hole. In C Company, Bill lay on his back near Roman, listening to the desert. During daylight hours, the encampment area was searched for nature's desert killers, snakes, and scorpions. With such desert critters moving about, the men in the holes often envied men sitting inside their armored units. However, if Russian heavy armor began rolling through the Khyber Pass, those men manning the Strykers, and Bradley units would be the ones envious of troops running for cover in the rocky cliffs and hills.

The Bradley could kill or at least disable a heavy Russian tank, but it would be in trouble if it was suddenly engaged by two or more tanks. The Stryker wouldn't have much of a chance. He really hated rumors and how easily they spread like wildfire, capable of causing apprehension and gut-wrenching fear. Still, he was incredibly proud of his Airborne troops, men willing to jump out of a plane and risk their lives on something a silkworm had thrown up. He imagined his men at this moment dipping into their pogey bait to help them stay awake and steady their nerves. He knew the mind could create a lot of monsters out there in the darkness. He whispered a prayer for the protection of his troops.

At 2106 hours, a single shot was fired, and Bill knew his sniper to the southeast had probably gotten a kill. *If that was a scout for those 50 Taliban, they're down to 49.* His main sniper, Corporal Herman Remmel, was out there, and Bill knew he could assume a clean kill. Bill had learned the Remmel family had immigrated from Argentina but originated in Kassel, Germany. In training at Fort Benning, Remmel shot 97 kill shots out of 100 on the 500-yard range. On the 1,000-yard range, he hit eight out of ten into the kill zone on the target. Bill had read about snipers in the past who scored kills at more than a mile away, but conditions had to be near perfect to hit one's target. After that one shot, the desert fell silent once more.

Bill hoped his other sniper, PFC Hobson, would learn from Remmel and become more focused on the job. This was his first deployment, and he had zero kills, but Remmel informed Bill that Hobson was a great shooter and he'd settle down once he made his first enemy kill. Bill knew that killing the enemy in the heat of battle was far different from sighting in on a target moving through the woods or the rocks. Although it was all part of being at war, a sniper mentally had to have a firm grasp of his actions to continue his job. A certain degree of coldness was needed to keep one rational.

At 2237 hours, Roman jotted down in the Company Log, "Automatic weapons fire coming from Remmel's location."

As the gunfire intensified, Bill knew those men were in trouble and probably retreating under fire. Grabbing the microphone from Roman's hand, Bill ordered, "All units, this is Yankee One, move to Bravo Alert—I repeat we are now in Bravo Alert status... Out." He knew that everyone woke upon hearing this and would maintain 100% alert until ordered differently. The Taliban had arrived.

Concerned for his sniper team, Bill wished he could dispatch a Bradley to cover their retreat. But the Bradley would become a target for half a dozen Russian RPGs. Those shoulder-fired rockets the Taliban used could kill or disable a Bradley if it hit the right spot. Bill believed Remmel's team would be moving down through narrow crevices to stay out of the line of fire. But, once they hit the desert floor, the Bradleys could open up on those cliffs with an incredible array of firepower to force the Taliban to seek shelter wherever they could.

As for the patrol, SSgt Becker was an experienced NCO and would get all his men back if it at all possible or find a safe spot where they could make a stand. He turned to Roman, "Get your helmet on, Sergeant. We could have shrapnel flying down here real soon, and I'd hate to lose you."

"Sorry, sir—I was focused on listening for our patrol." At that instant, SSgt Becker's voice came over the radio.

"I've got three wounded... on the move, we had to leave one KIA... unable to reach him. Going slow, advise sniper team we could use help about now—unknown if there are enemy forces between Yankee Station and us. We'll try to report back in a bit." There was another intense exchange of AK-47 and M-4 firing, followed by a series of explosions from grenades or RPGs. It was hard to tell from Bill's position.

Bill heard automatic weapons fire in the hills across the road from Becker's position, the sound of M-4s on auto fire. The Taliban were apparently staying off the road as they slowly made their way down both ridgelines on each side of the road. They had apparently learned about some of the American positions. Bill knew the Taliban unit had separated into several smaller units to stage their attack. He had expected that, which is why he had placed his people in those strategic positions.

The Taliban force was trying to get close enough to use RPGs to rain hellfire down on the FOB and the Chinooks. He realized he had to get more men up into the nearby rocks to prevent that from happening. He wasn't sure what Sam was thinking, but he broke into Roman's thoughts, "Advise 2nd Platoon to send two squads to hold the bottom of that ridgeline directly to our east. Warn them to watch for suicide sappers making a dash for those Chinooks. Keep both sides of the roadway under observation. Remind all units we have one squad across that road and another falling back from our side, so have them make sure of their targets!"

"Yes, sir," Roman replied.

"Advise all units, friendlies moving about up there to be sure of your targets." Bill snapped.

"Yes, sir," Roman replied. Right now, Roman really missed RTO Jimmy Olsen.

Only the glimmer from a quarter moon provided light to move around. No flashlights would be in play until the firefight had ended. All troops would have infrared devices pulled down tight over their eyes. Once a firefight began, those were rendered useless as the flash from their own weapons interfered with the night vision.

Lt. Sam Rayson had some minor difficulty using his infrared optics. Twice he had to pull them down and use the moonlight, limited as it was. Moving between positions, he stumbled a few times as he didn't see several small boulders in front of him or a shallow hole. So, he wasn't in the best of moods when he reached a D Company squad waiting to be assigned. He directed them to follow him. Sam left his senior officer behind to handle D Company's half of the perimeter as he moved up to support B Company with another squad.

Bill crouched down beside Roman and reached across to touch his left shoulder, "Roman, where is Chaplain Taylor?" Bill was concerned the Chaplain would be out comforting the men. He had warned the Chaplain numerous times not to be out and about during these alerts.

In this darkness, Bill didn't want to become a target for a Taliban sniper. Intel had briefed the senior officers before their first mission that Taliban officers and snipers had captured infrared gear or Russian hand-me-downs. Earlier in the war, the Taliban had carried some old Nam-era infrared scopes, thanks to the Black Market. These snipers were trained by Russians, Iranians, and Chinese. With the Taliban supported by the communists and the Afghan government supported by the US and their allies, Bill could understand why this lengthy war was often compared to the Vietnam War. He suspected it would end that way, too. The Allies would eventually give up using their money to support the Afghan government and the Americans would probably soon follow. The American people were growing weary of sending soldiers to fight in foreign wars. Bill suspected a growing number of Americans were no longer looking at the big picture of keeping the communists from taking over the world. They had seen too many flagged draped caskets, the growing number of wounded troops, and the money spent on such wars. Yet, for some, it wasn't always in that order.

"Sir, the Chaplain is with the Strykers, hopefully inside one," Roman replied.

"Okay, as long as he stays with them. This place isn't too friendly toward clergymen, and I don't want him getting lost and picked up by some Taliban scout. Roman, I'm moving over to that far Bradley, about fifty yards. If you need me, send a runner; otherwise, I'll be back in a few. Don't go anywhere!" Bill sprinted away, staying low as he moved across the desert stopping every few yards to listen, and then proceeded on until he reached the Bradley. He hoped to see his patrol moving in, as they were overdue. He exchanged a few hand waves with the men in the holes outside the Bradley.

A squad leader from the 2nd platoon came running over to see what Bill wanted, "sir, Sgt. House. What's up?"

"I have an overdue squad that should've been here before now. Remind your men they could be coming in at any moment and to hold their fire until they can confirm targets. I know we've been saying that a lot, but I don't want to lose anyone to friendly fire. Lord, I hate those words, nothing friendly about it!"

"Yes, sir." Sgt House moved from hole to hole to tell his people of the overdue squad.

A few minutes later, a voice called out of the desert to the East, right across the road from Bill's position. He recognized the voice, even though it was low and strained. Bill made the decision to call him across, hoping they hadn't been followed. He was somewhat surprised the wounded patrol was coming across the roadway from a position north of where they were supposed to. But he knew he'd have his answer soon enough as he advised the men in the Bradley of the patrol coming in. "Once they're across, keep a close eye on the desert behind them. They may have followers."

"Yes, Captain." A soldier at the door replied before turning to brief his sergeant.

"Move on across—do you need assistance?" Bill had to use a louder voice, but they'd just have to chance it.

"Two men to help with wounded; mah men are really worn out."

Bill thought about it for a brief second and then ordered Sgt. House to send two men to assist the squad. The men showed up quickly and knelt beside Bill. "Move across the road but watch your step because of all the holes. Join SSgt Becker and help carry wounded across the road. I'll have a medic here on the double-quick."

"Yes, sir," The two men whispered in unison and then made their way over the blasted section of highway. Looking at each other first, they knocked their knuckles together for good luck and began shuffling forward. They'd seen this road in the daylight, and though this section had been demined, they were not all that trusting of it. The 25mm cannon fire had left behind mounds of dirt, rocks of all sizes, and deep holes from exploded IEDs that could swallow a small car. It took them a little over a minute to cross the road's estimated 22 feet before reaching

SSgt Becker. He and his squad were either sitting quietly or lying on their backs near the road.

"Glad to see you, boys—now, which one brought the coffee?" Becker whispered.

The two men from House's squad shook their heads and grinned. One said, "Sergeant, can we get moving? I'd feel a whole lot safer on the other side of this road."

"Sure, we've got three injured troops, one with an arm wound I didn't know about earlier. Bullet went straight through his left arm above the elbow but didn't break the bone. He simply has no feeling in his hand, but we got him bandaged up. Two with leg wounds can barely walk; I'd like you to help carry them over. I'll help the man with the arm wound; he's real shook-up, lots of blood!"

"Sergeant, you take the lead—the captain is waiting across the road with a medic."

"Then let's do it! Lookin' forward to a nice hotel suite, with lots of beer, broads, and hamburgers—and a nice hot bath."

"You okay, Sergeant?" One of House's men asked.

"I'm fine, just a lousy patrol, soldier, a real lousy patrol."

Bill had sent another of House's men to locate the nearest medic. Keeping his eyes on the road, he felt like he'd been waiting for half an hour for that overdue squad to come into view, though in fact, it had been only moments. Finally, the patrol, seen through Bill's infrared goggles, crossed the road. It worried him when he saw how difficult a job the men were having with the wounded, but he was proud of them for not making any noise. Screaming in pain was a dead giveaway to bring the enemy to one's position—a fact drilled into the men during training.

In no time at all, the medic had the wounded on stretchers, running quick exams before transport. Another medic was summoned to lend a hand. Chaplain Taylor appeared and held up an IV bag. The Bradley crew kept the road under observation in the event any Taliban tried to sneak across. The Taliban had used this ploy before, following closely behind a returning patrol. Bill spoke briefly with each of the wounded men and as soon as they were taken away, he returned to his own position, surprised to find Sam there talking with Roman.

"What are you doing over here, Sam?" Bill asked.

"Quiet as a tomb on my side. Appears you've got all the action over here. How's the patrol?"

"Shot up; three wounded. They're well taken care of, but I'm still waiting for Sgt. Becker's report," Bill replied. He was impressed with SSgt Becker getting his disabled patrol this far without help. Still, he needed to know what had happened to the patrol.

Suddenly, a series of explosions went off to the southeast. Bill suspected this was most likely his men blowing up the cave where his men had captured the Russian and Iranian. "Roman, move everyone to Alpha Alert Three and inform the other patrol not to move this way unless absolutely necessary. I'll send runners out to notify the outer perimeter positions while you're on the radio."

"Handling it, Captain," Roman replied.

At that moment, several RPGs fired from Taliban positions in the southeast rock formations. Herman Remmel had cost the insurgents several lives since the car lot firefight began. Seeing the RPGs fired provided him with several targets, and he opened fire assisted by his team members.

A Taliban preparing to fire another RPG suddenly fell to the cliffs below, dead from one of Remmel's bullets. A second Taliban, who stood nearby, was killed. Then a third stood, hoping to grab the first man's RPG, but Remmel's next shot sent him plummeting to the gorge below. The Taliban attempted to locate Remmel with an RPG, but it landed over 200 feet south of his position. They had no idea where the sniper team was, other than somewhere on that eastern ridgeline.

Raising his voice, Bill issued an order to Roman, who worked the radio with his left hand, while holding his M-4 braced against his chest with his right. "It appears the Taliban have arrived. Contact Bagram and notify them that we'll need either armed drones or Apache gunships at daylight. We'll also need another Chinook to pick up our wounded and to bring out extra stretchers. We're using ours up too fast. Notify them we have one KIA and four WIA at this time, but we cannot reach the KIA until daylight. Let them know it's just beginning, and we'll keep them advised."

SIEGE

Suddenly, claymore mines began exploding on the open plains, south of their position. The Taliban had come upon the line of mines placed in front of that position. They had stretched the first line of wire 25 yards out in front but didn't hook it to any mines. The men knew the Taliban would see the first wire as they crawled forward and simply lift themselves over it. But the second wire, five yards closer to the Americans, was camouflaged with shrubbery, sand, and several trashed metal pieces from the car lot.

Sure enough, two of the Taliban caught the second wire and set off a string of mines that sent six Muslim terrorists to their heavenly reward. Two more were severely wounded when the troops cut loose with automatic weapons fire. Amazingly, the 16 men, a squad from each Company, held together and remained in position as the desert exploded before them. They survived without a scratch. Though nerves were stretched taut, those 16 men burrowed deeper into their fox holes as they waited for a rush of maniacal terrorists.

Several men pulled out extra knives from their packs and slid them into their boots, wanting to be ready if hand-to-hand fighting ensued. Staying alert, keeping their eyes open, they quietly uttered prayers. They scanned the darkness to the south while other troops had the other directions under observation.

Before the Taliban attacked in force, the 2nd patrol, who had been on the western ridgeline, came in at a fast clip, giving out the password to identify themselves in the dark as they dashed forward. The mine explosions gave them the opening they needed to reach the perimeter lines. Two men could be seen carrying a wounded man in. Nothing was reported over the radio because of the alert status.

Then, just as the patrol drew close to D Company's positions, insurgent snipers with infrared scopes on long rifles took advantage and opened fire. The remainder of the Taliban forces launched an attack. One young American in the patrol shouted out, "Here they come!" But failed to say where they were coming from. Screaming like banshees, more than 30 Taliban raced down the hillside to avenge those who had just been blown up by the mines. Most of them carried AK-47 automatic rifles, firing on full automatic at B Company's lines. The remaining Taliban arrived wielding long and short blade swords, swinging them wildly about through the air like ancient seafaring buccaneers. A few Taliban screamed words of profanity or maybe a promise, in an Arabian dialect, calling for the slow and painful death to all infidels. It had little effect on the troops since they couldn't understand this language.

The patrol made it to the perimeter line, using the pathway set up to avoid the mines. The Taliban, unaware of that pathway, triggered some of the mines. As they continued their frenzied rush forward, additional mines were set off, with a claymore claiming four of them.

Bill dashed to the southern perimeter, holding his rifle in both hands, its selector switch set on 'auto'. He jumped into the narrow trench line beside a couple of surprised soldiers. Together, they opened fire on the rushing Taliban fighters.

Within seconds, wave after wave of flaming cannon fire erupted from the perimeter as Bradleys began mowing down the Taliban like a farmer's scythe harvesting wheat. More Taliban rose up from behind the rocks and made their run at the Americans, firing as they ran. Bullets hit all around D Company's southern perimeter, but the men were dug in, shooting between sandbags that made it nearly impossible for the Taliban to hit them.

Less than 30 yards separated the Taliban from the southern and eastward positions. Bill's troops, supported by the Bradleys and Strykers, sent out a lethal wave of fire. The patrol who had barely made it in were forced to lay their wounded down to keep them from being hit by enemy fire. Medics draped themselves over their patients to protect them from a wayward bullet.

Several of the Taliban shooters who had remained in the upper rocks, as snipers, were targeted by the Bradley's 25mm gunners. Stryker gunners picked out those Taliban who had made their mad rush at D Company's lines. Bill spotted a Taliban fall over twenty feet, wedging a leg in a crevice unable to escape. He was shot by the second sniper working with Remmel, his second kill of the night. He was now officially bloodied, but he wasn't done.

Bill heard Sam some 20 yards to the west, moving with one of his squads to block the Taliban from escaping. Nearly a dozen Taliban hit D

Company's southern line, and the two sides became locked in deadly hand-to-hand combat.

Suddenly, grayish specters, armed with bayonets, rifles, knives, and a few sidearms tightly grasped in hand were in a brutal engagement. Some of the Taliban, unable to reload, dropped long rifles and began swinging swords in hopes of relieving some American of his head. This was a suicide attack. *The Taliban had to know they didn't have the manpower to defeat two entire companies of American troops, especially with armored units in support.* Though he could respect their courage, Bill knew these men would not surrender. He spotted a Taliban warrior rushing forward to strike one of his men from behind who was locked in hand-to-hand with another Taliban. Bill fired twice, his bullets hit the man's upper body and drove him to the ground. He took aim at another insurgent as he moved forward to help his men. The man went down, shot in the side, and grabbed a grenade from his bandoleer, but before he could pull the pin, Bill finished him off with a double tap to the head.

Mortar flares lit up the night sky, giving Bill a view of the remaining Taliban and his men engaged in quickly dispatching them. One soldier dropped his empty pistol and used both hands in an attempt to sink a K-Bar knife into the chest of a terrorist. Straddling the man who struggled to keep the huge knife in front of him, he was able to knock the American's helmet off. The American whose own eyes were filled with sheer determination glared into the insurgent's defiant eyes, gritted his teeth, and slowly forced his knife down to the man's chest. With one final burst of strength, he finally shoved the blade into the man's heart until only the knife's handle remained in view. Death was nearly instantaneous.

Bill exchanged fire with two other Taliban armed with swords. As the taller of the two went down under Bill's withering fire, the second went down to the last two rounds in Bill's magazine. To the west, Sam Rayson and his force exchanged a heavy concentration of fire with a few remaining Taliban. Sam was almost hit with a wave of shrapnel when a Taliban RPG exploded some 50 feet from him. One piece left a shallow inch-and-a-half long gash in the top of his metal helmet as the blast knocked him to the ground. Sam rose to his feet his ears ringing and staggered a bit before regaining his composure and continued firing from the hip. A second RPG round exploded closer, fired from a higher distance. But the men saw it fired and dove into the closest pits. A third round was prepared, but the Taliban shooter disappeared as the Bradley's 25mm cannon roared.

A ball of fire sailed through the air from the southern embankment and exploded sending out bits of metal and flames. Several other RPGs were fired, and later, the Airborne troops would say this was the closest they had come to witnessing hell on earth. Explosions went off all around them while Bradleys and Strykers laid extensive fire on the hillside until the RPGs ceased. When daylight arrived, the vehicle crews found dozens of hits made by RPG shrapnel. One Bradley suffered a broken track while its crew, though frightened, escaped physical injury.

Before the night began, a lot of the young men had never pulled a trigger or used a blade against the enemy. When the adrenaline wore off, some would need to spend time with the Chaplain. Others would brag, and war stories would be born.

Bill scanned the silent battlefield, still clutching his M-4 to his chest with a new magazine in place. He surveyed his men and admired their courage and tenacity. As he looked at the fallen Taliban, he knew he could never understand the fanatical belief that drove them to slay all infidels (non-believers). *I leave that to the Lord.* He thought as he turned his attention to his survivors, the wounded, and the dead. Bill knew the first kill was always the hardest to deal with; for some time, the enemy's blood would be hard to wash off. A new soldier would rarely admit to that and would usually try to bluster his way through the experience.

Bill still lived with the first man he had killed and knew it would be the same for these new warriors. He refocused and headed for the Chinooks to ensure everyone there was safe. The helicopters were miraculously untouched, and no one was hurt. He found SSgt. Becker's wounded where they had been set down while their stretcher bearers engaged the enemy. The medics had remained to attend and protect them through the firefight. SSgt. Becker, who had stayed close to protect them, lay on the ground nearby bleeding from a nasty shoulder wound.

"Son, you did a great job this night. You'll be flown back with your wounded brothers, and you'll all be in my prayers for quick healing. You've done Airborne proud! All of you. Roman's back there requesting a ride at first light. You've all done a hell of a job—got it?"

"Yes, sir," a weary voice replied. "Oh, three wounded to report—Roberson, Judge, and Loudermilk, sir!" SSgt Becker said.

"And you make four, SSgt Becker. Let the medic do his work; you'll be leaving soon enough."

"Airborne, sir!" SSgt Becker exclaimed just before passing out as a stretcher arrived for him.

"All the way!" Bill muttered in reply.

After glancing about, Bill moved to his foxhole and spoke to Roman, "Advice Bradleys four and five to open up on those higher rocks directly east of you. Fire for 60 seconds! Then cease-fire. When they stop, our troops will advance to that lower stand of rocks to reconnoiter the area for wounded Taliban." After the orders were given to the two Bradleys, he told Roman to contact B Company's Heavy Weapons Platoon and advise them to continue the parachute flares.

Then he took the microphone from Roman and addressed both companies, "This is Yankee One—Airborne troops now moving against possible Taliban survivors to our east."

He followed that with a radio message to Bradley Two telling them to use their 25mm cannon to rake the remaining Taliban's upper positions directly to the east. He wanted anyone up there to be running for cover, not wanting any snipers to remain. 81mm Mortars were ordered to fire three explosive rounds along the hill's crest to the northeast. Three more explosive rounds were fired into the open desert to the southeast in hopes of keeping the Taliban from fleeing that way. Bill still wanted prisoners.

Releasing a deep and weary sigh, Bill stood up and stepped out of his hole. He could see that Chief was organizing a platoon-sized force of men. Two mortar flares illuminated four Taliban, armed with only swords, engaged with three of his troops. The soldiers were blocking them with rifles in an attempt to take them as prisoners. The Taliban swung wildly at the soldiers, clearly having not gained any real training in the proper use of such weapons. Finally, Bill's force waded in from behind and used their rifle butts to club the Taliban to the ground. The last fight of the night was over, and Bill had prisoners to turn over to the Military Police.

The four Taliban were laid out, unconscious from their bludgeoning. One came to, struggling to raise his hands to show he was surrendering.

Bill ordered six more 81mm explosive mortar rounds to the south of the enemy's last position. He wanted to ensure the Taliban force was finished or fleeing the area. The Bradley's 25mm raked the hillsides, causing sparks to explode as the rounds impacted stone. The firing ceased and when the smoke from the explosions and flares cleared, the Bradleys' and Strykers' powerful searchlights illuminated the battlefield. They revealed an eerie scene as the dead and dying were left to lie for the moment as Airborne troops moved to help the wounded. Nine wounded Taliban had survived, 34 bodies were counted. If Intel was right about a force of 50, Bill figured half a dozen of the enemy were unaccounted for. But he also knew there could be bodies up in the rocks. He would have his men search after the sun came up. Meanwhile, the Americans retrieved their own wounded and dead.

Bill would later learn that the soldier lost on patrol was located. He had been wounded and lost his footing, taking a fall of several feet to rocks below.

Weary from the long night, Bill looked at his watch and estimated the fight had lasted less than 22 minutes. His morning patrols had found additional dead Taliban up in the rocks, clearly killed by the concentration of 25mm auto fire. The known enemy dead numbered 70 which indicated that the estimated force of fifty was a low number. Based on the updated count the number might be much higher had any of the Taliban escaped. It proved to be a costly mistake for the Taliban, but the Americans had suffered far too many casualties.

Bill called for his interpreters and smiled as both quickly popped up from a hole they had dug about 20 feet north of Bill's foxhole. "You have need of us, now, Captain, seeing we had no weapons to protect us, you wish to use our services?" Janke, a Kurdish Coptic Christian, asked. He was not happy to have been left unarmed, knowing the Taliban would have executed them both had they been captured. But Bill had had little choice; they were considered non-combatants and could not be armed. Orders had to be obeyed.

"Gentlemen, I apologize, but Interpreters may not carry weapons. That's the order. Sorry. Still, I'm glad to see you both made it."

"Okay, okay, what do you need now, Captain Bill?" During a briefing, Bill had given the Kurd permission to call him Bill, unlike other company commanders, who had always required military protocol. "Bill" had then become "Captain Bill" as a friendly gesture.

"We have prisoners, and they need to be interviewed; that's your department, okay?"

"Captain Bill, you want me to approach these vile creatures—these abusers of humanity and killers of women and children—and talk to them?"

"Hey, someone has too, and my Arabic couldn't buy us a bowl of— don't forget, my friends, it's your job. My men will accompany you. They've all been searched, and their hands and feet are bound. So, be brave and let me know what you can find out."

"Yes, Captain Bill, we will excuse your rudeness. We know it has been a bad night for us all. But please advise your soldiers to standby, as we do not trust these vile Taliban."

Bill grinned, "Thanks, Janke."

Chief had already given both companies the order to return to their FOB positions, as the alert was downgraded to a readiness status.

An hour later, Janke and Hanci reported to Bill and advised him of information learned from the prisoners. Janke spoke first, "Two of these men say they had only recently been taken out of their village by a Taliban enlistment force and handed a sword. One of the men who died was their village blacksmith. These men had to go or be killed for refusing and possibly their whole family. None of the men had any idea they were being used to attack the American force removing these mines. Villagers who had seen this reported it to village elders, and many were in favor of this. Other routes are far longer and more hazardous than this road."

Hanci added, "One prisoner says various townships along this road have buried fellow villagers who did not know about these mines and were blown up. No one argues with the Taliban, or they die. Three prisoners only spit at us; these are Taliban fighters who expect to be executed. They refuse to tell us where those who got away have gone. Maybe, your people at Bagram can get them to talk, but they won't speak to us as we are beneath them, as you are. All Christians and Jews must die. A fast way for the Taliban to get to their heaven is by killing their enemy. This is their way."

Bill recalled his dad telling him how the Viet Cong had seized villagers and forced them to become guerrilla fighters and provide aid to the VC. Bill saw it firsthand in this war, and it deeply troubled him. *Serve or die, a brutal way of enlisting troops.* "By the time we get back to Bagram, this one mission is going to create enough paperwork to fill a Navy trunk!" Bill said to Roman, as the Chief appeared.

"What's our stats, Captain?" Chief wished he hadn't asked when he heard the figures.

"You tell him," Bill said to Roman, who had the figures in his logbook.

"Umm... Yes, sir." Roman read from the page. "Last night's engagement, including sniper action before the attack—we suffered seven killed and 19 wounded between both companies. The enemy suffered a total of 57 killed, with the bodies we just found up in those rocks, and 11 wounded—four walking. Based on these numbers, the Taliban numbered at least 78, not counting how many may have escaped. Patrol found blood trails up in the rocks but no way to number how many got away."

Chief turned to Bill, shook his head with dismay, and said, "We were told to watch for a terrorist unit of 50. Supposedly confirmed by satellite, but instead, a force of nearly 80 sons of Allah come at us. I feel bad about some of the dead being enslaved men, but they all tried to kill us and would have had if we allowed any of them to breach our perimeter or strike our armor with an RPG. We lost seven good men last night and six more earlier, and that's 13 damn letters to write—and we've still got another 10 months to go!"

Sam had heard the Chief's heated words and stepped over to offer his contribution. "Captain, had you known there was a force of 70 to 80, allowing for one or two of the enemy to have escaped, would you have changed the positioning on our perimeter?"

Bill thought about it for a moment, "I'd have moved a couple more units into the outer perimeter. Maybe I'd at least put a couple Strykers on the line facing the open desert to the south. I also might have sent up a larger patrol through those ridgelines. But basically, 50 or 80, we were set to oppose them, and we did. I'm not going to play the blame game. We did what we did, and we're still alive and have a job to finish. Now get the men some sleep, keep two squads on alert and change the prisoner's guards every six hours so everyone can catch some shut-eye before tonight. We'll keep two Bradleys on alert, ready to repel anyone coming down from the hills. The important thing right now is to get our casualties and prisoners back to Bagram and get those Chinooks out of here. I'll talk to the Colonel and see if we can get some extra troops out here to assist. Everyone gets something to eat, weapons cleaned, and we'll see what our next orders are and when we can move out to finish this damn job."

Bill squeezed the bridge of his nose and shook his head to clear the cobwebs, then turned to Roman, "Get me some helicopters out here to handle our wounded, dead, and prisoners. Notify them of all stats; numbers in code; no sense alerting the Taliban how many men we lost."

"Yes, sir. Everything has already been called in. We can expect our first bird within 30 minutes—they had one on stand-by, and the On-Duty OIC will give the information to the Colonel at 0900 hours when he gets his daily briefing."

"Sounds good, Sergeant, make sure the prisoners are fed and have water."

"Their Muslim diet is a bit restrictive, but we'll do what we can. I've also got three guards in the hospital area with those prisoners."

"What about all the weapons recovered?" Samson asked.

"Sir, all the AK-47s and any side-arms recovered are piled up right over there." He pointed to a large boulder beside their foxhole. The magazines were pulled, chambers empty, and all ammo, including RPGs, was piled in a trench. The swords and knives seemed to have vanished, if that's okay with you, Captain?"

"Souvenirs?" Bill asked with a raised eyebrow. "Americans are big on souvenirs—I'd rather call them that over war trophies. Okay, but get me the numbers of swords and knives collected for my report." Bill knew if he turned them in at Bagram, the Fobbits would steal them to take home. Fobbits, a word created from the "Hobbit" movies, was used to name the men who lived on post and never went out on patrol. Bill had heard stories of several Fobbits being caught for attempting to smuggle

AK-47s, rifles, Russian pistols, and numerous other things home. It happened in every war; troops took home little reminders. Battlefield souvenirs brought to mind a tale from his dad that he had shared with Roman, "A Green Beret Bird Colonel tried to smuggle home the uniformed body of a dead North Vietnamese officer. When the body was discovered by Customs personnel, the Colonel tried to pull rank, 'He's mine, and I'm shipping him home to my wife. I want him stuffed!' The officer in charge of the U.S. Customs area notified the hospital that a doctor was needed. The Colonel was sedated and flown home. The body was transferred to Graves Registration."

"I'd like to have seen the wife's expression when she opened the crate," Roman replied.

Bill turned to the Chief, "Chief, make sure all the captured weapons —the items we have on hand, that is, go to Division Intel. Search those dead Taliban one final time for any documents and then move them to a new hole. We'll get one dug soon. One big mass grave will do. Any and all Taliban documents, letters, or whatever will be carried back to Bagram aboard the Chinook with the prisoners." Bill drew closer to Roman and knelt beside him. "Advise Bagram we are holding our position pending new orders. Request the latest data on satellite or drone images of this area. Use the satellite phone; it's a bit more secure. Far as I know, with that possible leak at Division, the Taliban may already have a copy of our code book."

"Yes, sir," Roman replied.

"Sergeant, you've been doing such a great job out here I might have you stay on and let Jimmy Olson move back into 1st Platoon as squad leader, when and if he returns. What do you think about that?"

"Sir, I'll leave that up to you, but I do know Jimmy prefers his RTO position over humping with advance patrols. However, if you need me, I'll be the best RTO you've ever had, and I'll even extend for another two years. That'll give a big boost to my monthly retirement."

"Trying to make deals with me, now, Sergeant?" Bill smiled.

"My job as an enlisted man, sir, is to provide you with options. How do you feel about bribes?"

Bill patted Roman on the shoulder, "Maybe a week pulling KP in the Bagram chow hall will help to remind you that West Point graduates are above such things. Having said that, and don't let it go to your head, I've already nominated you for your master's stripe. A field promotion if the Colonel agrees. Chief supported it, and that'll most likely get the Colonel to come on board. The Bronze Star I'm recommending you for will help a bit. Once I get a new RTO, I'm moving you into Assistant Platoon Leader for B Company's 2nd Platoon. But you've got to stay here as RTO until Olson returns, or until we get another RTO who knows which end of the radio to speak into and can take code quickly."

Roman nodded, unable to speak from amazement. Finally, he blurted, "Thank you, sir!"

"Now get it done, Sergeant. Lots to do."

"Yes, sir!" Roman picked up his logbook and began filling in the lines with Bill's orders. Afterward, he grasped his satellite phone and called Division at Bagram. By the time he was halfway through his messages, he could hear an approaching helicopter. He knew this was the medivac Chinook escorted by a well-armed Blackhawk Helicopter.

"Sam, would you put together a guard detail to escort the Taliban, make sure they're ready to go with the wounded and well secured on board that bird."

"I'll use a squad from the 3rd platoon. They've had the most sleep until we went on full alert status, that is."

"Sounds good. I'm going to check the perimeter with the Chief. Holler out if you need me or send a runner. We know the Pakistani are monitoring our radio traffic. That's why Headquarters was speaking in the clear; so the Pakistani would know we have no plans of invading. Hopefully, they believe it. I'm also betting Iran has probably sold the Pakistani some drones, maybe Russia, to watch the borders. Those 100 tanks were perhaps just a show of force or possibly maneuvers. What do you think, Sam?"

Sam shook his head and replied, "I refuse to answer on the grounds I might incriminate myself—I think I heard that on an old Perry Mason show—or maybe it was Dragnet or Adam-12? My mom was into cop shows, and I inherited it."

Chief looked off to the southwest, his imagination giving him a visual image of the awakening desert plains. "If we ever do enter

Pakistan, it'll be a replay of World War II, when the American and British forces fought the Germans for every foot of sand."

"Yup," Bill agreed. "No more snowy mountains to contend with, at least to the southwest. The desert out that way is pure evil. Makes me wonder why the Good Lord didn't put his chosen people in a milder climate, like Hawaii."

The two large helicopters flew overhead, and the Chinook settled down for a landing. The Blackhawk remained in the air, circling. The seriously wounded were loaded first. Then came the walking wounded, followed by the prisoners, along with a five-member guard detail. Janke, the Interpreter, returned to Bagram with the prisoners and would fly back in the afternoon supply bird. Janke's job was to sit near the prisoners and listen for anything that might be important to U.S. Intel.

As the Chinook lifted off, the Chief and Bill were back with Roman for an MRE breakfast. Chief held a half cup of fresh hot coffee in hand as he addressed Bill, "I almost couldn't believe it when you were talking with Roman. It was the first time I've heard him lock up, unable to speak when you told him about that promotion. He told me earlier he didn't think you liked him much, and he was trying to figure out a way for you to consider him as your senior RTO. Apparently, he's good at his job, he's grown weary of being a medic."

"Jimmy is a great RTO, but he needs to gain additional field experience in leadership to earn his next stripe. I had planned to move him to the squad leader's position for the last six months of our deployment and bring up an RTO he and Roman can agree on. With everything a Company RTO has to do, we need a knowledgeable man for the job. Roman is a great medic and does a fine job at RTO, but he needs more experience leading combat troops. That's why I want to move him as soon as a replacement RTO can be found." Bill stood up and checked out the rising glimmer to the east. The sun came up fast over here in Afghanistan; once it rose from behind the faraway mountains, the whole sky became illuminated. Not a cloud in the sky, and already it was warming up.

"Pertaining to our mission, Captain, how soon before we move out and continue on with this little venture of ours?" Chief asked.

"Our troops need a few hours of sleep. I'm hoping to get permission to hold off until tomorrow morning. After last night, we'll need additional ammo, from 25mm down to M-4s, mortar flares, grenades—the whole list. Work with Roman and our platoon leaders to make up a wish list and send it in. We also need additional medical supplies, so get with Sam, and we can send that list in all at once. Make some supply sergeant's day.

"We have to stay ready to fight a pitched battle, possibly against the Pakistan Army. I'm not into throwing spears and rocks or fighting with knives. Let the Colonel know we burned through a lot of ammo last night. I don't believe the Taliban are done with us, not yet. I just wish those Intel people could better estimate how many are in the Khyber Pass area. As far as we know, they could have another 500 sons of Allah up in those hills. Just a good thing they don't have tanks and aircraft."

Bill left to make a visual inspection of the troops and vehicle crews. He was relieved to find B and D companies were still in pretty good shape. Chaplain Taylor reported that six men had come to him in need of counseling after last night's attack.

After talking with Taylor, Bill talked with Sam while refilling canteens at a water wagon. "I want another patrol—two squads from D Company this time. My guys went on the last little jaunt. Their platoon commander can provide names to Sergeant Roman. He's our official logbook scribe and our company clerk. I like to know who I'm sending out into harm's way. What I want is another search of all those caves along that next ridgeline. Have them patrol until they reach the end of the road we've already demolished. That way, they'll be protected by Remmel's sniper team, so make he's out there. Remmel's real good about camouflaging his position. His last report shows no one moving about up there. B Company's 3rd Platoon will provide a squad on stand-by to reinforce your two squads if they run into trouble.

The men are not to go over that far ridgeline to the east. We have no idea what may be out there, and I don't want them walking into an ambush. We'll send one of the EOD boys with them to check for booby traps before entering any caves. Have the RTOs get new batteries. Sorry, Sam, you already know all this stuff. I just need a few hours of sack time. I'll be over at my home away from home with a damp towel over my face.

Come get me if anything comes up. Roman will wake me if new orders come in or your patrol needs anything."

Before taking a nap, Bill discussed a few more things with the Chief, "Let them sleep in shifts; those who are awake can check their equipment. Keep them busy and remind them we're still on readiness alert status. Helmets and rifles. Be prepared for additional air assets and that road crews' arrival. They should be catching up with us pretty soon. Any questions?"

"Bill, I'll awaken you if the balloon goes up. We can handle the rest; get some shut-eye before you fall down. You haven't slept for the last 48 hours, and it's starting to show."

"Really? Okay, Chief. Wake me in five hours, or if it hits the fan." Bill was asleep within moments, with a slight snore that made Roman grin.

1 0

NEW OPERATIONS & NEW BATTALION

THE LENGTHY SUPPLY list for the two companies had been sent in and troops rotated from alert status to standby to catch some sleep. MRE packets were ripped open as troops sat down for dinner. Bill and Chief nit-picked through theirs, both wondering, *Am I really hungry enough to eat this crap?* A question soldiers have been asking themselves since the beginning of those distasteful K-rations.

"At least we have hot coffee. A man can go without eating for a time but not having hot coffee—that's got to be some sort of war crime," Chief said in a low voice.

Bill agreed, "You'd think that a government with our current technology could create meal packets that contain steak, roast beef, or a pork sandwich. Maybe a freeze-dried Big Mac or even a Whooper—I could sure go for some tasty tacos right now—oh, man, I'm about ready to send Roman out to shoot a couple of those Afghan goats. We could roast them over the fire." Bill shook his head and shoved his MRE packet back into his field pack.

Chief pulled out a clear quart-sized plastic bag that contained his version of trail mix: dry roasted peanuts and cashews, raisins, almonds, several chewable vitamins, a double handful of honey roasted oatmeal flakes, coconut flakes, and semi-sweet chocolate chips. He had learned that semi-sweet chocolate chips didn't melt as fast as milk chocolate. He also carried a separate packet of dried beef jerky.

Roman looked on with envy and was appreciative when the Chief offered him a handful and then poured some of the mix into Bill's waiting hands. "Thanks, Chief."

"What about the jerky, Chief?" Bill asked a look of anticipation in his eyes, his right hand extended toward the Chief.

"Sir, my supply is running low, but I'll split a piece between you and Roman."

Bill produced a couple of energy bars and handed one to Roman and one to the Chief. "Kitty gets them at some mom-and-pop Health Food store. They taste a lot better than most of those big chain bars and cost less. She mails me two dozen bars every week. He tossed one each to his two very appreciative runners.

Chief noticed one of the runners looking at him, eyes and facial expression showing desire for a hunk of jerky. The Chief shook his head, "Forget it, young'un. All that sugary pogey bait is great, but you need protein to make it out here. When we get back to Bagram, hit the Exchange, and make up your own mixture. Think about protein, some fats—and see what kind of health bars they carry. This heat melts the chocolate-coated ones, so avoid those, or you're stuck with a big sticky mess. I use semi-sweet chocolate chips; other things in the bag keep the chips from melting. Learn to read the ingredients on the back of those energy bar packages. Just because it says Nestle's, or Hershey's doesn't mean it can handle your needs out here. And, by the way, another life-saver is a small jar of crunchy peanut butter. I forgot to bring one out with me, so that should show you this old chief is fallible, too."

"Captain, may I ask a question?" One of the runners, a PFC, asked.

"Speak freely, Private—we're relaxed for the moment," Bill said.

"Well, sir, I heard your old pastor friend speak about your father that day on the track. Did your dad ever complain about those old C-Rations?"

"Sure, he did. Soldiers have complained about GI chow since day one of this man's army. Those old C-rations came in cans, except for a foil container holding packets of salt, pepper, a narrow package containing three cigarettes, a hot chocolate packet, and a lemonade packet. Some dated back to World War II, and the medic warned the guys not to use them. Hopefully, the box contained a little can opener, a P-38; most guys took to carrying one on their dog tag chains. Otherwise, they had to use a bayonet to get into the cans. They came to the field in a box of... I think it held 12 meals. Each meal contained four to five cans. Made the field packs a bit heavier than our MREs. He told me when going into the field, you'd often carry three meals in your pack, and most of them were edible. I heard the beans-and-weenies were the favored meal in Nam—that and the pound cake and a can of fruit cocktail."

Chief added his two cents, "Not only was the field chow a problem, but the troops had some serious problems with their M-16s. They kept jamming due to all the mud and rain. All those plastic parts didn't help. It made the weapon lighter to carry, but it sure disliked the jungle and all that moisture. You could toss an AK-47 into a rice paddy and come back for it in a couple of days, clean it off, and it was ready to fire. But not the M-16. They took what they learned from that war to finally produce the M-4 you carry today."

"How come the government sent all those troops to war with such a faulty rifle?" The second runner asked.

"That's a good question, soldier," Bill said before the Chief could reply. "When you find the answer, let me know. I imagine it came down to cost, big deals between arms dealers and politicians, and probably some kickback. It's sad, but it's not always the best company that gets those billion-dollar contracts—greed and human error become a major problem."

Bill looked at his two young runners, and for a moment, felt like a history teacher. "Basically, from what I was told, our military was in a hurry to replace the M-14, which a lot of Marine units carried in Nam. Most of the troops were not all that crazy about the new M-16. They called it a Mattel toy. In their hurry to get the M-16 into the field, they didn't run it through enough combat scenarios. Unfortunately, some of those jungle firefights lasted for a whole day, or even longer, and the rifles started jamming.

Here in the desert, you can see a long way during the daytime, but in those jungles of Nam, you were often lucky to see the man walking in front of you. Our troops found the same thing during the island campaigns of World War II. In Nam, there were poisonous snakes and those accursed booby traps. A well-known one was the punji trap, where a trip device was triggered causing the victim to fall onto sharpened bamboo spikes. The VC would crap and pee on them, which poisoned the blood system. Early on in that war, doctors were troubled by the number of men who died from what looked to be non-life-threatening wounds. When they finally learned why, fewer men died. Just like the IEDs— experience is always the greatest teacher. My dad fell into one of them, but it was so old the bamboo snapped off without causing an injury. He and his buddies figured it was left behind by the original Viet Minh, who were at war with the French in the '50s. But it still took him a moment to get his heart back to a normal rhythm."

"Captain, radio call for you—it's Division." Roman handed him the microphone and an extra headset. Roman stayed connected, prepared to jot down notes in the logbook. "All set up, sir," Roman said.

"This is Yankee One—go ahead." He looked over at Roman, "We're on the alternate frequency, right?"

"Sure thing, sir."

"Yankee One, stand-by for Command One... Over." The voice failed to identify himself, but Bill knew Command One was used only for the General.

"Standing by... Over."

"Be advised your new radio designation is Charlie Operation Post Alpha Three, as in Command Operations Post—Alpha, as in Alpha for Airborne, and three for your current special operations. Here is Command One," said the unidentified voice.

"Can you identify my voice... Over."

"Yes, sir... Over."

"Everyone around here is worried for fear the Russians or Pakistani, the Chinese or ISIS may have broken all of our radio signals and codes. But I have more faith in my troops than those feather merchants back in the states." Bill hadn't heard the phrase 'feather merchants' in a very long time. He knew from his days at West Point that it was a term used to describe politicians and military officers who had never served in combat. "Washington has issued new orders, and your unit is involved. Do you hear me? Over"

"I copy you... Over."

"You'd think with all this new tech, I could at least hear you breathing. You're to set up your FOB as a temporary Base of Operations, three miles east of your present location. Do not enter the pass, stay south of the road. At 1700 hours, those hills to your south will be receiving airstrikes in hopes of removing any hidden enemy forces. Pilots know where you'll be positioned, set out today's colored air panels to mark your FOB. Your Operations Field Book should have the color—use them. I don't want to send any bodies home because those jet jockeys failed to see those panels, and overshoot their targets... Over."

"Yes, sir. Panels will be out, but sir, I've got patrols out in those rocks... Over."

"Get them out, Captain. I cannot postpone the attack. Do you understand? Over."

"I copy, sir... Over." Bill looked at Roman, who sent a runner to advise Lt. Sam Rayson to recall his two squads ASAP. He was also instructed to report to Bill right away.

The General continued, "At 1600 hours, a Blackhawk will be arriving at your new homestead; you and Lieutenant Rayson are ordered to return here. You will report directly to me for further orders. Do you Copy, Captain? Over."

"I copy, 1600 hours, and we report to you... Over."

"I know you've got other junior officers with little or no experience, but for the time you're gone, I want that new Chief Warrant Officer of yours to take charge. Do you understand? On my authority, he will be the acting C.O. ... Over."

"I concur... Over."

"I'll see you at 1700 hours—oh, I'll have a vehicle waiting for you at the helipad. That's it for now... Out."

Bill was set to reply that he copied, but the General had signed off. Bill's mind filled with random speculation. He tried to understand why the General would want him and Rayson to report in person. No matter, the General had issued the orders. Bill needed to be ready to go for another helicopter ride. First, however, he needed to ensure the squads had returned. He also needed to look over his area map to see where his new home would be located. As soon as he briefed Sam, the two companies would start packing up. "But we can't leave here until the crews are done with the car lot. Send a runner over there and ask that Major how much longer he might be and tell him we've got orders to move. He may have to bury everything else; I'm sure he doesn't want to remain out here for another night without protection." Bill rubbed the stubble on his chin and realized he needed a shave before reporting to the General. "Roman, you heard the General. Contact Remmel's team, and order them to pull back to this location with those two squads from D Company. I want everyone clear of those ridgelines within the hour. I also want a Commander's Call for all officers and senior NCOs to be held here in 30 minutes. Then we move up three miles or so and do it all over again."

"Yes, sir," Roman replied, and began contacting Remmel and the other platoon commanders.

Bill looked over at his runners, "Send the word out to all those vehicles, advise them we should be leaving here in one hour for a short drive up the road to set up a new FOB. Load up as many sandbags as they can handle to save time filling new ones at our new location." He pointed to the nearest runner, "You take care of Bravo Company!" He pointed at the second man, "... and you take Delta Company. The first man back is to assist Sergeant Roman. Now get moving!"

Suddenly, in a mad dash, the runners were on their feet and jumping out of the foxhole. One man stopped abruptly and returned for his helmet, glanced back at the Captain with a sheepish grin, and then turned to make a run for D Company.

When Bill looked back at Roman, he learned that Remmel didn't want to leave his new duck blind but was in the process of uprooting his team. "He should be back within the hour. I think Remmel found a sweet spot and hates giving it up—the man sure likes his job."

"Roman, he's good at what he does. When he's done with the Army, I'm sure the CIA or Secret Service will be offering him a new career. With his growing record, I'm betting he'll be getting an invite to join the Green Beenies. They're always looking for top shooters."

"What's going on, Captain?" Chief asked. His helmet was off, attached to his belt hanging with his right-side canteen, behind his pistol. Bill knew no one, including himself, would tell the Chief the helmet belonged on his head.

"At approximately 1700 hours, our Air Force and possibly some Marine fighters will light up these hilltops in a massive air attack. The General wants us to relocate a minimum of three miles up the road and set up a new FOB. That will put us real close to the actual entrance to the pass. You're liable to be in charge of this operation. Lt. Rayson and I are catching a ride at 1600 hours to report to the General for our new orders. I imagine the Colonel will be in on the briefing, at least I hope so. This means we don't have time for a lengthy Commander's Call. By the way, the General himself placed you in charge while Sam and I are gone. I'll make sure the other officers know you're running things. But with your experience, I don't imagine a single one will object.

The helicopter will pick Sam and me up here unless we get out of here before it is due, and they can pick us up along the way. I have no idea if we'll get back before dark, so get our new FOB ready for the night, with the same setup as here. Get the men dug in, perimeter defenses in place, and hopefully, I'll be back before nightfall. Oh, we're to put out today's colored air panels so the pilots can see that our new location is filled with the good guys, and we don't get bombed or strafed. Roman has the book with today's panel color, so get them unpacked. I want to have them handy when and if our ride arrives before we reach the new location. I think today's color is red, but make sure."

Roman was pulling the rolled-up panels from the Company Command bag as Bill spoke. The green canvas bag held four different colored sets of air panels, all tightly rolled up. There were also assorted maps of the region, colored smoke flares, and, among other things, extra batteries for all the radios.

"I sure hope—never mind, we'll get it done, Captain," Chief said.

"While Sam and I are gone, just pray we're not being ordered to occupy the Khyber Pass for an extended period. I can only imagine the nightmare that would be... The Taliban know that place like we know our old neighborhoods back in the states. Home field advantage would be all theirs."

"Yes, sir. I'll also get the Chaplain busy with the prayers."

Remmel and his team arrived, and the last squad was within sight. The units prepared to move up the road, with piles of sandbags on every vehicle. No one was happy about it. Driving three miles only to dig in again sounded too much like make work. Bill held Bravo Company's 2nd platoon in the old position until the last armored unit disappeared in the distance. With the pass narrowing, Bill didn't like being close to the road not with the entrance so near at hand, so had remained off the road. From what Bill could see, finding a suitable spot to set the two companies up would be right at the pass entrance. This made him uncomfortable as both sides of the road led up to towering massive rocks which led to a higher elevation of mostly stone ridgelines leading to more prominent hills and huge mountains. Unlike the mountains Bill grew up with in Southern California, like the San Bernardino Mountain Range, there was little foliage and very few trees here. These hills were mostly solid rocks with steep cliffsides.

2nd Platoon was left as Tail End Charlie to ensure the Taliban didn't attempt to follow the armored units. With pillars of desert dust lifting into the clear sky, it would be easy for the enemy to follow. Since 2nd Platoon would be on foot those three miles, Bill assigned a Bradley and a Stryker to escort them to the new location. However, before following the two companies, they were to ensure that the Civil Engineers and the Chinooks departed the area safely. By the time the two companies began moving across the desert, remaining parallel with the road, the Chinooks were airborne and returning to Bagram with the goods from the Taliban car lot. Everything else was buried and covered over with sand and large boulders moved into place with the help of the Bradley plow blade.

Scouts reported seeing several small groups traveling toward Kabul. They turned out to be locals, primarily women, kids, and some older people also avoiding the roadway. The short drive was made without incident, and a suitable location was found for the new FOB about 2.3 three miles from their old encampment. Unfortunately, the pass itself didn't provide adequate space to set up a FOB. The spot selected was inside the western edges of the Khyber Pass which meant the nearby hills were easily within sniper range. Bill sent patrols to clear the nearest rock formations, fortunately without encountering any Taliban. The air panels were put out, and a small helipad was established for the Blackhawk coming in to pick up Bill and Sam.

The troops set up their new defense perimeter, unloaded the filled sandbags, and dug new holes. Additional sandbags would be needed, so everyone had a job to do. They had only traded one piece of desert for another, but the work kept the men busy. Each man glanced behind him to the massive rock formations nearby and kept a close eye on the few civilians walking by along the road. Occasionally, a local would speed by on a motorcycle. This section and the next five miles had already been demined, but the locals were not too trusting and stayed with the desert. Occasionally a herd of sheep or goats used the roadway. With the number of locals, many soldiers wondered where the villages were. Townsites were not visible from the road, and the military didn't seem to know how many hamlets were under Taliban control.

TO BAGRAM

On the flight in, Bill spotted two flights of four Cobra gunships headed southeast, and above them, two flights of five F-15 Eagles. Using binoculars, he could see that the aircraft were headed for the Khyber Pass loaded with 250-pound bombs. Such a load would make for thunderous explosions as the hilltops were bombarded. He didn't feel sorry for the Taliban; he had lost too many men to be concerned about these fanatics. His thoughts turned to his own men and their need to survive the next 10 months and again wondered what plans the General had waiting for him.

Bill was tormented with the thought of being relieved of his command after losing so many troops in just two months. This forced him to consider this might be why Rayson was accompanying him, to take over the unit. But playing all sides of the situation, he still could not find any fault in his decision-making and pushed those doubts away. As the Blackhawk settled down for a landing, Bill saw a Humvee sitting beside the helipad. It appeared their ride was at hand.

BACK WITH B AND D COMPANIES

While Bill and Sam waited in an air-conditioned office at Command with ceramic coffee cups in hand, things began jumping back at the new COP Alpha-Three. A Blackhawk Helicopter landed and offloaded three people and their equipment. Chief had no advance warning of their arrival. The pilot had requested his presence over the radio. The passengers were Major William C. Garnett, SSgt Arnold Underling, the major's RTO, and SSgt Oscar Ryan.

Major Garnett was a Forward Air Controller (FAC), and the two NCOs were his support staff. Their job was to guide the air assault, staying in touch with the pilots for the upcoming operation. "Who's in charge of this outfit?" Major Garnett bellowed to be heard over the departing Blackhawk.

Chief identified himself and offered his hand, "Sir, I'm the acting CO. My commander is back at Division and should be returning before nightfall. What are your orders, Major?"

"We're here to play mother hen to a flight of F-15s and helicopter gunships that should be arriving shortly. I just need a place to set up my RTO; I already have all the coordinates for the strike. But you might tell your troops to have earplugs handy, it's about to get real loud around here and a sight to behold."

"Yes, sir, if you'll follow me, it's just a short walk to where you can set your equipment up. We're in the process of setting up a new FOB and only arrived here a short time ago. But if you need anything, just sing out."

"You got it, Chief—thanks for meeting me. I hope to be out of your hair within the hour." The major turned to his men and advised them to follow, "We don't have much time, so let's get set up quickly. Those birds will be overhead shortly and demanding final target coordinates."

Major Garnett, an Air Force officer, didn't complain about not being saluted in a combat zone. He was just a little taken back to find a Chief Warrant Officer, a crusty looking one at that, in charge of this FOB.

"Welcome to the Khyber Pass, Major?" Chief said questioningly as he led the men toward a small rise he felt would be a safe location for them to set up their operation. He pointed at the spot where Roman and the two runners were in the process of digging out their new home. "There's our new headquarters hole; you'll be about 15 yards to the right on that small rise. It should give you a good view of those hills."

Garnett gestured his men forward and watched as they hurried to set up their radio. Theirs was a good 20 pounds heavier and six inches taller than the one Roman was using. "Okay, Chief, let's get a quick look-see at your southern perimeter, and you can show me this location on my map. I want to ensure I have us in the right spot. I'd hate to have one of those pilots drop an egg or two in our laps. Glad to see you have your air panels out; that's a big help in keeping accidents down."

Chief showed the Major the road and gave him a quick rundown on the perimeter positions. "Normally, I'd have sent patrols into those rocks just south of us. But that would be too dangerous with this attack about to begin. Bomb shrapnel will be flying, so I'm keeping our troops close to their holes. I've seen what these planes can do from previous operations. Even watched as one bomb failed to explode on contact, it just bounced along before finally exploding some 200 yards or so from the intended target. Unfortunately, it killed and wounded a couple dozen civilians."

"Chief, between you and I, I don't understand what the General wants done here. He only told me to come out here, flatten these rocks below us, and then explained that the Afghan military had opted out of this operation. They wanted us to handle this job. Makes one wonder who our allies are out here. But apparently, they say they don't have the bombs and missiles to get this job done. This is one massive rock range, and the General says it's a natural haven for the enemy. To tell you the truth, I was expecting a much smaller target. I'm not sure we have enough bombs to do this job. Be a much better assignment for a flight of B-52s or B-1s. Still, we go with what we got—right?"

"Sir, maybe he simply wants to scare the remaining rats out into the open, though I'll be surprised if they're many left if any. We've been here for almost 14 years. The Taliban are likely expecting this and cleared out. We fought a pretty good firefight near here last night, took out nearly 80 Taliban, and that's a large force. So, we might just be clearing a lot of rock and giving our pilots some practice."

"Orders are orders, Chief. It'll put on a big show for the people in this area, seeing the power we can bring. Thankfully, there are no villages in the target area. Who knows, we might end up clearing a large area for all those goat and sheepherders, make new pastures." The major broke out his map case and unfolded a map of the area. "Okay, show me where we're at."

Chief looked over the map and then pointed to the spot, "That's us."

"Good, having this established road here makes for a good boundary.

I'll have the F-15s make their first run from west to east. They'll make two runs, then helicopters will move in to mop up if they see any movement or possible caves."

Chief set up the Bradleys to provide 25mm cannon fire to support the F-15s if fired upon by the Taliban. The major agreed.

Remmel and his spotter established a position on top of a Stryker to pick up any nearby terrorists fleeing for their lives. Chief issued orders that if any Taliban had his hands up to surrender, Remmel was to hold fire. There was always the possibility that slaves and kidnapped villagers were being held in caves. However, the General did not want to risk losing any more men by holding off the air attack and searching several miles or more of these mountains.

Chief asked a question that had been pestering him ever since they had taken up positions. "Sir, do you think we're making this effort just to show the Pakistani how much power we have in hopes of getting them to cancel any planned invasion of Afghanistan?"

"Chief, I heard that rumor back at Division, but that's way above my pay grade. With all your time in service, you know as well as I that anything is possible. He could have ordered in the big bombers if it was only a demonstration. I once saw a film on an arc strike B-52's made in Vietnam. The sheer force of that attack was—it was the closest thing to what Hiroshima or Nagasaki might have been like. Nothing can survive under that degree of destruction. That arc strike turned a square mile of ground into a square mile of ash. I doubt anything is growing there to this day. This is just barren desert so I doubt very much that that that type of demonstration would do much to deter the Pakistani." He pointed to the west to show the Chief that the flight of F-15s had arrived. "Time to go to work, Chief. Tell your men to get earplugs in and helmets on; it's gonna get fierce!" His left hand held the microphone his RTO had just handed him, and he turned his attention to contacting the lead pilot.

Chief dashed off to issue orders for earplugs and helmets, "Keep your heads down! It's going to get loud. Wait for the all-clear before moving!" The planes had ceased to be distant dots in the sky; they were easily visible as first one, and then another peeled off from the flight. Chief looked down at Roman, "Repeat my orders over the radio—everyone to remain undercover, helmets on, and earplugs in place. No one moves until I give the all-clear."

Roman nodded that he understood and repeated the order in a surprisingly calm voice.

BACK AT BAGRAM

Bill and Sam were a bit stymied following the meeting with their Commanding General. He had relayed his instructions in a clear and concise voice and dismissed them abruptly, leaving no time for questions. Written orders were handed to them as they walked out. Bill was placed second in command of three companies of Airborne troops, to be known as the 4th Provisional Battalion, a position generally held by a light colonel or at least a major. The battalion would consist of Bill's two current companies (B and D) and A company which was due to land at Bagram before nightfall and board Chinooks to ride out to Bill's new FOB. Bill was stunned when the Colonel informed him about the new provisional 4th Battalion, 501st Regiment, 3rd Brigade (Airborne) of the 25th Infantry, 101st Airborne Division. *What a mouthful!*

The undersized battalion would be commanded by Lt. Colonel Hiram Rogers, who had been very recently assigned to the General's staff. Rogers would remain at Bagram. Though not Airborne qualified, he was known to be an excellent strategic planner. Still, under the Colonel's orders, Bill would remain field commander for the provisional battalion. He knew that the word provisional was often used to mean temporary. Bill wondered why he was so blessed as he and Sam discussed the new development. "On one side, you could look at this as another move to give you command experience and prep you for a major's leaf when this tour is up. But, on the other hand, Bill, it could be using a lowly captain to become a scapegoat if things turn sour. Colonel Rogers would escape being seen as a failure if we all get our asses blown away when the balloon goes up. Can I have a transfer now, sir, maybe guarding a visiting USO troupe of lovely blonde ladies?"

"Oh, shut up!" Bill said trying to match Sam's suddenly light teasing tone. "Remember, lieutenants should listen and refrain from speaking. Don't you remember that from your platoon leader's course?" He remembered the last words of the General, 'Captain, I made you the XO because you've proven yourself to be a good battlefield officer. Company A's commander is also a captain but with more time in grade than you. He's also four months away from making major. However, Captain Tyler has no battlefield experience, as this is his first combat tour. He knows you're my field commander, I do not want any turf wars out there, and by the way, he's also been made aware of this. He won't do anything to jeopardize his promotion, so instruct the man and show him how things are done in combat. I'm sure he'll learn a lot from you—things you've gained from your previous two tours, and from what you've gone through since your arrival here. Your Colonel recommended you to lead this band of cutthroats, and from what I know, you darn well deserve it. Questions?'

"Sir, you said his name was Captain Tyler. By any chance would this be Mark Tyler—a West Point grad? There was an upperclassman of that name two years ahead of me."

The General looked to the Colonel, who replied, "Yes, Captain, A Company is commanded by Captain Mark Tyler, a West Point graduate. He's only been in command of A Company for just over two months, so he's new to his people. He's also new to the 101st, having transferred over from the 82nd, and his only overseas assignments have been in Europe. Any other questions, Captain?"

"Uh... uh, no, sir. Thank you, sir—and thank you, Colonel." Bill looked over at Sam, who also wore a look of astonishment on his face.

They hurried to the Humvee the General had provided, with an armed escort. As they approached the airfield, Bill noticed that four Boing AH-64 Apache Helicopters assigned to his new battalion were being refueled and readied to escort the Blackhawk back to their unit. With the current armor, his battalion was rapidly becoming a strongly reinforced fighting unit. But he knew that if things turned sour on the job ahead, he would need every single man and every killing machine to get them safely out of Dodge. He just hoped he was up to it; doubts, he had to keep to himself.

Bill had asked the Colonel for extra rations and additional water wagons. After a few phone calls, four extra water trailers were filled and delivered to the tarmac to be airlifted out to the FOB the following morning. When Bill and Sam were dropped off at their Blackhawk, they were told that all aircraft would be prevented from entering air space near their FOB's immediate area until all bombing runs were completed to avoid endangering fighters and any arriving helicopters.

The delay gave Bill and Sam a chance to walk over to Base Operations to make a few purchases. There was a small Exchange where they could pick up snacks, new socks, and underwear. Bill purchased socks for the Chief, Roman, and his runners. Roman had been complaining about the socks he received in his last issue, 'Captain, the material is so cheap, I've already worn holes in them!'

"You know how it is; government contracts always go to the lowest bidder. I guess we should consider ourselves lucky we're not out here in sandals."

Both Bill and Sam carried full brown paper bags back to their bird and waited for the all-clear order. Bill's thoughts slipped back to his days at West Point and memories of a cadet named Mark Tyler, who now commanded A Company. He spoke aloud to Sam. "If this is the same Mark Tyler I know, he played football at the Point, and my impression of him is favorable. But I'm surprised this is his first tour into the Sandbox. I wonder what he's been doing in Europe and why'd he left the 82nd?"

"I'm sure we'll find out," Sam replied.

BACK AT THE FOB

The F-15s came in hot, dropping their first load of bombs at well-spaced intervals along the first string of low stone mountains. The scene instantly transformed into one massive storm-like front as black clouds and fiery blasts billowed up. Within seconds, the ridgelines were obscured in dust, dirt, and flying debris. Not only was there shrapnel to be concerned about, but each explosion sent out lethal showers of stone slivers and rocks of all sizes flying in all directions. The ground beneath the Americans rumbled and trembled as if a 6.0 earthquake held the area in its powerful grip. Troops inside combat vehicles grabbed for handholds as the vehicles shook.

Seeing and feeling all this, the men of B and D Companies dug at the ground in a frantic attempt to go even deeper into their holes in anticipation of the shock waves. The Major and his two men braced themselves as the officer barked out orders to the pilots. To Chief, it was clear that the tactical air control specialists had weathered many such poundings before. And he could see that the magnitude of carpet bombing had rattled his own troops. Later, when it was safe to move around, the men would see large rocks and small boulders scattered about the area by the sheer force of the explosions. One man remarked that a small stone had bounced off his helmet. Several of the armored vehicles had been rained upon, but no damage was done.

"Man, we're miles away from that blast. Imagine what it would be like to be up in those same mountains when those bombs fell—never seen anything like it and hope to never again," a shaken PFC said to fellow hole mates.

The bone-rattling thunder of the F-15s barreling in overhead was so loud the troops wouldn't even look up. Several remarked later that they had held their breath as the Eagles screamed in over their position. Most of them would not soon forget this experience. SFC Roman squeezed his headphones tight with both hands as the last 250-pounder fell all too close. He watched as a small piece of shrapnel struck and bounced off the side of a nearby Bradley.

Then the second wave of F-15's dropped low and thundered in, dropping their loads farther south. The pilots knew there was no way they could flatten these hills; there simply were not enough bombs to accomplish that task. After the Eagles completed their second run and the dust settled and smoke faded away, the hillsides were left cratered, the tortured earth torn and ripped apart. The General knew this; otherwise, he would have requested bigger bombers. He simply wanted a show of force in an attempt to drive the Taliban out of this immediate area for the forthcoming operation.

Major Garnett was on the radio with a flight of Apache Helicopters, whose arrival had surprised the Chief. "Apaches, great, but what happened to our Cobras, Major?"

"Phasing them out I guess. Probably being shipped to Iraq or some South African Army we're allied with. I've found the Apache to be a real killing machine. They're agile enough to escape an RPG or knock it out with one of their small missiles or guns. The AH-64 Apache can carry three Hellfire Missiles, Hydra rockets, and a 30mm M230 chain-gun. They can knock out enemy aircraft if they engage one, Chief, though they lack the speed to catch one. Right now, their mission is to locate any surviving caves or trails and make them disappear. Someone wants to turn this area into 'do-not enter' territory."

"They sure look deadly enough, I don't believe anyone up there could have survived. If the caves are destroyed, we'll never know for sure if there was anyone or if any survived or got away. My main concern is for possible prisoners. The Captain and I firmly believe some of the forces who attacked us last night were, in fact, prisoners taken from nearby communities who were forced to fight or be killed. Instead of rifles, they were only issued swords though a crazed man swinging a long sword can be pretty intimidating."

"I'd heard rumors of that, Chief. But this order was given back at Division."

The Chief could only shake his head in response.

19 minutes had passed since the first aircraft made the first drop; the Apaches were done, their loads expended, and they turned back to Bagram. Before the Major could pack up his radio, his RTO picked up incoming traffic. Four other Apache Helicopters were inbound to the FOB and requesting landing instructions. Within minutes they circled the western flats before descending in slow procession. Chief sent out two of the Strykers and a squad of troops to guard the birds, which were 100 yards west of B Company's position.

Each Apache carried a pilot and a weapons officer, in the rank of either a warrant officer or commissioned 1st lieutenant or Captain. Chief would learn the ground crews and armorers, along with the bird's munitions, were due to arrive the next day. As the Chief admired the birds, he thought they reminded him of a praying mantis. Once tied down with the help of the closest soldiers, the pilots completed a walk-around check. Satisfied that nothing had fallen off and nothing appeared amiss, they walked to where Major Garnett was standing beside the Chief.

Captain Andy Salsby, in command of the Apaches, saluted the major and nodded to the Chief. Behind him stood the other three Apache pilots: 1st Lieutenant Jack Summer, Captain Teddy Barnes, and 1st Lieutenant Andie Sharpe; weapons officers 2nd Lieutenant Augustus

Reddington, Warrant Officer Al Brightly, Warrant Officer Fred Starling, and Warrant Officer Steve Railsback. Lt. Andie Sharpe was one of only a few women pilots who currently flew the Apache into combat. The pilots were introduced, but the Chief raised an eyebrow as he shook hands with Lt. Andie Sharp. Being old school, he just wasn't too sure about "girlie" pilots. He didn't think women belonged in combat, having been brought up at an age when men protected their women, not the other way around. But being a professional, he welcomed her to the group.

"If you need a hole, I can give you shovels and a couple of soldiers to help out," Chief said to them as a group.

"No, Chief, we'll dig our own holes, but if it's all right, we'd like to set up by our birds," Captain Salsby replied. "But I will take you up on those shovels. That's one thing these birds don't carry—and some water, please."

"You got it, Captain," Chief said as he turned and hollered out for shovels. They appeared as by magic and the Chief handed them over to 1st Lt. Summer. Then he introduced Major William Garnet to the crews, and again, there were quick handshakes.

"Major, we've worked with you before; my pilots appreciate your calm voice feeding out instructions for the strikes. You make a great Forward Air Controller, sir," Captain Salsby said.

"Thank you, and Chief, I just heard that your Captain Warrens and Lt. Rayson have already lifted off from Bagram and should be arriving soon. I'm to standby until tomorrow when another load of troops is due to arrive."

"Sir, we're getting additional troops? This is the first I've heard of that," Chief said.

"Sorry about that Chief, I just got word on that a moment ago, too. Your commander knows about it. Company A has been assigned to the new provisional 4th Battalion; that's about all I know."

"I wonder who we might be getting for a new commander? Three companies call for at least a major. Out here, it should be someone with some combat experience. Curious... damn... excuse me, ma'am...I mean Lieutenant. I'm a tad upset about losing my Captain. He's a good man and has a lot of experience in handling the Taliban."

"Not a problem, Chief." She smiled to show the Chief she wasn't offended by his profanity. She had heard much worse as a teenager.

Chief told the pilots that they would be advised to swap flight helmets for soldiers' steel pots while with the ground units. "I'll see about scrounging up enough helmets for you."

"Thanks, Chief. These flight helmets carry a lot of technology, but they won't stop a bullet or a good-sized piece of shrapnel. So, we'll gladly accept your helmets."

"You're all carrying sidearms, Captain, but are you carrying anything bigger?" He directed the question to Captain Salsby.

"Chief, we fly knowing at any moment we can be shot down. Each man is prepared for that moment with M-4s and 4-banana clips of ammo." He gestured to Lieutenant Andie Sharpe and said, "The Lieutenant can outshoot us all—she's the best rifle shot in our squadron—raised with a rifle in her hand from age three from the way she tells it. Sometimes, she's even gone out with a sniper during downtime. Last I heard, she has three kills on the ground, but that was way north of here when we supported the Marines."

"Sounds good, Captain. I won't have to worry about her then." *I wonder how Remmel would feel about taking this young lieutenant out for some sniper work? With his heritage, he's probably much like me; women belong in the kitchen and having babies. But this man's Army is now also a woman's army. Good thing I'm going to retire, my way of thinking is old-fashioned. We even have female generals now. Good Grief!"*

The sun was heading for the western horizon, and Chief knew they had about 40 to 50 minutes before it vanished, and darkness began to blanket them. The humidity would be high tonight. Lights would be going out soon to prevent Taliban snipers from having a target.

The men in the command hole heard Major Garnett speaking on the radio but could not hear well enough to understand his words. Then they noticed Garnett, followed by Roman, point to the northwest. A Blackhawk approached from that direction, and Chief assumed it would be their new commander. The bird settled down on the ground close to the tied-down Apaches. Chief made his way over to meet his new boss and was surprised to see Bill and Sam, with paper bags in hand and M-4s slung over their shoulders.

Standing at the Chief's side, Roman said, "Don't worry, Chief, you'll know all about it in a moment."

Captain Bill Warrens stopped when he saw the questioning expression on Roman's face. "What's wrong?"

"The Chief expected our new battalion commander, and you arrive without a new senior officer accompanying you. We're a bit confused."

"I'll tell you all about it after I unload my stuff. Where are the pilots for those Apache's, Chief?"

"Digging out their new lodgings. I offered them some enlisted help, but they refused. Seem like a good bunch, and one of them is a female—sir."

"It's the new Army, Chief, get used to it. Before long, they'll start putting them in the airborne, and that's goin' to be mighty interesting. C'mon, I brought back some new socks for both of you. Size 12 for the Chief and 10 for you, Roman—right?"

"Thank you, sir! How much do I owe you?" Roman replied.

"It's a gift. I couldn't stand how bad your feet were looking or the stink. So, go change your socks!"

"Yes, sir." Roman grinned and sat down to change socks.

Sam broke away to join his own company, leaving Bill with the Chief and Roman. In their foxhole, Bill told both men what had happened back at headquarters. They shook their heads in disbelief. "This Army keeps changing..." Chief muttered. "I think I'll retire when this tour is over. Women fighting beside us—hard for an old warhorse like me to get a handle on all this."

"I think I know this Captain Tyler; he was two years ahead of me at the Academy. From what I recall, he was a decent sort. What I don't understand is why this is his first tour to the Sandbox. A good number of officers ended up in Europe where they trained for the day the Russian balloon goes up. Maybe he just got tired of training and wanted to see some action."

"The major, our Forward Air Controller, said that A Company is due to come in tomorrow. What then?"

"Give me a moment to catch my breath, Chief. I've been stressed out all day, and now it's time for chow. I'll fill you in after I get something in my stomach, okay?"

"Yes, sir," Chief replied and hurried away to ensure all the night positions were covered. Though he didn't expect any visitors, he knew he could never count on that, even with the bombardment the nearby mountains had taken. He saw the Taliban as snakes that burrowed deep and sneaked out under cover of darkness. He wanted his people ready.

With frequent radio problems, it was an added security measure to use runners whenever possible, to ensure everyone, platoons, armor, and now the Apache pilots, knew what was going on. The runners came in handy as Roman could not make radio contact with two of the platoon commanders caused by an equipment malfunction and an RTO who failed to change batteries. The night perimeter posts were manned and ready by the time darkness descended on the desert.

Having eaten one of his energy bars and a handful of peanuts he got back at Bagram, Bill was ready to brief the Chief and Roman. "Those four Apache gunships are ours. They'll be our observation platform as we move east through the pass and our support if 'it' hits the fan. I was stunned to find myself Battalion XO in the field while our commander remains on Bagram. The Battalion C.O. is Lt. Colonel Rogers, who has no field experience but is known as a great war planner from what the General told me. With your support, I hope to prove myself worthy of holding this group together. I'll be calling on a lot of help from you two. I'm not above taking advice or correction as I've learned to value both of you. Our mission is this beautiful recreational site all around us, henceforth known as Eagle One. Sergeant Roman, the command's main RTO and Battalion Keeper of the Record, will be handing out new call signs for each of our three companies. I'll give you the new lists when we're done here. Chief—by order of our beloved Colonel, and at my suggestion, you are the acting commander of B Company. I cannot be both the XO and B Company's commander. You'll have already been given your promotion, and I doubt your lieutenants will give you any problems. They're already scared of you, which helps. A Chief Warrant Officer makes a lot more money than a lowly 1st Lieutenant—I should know."

The Chief shook his head in wonder—he was a company commander, and it had all happened fast.

Bill smiled and continued. "Orders for this new unit—Eagle Base; us as a whole—is to carry out three different operations. Lt. Colonel Rogers is Eagle One, I am Eagle Two. I'll be meeting with the other company commanders tomorrow after A Company arrives to hand out their new call signs. A Company's Captain Tyler will be Eagle Three, B Company — the Chief—is Eagle Four, and D Company's Lt. Rayson is Eagle Five. Easy to remember. Our first duty is to finish removing the mines on this road. Our allies will be right behind us with their road crews. We are to go all the way to the end of Khyber Pass and avoid the Pakistan border, which will be hard to do as the pass leads almost right up to it. The Pakistani fear a possible invasion, no matter what we try to tell them. Probably because the Russians, possibly Iran, or the Chinese are telling them just the opposite.

We know they have a force of one hundred tanks within 100 miles of the border and south of the entrance to Khyber Pass. It is believed that to some degree this armored force, supported by infantry, may move in to engage us if we close on their border. This we will not do. We have explained numerous times that this demining operation will be completed, just as we've told them—we do not plan on invading their land. Our job is to make this road safe for all to use, including their civilians when passing over the border. Before hostilities blew up between Afghanistan and Pakistan, there were minor border skirmishes. Pakistani traders have journeyed to Kabul with their wares for decades. Hopefully, this will happen again, maybe even help end the friction between these two countries.

I asked about patrols for the pass after our units are finished. Someone has to make sure the Taliban don't simply return to do it all over again. I was not provided with a response, so for now, this issue is out of our hands."

Our second assignment is to search the area surrounding Khyber Pass to ensure it's free of Taliban influence and to create a safe zone for locals to pass through. We'll remain for a short time as a primary response force but using Airborne for security makes no sense at all to me, so I'm hoping Afghan infantry will replace us shortly. After the flyboys tore up every inch of those hillsides, our men will have to become mountain goats to scour new rock formations to see if there are any caves or crevices for rats to hide in. In any event, we'll need eyes up there as soon as possible—I'm talking about tomorrow.

Our third assignment is a bit more complicated and will involve all three elements of our new provisional battalion. We have limited armor and two Apache gunships to cover one entire company and our men will be searching five nearby villages for Taliban and arms caches. We suspect the Taliban have kidnapped townspeople to serve in their ranks —pretty much as *cannon fodder*. I can see why that term keeps coming up; it's rather fitting. Last night we fought a large force of Taliban, some obviously either untrained or poorly trained and with limited weapons which could support the theory that at least some of them were, in fact, slaves forced into battle. Men with only swords to pit against guns, to provide a distraction while Taliban soldiers brought RPGs and AKs into play. Our Intel has reason to believe most of these men were fighting for the safety of their families. Fearful of what the Taliban might do to their people had they refused.

We'll search these communities and show the locals we stand ready to do battle against the Taliban to defend them. Hopefully, in the process, gaining supporters who will provide us with information about real or suspected Taliban, Russian, and ISIS activity in this region. Our interpreters are returning tomorrow. They'll be a big help getting the local people on our side. If we show we're serious about helping them, we may gain some new friends. They're used to the Afghan Government making empty promises. At least one platoon will remain as a Rapid Response Force to respond to the security needs of these communities. Two Chinook Helicopters will be assigned here on standby to deliver a force in any direction, where and as needed. The Battalion's remaining men will stand ready as a backup force with the Apaches. This also means beefing up FOB security.

I'm hoping our unit will be relieved before winter hits, but the General wouldn't guarantee it. Be prepared to spend a cold winter in this beautiful vacation spot, Just in case, winter supplies and clothing will be provided before it gets cold—we hope. I'll have the wife send over the LL Bean winter catalog as soon as it comes out. I recommend your men contact wives, sisters, mothers, or girlfriends to start knitting dark green wool scarves, mittens, and wool socks and buy long underwear to help keep them warm.

We'll try to get men rotated back to Bagram for medical visits, supply runs for pogey bait, decent chow, and hot showers. The General promised extra chow to supplement our outstanding MRE cuisine. I mentioned having the chow hall make over a thousand PBJs, but the General didn't appreciate my sense of humor.

A rumor floating around Bagram Command mentioned the 82nd Airborne or another regiment possibly, I repeat possibly, relieving us and the 101st being moved to Iraq. Let me remind you, this was only a rumor among office personnel.

Rumors aside, I want armored units checked for ammo, parts, and supplies. Roman, you put that together, let me see it, and then call it in over the satellite phone. I'll need shopping lists for the men as well. Additional water wagons will be refilled from bladders carried out aboard a Chinook at least once a week—that's a standard seven-day week. So, advise the men to be stringent in the proper use of water in this fiery desert. I know I keep repeating it like a broken record, I don't want anyone passing out from dehydration.

In my upcoming meeting with our Company Commanders, we will be discussing actions if the Pakistan Army just happens to decide they want to make a war of it. They might want to annex the Khyber Pass and call it theirs for all I know. All options are being bandied about at Command. There is still speculation that this is only a ploy by other international forces who dislike us.

Lastly, I want all troops to be inspected every day. I do not want to see our troops walking around in shoddy-looking uniforms with torn socks or none at all. They can be in t-shirts for work details, but helmets and personal armor are to be worn at all times. We never know when an RPG or mortar round might drop in. All men will be clean-shaven unless they have a medic's written excuse that has been counter-signed by the Company Commander. I understand that some men cannot have a close shave due to skin conditions, but I want beards to be minimal and tightly groomed. We are the 101st Airborne, and I'm respectful of our proud history. No one will bring dishonor to our record, and if they attempt to do so, they will be very sorry. Many of us have worked hard to be part of the 101st Screaming Eagles.

Our recent Russian guest appears to be a real talker and no longer a strong supporter of President Putin. His information, which has been verified, is another factor regarding the formation of this Battalion. Supposedly, there are some allied prisoners up there with a few missing Americans.

Okay, that's about it. You now know what I know—this battalion is now on standby waiting for the go order and the arrival of A Company. Unless there are any questions, you are dismissed."

Later that afternoon, when Bill and the Chief returned to their foxhole, Roman waved and asked Bill to step over to the radio. "Captain, the 'go order' just came down, but they need you to call 'em back and confirm *you* have received it. I think whoever I was talking to at Division is under the impression that A Company is already here."

"All right, put me on the radio with them."

Sure enough, things had gotten a bit confused about A Company's location. Division knew that a third of the Battalion had yet to show up and was not due to arrive at Bill's encampment until the following morning. As a result, the 'go order' was delayed a day. Bill could only imagine how the senior officers at Division felt about this snafu and another delay. *But that's way above my grade—I just follow orders and say, 'yes, sir!*

"Sir, do you think the Taliban, or whoever has broken our security codes, is jamming things up?" Roman asked.

"With all those beautiful Eurasian women hanging around feed joints back at Bagram, and the ones wandering about the streets of Kabul, I can imagine some horny G.I. might succumb. Any secret can be compromised if enough money, alcohol, or favors is offered to the right man or woman. Or they're blackmailed into it. It's happened in every war since… since mankind began fighting wars. Before long, codes get broken, and new ones have to be created. It's a game, and we all play it. Intel operatives set up operations to ensnare a foreign agent or come up with the right price to turn. It's simply another part of waging war or preventing it."

Chief nodded, "Sometimes traitors are found out. In the old days, they were either executed, committed suicide, or died 'mysteriously' in some sort of training accident."

"Chief is right. During the first Iraq War, all four military services appeared to have a lot of training accidents. During our 10 years in Vietnam, a lot of secrets were sold, and they weren't always traitors or the victims of blackmail. Intelligence people arrested one North Vietnamese spy posing as a South Vietnamese officer. For 11 years, he worked in some highly placed intel jobs. When they took him away, he was working in Saigon's Command Center—really embarrassing! So, Roman, next time you check out that beautiful Eurasian or Indian gal with mixed blood and think she's some princess, remember this little chat." Bill patted his shoulder and added, "Live and learn, Sergeant."

"Right, thanks for that, Captain. But I'm a faithful husband who doesn't want to lose his family on some fling. I sure don't need to go home with an STD on my medical record, not to mention having to look into my wife's eyes and my children."

"Good man!" Bill declared.

MEETING TIME/ NEXT DAY

A Company arrived just after the sun vaulted over the mountains to pour blistering heat across the desert. The newly commissioned 4th Battalion Command foxhole hosted a meeting attended by Bill, Sam, Roman, the Chief, Company A's Captain Tyler, Captain Salsby, representing the Apache gunships, and Major Garnet, the Forward Air Controller. Major Garnet had been advised that he and his two people had been temporarily reassigned to the 4th Provisional Battalion to assist with the Apaches and Chinooks.

Bill requested the three company commanders and the chief pilot conduct their own briefing with their officers and senior enlisted personnel. Coffee was served by Bill's two runners and Roman, who managed to jot notes in his log at the same time.

"My first thought was to leave unit assignments to chance—tossing a coin in the air or drawing cards. But then I remembered I was a Battalion XO, though a very low-ranking one, and couldn't justify making critical decisions in such an ignorant way. After some thought I decided to base assignments on each company's experience, but know this, Gentlemen, each assignment can lead to victory and awards, or deaths and severely wounded troops. We need to stay alert and be ever watchful for booby traps or those oh-so-deadly IEDs. Never take this desert for granted or these people. A kind villager—man, woman, or child—could stab you or one of your men in the back. Advise your men to be careful, suspicious, but also friendly in dealing with villagers we encounter.

Saying all that, here it is, and, please, no complaints. We will rotate who goes into villages, which means you'll all have your chance to experience a shooting war. Since we arrived here, I can tell you that B and D companies have lost far too many good men and sent home a lot of wounded. This made us a bit shorthanded, so we are truly fortunate to have A Company join us. We are also lucky to have gunships and an experienced Forward Air Controller with us—Major Garnet and his two men."

Bill pointed to Captain Tyler, "A Company will get the first shot at the locals. You'll be taking a long hike up into the hills to the north side of this road to reach our nearest known village. I wish we had guides, but we don't. However, we do have maps." He smiled as he looked around. "You'll have the two Apaches for air cover and surveillance. Your senior RTO will need to spend a few minutes with Major Garnet and Captain Salsby to go over proper radio procedures. I'd like to assign you some armor, but they would never make it up into those hills, which is why the Apaches will be in the air. If they need to fuel or rearm, you will not be abandoned, they will be relieved by our other two craft. Fuel bladders should be delivered soon. A Company will leave here tomorrow morning at 0700 hours in order to reach the village by 1300 hours. Few of these villages have formal names so to simplify things, we'll just call this Village One for communication purposes.

Captain, since this is your first experience in Afghanistan, you'll need to ensure your men are changing socks daily and that your medics carry an ample supply of foot powder and ointment. Both companies have already experienced early signs of Trench Foot. Temperatures have reached as high as 135 degrees since our arrival. Feet sweat and, if not cared for properly, can disable a man. The medics can tell your people what to look for."

"Thank you, Captain. Most of my troops are on their first combat tour, and I can use any advice you can offer."

"What about your NCOs? Are they also new to Afghanistan?" Chief asked.

"I have several NCOs on their second and third deployments here."

"Good, you'll have some experienced men with you," Bill replied. "When you reach the village, there's a strong possibility that the people are either sympathetic to or under dire threat by the Taliban. We know that men have been taken from villages and forced to become fighters, usually through coercion or by threatening families. Your main goal is to prove to these villagers that we are the good guys here to protect them from the Taliban. Be on the alert and search the village for hidden weapons caches. Remind your troops—just because there are women present, those women can kill. Same for older kids. Treat the village as hostile, but do not harm anyone unless you have no choice. One of our interpreters will be with you to give you a hand with the language. Both of these men have aided the US for years and have earned my trust and that of previous commanders. I can show you on the map the safest route to this village. I want hourly radio checks while you are out. Watch for traps, and make sure your scouts watch for side trails and caves. We've already taken prisoners hiding in caves, both Russian and Iranian.

"Captain Tyler, among your men, do you have many Afghan or Iraq veterans?"

"Yes, Captain, I've got numerous combat veterans on their second and third tours over here."

"Good, rely on them; they'll know what to expect. How about your officers?"

"I have two platoon commanders with combat experience."

"Glad to hear that, Captain. It won't take you long to gain that experience. This is my third tour, but I've got men on their fourth and fifth tours, a real plus to have. Chief here, well, he's been around the block many times and all over this world. If you have any questions, he's a great one to talk with. This is one of the reasons he was recently promoted to Warrant Officer III."

"Thank you, Captain, sir. And congratulations Chief. Captain, can we speak later, between ourselves?" Captain Tyler asked.

"Sure, right after we break up here, Captain." *I wonder what that's all about?*

"Okay then, when you arrive at this first village, Captain, you're liable to run into a lot of angry women because I firmly believe this is where slaves were taken and forced to fight us. By now, the Taliban will have told them that we have killed their menfolk. Let your interpreter smooth the way for you. Watch the animals in the village. If there is anything afoul, these critters will react to it. They'll be jumpy; a donkey, camel, or sheep, and goats might try to bite you. I was bit by a goat on my first tour in Iraq. The animal hadn't been fed regularly due to insurgents using the village as a base of operations. The people were tense, and the animals felt it. Thankfully, I had some experienced men with me, and they sensed it watching the people and animals. We ended up taking half a dozen prisoners. There's no need to shoot animals unless your life is at risk. For each animal shot, I'll need a report stating who, why, where, and the owner's name, as we will need to compensate them for their loss. If one of your men kills for pleasure only, you will relieve him of his weapons and ammo and place him under arrest and he will be charged with Dereliction of Duty and Disobeying an Order. Make sure everyone understands that. We'll probably still have to pay for dead critters if it was life-threatening. The General is an animal lover, and he's the one who gave this order. It's a strange business, but you'll get used to it in a short time."

Bill took a deep swallow of sugarless black coffee, only to find it had cooled. He threw the rest out, laid his paper cup on a sandbag, and looked directly at the Chief. "B Company, Chief Johnson's new command. So you all know, this assignment came directly from Division, but I believe it to be for the best due to the Chief's experience. B Company will patrol the next five miles of ridgelines to the south side of the road. Chief, try to find a suitable encampment for tomorrow night. I'm not sure if there's a spot large enough inside the pass. If not, our FOB will remain here. At this stage, I would prefer to use our troops to recon, as I don't wish to lose a helicopter to some Stinger in the hands of a Taliban. You know what to expect, having been here for two months and all those other treasured visits you've made here in the past. Captain Tyler, the Chief, here, has been wandering this and other deserts for many years."

"Captain, thank you. Stingers are hard to avoid," Captain Salsby interjected.

"Remember, prisoners, are preferred over dead bodies, when possible. Be on the lookout for 'slaves' who were captured by the Taliban and forced to fight. Some villagers may be hiding in small groups or alone, afraid to return home. Chief, you will have support from one of the standby Apaches if the shit hits the fan. I want one of your squads to stay back and support the Bradley plow and protect it from being taken out by the Taliban. Pick your best man to lead that squad—you already know this. I feel like a student instructing the professor!" Bill checked his notes, "When on standby, the Apaches are to be ready to move out in the event of an emergency. Your Apaches can save the day.

Oh, I almost forgot. Captain Tyler, I'm assigning one of my EOD troops to your company. Try to keep him out of the scrape if you can, these men are highly trained and extremely valuable. You might consider assigning one of your men to accompany him as added protection. I want him with you in the event you find any IEDs or weapons caches. Let him inspect any cache for booby traps before entering. Sometimes, you simply have to recon by fire, we've seen times where a good EOD might have saved lives.

Sam—D Company—you will patrol the next five-mile stretch of hills on the north side of the road. Try to stay within 100 yards of that, it's easy to get lost, I know, I've done it. You'll be going well past the point where the demining has stopped temporarily, so do not attempt to cross after that point. As far as we know, this whole road is mined possibly all the way to the eastern end of the pass. Again, you are to make hourly security checks with Sergeant Roman. I'm told that these hills reach over 400 feet or better, and behind them, the mountains begin. You and your men are not mountain goats, watch your step, a good part of that ground has been disturbed, rocks and ground like that tend to be unstable. Look for caves, drop-offs, and as always, Taliban goodwill gifts—tripwires and IEDs. I'm not all that sure how long it will take us to search this pass —could be a week or more, and will, of course, depend on what sort of 'Welcome to the Khyber Pass' party we receive from the Taliban.

For the benefit of our new arrivals, there's a lot of speculation about rumors of the Pakistan Army planning to invade Afghanistan specifically through this pass. Anything is possible, but this unit will operate as if this is only a rumor. We've got drones, satellites, and aircraft up there watching 24 hours a day. If they do invade, the 101st will engage.

When we do complete the current project, I want you to ensure that not one of your troops makes a dash for the border just to say they were the first American soldier to cross the Pakistan Border. This happened a few times on the Korean Peninsula. Certain soldiers, including officers, crossed illegally into North Korea simply to say they did. Some were killed in the process. I do not wish for that to happen here. As far as I know, their side of the border could be mined. If some troop decides to be the first American into Pakistan, he will be charged and court-martialed for 'Disobeying a Lawful Order in Combat'—if he survives, and probably sent to Leavenworth for 20 to 30 years. Make sure you drill this into your men, and the same thing goes for the pilots. Those Apaches will not fly within a mile of that border because right now, there's a good chance people over there have ground-to-air missiles in the area in the event we've been lying to them. And just to add to your jitters, remember Pakistan has nukes."

Bill paused to check his notes and then addressed the group again, "Remind your men that heavy barrage on the hillside could have caused deep holes and fissures, collapsed old trails and caves, some deep enough to swallow a man or a squad. Watch for unstable cliffs, boulders, rocks, and slopes. Snakes and scorpions will be searching for new homes. No shooting across the road—you might hit a troop from A Company or one of our other units. If fired upon, report same immediately to Roman.

This leaves the armored units, which will move up slowly as we follow the plow tank. Make sure the crews remember we have friendlies up in those hills, on both sides of the road. No shooting unless fired upon, and only after the target has been identified as an enemy. The only exception is if a suicide bomber jumps out from behind a rock and tries to nail one of our vehicles.

Unless you have questions concerning the Battalion as a whole, you can check with me following this meeting. SFC Roman will now advise you of all new radio calls signs."

Roman read from his worn, dog-eared logbook. "Gentlemen, as you are aware, Eagle Base is headquarters right here where that big coffee pot sits. Lt. Colonel Rogers is designated as Eagle One—he's back at Bagram, and Captain Warrens is Eagle Two. Alpha Company is Eagle Three—Bravo Company, Eagle Four and D Company, Eagle Five. Reasonably easy to remember. Platoons will be given a 'Papa' designation, in other words. 1st platoon is Papa One, 2nd platoon is Papa Two, and so on, this can get complicated, so be patient with me. Squads will be identified in the same manner except that Sierra is used for squad and numbers one thru four. Oh, and the Heavy Weapons platoon will be Papa Four.

For example, 'This is Eagle Six, Papa Three, Sierra Two,' will be D Company, 3rd Platoon, 2nd Squad. Any questions so far?" There were none. "When possible, RTOs should go through their own companies, and the company RTO can talk with me so I can brief the captain. Emergencies will happen, I'll try to monitor as much traffic as I can. Codes should be used, but in an emergency, that's not always possible. Your company commanders have satellite phones; use them when the message is vital, and you don't want the neighbors to listen in.

While in the air, Captain Salsby and his Apaches will be 'Eagle Flight one through four, very simple. Bradleys are just going to be Bradley one thru eight. Same for the Strykers, one through ten. Humvees will simply go by Mobile one through—damn, I forgot how many Humvees we have out here! But I'll be handing out lists for everyone to give to your RTOs later today. The Bradley with the blade is designated Clunker One.

Oh, yeah, your assigned sniper teams will go by Deadeye one thru three for A Company, Deadeye four thru six for B Company, and Deadeye seven thru nine for D Company. Please let your shooters know these numbers are not based on skill level. I'm not out to belittle any of these fine men.

It is vital to keep two extra fully charged radio batteries with your RTO, and that's for each radio. They can see me about the battery issue before dark. This desert heat is rough on batteries. Are we all clear so far?" No one said anything, so Roman looked over at Bill and said, "Captain, I believe that's all I have."

"Thanks, Roman, you're doing a fine job, and pass that down to our runners. Okay, the last item on my list—yes, I'm trying to cut this meeting short, so you all have time to cook up a hot meal before 'lights out.' I wish to add something about our men's morale—at the moment,

Bravo and Delta Company are living on a high that can only come from being the victor of a really nasty firefight. The subject of souvenirs or keepsakes has come up a lot. I do not mind souvenir hunting in the field, as long as it is done safely. However, let your men know that I will not allow any automatic weapons to be shipped home. Intel needs to investigate every captured American-made automatic weapon, including pistols, to determine their origin. They will be turned over to the proper authorities. It's a way to stop black-market weapons from showing up here in the hands of the Taliban and other factions. Older rifles from World War I to foreign jobs, non-automatic can be kept, but paperwork still must be done to allow them to go home legally. As for enemy knives, swords, spears, and hatchet-style weapons, I can care less unless it is of some historical value. We recently obtained a sword that nearly killed one of my men that could be 200 to 300 years old and of some historical significance. We need to clear such finds through the Afghan government, but that's only for the fancy jobs. Most of these hand weapons are made from old auto parts."

Bill turned to Captain Tyler, "I'm not sure if you've read the report, but during one of our first engagements here, we were attacked with bow and arrows with Russian-made hand grenades strapped to the arrow shaft. An impressive sight. The Taliban are very resourceful. Sticks of dynamite can also be used, which they probably got from watching one of our old westerns." Captain Tyler shook his head in amazement as Bill continued, "Speaking of keepsakes—no one in my command will make prizes of scalps, eyeballs, penises, ears, gold and silver teeth taken off an enemy. Let your people know this is unacceptable in this battalion. I learn of a man taking such trophies his time in the military will come to an abrupt end." Bill sighed deeply, "Enough on this subject, this meeting is officially over. We will meet tomorrow at 0700 hours, right here and the coffee will be hot. If you have questions, this is the time, but I will be sitting down to enjoy the setting sun. I just noticed Pastor Taylor has again gotten a lift out here, so I believe he'll be holding service tonight and in the early morning hours. Check with him when you leave to ensure times. Hopefully, we will have a quiet night. That's it for now!"

Captain Tyler remained behind. "Thanks, I just wanted to clear the air between us. As you know, I'm about to put on a major's leaf; the

General was a bit concerned this would cause friction. It won't. I'm a babe in the woods here. I spent much of my time in Europe or back in the state's training; I need battle experience, and this is the only place to get it, so I transferred to the 101st and volunteered to come to Afghanistan. I want—need to learn from experienced men, such as yourself. I was concerned I might find myself leading a battalion in the 82nd, going up against Russian troops with no combat experience to base my decisions on. So that's why I'm here, Captain. I just wanted you to know. I remember you from the Point; there weren't many Medal of Honor offspring running through the academy. You played pretty good football in your sophomore year. I just wanted to say I feel fortunate to be placed under your command—that's all."

"Thank you, and I was glad to hear about your coming promotion to Major. If you have any questions, I'm always open, but my best advice is to watch the Chief. The man truly knows his business better than most. He's former Delta, wore the Green Beenie, and has more jumps than anyone I know. I'd say that if he always traveled with a passport, he'd be on his third book by now. He rarely talks about those assignments, but maybe someday he'll write a novel based on his life. Be worth reading."

The two men walked to A Company's area so Bill could meet some of the company's key figures. He recognized several men he'd seen back in the states or on past assignments to the Sandbox. When Bill finally got back to his own foxhole, he found Roman watching the stars in the sky. The Chief was with his new company, going over things with his platoon commanders.

11

THE MISSION IS A GO

THE LONG NIGHT went by without a shot being fired, a claymore triggered, or a word raised in alarm. In the dark, troops continued quietly preparing for the next morning's roll-out. Gear was checked and re-checked to ensure needed items were easily accessible and in sufficient quantity. Not necessarily new, but clean socks were put on. Medics met to trade supplies to ensure they had the items required to handle the wounded. With everything in order, the men waited for the order to move out. Some wrote letters under a rising sun, others ate breakfast, while a few lined up to have a chat with Chaplain Taylor. Nobody made snide remarks or repeated 'Holy Joe" jokes about the believers. In war zones, many young men draw closer to the Lord. Weapons were inspected, some platoon duties assigned, and gear loaded into vehicles.

It was the waiting that everyone hated, anxious to receive word to move out. With that one order, anxiety would transform into alertness, and for most of these men, fear would take a back seat. These were veterans, some who had fought in Iraq and Afghanistan and knew what lay ahead, and the new ones who had recently experienced their first firefights and understood what was expected of them in the days ahead.

MORNING MEETING

The sun was just over the mountain range when Captain Tyler of A Company appeared at Bill's foxhole and slipped onto a seat in the sand across from Bill. The sandbags that had surrounded the hole had been loaded atop a Bradley. The extra cover made the gunner happy, as he placed the sandbags in the best spots to protect the crew and soldiers inside.

"Good morning, Captain Tyler. Care for a cup of Sergeant Roman's camp coffee, guaranteed to pep you right up and possibly burn the lining of your mouth," Bill asked with a grin.

"Thank you, sir, but I'm coffeed out... Just wanted to report that A Company is ready to go. I have a few nervous young'uns and a couple sergeants on their first tour. As for me, I feel like I'm getting ready for my first date."

"We all felt that way, Captain, but it will pass quickly enough," Bill replied.

Others arrived as coffee service was completed, and Bill started his briefing. Most items had been discussed the night before in order to make the morning briefing short and sweet. After being assured that troops and equipment were battle-ready, Bill ended the meeting. "Any questions?"

Tyler spoke up first, "Captain, what if the cherry is blown off the sundae and my company is engaged by a major force of Taliban? Do we fall back to keep from destroying one of the villages and harming the friendlies, or do we light the place up with the help of our gunship support? And, how long before you'll be able to be on scene with assistance?"

"Good questions and I apologize for not bringing that issue up myself last night." Bill stood, glanced around at those crowded into the foxhole, and chose his words carefully as he addressed his leaders. He did not want it to sound as if the troops were expendable and unable to protect themselves nor did he want a blood bath on his hands. "If engaged by the enemy, your primary responsibility is first, the safety of your troops, and second, but no less vital, the protection of civilians. This especially goes for women and children. Maintain your position if at all possible; radio in what is happening. I'll be on my way as soon as I get your call for help. You'll already have Apaches flying air cover, so use your RTO to direct them; the Major will also monitor all ground-to-air traffic.

As I said before, there could be Taliban in this village, and you should go in expecting that. There will be those who are sympathetic to the Taliban cause. You'll find that these desert countries are more religious than what we are used to back home. We take a multi-religious culture for granted in the US—Christian, Jew, Buddhist, Catholic, Mormon, Jehovah's Witness, Ba Hai, Muslim. Here, it's overwhelmingly Muslim, and they're deadly serious about it. Back home, a person can mock your belief in God, and the worst that might happen is a whack to the jaw. But here, a person would likely be killed for mocking Allah. Make sure your new troops understand that. You might find an ISIS agent or a Taliban crew out recruiting. Our recent action and the deaths of their men is an excellent inducement for women and other family members to become involved in the Taliban cause.

"Remember, Taliban, ISIS, Russian or Iranian prisoners make our Intel people happy, which makes Command happy. I'm curious to see if there are any other Russians running about in these villages, so try not to shoot them unless you have no other choice. I'm really hoping it's only Russian advisors, as I'd hate to get into a shooting war with the Russian Army. All too quickly, it could go nuclear, and that would really upset my wife. If things go sour for you, make no mistake, we will be on our way." Suddenly he recalled the last item he had to acknowledge. For a moment, he felt overwhelmed. *As a Battalion XO, I've simply got to learn to write down as much as I can. I'm just too swamped to remember everything I did as a single company commander.*

"Gentlemen, keep your ears open for any words that don't sound like Afghan language. Janke will be with you to help interpret, and he speaks multiple languages. What we're looking for are Pakistani spies, illegal border-crossers, and identifying any Pakistani sympathizers. You might hear Iranian, Russian—possibly even Chinese. I'd have a hard time distinguishing an Afghan, Iranian, or Pakistani. Many have ancient family ties when the desert people here were separated by respective tribes. Just be careful—I don't want to fill any more body bags." He hesitated as he glanced around at the gathered men, "Questions?" No one moved, and Bill continued, "Remember, the Taliban are all true believers, fanatics fighting for Islam, against anything Christian or American. They despise the Afghan government for allying with America and our allies. They hate us, that's simple enough, and they're very crafty. They know how to fight in these remote rugged lands.

Religion aside, try to recall American History during our Revolution. The Taliban are the citizen volunteers, and we're the British—remember how that worked out for the Brits. We don't want to repeat their mistakes. But don't worry, we'll still make enough on our own. They've had nearly two decades to train their current army of fanatical warriors, and we helped train them early on to fight the Russians. We taught them how to be sneaky soldiers, trained by our own advisors, the Green Berets, and CIA. Makes me wonder if the Taliban might have forces across the border in Pakistan. Big desert out there to hide in, and we can't touch them." Bill gave them a few silent seconds, gazing into each of their eyes in hopes he's reached them with his insight. Bill was mainly concerned with the leaders from A Company. These officers were still an unknown factor.

The Heavy Weapons platoons will remain with me, in the event we're attacked, so you won't have to worry about lugging mortars up into those mountains. Bradley Clunker One will begin tearing up road shortly—got to be noisy work for the crew inside that plow—even with headsets on. However, the plow will stop when you and your men come within range to prevent accidental wounds from flying shrapnel. Just make sure no one goes any further on that roadway than Clunker One. You've all been provided new call signs; make sure your RTO keeps that list handy to hold confusion down to a minimum. If there are no additional questions, you may move out as soon as the order comes down from Command. But make sure you notify Roman when you do so he can log the time. And don't forget those hourly check-ins based on the moment you depart the perimeter. That way, not everyone is trying to check in at the same time. If we don't hear from you within fifteen minutes of that scheduled time, I'll send an Apache out looking for you. Oh, and make sure Roman has any last-minute mail that needs to go out. God Bless you, all."

Captain Tyler made eye contact and nodded at Bill before leaving the hole, but Chief smiled and moved over to place his right hand on Bill's shoulders. "You're doing great, Bill—don't fret over forgetting an item or two. I've seen three-star generals forget what they were talking about only seconds before. We're all under a lot of pressure here, there's a lot to take into consideration. Just slow down in that gray matter and take your time to go over what you know. You've got this. You're just anxious with the new title. Responsibility's the same, jobs the same, just a few more men and equipment to move around. Don't overthink and get lost in the fluff."

Bill nodded, "Thanks, Chief. Now you'd better get ready as I expect that order to move any minute. Be safe up on those hilltops—I can't afford to lose you to some slippery rock or a frightened snake."

"Yes, Captain, sir!" Chief said as he stepped over to Roman and slapped him on the side of the helmet. "You keep your ears open, Sergeant. I may be needing a medivac after climbing through all those hills. I believe I'm startin' to get a wee bit old for such antics."

"Not to worry, Chief. They'll find you a nice desk job when we go home."

"Like hell they will! More likely send me over to some training command, and I'll be dealing with brainless ex-civilians with big dreams of becoming heroes."

"That's us, Chief—certified Airborne heroes—you be careful, my friend."

"Thanks, back at you, Louis-Paul." Chief returned to B Company for one last inspection before they stepped off. Under a cloudless sky, the temperature was already reaching up to 100 degrees. It was nearing time to step off and once more enter the war. Eight minutes later, Roman advised all units that orders had come down from Command to move out.

THE HOT-SEAT OF COMMAND

By 1130 hours, Captain Bill Warrens was looking over his nearly empty camp. Four hours earlier, three companies of troops had set around in newly enlarged foxholes. Only the crews of heavy weapons platoons remained along with most of the armor. The two Apaches assigned to A Company had taken off to get an extended view of the surrounding area for any movement that might indicate the presence of unwanted company.

Men who had pulled security watch the night before had made valiant attempts to catch some sleep. Camouflaged tarps, braced up by whatever deadwood the men could find, covered the foxholes to provide some degree of shade and privacy. But with the afternoon sun, those areas quickly became saunas. Whatever was used, the order was to make the site look natural if seen from a distance.

However, nothing could be done about the loud rumbling made by the steel plow as it shoved and pushed dirt aside to expose live mines. Most of them exploded in a burst of fire and smoke when the heavily reinforced plow blade made contact. A shower of rocks, dirt, and lethal shrapnel shot out in all directions and rained down over the immediate area. A heavy protective screen, made from metal plates used primarily to make temporary runways and helicopter landing pads, rose one foot above the Bradley's roof to prevent falling debris from striking the vehicle. The driver and his spotter were well protected, with unique ear coverings under their steel helmets, but it was still a brain-jarring job.

The EOD Specialists stopped the plow every few minutes or so to disarm or dispose of unearthed mines that had failed to explode. There were a few stressful moments for the EOD men as they removed arming fuses and carried the mines to the side of the road to be recovered later and destroyed at a safe distance.

Bill was amazed at the number of mines that had been placed along the highway. They unearthed IEDs, Russian mines, and devices bought off foreign trade. Bill understood why this work needed to be done and probably repeated every now and then to ensure the road was safe to use. He had been told that most of the locals in these mountain villages moved across the open desert but would likely return to the road once it was repaired. He had also learned the locals had uncovered a few mines in the desert that dated back to World War Two, made by Britain, Germany, or Italy. It was impossible to know how many of those remained or how many innocent civilians had died or were maimed over the years since that war. Bill's provisional 4th Battalion was expected to complete demining work in the next eight to nine days. He only hoped the drivers of the plow beast lasted that long. By then they would certainly have earned commendations—it was a horrible job to be assigned.

An hour and a half later, while refilling his canteen at the water trailer and checking the water supply, he heard two of the Apache gunships as they scanned the terrain from above, the two birds piloted by Captain Andy Salsby and Lt. Andie Sharpe. *Apparently, it's pretty quiet out there, but Lord, for how long? Lord, protect my men, on the ground and in the air.*

WITH B COMPANY

Chief's knees felt the strain of climbing slopes, but he wouldn't let it slow him down. Many of the men in his company kept a close eye on him as they hiked the rocky hillsides, circling gaping holes and jumping across others, skirting boulders and slipping on loose rocks. He appreciated their concern, but he knew what he was capable of.

Snipers moved ahead, securing positions until the first patrol approached, then quickly moved forward to secure the next. Chief knew sending the sniper teams ahead as scouts might force a well-concealed enemy to reveal his position before the patrol walked into an ambush. If that happened, his whole company would move up to engage the enemy. As he moved through the rocks and climbed ever higher, he wondered how many different armies had been through these same hills over the last couple hundred years. *Soldiers, desert tribesmen, maybe even Alexander the Great and his vast Greek armies, and Roman legions may have climbed over these same hills. A lot of history in Khyber Pass.*

He stopped to look around and sent an order through the company's ranks to widen the space between men. This would make them tougher targets for any shooters. The three platoons were already separated by at least 20 yards and maintained a loose file as they headed east. He was proud to see how quietly his men moved. They knew they were in a hostile area and wanted all their senses on high alert. Some of the trails on the hill slopes seemed naturally formed while others had been deeply grooved by animals, local herders, villagers, and the elusive Taliban. Off in the distance, the chief spotted a couple of goats and suspected a herd might be nearby.

3rd Platoon's 4th Squad was assigned as tail-end Charlie to keep an eye on their back trail. Everyone was vigilant, no one wanted to be surprised by a Taliban or ISIS warrior sneaking up from the rear or leaping up from a crevice in the rocks or a well-camouflaged cave.

Knowing what was expected of him, Chief maintained a minimum distance of 15 yards behind the last man of 1st Platoon. He wanted to be ready to dash forward if summoned by a squad leader or MSgt John Hallsworth McCullough, 1st Platoon's acting Commander. So far, the two officers promised by the Colonel had failed to appear. Chief knew the longer McCullough remained in command and did a good job, the closer he came to gaining his next promotion. The previous night, Chief had worked out the line of march with his platoon leaders and knew Lt. Parker's platoon had only 17 soldiers. They'd taken some wounded the night of the camp attack, and replacements had not arrived in time for this morning's departure. *I sure got me a lot of new chicks out there, and I'm responsible for each and every one. I really hate writing those kinds of letters home; most of these boys I hardly know anything about. I'll have to work on my social skills, and listen to their concerns, worries, and feelings—I'd rather be leading a squad right now.*

Chief ordered 1st through 3rd Squads of 3rd Platoon, commanded by 2nd Lt. Dave Thomas Parker, to take a trail that ran parallel and a bit higher up the hillside. Parker was an ROTC Graduate on his first combat tour. Chief knew him to be another smiling Christian, which concerned him some, but he knew the man needed some time to either prove himself or fall flat on his face. The problem was how many young troops might end up dead or wounded in the learning process. At this stage, Chief's only option was to keep a close eye on him. *Training is fine, but instinct has to be learned. Often this learning process can be painful for the learner and the men they command.*

The three Squads, under Lt. Parker, were given the duty of watching the company's right or southeast side. Chief didn't want to be surprised by a sizable force of Taliban hitting his command from the mountainsides although he was sure the choppers would give him advance notice if they caught movement from their vantage point in the sky. Parker's men were a reasonable distance away, between 100 to 160 feet on the trail above. He didn't want too much separation as the trails veered back and forth but they also had snipers out in front as scouts.

Some of the stone faces were steep cliff sides rising from 20 to 50 feet high, with rocks broken and loosened by the bombing. Sharp, jagged rocks not only lay underfoot but projected from the cliff face itself. Large boulders with sharp jagged edges blocked the path in places and had to be carefully maneuvered around because they could not be climbed over. The downhill ground in front of some was soft and unsteady in places and extra care had to be taken to make sure the boulder did not displace. He sent back a reminder to the men to remain thoughtful of their surroundings, where they placed their hands and feet, but it also slowed them down as they moved across the rugged and formidable terrain. They were surrounded by damage the F-15s had done with their bombing and the men were grateful they had not been up here then. Chief began to wonder why the General hadn't requested the big bombers. He knew Bagram had suitable runways to bring in the B-52s and B-1s and even the B-2s, but he doubted that they would let the B-2 land here as much of the plane was still classified and highly regarded as a potential target.

B Company was well past the demining operation, though they could still hear the explosions in the distance. The soldiers knew the road below was highly dangerous and avoided it. The latest obstacle B Company faced was the growing height of these massive stone hills. They would come across a trail here and there, but the bombing had obliterated most of them. They found a few holes, which might have been air-holes to a Taliban hideout, but there was no evidence of an entrance to an underground cave big enough to serve as a shelter. The holes could just as easily have been used by snakes, spiders, and scorpions. If the hole was big enough to merit attention, the answer was to drop a grenade into it and quickly take cover. It was doubtful anyone could have survived the severe bombing concussions in any underground shelters close to the surface. Without heavy equipment, there was no way to reach survivors in deeper caverns.

Chief advised his men, "Chances are any Taliban up here in caves would be dead from the concussion waves those bombs caused. But we'll waste a couple grenades just to make sure."

B Company would find a spot to shelter for the night, eat cold chow and be on 50-50 alert watch until midnight and 100% alert status until dawn. Chief and the platoon commanders would move about some, but Chief advised the squad leaders to remain with their men. Sniper positions would also be set up to protect the company on three sides, with Remmel's team holding the high ground. 3rd Platoon's 4th squad was stuck with the 'sweeper' position sometimes referred to as the rear guard. If B Company came under fire and was forced to retreat, 4th Squad would hold their position and remain in place until the rest of B Company fell back. It was up to nine soldiers to keep the enemy off their buddy's retreat. They could not fall back until everyone had passed them. When Chief wrote up his plan for Bill to look over, both knew retreat would only occur if the Pakistan Army invaded, or they had come across a considerable force of Taliban.

Bill had reminded him, "Let's say this invasion does occur—our Bradleys on the highway would come into play once B and A Company are out of harm's way. We'd also have our Apache gunships, and before long, Bagram's Air Force and Marine fighters would be overhead and add F-14s and F-18s off the carriers—I doubt there would be anything left of a Pakistani tank brigade—unless the Russian Air Force entered into it— but by then, we'd probably all be looking at World War III."

"That might be something to see, Bill. All those fighters screaming in to strafe and bomb Pakistani tanks and their infantry. Be like when Patton stood off the German Army in North Africa. Lots of explosions and burning tanks. I think the whole thing is some kind of con job, and we're out here just to show the colors. You don't think those Pakistani generals would march their troops in front of their armor, do ya? The Germans did that in WWII to set off landmines and save their precious tanks. Saw it in that movie, "Battle of the Bulge" at the Cinerama Dome in Los Angeles—one of those curved screens. Great movie!"

"Chief, in my time fighting Muslim fanatics, I haven't come to understand how their minds work. Nor have I come to understand their faith. I know many great Muslim Americans, I've served beside them, and now I lead a few. But the fanatics—nope. I've only met a couple Pakistani officers who were guests at social events in Iraq and they were really arrogant and pompous. I suppose it could have been a shield to hide their fear of being surrounded by so many allied troops. India is really concerned with Pakistan, especially since they both have nukes. Just about everyone has them these days. Maybe we'll wake up one morning and the whole world will just blow up in one giant flash."

"I thought you were a Bible believer."

"Oh, I am, Chief, but the Book of Revelation doesn't have any set dates in it. When it calls for that Heavenly trumpet to blow, it could be thousands of years from now—or it could be tomorrow. I guess that's what having faith means, leaving it to the man upstairs to know the right moment. Glad it's not in my hands; I probably would've given up on this whole human race a long time ago. We just keep making the same mistakes, only now with a bit more technology behind us."

BACK TO THE ROCKS

The sun was sinking toward the horizon, its fiery colors exploding outward across the sky at the same time the squad leaders were ordering their men into night positions. Listening Posts were established, sniper positions manned, and squad leaders checked food and water supplies. It was hoped the men would still have one half-full canteen on their belts and two full ones in their packs, but there were always a couple of new guys who would drink too much too fast. One of the new men in B Company had used up one entire canteen during the long hike. His NCO did not mince words over the issue, "You just remember, Soldier, when you use up all your water, the others will not be sharing theirs. But I will give you a shovel to dig deep, in hopes you might strike a spring to replenish your supply. Legends speak of a large river running underneath us, who knows, you might punch through to one. So, go easy on that water, or I'll take your canteens away and only give you a sip during our breaks, got it!?"

Chief wondered how the men of A Company were doing. *Coming from Germany and into this blast furnace without time to climatize, gotta be tough on some of them.*

On the north side of Khyber Pass, Sam's D Company remained in place. They formed a tighter circle since the other two companies entered the pass. Though well protected by the armor, Sam had set up four two-man listening posts to cover the four directions. Tonight, he shared Bill's fox hole; tomorrow morning they would move up to whatever position the Chief had found for them. Both Sam and Bill were hoping for another quiet night, but they went to a 100% alert status at midnight as caution dictated.

The road crew stopped with the coming of nightfall and returned to D Company's position. A single squad remained within visual range to keep an eye out for any Taliban returning to set up new IEDs in the cleared roadway. If a firefight developed, Bill would send the Bradley up to reinforce them, supported by a platoon from D Company.

A Company had stopped moving forward when the sun hit the horizon and from their vantage point could clearly see the village and the locals moving about. The two Apaches avoided flying over the village so as to not alarm the locals or warn any Taliban in attendance. Captain Tyler thought about entering the village after midnight, rousting the locals out of bed and searching for the enemy, but Bill had shot that idea down. He ordered Captain Tyler to wait for morning.

Over the radio, Bill's voice advised Tyler, "I'll not send those Apache's up at night; it makes them too easy a target, and it's hard for the pilots to distinguish between the enemy and the good guys. I don't want to alienate the villagers, if at all possible, by frightening everyone. This is their home, and the Taliban and the Afghan Army have already used scare tactics. Your men have had a long hike. So, set up your security positions and get some rest. In the morning, you can move in once you see the locals moving about, and you'll have air cover. Secure your position, and if it hits the fan, help will be on the way."

The two Apaches were back at the FOB, and the aircrews were resting from a very long day of flying. One Apache was kept on standby for emergencies, and the rest of the crews were close by if needed.

Roman kept most of his radios working with the three companies on different frequencies or coded. He wished he had six arms or three more RTOs to assist him. At least with B and D Company bedded down for the night, he could use one of his runners to help monitor A Company.

At 2310 hours, the message Bill didn't want to hear came over the radio, "Sir, it sounds like Alpha Company—Eagle Four has uninvited company. They're calling for immediate assistance."

Captain Warrens sent runners across the FOB with the news. "Get D Company's 1st Platoon moving out to proceed in their direction. Advise 1st Platoon's Strykers to get ready to move out as soon as they're loaded. Send Bradleys three and four with them as fire support. Those vehicles won't be able to go any farther than where A Company started climbing that trail. Send the squads assigned to those Bradleys along to guard vehicles. Remind crews they are to maintain 100% alert. Remind gunners and troops to be alert to friendlies retreating down the trail, both our guys and fleeing villagers. No shooting unless they can identify the target as being unfriendly.

He yelled to Roman, "Send runners out to notify all vehicles to stand ready for a possible attack! The Taliban may try to attack us here while others engage A Company at the village. Advise B Company what's happening with A Company. They've probably heard the shooting, I'm not too sure about the distance between them. Mountains tend to distort and interfere with sounds. When you have them on the line, advise the Chief he is not to cross that road to assist A Company; we'd probably lose too many men to mines. They're to maintain position until told otherwise—you got all that, Roman?" Bill wanted to respond to the fray, but as the Battalion XO, he was forced to remain at base camp and handle everything over the radios. Briefly, he wondered how Captain Tyler, on his first combat assignment, might be handling this situation. Bill was beginning to understand why so many senior officers have gray hair before they turned 50.

1st Lt. Sam Rayson stood ready, advising his men to stay alert as he moved from one position to the next. The Chief was doing the same thing with B Company. He had heard several shots in the distance. The mountains made it difficult to monitor the events that A Company was caught up in. Chief had to agree with Bill; moving down this mountain and attempting to cross that uncleared roadway was suicidal.

Officially, the first shot was fired at 2258 hours, and it only took 12 minutes for Captain Tyler to realize he would need help to drive the ferrets out of the village. Gunfire erupted from over two-thirds of the structures, which were not much more than stone or mud huts.

"Eagle Two, we're taking heavy fire from Village One. We are not, I repeat, we are not withdrawing, our position is secure. We cannot move on the enemy until morning. Estimate enemy strength at twenty to thirty shooters. With civilians present, I've ordered my men not to return fire unless they see someone with a rifle in their hands. Recommend we hold here until daylight at which time I will engage with Apache assistance. Over."

"This is Eagle Two; I copy and agree. The birds will take flight at first light. I will advise when airborne. D Company has a platoon standing by where you left the roadway. At daylight, they will proceed to your location to assist. Over."

After Tyler confirmed Bill's orders, Bill contacted D Company's platoon and gave them orders to move up to join Tyler at first light. "Soon as you can see the trail, start moving up to join Eagle Three." After signing off Bill contacted the Chief. "Eagle Two to Eagle Four, what's your status?"

"Eagle Four to Eagle Two, on 100% alert, but so far, all quiet our end... Over."

"Copy, Eagle Four, stand by for a phone call. Out!" Bill took the satellite phone from Roman and called Chief's phone. "B Company," Chief answered. "What'd Tyler walk into?"

"Sounds like Village One might be a Taliban stronghold. He estimates twenty to thirty shooters firing from huts. They had to have seen A Company moving around. Not too sure why they opened up. They could've waited until A Company entered the village and then ambushed them, using villagers as cover. I'm sending a platoon from D Company up to reinforce A Company. They'll move in as soon as we have those Apaches flying cover and taking a look-see. I'm just hoping those Taliban don't have any stingers. The aircrews are trained for such things and how to approach a ground target. I'm only concerned about a lot of civilian casualties if we go in too hard and too fast."

"That's why you get all that big money, to carry this kind of responsibility and make those big decisions. It could be a bunch of older boys with their daddy's AK-47s—and that's why they remained in those houses—lack of training. We'll know for sure come morning. If they are

Taliban, they may have fired a few magazines to get Tyler to hold off attacking, to cover a back door exit and head for the hills."

"We'll know come morning. Contact me if you get any movement in your area. Oh, did you come across anything wide enough for our battalion?"

"No, not a thing. Appears we might have to keep the FOB where it is, at least until we find something deeper in the pass. But after looking around up here, I doubt we will."

"Hope you have a quiet night, signing off." Bill hung up and handed the phone to Roman. "Anything more from Tyler or D Company's platoon."

"Negative, sir." Roman was logging down the items discussed in the battalion logbook. The information in these logbooks would later be transferred into a report placed into the files for historical reference of actions taken during this tour. Particular facts were recorded in the Division's historical records.

A Company had positioned themselves behind a hill made up of massive boulders. The village had gone silent, and Tyler was concerned the Taliban might be escaping to the east of the village, he had no idea what the area looked like. He agreed with Bill; they would have to wait for daylight, and then with the Apaches on site, they might be able to see where the enemy had gone. Three men had been wounded, but the medics advised him they were not critical.

Bill had never been into this village before and Intel on the villages in this pass was very limited. He could imagine the place was nothing more than a hamlet of maybe 200 people, with herds of goats or sheep, now scattered by weapons fire.

Taking the satellite phone back from Roman, Bill contacted Tyler, "What's your situation, Captain?"

"No more shots but we've seen a lot of movement on our side of the village with infra-red. No light and no fires. It appears civilians are fleeing to take refuge in some rocks just east of the village. I suspect the Taliban have fled to the north. Looks like civilians want to be out of the way when we decide to move up and hit their homes. Probably concerned, we might shoot them all, believing them to be the enemy. At least that's what might be going through my head if I was one of them."

Tyler's RTO addressed him quietly, "Captain, I just heard from our 3rd Platoon; they're the closest unit to the village. They estimate 50 to 60 women and children, maybe 200 yards from the south end of the village, hiding in a dry wash. He believes the village is empty of innocents and wants permission to bring heavy fire down on those structures."

"That's negative—*no* cowboy actions. Unless fired upon, we are under orders to hold until daylight. I am not going to shoot up these people's homes if the enemy has abandoned this position and fled. Advise him to keep an eye on those civilians and report any movement by them or anyone else moving around in that village."

"Yes, sir." The RTO radioed the message to 3rd Platoon.

"I've got a young and spirited Texas boy with a gold lieutenant's bar who wants to play John Wayne. He'll learn. Admittedly, I thought we were about to get our butts kicked when those AK-47s opened up. Scary, I can see why it takes time to learn this stuff. No book or professor can make it real for you until those bullets go zinging over your head. And this is your third tour, Bill? I'm only hoping I survive my first patrol. Do you ever get used to it?"

Bill was amazed by how honest Tyler was being with him, which boosted his approval rating for the man. He could see why Tyler was about to be promoted to Major. "I can't say you'll ever get used to it, but eventually, you take it all in stride. Now you begin to understand why we have so many soldiers with PTSD problems. After a year of this, you either turn to religion, booze, or you get a little bit unhinged. The first person who says they enjoy this stuff is the one ready for the rubber room. As soon as D Company's platoon makes it to your location in the morning, move into that village. The birds will be in the air to cover your advance. I'm thinking like you, if everything is quiet, it's only because the Taliban fled through the back door. Be careful of traps when you recon the town; they love their IEDs. I'll check back in with you at 0630 hours, but make sure your RTO keeps up with his security checks, so we know you're all right."

"Thanks, Bill. Talk to you in the morning." Both men hung up, and Bill tossed his phone to Roman.

Tyler checked on his men and low crawled over to the medics working on the wounded men. The adrenaline was wearing off, and he had a minor case of the shakes. He called his platoon leaders in for a quick meeting to advise them what would be occurring come morning. He also let them know additional support was on the way. "We have another platoon moving up to support us, so make sure our back door knows that company is coming. Just make sure they're friendly, as we still have Taliban out and about."

After the briefing, Captain Tyler found the interpreter Janke, "I'd like to send you down the hill a ways with a patrol to see if you can get within range of those women and children. We need them to stay in place until we feel it is safe to return to the village. Can you do that for me?"

Janke clutched the pistol given to him by Bill for this patrol, he thought about it for a moment, "I'll tell them, but they might think it's some sort of trick. These people have been lied to by both sides, and now they worry for their men folk. But, yes, I will go."

"Good man. Thank you. I'll have the squad leader come get you when he's ready to move out."

When Janke was able to get close to the civilians, he called out to them, and at first, no one replied. Janke identified himself and told them he was with a force of Americans. He gave them instructions for remaining out of danger when the sun came up. Janke knew how frightened these people were, especially the children. If the information they had was correct, several of these women had recently been made widows by the recent Taliban attack on these same American soldiers. Since becoming an interpreter and being among these people, Janke believed the children were formed into a tight bunch encircled by heavily clothed older women, all armed with knives to protect them.

Finally, after trying different languages, a woman replied, calling out to him in Pakistani. Janke was surprised, he had believed these people were probably Afghan or Kurdish. Many Kurds had fled Iran and Syria after those countries began killing the Kurdish people in large numbers. Janke advised the women to remain undercover and not move until he contacted them in the morning. He learned that none of them were injured or armed with weapons. Though Janke knew the women would likely possess knives, she was talking about firearms. He reported back to Tyler with the information he had obtained.

Tyler contacted Bill on the sat phone and relayed the new information, "Bill, according to Janke, these people may all be Pakistani. So, what happened to the Afghan people who lived here, and who were the shooters? Are they Taliban or Pakistani troops who filtered in here to secure the pass? Possibly working with the Taliban?"

"I don't know, but I'll pass that info on to Command and advise them we'll have more information after you've secured the village. It could prove to be real interesting, so use caution when you move in. Gather as much Intel as possible. Once the village is secure, send Janke in to get some numbers on how many are Pakistani and who else might be there. Maintain tight security as those shooters might try to return to keep us from learning more. When you can, take a look around for mass graves. According to my information, that village has been there for some time. If Pakistani people have moved in, we might find a lot of dead Afghans."

The four Apache gunships took to the air at daybreak and flew over the mountain tops, all four loaded for bear. They had been advised of civilians to the south and to avoid them at all cost. Tyler kept one squad 100 yards to the west of their position with orders to keep an eye out for anyone attempting to reach the non-combatants. The squad's RTO was under orders to report any movement in the area so Tyler could alert the Apaches. The aircrews were also keeping an eye out for any activity in the hills beyond the town.

When the four birds flew over the village, they were not fired upon, and Tyler's troops began to move in. A Company, with the platoon from D Company, moved into the village from three sides. The village was deserted; two squads moved to where the women and children hid and escorted them back into the village. All the knives had been taken from the women, and kids were searched to ensure they were not being used to hide weapons. No firearms were found. Within the hour, the women and children returned to what was left of their homes. Janke spoke to them and what he learned shocked him, he passed the news to Captain Tyler.

Tyler was astounded to learn that these villagers were actually new to the area. Several months before, the Taliban had arrived and murdered everyone in the village, then moved in their own families hoping to look like an ordinary Afghan mountain village and not a

Taliban stronghold. The murdered Afghans had been buried during one long night of nightmarish events. When the mass grave was found, it was estimated that more than 200 people had lost their lives at the hands of a joint force of ISIS, Taliban, and their sympathizers. Three of the women Janke spoke with, advised them there had been Russian and Pakistani military officers among the men. Six Pakistani women were brought here by their husbands, who were reportedly Pakistani traders. These women would later be turned over to the Afghan government after US Military Intel finished talking with them about their husbands' activities.

"According to these women," Janke advised Captain Tyler, "the Pakistani traders went back across the border to obtain additional goods. I do not believe them; I think their men probably fled with the Taliban last night. ISIS and Taliban fighters wanted this town to resemble an Afghan township but were using it to store munitions and weapons for resupplying the men in the upper mountains to the north."

A large cache of weapons was located underneath one of the homes, including two large metal containers which held U.S. issue shoulder-fired Stinger Missiles. This was a significant find, but unfortunately, the Taliban had escaped.

Tyler learned of others who had been killed after coming to the village to visit their families. The Taliban did not want to risk anyone reporting missing people from this village to the Afghan authorities. These visitors were buried in unmarked graves, the exact number of those killed would never be known. But one older woman advised Janke that there had been between twenty and thirty people.

Janke added, "Since we have no report of missing government officials, I believe there haven't been any Afghan officials to this place for the last several months. This is unusual as tax collectors come around more often than that. Unless the official has been bribed to stay away. Or maybe the official got wind of the atrocity and simply stayed away It's also possible that an official was a Taliban plant, an old story in Third World Nations."

Although Janke had been doing this for some time, he was still shocked by what he learned. He suspected the Afghan Army would soon arrive to remove all the women and children and hold them for a lengthy period. Janke advised Tyler that this village would be considered cursed by the Afghan people. According to the old ways, it would be left to vanish under the desert's hot sun and Afghanistan's cold winters.

Tyler handed Janke his canteen and told him to drink, and then he was given new orders. "Janke, go back and tell them that except for the Pakistani women, we will be leaving the rest of them here, to be contacted by their Afghan government. The Afghan government may have this village bombed within the week because it was used by the Taliban, and all the people murdered here. They might wish to move along and find another village. I've been told to leave any food and water we can spare. There are also numerous goats and sheep. Command will notify the Afghan government of what transpired here and leave what comes to our allies.

Munitions and weapons found would be destroyed, other than the Stingers. Tyler's men would have to lug those down the mountain to turn over to Command. Unfortunately, the Apache gunships were not equipped to carry such items. American goods found in the homes, other than food or medical supplies, were to be itemized, photographed, and destroyed.

Tyler got on the sat phone and advised Bill of everything they had learned. "Good job, Captain. Your men deserve a lot of credit for this, but it is unfortunate about the former villagers. Give the men a pat on the back for me, let them get some rest, but maintain your vigilance as those Taliban are still out there. I'll keep two of the Apaches on standby here and have the other two make a wide search for the missing Taliban. I want those birds back here before nightfall. Tomorrow at daybreak, proceed to your next objective. You'll have air cover; according to my map, the next village should be reached before sunset. With what happened last night, they know you're coming. So be prepared for ambushes and especially for boobytraps. Contact me if anything else comes up and continue the security checks. Good job!"

"Thanks for the break—my guys and I can use it." They both hung up.

An older squad leader stopped by Captain Tyler and remarked, "Funny, I've been examining this place, thinking I'd seen it before. It came to me that this place sort of resembles a bit of Old Tucson back when they made most of the structures out of dried mud and whatever wood they could scrounge—Pre-Civil War—and not much more than a stopover in mid-1800s Arizona. I watched a black and white movie where they built a replica of the old adobe communities. Now, here it is, in the 21st Century. Sort of weird, sir."

"People do what they do to survive and are forced to use what they can. I doubt these people see more than thirty dollars a year, or whatever they call their money over here. Mostly barter and trade—like that Old West you spoke of."

Tyler held a platoon leader's briefing to advise them to dig in, they would depart for their next village at daybreak. "Get your men fed, check water supply, and hands off the goats and sheep. They belong to these people and advise them to avoid any fraternization with these civilians. They've been through the worst night of their life, and they're related to the Taliban, or members themselves. I'm not too sure about female Taliban the way their religion is. Just don't take any chances. I once read that female VC were worse than the males, and Buddhists are supposed to be non-violent. Remember, vengeance is a big thing over here, and I don't want to lose a man because he tried to sweet talk some woman or play ball with one of those kids—so, hands off! We've already removed knives from those ladies and a couple of the older boys.

All right, return to your men. We're on a 50-50 alert until 2200 hours, then we go on full alert. And remind your men that there are still Taliban in those hills to our north. I want security posts and sniper teams out there before anyone takes a break. That's it, you know your jobs, pass it down. The men did a fine job, especially for our first engagement."

Janke approached Tyler, "Tell me, sir, have you known many Muslims back in America?"

Tyler grinned in response, "I've got a couple Muslims in my company, and our three companies have probably a dozen or more who hold with that belief. We also have Jews, Christians and people of other faiths, and some atheists. Our problem is with the fanatics. If you know your history, it was much the same way back during the Crusades. Many European and British Crusaders behaved as fanatics back then, slaughtering Muslims or anyone who didn't profess to be a Christian. History continues to repeat itself. Only now the wars are much larger and the technology more frightening. Why do you ask?"

"Curious, I've been working with you Americans for some time, heard of your different religions, and how you get along so well is confusing to me."

"Oh, I agree, but our U.S. Constitution allows for the freedom of religion, and we've kept that policy for over 200 years. But, we still have our squabbles."

Roman gave Bill the current status report, and with his approval, sent it to Command and Lt. Colonel Rogers. After reviewing it, Rogers passed the information to the Colonel, who would brief the General. All three senior officers were interested in the report of Russian, Pakistani, and ISIS influence in this area. They were both saddened and enraged to hear about the villagers having been wiped out by Taliban invaders. The Colonel ordered vehicles to transport the Pakistani women to Bagram. Intel desired further information, and these civilians could serve as a potential source if handled correctly.

Bill received orders, which he sent on to Tyler, to have Company D's platoon escort the women to the road, where they would be picked up and returned to Bagram. When Janke advised the women of this, it frightened them. Janke assured them this was for their safety and well-being, but only two of the women believed him.

Once the women were interviewed by Intel, a senior intelligence officer reported their findings to the General. "Sir, based on what we've learned so far, it would seem that ISIS recruiters are assisting the Taliban and recruiting additional operatives. It appears that the Pakistani Intelligence Force is also involved out of fear we or the Afghan military might be planning to attack them. It's their belief that the Americans would support them. I suspect three of these ladies work for or with Pakistani Intelligence. There is some indication that the Russians may have been feeding this suspicion to increase weapon sales to the Pakistan Government, and quite possibly, the Chinese, for the same reason. We know that China sells nukes to Pakistan, who fears India might invade. As it stands right now, Pakistan is surrounded by unfriendly nations, and they are extremely fearful."

"Type it up and send it to your people in Washington, let them hash it out," the General ordered. He knew it came with the job, he never trusted Intel operatives, even his own. But he kept that to himself, as he was considered a politician because of his stars. *That's the one thing they don't prepare you for at West Point—learning how to be a politician. Some never grasp it, and others go on to become an ambassador or Secretary of Defense. As for me, I'd rather be out playing golf!*

JIMMY OLSON RETURNS

"Jimmy, you're back!" Bill was delighted to see his friend and quickly shook hands with him.

"Good to see you too, Captain! I hitched a ride out in one of the supply birds. Roman's been filling me in on what's happened with the unit since I left. Seems I've missed a lot of the action."

Bill grinned, "You up to handling the radio again? Now that we're a real battalion, I could use both of you."

"Yes, sir—if that's where you want me, then that's fine, sir."

"Well, you'll work for Roman, but I need to move you around, too, get you some command experience. So, we'll play it by ear for now—you may find yourself leading a squad, it'll look good on your record. Okay?"

"Sounds good to me, Captain. Give me another opportunity to see how the other half lives. Fine food, best of drinks, and all the charming women. My kind of war."

"Jimmy, you spent too much time back in the states. Go get settled, which won't take long out here, then relieve Roman so he can get some shut-eye. He's been on the radio all night and looks like he's about to pass out from fatigue. He's an old man, after all."

"Hey, I heard that!" Roman said raising his voice, but he was smiling.

"Any radio traffic right now, sir?" Jimmy asked.

"I'll have some priority messages for you in a minute," Bill said.

He turned to Roman, "Give me the latest on B and D Companies." Bill sat down on the edge of the fox hole, pulled out his full canteen, and took a long swig of warm water. He pulled the empty one off his belt, removed two empty ones from his field pack, and glanced at one of the PFC runners. "Could I get you to fill these up for me? I prefer them without spit, please do not pee in them and I really hate the bottom of my canteen filled with sand... Okay?"

The PFC took the canteens, "Yes, sir, I got it." The young man was off on a casual jog making his way around scattered foxholes, to reach the line of men waiting at the water wagon. A Staff Sergeant supervised the filling of canteens to prevent a childish water fight from breaking out, it had happened before. But these men had learned how valuable every drop of water was in this vast desert, and they made sure every drop made it into the canteens. During his first tour, Bill had watched as company punishment was dished out for a fight over some stupid issue. A squad's water cooler was knocked over during the fight, spilling the life-giving fluid into the dry desert sand. The captain had kept the four men from having any water for 18 hours. While the temperature was in the high 90s, the men's throats dried and began to swell slightly from lack of moisture. They reportedly pleaded for drinks from buddies, even offering to pay, but the sergeant made sure no one gave them a single sip. The captain responsible for the four hooligans had kept a medic on standby. The Doc had told him that though it might get uncomfortable, 18 hours without water would not cause harm. But they did learn from it. Bill told this story to his men and prayed it soaked in.

Bill reviewed his radio messages from Post Supply and the mechanic shop. The parts he needed for a broken-down Stryker had arrived. Extra coffee and field meals had been delivered. A case of new canteens had been misplaced—probably given to another unit. By the time he finished, the runner had returned with his full canteens.

"You want me to put them anywhere, Captain?"

Bill looked up, his hands full of paper messages Jimmy had handed him, recognized his PFC, and grinned. "Thanks for doing that. Give me one, and you can put the other two inside my field pack... It's right over... that rough looking one." Finishing a review of the messages, Bill said to Jimmy, "Eagle One—that's Lt. Colonel Rogers, our Battalion Commander back at Bagram—wants a count of how many structures were in that village and the number of animals killed. It's all in the logbook. And take a moment to try to memorize all our new call signs. We've added some since you went on vacation."

"Sir, if I may, you might want to grab a few winks of shut-eye. Not wanting to sound disrespectful, Captain, but you're looking pretty dragged out, sir."

"Maybe you're right. But Jimmy, wake me up in two hours, and only two hours, you got that? Unless, of course, an emergency pops up. Remind Lt. Rayson his two platoons remain on standby for those two companies we still have out there in the rocks."

"I hear and will obey, ol' gracious leader."

"Hey, you forgot to give me an update on those other two companies. Man, I must be tired." He gave Jimmy a thumbs up. "Give it up, Jimmy," Bill gestured with both hands.

"I'm sorry, sir, but when I sent Roman off to lullaby land, he hadn't passed anything else on, and I'll have to review the log."

"Then check the log. You should have done that when you relieved him.

"Sir—I do apologize."

"I'll cut you some slack this time, Jimmy, but open the log and review what's come in from Alpha and Bravo Companies."

"Yes, sir."

"Read, so I can go to sleep knowing my men haven't been either killed off by the Taliban or carried away by some ravishing Amazons in search of mates."

"I bet your kids love your imagination, sir," SSgt Stoneville said as he dropped into the foxhole. When Bill was on his first tour in Iraq, he had been a young PFC and had recently become the Assistant Platoon Commander for B Company, 2nd Platoon.

"I wondered where you were, Steve. I heard a swollen ankle kept you from going out with the Chief, but you look fine now."

"You forgot, sir, this ankle always swells up in this blasted desert. But this is where the war is, and I'm not going to let some genetic ailment keep me from coming over here. Don't forget that swell overseas pay and the new combat pay we've been promised. It keeps my kids in chocolate, and that makes things easier on my wife. While the Chief is out there, I'm pulling night-guard."

"How'd you ever get that ankle past the doctors?" Bill asked.

Steve, who suddenly looked somewhat devious, replied, "Physicals are always done stateside, and it's this country's high humidity, mixed with this damned infernal heat, that produces the swelling. Oh, don't get me wrong, sir, I'm not an idiot. If we were ordered to make a jump, I'd have said something. I'm not about to be crippled for life over this one swollen ankle. By the time I'm in my fifties, I'll probably have arthritis."

"Well, until that swelling goes down, Steve, you're assigned to my little headquarters branch as a rifleman. Keep the bad guys from getting to my people here."

"Wherever you want me, sir—just please, let me finish out this third tour. I'll not let you down."

"You never have, Steve." Bill punched him in the left shoulder and waited for Jimmy's update. It came after Bill sat down to relax with a steaming cup of black coffee.

"I often wonder how, in this unbearable heat, a cup of scalding coffee can still taste so good? Oh, you can go ahead, Jimmy, I'm listening."

"Captain, B Company reached their destination without enemy contact and in process of setting up for night operations. They report scouts can see the border and the Pakistan Desert a ways off. They've seen no tanks or evidence of enemy build-up within view. They reported finding bodies and partial bodies of four suspected Taliban up in those rocks. No paperwork and no weapons." Jimmy read from Roman's latest notes.

"How about A Company?" Bill asked. The coffee was a bit too hot, and he winced when it burned the right corner of his mouth.

"A Company last reported they were one, maybe two miles from their objective. Trails are in terrible shape, and it's slow going. They also report finding a couple of bodies, both pretty beat up probably from the bombing done by the F-15s. One broken rifle was found nearby—but no papers. They're proceeding to their objective."

"Sounds good. Contact both A and B Companies, advise them to remain on high alert, and go to a 50-50 watch when the sun goes down, with security checks every 30 minutes with Eagle Base—that's the new designation for Battalion—I'm Eagle Two. Did you review those call signs yet?"

"In the process, Captain, when you asked for those updates. I'll get back to the swing of things, sir."

"Between us, I'm hoping to receive orders sometime tomorrow, recalling B Company. I really doubt we'll be entering Pakistan, nor will they be invading Afghanistan. But I still want them on a 50-50 guard all night, with LPs posted and sniper teams in place. Advise them I'll contact them before lights out."

"Will, you get some sleep now, Captain?" Jimmy asked.

"Yup, if the heat doesn't make it impossible," Bill replied.

12

PARADISE- AFGHAN STYLE

THE HEAT, even at 123 degrees, did not interfere with Bill closing his eyes and getting a solid two hours of uninterrupted and glorious sleep. The hard part was waking him up. Bill was in a dream involving his family and didn't want it to end. Finally, Roman, who was also awake, took some canteen water to dribble over the captain's face. He was soon up and glaring in Roman's direction.

"Roman, only the fact I like you keeps me from having you dig a deep hole and have you placed in it. I'd hire some local to catch me one of those gigantic camel spiders to dine on your eyeballs I was right in that place where the dream seems so real, and Kitty—never mind—anything new?"

"Sorry, sir. Only thing to report is the Bradley plow has only about three miles left before reaching the end of the pass. The Sergeant in charge feels he can finish the project before ten hundred hours tomorrow if he stops at nightfall and hits it again with the rising sun. He added that they're encountering fewer mines. Looks like the Taliban might be running out."

"Contact that sergeant and inform him his plan for a ten-hundred-hour completion time sounds good. Also, advise him, via code, that both A and B Companies will be on a 50/50 watch tonight from lights out until dawn. He's not to try to contact them—to do so would risk harm to his people in a shooting accident. I want him and those Bradleys on 50-50 alert, with gunners on full alert. Make sure there are enough sentries around those vehicles through the night and monitor radios in case the other companies pick up movement or engage the enemy. I should have new orders for them once this little chore is completed, so have them stand by out there. Tell them to stay within the pass's natural boundaries and not to enter the open desert. No sense taking any risks with those Pakistani."

"Are you ready for chow yet, Captain?" Roman asked.

"Not yet. Where's Jimmy sleeping?"

"He took over my place under the large tarp, the one next to that watermelon-shaped stone standing up on its base."

"Okay, I see it—how many troops you got under there?" Bill asked.

"The last count was five, but after lights out, we'll probably have to charge hotel rates."

Bill grinned, then added, "I need to fire off a message to the Colonel at Bagram, probably by code—tell me when you're ready to copy."

Roman opened his logbook, grabbed a wooden pencil, and announced he was ready. He jotted down what the captain dictated and narrowed it down before converting it to code. Fourteen minutes later, Roman reported it was ready, and Bill gave him the okay to send it. In less than a minute, the Colonel's communications officer received it at Bagram and decoded it for the Colonel to read. He'd also made a copy of the message to have ready if the Colonel wanted it sent on to the General's office.

As the sun began its downward plunge for the western horizon, a beautiful fiery blaze spread across the sky. Roman received a coded message from Bagram and signed off to decode it for the captain to read.

That evening, under cover of a large desert camouflage tarp and illuminated by a single military flashlight at the floor of the hole, Bill read their new orders. He had watched the sunset thinking, *'Red sunset at night, sailors delight'* and hoped it held true for land troops as well. Still awed by the flaming red sunset, he turned to concentrate on his messages. "According to Bagram, there was no evidence of an invasion underway or in the Pakistan Army's planning stages. It added that neither the US nor the Afghan Government was planning on invading Pakistan. It was felt the situation had been created by either the Russians or the Chinese, and maybe both to simply stir the pot and increase weapon sales.

"We are to complete the road demining project but only to the exit of the Khyber Pass. We are also told there may be other mines along the border, set in place by the Afghan or the Pakistani military, or both, and to use caution.

Tyler's A Company will discontinue their search of the villages and withdraw from the Khyber Pass's stony hills. He will return to the 4th Battalion to await further orders. Bravo Company will remain in place to keep an eye on our road crew. I was also notified that the four Apaches and Major Garnet, the FAC, will remain assigned to the 4th Battalion for the time being.

Looks like our armor will remain assigned to us. When the Chinooks come in to pick up our excess gear and non-burnable trash, we'll be ready to move out. D Company will remain at Eagle on full alert while Bravo and Charlie convoy back to Bagram. Then D Company will withdraw. Two Apaches will fly escort for A and B Companies, while the remaining two Apaches will protect D Company and escort them back to Bagram. Sounds good so far.

The General has also ordered that when Eagle Base breaks down for return to Bagram, the area will look as if the base had never existed. All holes are to be filled to keep the Afghan allies happy. We can use Clunker One to help with that."

That night, everything was quiet, and there was no contact with the Taliban. The next day, with the completion of the road demining, all elements of the 4th Provisional Battalion were ordered to prepare to return to Bagram. Everyone pitched in to expedite the order and the camp was quickly packed up and loaded onto transport vehicles. It was with great relief that on their return trip, there was no contact with the enemy.

The troops were happy to see their enclosure again, enlarged to make room for A Company. Captain Tyler and his men were surprised by the distance to their showers and the chow hall, but they got used to it in time. Once all the housekeeping chores were completed, Bill issued orders for the company commanders to begin letting their men have some time off.

Training sessions began the following day. All personal equipment was cleaned, items needing repair were turned in, and vehicle maintenance was scheduled. Duties were assigned, and within 24 hours, the men were settled back into life at Bagram base awaiting a new assignment. After three days of light training, the troops returned to a full training schedule while the men wondered how much longer the 4th Battalion would remain together.

REPLACEMENTS FOR THE BATTALION

Two weeks had gone by since the road operation was finished. The men finished up three days of Desert Warfare Training as an under-strength battalion. They were minus a C Company, and Bill wondered if another unit was forthcoming or would they continue on as a three-company battalion or be split up.

Since returning to Bagram, Bill had written four letters to Kitty and one to his mom. Mail went from Afghanistan to either England or Germany, so Kitty often received his mail in clumps. Occasionally, she would get her letters out of order, but she had grown used to that and was excited to get every letter from her loving husband. She often wrote him a letter every night. Satellite phones and the newer cell phones made it possible for near-instant contact with a friend or loved one back home, but each caller realized such communications were continuously monitored by the government, the enemy, or an unfriendly country. The United States oversaw most international communications through the new supercomputers in Nevada which were a great help to the combat troops dealing with the initial stages of PTSD.

The one item Bill refused to send Kitty was an up-to-date photo of himself. He didn't want her to fret over his loss of weight and the shallowness evident in his eyes. Most of it came from lack of sleep and the meals that were almost but not quite palatable. In the three months since arriving, he had lost 17 pounds. In the last letter from her, which he had just finished reading, Kitty complained quite a bit about his mother. "Honey, she's always right over my shoulder, popping off 30 different ways for doing this or that—driving me crazy! I'm ready to put her into a retirement home—either your mother or I need the rest. I do love her so. She's just middle-aged, lonely, and worried about you." Bill had been the one to suggest his mother come to stay and help with the kids. But it seems the situation had turned into a movie version for "The Thing from the Fantastic Four meets the Hulk."

Rubbing a sore right knee earned jumping down from a 10-foot-high cliff and not managing the roll as he should, Bill watched as a Deuce truck stopped at the gate of the Airborne enclosure. With the addition of the other Army units, Airborne's camp resembled a small township, made up mostly of ugly metal Conex containers and barrier walls. Over 550 troops occupied this massive chicken coop, with four men to a closet-sized room and only eight new double-wide portable latrines. They hadn't increased the number of shower stalls, so everyone, including officers, was limited to five-minute showers and long lines. Division had sent the word down that the new alert status was changed to 'orange', which produced a minor change in guard duties as the security level was lowered.

Bill watched as eight men jumped off the truck and knew these were his new replacements—seven brand new Private First-Class troops, and one Corporal Walter Mayer, from Los Angeles, California. Bill would learn this was to be his first combat deployment. Putting the line of men at ease, Bill welcomed them to the 4th Battalion and then looked over the new men's orders. The fine young specimens of manhood had all finished Advanced Infantry School, and Airborne Jump School, and were ready to participate in the Afghan War. The men were not HALO qualified, and it made Bill wonder if they had stopped HALO training in the 101st Airborne. *These soldiers are replacements for the men I lost—that was swift action for today's Army Personnel Department.*

Bill read the names on their orders out loud so he could put a face to the name. "Hold your hand up when I read your name. "PFC Richard Sessions out of St. Louis, Missouri; PFC Edward Nightly from Sacramento, California; PFC Chuck Jones out of New York City; PFC Bob Harrington, from Houston, Texas; PFC Rex Corrington, from Salem, Missouri; PFC Percy Jackson from Albertville, Arizona, and PFC Cole

Porter from Seattle, Washington." He looked at Corporal Mayer, "This is your first tour to the Sandbox. Where else have you been stationed?"

"Sir, I pulled two years as an instructor in training with the Division, but I wanted to serve overseas, and they granted my request to return to a combat unit. It's all in my file, Captain."

"Welcome to Afghanistan. I am your Battalion Executive Officer, and I will travel with you on every deployment unless smaller units are required. Lt. Colonel Rogers is the Battalion Commander and will usually remain here at Bagram. Now, listen well, the U.S. 101st Army Airborne has graciously sent all of you to me to replace fallen men. These men lost their lives in what I will refer to as a hand-to-hand, bare knuckle-dragging brawl, often by knife versus sword or the modern weapons of warfare. The Taliban like their swords. I nearly lost my RTO in one such attack. His name is Olson, and you can talk with him for the details. We have a strict policy on what is suitable for souvenirs over here, but I'll let your platoon leaders handle that.

You've all graduated from our primary training schools, telling me you're all physically fit and ready to handle Afghanistan. This is not my first tour in the Sandbox, and to be completely honest with you, I still don't understand these people. It's the same in Iraq, Iran, and a hundred other third-world countries. The Taliban is our enemy in this. They are very proficient in tribal and desert warfare and totally ruthless. The Taliban will often execute prisoners by cutting their heads off, so surrendering is not an ideal option. They want all foreign powers to leave or die, and then they can run the country under their stiff Muslim regime. ISIS is involved here, too. There are a few Russians and maybe some Chinese influence.

Since arriving some three months ago, this unit has apprehended a Russian Colonel, identified as an Intelligence Officer. An Iranian Army Major and an ISIS thug were taken at the same time. We learned several things from these prisoners—I'm only saying this as a way to show you how important it is to take prisoners. We only kill when we have to—to protect ourselves and our fellow soldiers—oh, and our allies. Always remember how essential prisoners are.

You guys can be at *rest*, and smoke if you want to, but make sure to break down butts and trash them. We strive hard to keep our enclosure trash free and if you see any litter on the ground, pick it up. We do not employ locals to clean up our grounds. Besides being clean, we never know when a congressman or woman may make a surprise visit.

You'll find that I run a relaxed ship unless we're on a high alert status or on deployment, then it's completely by the book. No salutes in the field; snipers would just love to have us pointed out. Just a friendly nod will do, and sometimes a slice of pizza or a chocolate candy bar." There were more than a few grins in response, and the men began to relax.

I know it's not easy moving into a new platoon, but we have good people here—" Bill stopped when Chief approached. "Gentlemen, this is Chief Warrant Officer Johnson, B Company's new Commander. I'll turn you over to him. He's been at this racket for a long time, so listen to him."

Chief stepped forward, "Get your duffle bags and anything else you're carrying and follow me in a run. See how you like the desert heat —I've heard it's supposed to be very healthy for you young'uns."

The troops displayed some discomfort carrying all their gear as they moved into a jog. Chief shouted out, "Soldiers, helmets will be worn at all times when outside the wire or on special work detail. The same goes for your 'Superman' vests. Those vests and helmets saved a lot of lives during our last assignment."

Chief continued shouting, "Unchambered M-4s will be with you at all times, except for work details and then the weapon will be within grasp. Now, this is it, welcome to B Company's magical kingdom. You'll have to find seven empty bunks. If death scares you, get over it. Combat soldiers don't die in bed. You're Airborne, and we're not scared of noth-in'!" Chief walked away, knowing the squad leaders assigned to watch over these lost children would take over.

"Hooah!" rang out from numerous soldiers sitting outside their rooms where the heat was less stifling. A tall squad leader approached them, identified himself, and addressed them in a raised voice, "You men are going into C Platoon. 'C' as in Charles and your platoon leader is 2nd Lt. Dave Daniels. He's a good officer who's on his first tour here, but he's got three months in-country and he's learned a bit in that time. Listen to him, listen to the others who have 'seen the elephant'; it might keep you alive." The men had heard the elephant reference in Boot Camp and again later. So, they understood it to mean, *I've gone and seen my war, and I'm forever changed.*

"When off duty, we have most things here on Bagram that you would find at a stateside base, but if you decide you want to see Kabul, you will obtain a 12- or 24-hour pass and have it signed off by your platoon leader. The army doesn't like to lose its men only to find them in some dark alley with their throats sliced and manhood removed. I think you know what I mean; Kabul is not safe after the sun goes down. Stay in groups of three and four; even if you go to the main base, you should have a partner with you. Some of our allies are genuinely not who they seem, and the Taliban are always out and about. Some of them working right on this base.

Besides the Taliban, we've got ISIS agents and your basic slave traders, who'd sell you to another tribe in southern Afghanistan in a heartbeat, and there are plenty of fanatic sympathizers or the various insurgent groups. Added to this, we have the ever-tried and true killer thieves. Here, the locals see us all as millionaires. They watch our movies and television shows, so what else could they think? A lot of these people see stories of American poor, and it makes them laugh. Either they don't believe it or consider our poor to be far wealthier than they are.

We've got pizza and burger joints, some ritzy eateries, and stores; you can even have your picture taken atop a camel, or an ox, or a donkey —but they all bite! You'll learn soon enough that Afghanistan is not like any country you've read about or visited. You can be walking down a major roadway in Kabul. A suicidal Muslim will explode himself right in front of you. Then I've got to write a letter home to your wife or parents and try to explain the training accident that took their son. So, be vigilant of your surroundings, even inside this enclosure. We do have a snake problem here—both human and serpent. Afghanistan has these fantastic Camel Spiders, about three to four times larger than your basic tarantula, and they're vicious. Don't even try to pick one up! When you get the okay to see the town and its bright lights, remember you represent the United States of America. We never leave anyone behind, even if we have to drag him kicking and screaming. Or the body of one of our fallen. The live ones will thank you later because those assassins would love a new set of ears or your balls to put on display.

Rumors have spread that a canine handler, taken with his highly trained pup, is worth $25,000 to the ISIS Front. These dogs have a tattoo on the inside of one ear. This means they only had to take the ear in, not the whole hound, which probably got ate. I'm telling you to have all the fun you can in this no alcohol allowed town. Yes, we follow an old Muslim Law about no booze or drugs that have our NCO and Officer's Clubs serving fruit drinks, soda, iced tea, milk, and coffee. However, being Army, we have our own moonshine, but I wouldn't trust it; it'll cost you a stripe if you're found drunk.

Water. Our Battalion drinks and cooks from those Water Wagons over there—they supply almost 600 men. We use up six of those 500-gallon wagons every 24 hours. On a personal level, you have three canteens in your desert issue. I'd recommend you get a fourth. Keep them full. In camp, if you walk by the water tank, check the level in your primary canteen and refill it. Water will help you survive. Rotate your pack canteens with your belt canteens; it'll help keep the water from going stale, and you'll get used to it being warm.

Showers and the chow hall are down that road about a mile. Showers are limited to five minutes. If you're on your first tour of combat duty, the more experienced troops might shy away from you. That often happens until they see how you handle yourselves during an attack or an operation in enemy-held land. It's hard losing a friend and tough making new ones.

Remember, just like they told you in school, your M-4 will save your life. Keep it clean and treat it nice. It's a good weapon, and best of all, it can handle the desert. Anyone wanting to become certified as 240B, M-60, or SAW gunners will have to prove themselves on the range. Tomorrow, B Company has it reserved, and you will be shooting. Your rifle is unloaded while inside this base, which means you may carry a magazine in it, but un-chambered. When we leave the base for a job, we get the order to chamber a round. If I find you with a chambered rifle inside the wire, you'll be transferred to the chow hall for a week, and that's really nasty duty. Knives will be sharp and cleaned every day; this wet heat can quickly cause rust. When our men were forced into a recent brawl with the Taliban, they were happy to have knives.

You will now shave and get cleaned up; this is not the Navy, nor the

Air Force. You will shave daily unless you have a signed excuse from a medic that has been counter-signed by your company commander. We want our men to give these people a good impression of America."

The sergeant's weapons inspection showed the men had been issued brand-new M-4s that hadn't been sighted in yet. The new guys didn't have extra ammo pouches but that would be remedied tomorrow when they went out to shoot. Their knives were new and shiny except for a diver's knife one man planned to tape to his combat suspenders with thick black tape. "Sorry, that plastic handle won't last here; you'll have to find yourself another knife." The replacement didn't have handguns, either. That had to be done at Battalion level. However, the 4th Battalion had not been shipped a supply of pistols, which meant the Chief would have to do some horse trading with another Battalion.

THE LETTER HOME

Later that evening, Bill sat down and wrote a letter to Kitty-

Hi, Babe

I'm sure hoping you got the last four letters in order, one a day because this is the fifth letter regarding my inner thoughts you wished to learn about. If they arrived in the wrong order, look for the date in the right corner. It might not make a lot of sense if you read them out of order.

First, I love you so much, Honey, more than I thought possible. My heart aches to have my arms around you, my lips nibbling at your ears. My hands feeling the warmth of your skin.

Sorry, had to stop for a moment. A fight broke out in B Company's 3rd Platoon. One of my new replacements was having difficulty fitting in and understanding the pecking order. The rest were making bets on the winner. No real harm, lesson learned.

Thought I'd finish off this note and put it aside for a couple of days. I talked with our new guys, all first-timers. Fine young men, and it's my job to make sure they survive.

I lost seven men on our last outing and 16 wounded. You do not need to hear this crap. Still, it does give you a view of my 'soldier in combat' side. Taking over as Battalion Executive Officer, no promotion or pay raise, just the responsibility for some 600 men.

My new Commander appears to trust me and lets me run the day-to-day operations, so, I'm getting a lot of leadership experience. We have our old full Bird Colonel from back home; he got moved over here for some reason. Maybe just further command experience, as I think he's about to be promoted to General. The General, the man who commands Bagram, is a tough but intelligent man. I honestly believe if this General changed his faith to Islam, he'd be elected Kabul's new mayor. He is very popular among the locals, but also with his officers and men. I'm still asking myself why he made me Battalion XO. Though, I wonder how long that will last once we return stateside. The paperwork for this size of force is impressive. I'm thankful for my support staff, as they are extremely helpful.

I came over here hoping to spread the Lord's word when the opportunity arose, but it never has. Now all I want to do is destroy ISIS and Taliban thugs. Thugs are my name for them without indulging in profanities. I will definitely need help when I return home because I know I've gotten sloppy with my adjectives and nouns.

We killed so many of them in a two-day encounter, but these brutal, evil men have accomplished so much harm to their fellow Muslims. For a westerner, it just makes no sense. How can one Muslim do such vileness to a fellow Muslim? A man who follows the same strict religion. I try to read my Bible every day, but I'm lucky if I get it done three days out of the week. Pray for me concerning this, Babe.

My heart has many dark times, actions I've taken and dealt out, but no war crimes; you do not need to be concerned with that. Still, when I combine my first two tours here, I feel ill. It's a sickness of death, the smells of battles filling my senses, and the cries of wounded or dying men. I remove the photos of loved ones from their bodies, placing them in a pouch with their wallet, rings, watches, dog tags, coins, and paper money. I used to make sure there's nothing present in packs or foot lockers that might hurt a wife or parents' feelings. Others handle that duty now. Porn is not allowed in Afghanistan, but the troops are good at smuggling it in. Even booze makes it in, along with some dope. Yeah, just like the stories my mom used to tell about my dad's time in the military.

Kitty, I'm beginning to have those dark dreams again, the frightening ones. But I can't tell my Colonel. He'd probably have to relieve me and ship me to Germany for evaluation and then some military hospital for the insane. I'd most likely be held there until they have my medical retirement set up and eventually a special room at a musty VA hospital back in the states. You wanted to know this stuff, remember? I hope it helps your prayers on my behalf.

Maybe there are many here enduring the same dreams. I've had a chat with our Chaplain. He doesn't feel my case has reached a severe status yet. I believe him to be a good man, he really loves the men of our Battalion and will go the extra ten miles for each of them. He has, of course, never killed anyone or felt the burning feeling that runs through your body, and often or not, the shame that wants to rip your guts out. He's gone into combat with us, gaining all the men's respect, even the atheists. I've noticed the lines to see him have gotten longer since we arrived here. Chaplain Zachary Taylor the Fifth holds the rank of captain. He comes from the New Hope Church, a non-denominational church in Salem, Oregon. I believe I'd like to attend his church once or twice to hear him preach when we all go home. This is his second tour; the last time he received a Purple Heart. He is a German Jew, and still follows the traditions of his Hebrew forefathers. Yet, he's a hardcore Christian and fast becoming a friend and confidant since I command everyone else. It makes it difficult sharing my hurts and feelings with anyone else during this deployment.

Oh, I often talk with Chief concerning my inner thoughts, and he tells me not to worry, how I'm not over the edge yet.

When I lost those seven men, I almost ordered the execution of our half dozen Taliban prisoners, but Intel needed them. I was just so angry; I kept thinking of my guy's parents, wives, and children. Fortunately, only three out of the seven had wives waiting for them to come home. One was the father of a five-year-old boy, one had two-year-old twin girls, and one expecting a baby he will never see. Now, they're flying home in silver-colored caskets with American flags draped over them. They were good men.

I had to walk away from the prisoners, briefly. I picked up a stone about the size of a marble and placed it in my mouth. I chewed on it to cause pain, to take my mind off the bodies of my men. I kept thinking I'd done something wrong, that I should've been killed instead of them. But the Division's Military Board of Review, who reviewed our operation, found that I had acted in the best interests of the U.S. Army, whatever that means.

The Chaplain and I are playing chess now; it makes it easier to chat. I haven't won a single game yet. Can you cheat at chess? Just kidding. My dad and I used to play chess when he fought the DTs, and occasionally, he would throw a piece at the wall. So, we used those cheap plastic sets. The chaplain's set is made of Myrtlewood, a tree from the coastal forests of the Pacific Northwest. All of the figures are a soft gold color, but one set has a metallic blue band at the base of each piece, the other set has a candy apple red band. The Chaplain says he always gives the red pieces to his opponent to remind them of Christ's love.

When I see my unit, all decked out for combat, I think about Dad making that climb up Hamburger Hill. I fight the desert and its terrible wave after wave of 100-plus degree heat. Had a couple days that hit 135 degrees; it was miserable. Dad, up on Hamburger, fought that mountain, with its slop-like mud from monsoon rains that seem to have no ending and.

No, no more talk about Hamburger. I find myself telling the story of Dad's heroism all too often over here when men ask me about his Medal.

I'm being hailed, Kitty. I'll seal this later tonight. Let's get back to sharing our dreams. This real stuff just brings me down. Isn't that a song? I love you, Bill.

"Captain Warrens, they need you over at Battalion Headquarters," one of the runners said from outside Bill's office door.

"I hear you," Bill called out. He was stripped down to his underwear and didn't want to frighten the runner with his hairy body. *That'll really give him a nasty case of PTSD,* Bill grinned and went for his fatigue pants.

"Captain, Colonel Rogers wants you ASAP; he's sending his Humvee over to bring you to headquarters. Do you want anyone to go with you?"

His new RTO asked. Roman had yet to come on for his 12-hour shift, but Bill realized it was only 14:58 hours.

"Yeah, get the Chief over here ASAP—I want him to accompany me to the Colonel's Office."

"You got it, Captain." A radio call was made, and the RTO talked directly to Chief Johnson.

Bill knew he would need the Chief's insight; he had a feeling new deployment orders were at hand. Not a single company had gone outside the wire, except for training purposes, in the last two weeks. This was unusual, especially for men who had been in the country for only three months.

When they arrived at the Colonel's office, Bill and the Chief were surprised by the Colonel's new assistant. Chief Command Sergeant Major Doug Packa was on hand to serve the two men coffee. Lt. Colonel Rogers came into the room and shook hands with both men. "You've been doing a hell of a job out there, Bill. I couldn't be more satisfied—and that goes for you too, Chief."

Chief smiled and moved over to speak with an old friend, "Doug, I thought you pulled the retirement pin five or six years ago. What happened, and what's with the coffee? This is just weird to have you serving us coffee! Where are the other office people? I haven't gone through such tight security since TSA was examining my shoes and threatening to steal my homemade chocolate chip cookies."

"Hey, if I learned anything in this man's army, it was how to serve a decent cup of coffee—sorry about the lack of whiskey to give it a boost. As to why we're here alone, this meeting has been Classified Top Secret for a reason, and that's why you're here. To answer your question about retirement—you might've heard my wife died a few years back, and the kids have no time for me and my beliefs. They're worried I'll try to talk my grandchildren into joining the military. I had nothing else to do, so I shipped over for another four years. That was four years ago. You know how it is; who's going to tell an E-9 to quit as long as he can pass the physicals? I've got a few prominent generals guarding my backside. Men I helped survive as young 2nd Lieutenants and our current Chief Command Sergeant Major in D.C. He works directly under our Army Chief of Staff. As to why you're here, my mouth is zipped closed, but it's important for Army Airborne. You want cream? Sugar? Maybe some dancing girls?" Chief Packa asked.

The door to the Colonel's office opened, and he gestured for all three men to enter. Only then did Bill and the Chief notice two MPs standing inside the office, who stepped out to post a sign that read, "The Colonel's Office is officially closed for a security matter."

Chief was glad to see Doug. They hadn't spoken face to face for eight or nine years, but there had been phone calls between them and a few letters. Neither one could remember how long it had been or where it was. Chief was a young SSgt going through NCO Advanced Training, and the class was led by Master Sergeant Packa who became known as the youngest ever Command Sergeant Major and the youngest Chief Command Sergeant Major. He earned his E-9 rank after 19 years in service.

Bill noticed the specialty patches Doug wore over his left fatigue shirt pocket; Combat Infantry Badge (CIB) with three combat stars. His airborne badge bore three combat stars to signify three combat jumps into war zones. He served time with an Air Cav unit, flew 167 missions as a door gunner, and earned himself the Basic Aviation Air Crew Wings. He wore the 101st Screaming Eagle patch on his left shoulder, but he had also served with the 82nd Airborne. His foreign wings and other awards filled a jewelry box, which he kept back in his room. His Top-Secret files would show he had worked in Delta Force and handled several Green Beret assignments. He kept a Top Secret "Letter of Commendation" signed by then-President Ronald Reagan for his participation in a *"Black Operation"*, where no medals were ever rewarded. The three troops who died on that particular mission were listed as having died in a training accident. When the Colonel called in need of a good man, Doug flew over from his office at Fort Benning. His travel orders and Temporary Duty Assignment was rushed through in less than six hours.

Doug sat in a chair beside the Colonel's desk, taking notes in his own unique shorthand that only he could read. For nearly three hours they talked, going over ideas and plans. When Bill left the Colonel's Office, he carried two armloads of plans, directives, maps, and a locked satchel containing Top Secret operational plans for Operation Camel Rider North, where even the title was Top Secret. Lt. Colonel Rogers knew all about the operation, having contributed to it. But Colonel Rogers would only be handling logistics, including communications and equipment needs. The General had made it clear that he wanted Bill to handle all the off-base operational duties, which was highly unusual for a mere captain.

When the Chief departed, after arranging to have dinner with Doug once this whole mess was completed, he too was loaded down with an equally impressive amount of paperwork. It had all been piled on one desk, and then one by one, the various needs and orders were provided to them.

An MP escort was provided for their return to the enclosure. When they arrived at headquarters, an MP was posted outside Bill's door. Other MPs were posted outside battalion headquarters, and new security procedures were underway. Everyone going into Battalion Headquarters had to be cleared, no cameras were allowed inside. Back at his desk, Bill unlocked the new satchel from his left wrist and began reviewing the enclosed papers in depth.

Within 10 minutes, a squad of men from B Company, 3rd Platoon, 2nd Squad, had been assigned to provide added security for their headquarters. Engineers showed up with a deuce carrying razor wire. In short order, it was three strands high, making Battalion Headquarters resemble a correctional facility. Additional security lighting was erected; next came a dog handler. A new M-60 sandbag bunker was placed near the new entry gate to headquarters. Until told otherwise, everyone but Bill and the Chief was patted down before entering and leaving headquarters.

The new security measures put the Battalion troops on edge, knowing something big was in the works. They knew that eventually they would be briefed on what lay ahead. Of course, rumors started flying as soon as Bill and Chief returned from Command with an escort followed by more MPs. One rumor included the invasion of Pakistan. Another story going around was the possible invasion of either Uzbekistan, Turkmenistan, or Tajikistan, which all bordered northern Afghanistan. All three were known to be under strong Russian influence. Military Intel reported that Russian military forces had been sighted in these three countries. Some suspected the Russians were planning to re-invade Afghanistan, but the Russian military buildup in these countries had been minimal. In any case, the men of the 4th Battalion did not like any of these rumors.

Non-U.S. military vehicles were no longer allowed into the 4th Battalion's enclosure, which had been placed on a 'high orange' alert status. Except for traffic whizzing by on Bagram's major roadway, the Airborne enclosure posted a 'no-go zone', which only increased curiosity as they drove by.

4th Battalion headquarters was transformed into a Top-Secret Operational Center, leaving the Captain, Chief, Roman, and one other RTO to work inside. Everyone else was moved to another building, along with telephones, radios, computers, file cabinets, desks, and chairs. All the paperwork concerning the upcoming operation was set on hastily put-together plywood tables. No paperwork was allowed to leave the room, and all communications were monitored by military Intel.

Coffee and water were delivered all hours of the day and night and left at the MP's temporary guard shack. Four boxes of MREs were brought in after they had been ripped, opened, and inspected by the MPs. Anything that appeared to be tampered with never made it past the checkpoint.

"I haven't seen security like this since my last tour over here—I feel like I'm working in Fort Knox," Bill said to Roman.

"Sir, would you get the word out; I need some chocolate," Roman insisted. Within a short time, two sealed boxes of chocolate candy bars were brought to the MPs. After ensuring it was not tampered with, it was brought to Roman. Grateful, he shared part of a box with the MPs.

The two RTOs went to work, using new operational satellite phones, for all contact between 4th Battalion and Bagram's Main Command Center. The phones were to only be used concerning this new operation. All other communications went through regular phone lines or over the radio.

"Sir, how many aircraft do we get for the jump—and do those forward air controllers jump with us?" Chief asked, between sips of his cold coffee.

"Our new operational plans call for four C-141s, and yes, this will be considered a combat jump. This means combat stars for all jumpers.

However, our forward air controllers will be delivered to the site via Blackhawk accompanied by infantry troops to safeguard them until we arrive. The infantry will return here. I've requested Major Garnett for this job, as he did an excellent job for us during our last operation. He's also got a couple good NCOs working with him, but none of them is jump qualified."

"Bill, this whole thing makes me wonder when this plan was initiated. Survey work had to have been done recently, checking the surface strength to see if the desert out there can even handle an active runway. We get this hurry-up push to get ready to go—sure, it was probably due to secrecy, but when did Washington decide to make Operation Camel-Rider North active?" Chief stopped long enough to remove a dessert pouch from his meal package. "I need sugar right now, more than I need instant protein."

"It's your gut, Chief," Bill said, and added, "I did some checking on Operational Plans for Afghanistan, and all I can tell you is that our operation had three older sisters, Operation Camel Rider South, Camel Rider East, and Camel Rider West. All three were canceled, and I can't find out why. Since this Afghan war began, there's been a lot of cancelations for any number of reasons."

"Sir, this plan makes me a bit nervous. I've never heard of a massive jump like this since we arrived in Afghanistan. I mean, we're planning on dropping our whole battalion into northern Afghanistan, an unoccupied area surrounded by hilly desert country. There has not been such a large combat jump since the 82nd and 101st jumped into Normandy in World War II. Korea and Nam only saw a couple of large jumps, but they were only company-sized at best—at least as far as I know."

"We won't be using C-47s, but four C-141s and they're going to fill the skies with open chutes. I just pray we don't have any streamers," Bill said as he pointed to the map in front of them. "Once the desert floor is deemed useable, heavy equipment will be brought in by helicopter. As soon as the strip is built, the first of three C-5As can start bringing in Heavy Weapons vehicles. The plan calls for heavy artillery. Once completed, Camel Rider will be a mini-Bagram. Water wagons will be flown in by Chinooks, along with the first of our regular supplies. A tent city will be erected, and our troops will eventually be replaced by the infantry and probably some Marines. All I know is, this will be a big surprise for the Taliban and their Russian allies. According to the operational plans, once we're on the ground and Major Garnett is up and running, we'll start receiving Chinooks, Apaches, and Blackhawks. Hopefully, if the strip can't handle the bigger birds because of unsuitable surfaces, some C-17s and C-130s can still get in. We might even see Clunker One again, but this time it'll be using its blade to make a strip. Or they may airlift out a couple graders. Our operation calls for an Air Force Para-rescue Outfit to be on hand. There'll be a lot of birds flying through these not-so-friendly skies."

Chief threw in his own two cents, "Our newly constructed North Base is liable to make some of our neighboring countries a wee bit nervous. There are no roads, and the bad guys can only reach us by going across 200 odd miles of open desert on three sides. Our satellites would pick them up right away, and a flight of bombers would decimate their armor. The only way the Russians could get at us would be Air Force or missiles, and then we're all smack in the middle of World War III. Those mountains to the north, across the border—the Taliban could have a few strongholds up there. Probably where the Russian advisors are training and equipping them. This new operation is going to drive the Taliban crazy, moving right into their backyard."

Bill nodded, "I think this will affect Al-Qaeda operations and possibly even the Hamas. However, our major concern will be our Russian friends and possibly the Chinese. They will not like having such an active military force so close to borders they control. But they can't stop us, and they won't know of it until we start dropping in. Thanks to all those rumors the Russians may have started, they might just believe we're building up our forces along the Pakistan border—surprise!"

"Right," Chief replied, nodding. "But now we need more hot coffee." He turned to the RTO, "Would you signal the kitchen staff, order up some more coffee, please, and remember to tip the waiter."

An MP arrived shortly with a tray of coffee cups, a loaf of bread, and a jar of peanut butter. "That's the best they could do for now. The bakery staff at the chow hall doesn't come in until 2200 hours, and all of today's goodies are long gone. I heard the peanut butter supply at the Exchange is all sold out. Be another day or two before new supplies are brought in. Seems your 4th Battalion has emptied the shelves."

"Hey, you can't go wrong with Skippy's Peanut Butter, and the chow hall's bread isn't that bad," Chief said as he opened the bag of bread. He reached into the desk for a letter opener. Finding none, he used his folding knife to slap the peanut butter onto the slices of bread. As he handed a slice to Bill, Chief said, "Your Doughnut, my Lord. I do hope you enjoy it."

"Wow, that coffee just took the outer skin off my lips again. I'm going to go home with scarred lips and have a heck of a time explaining my wounds to Kitty. But I gotta say, that's the way to scald coffee—nice and strong."

They worked hour after hour, putting together the Airborne's part of this wild operation to place a new joint service base in the northern country and have it operational within 24 hours. At least that was the plan.

13

IT'S ON!

OPERATION CAMEL RIDER North took off like a book-perfect deployment. Not a single in-flight emergency for all the aircraft that made the long flight to the new installation. Over 600 jumpers landed without casualties, other than a couple of sore ankles and one complaint of a sore back. The medics handled the injured men, as none of them needed to be returned to Bagram. Eventually, a field hospital would be erected, using the Army's massive tents, making the hospital resemble an old Korean War MASH unit. Additional medics, four combat nurses, and four field doctors would also be brought in. Division hoped to eventually treat the local tribesmen and villagers once Camel Rider North was up and running. Providing free medical care had proven to be an excellent way to make friends with the locals.

Troops dug more than 600 yards of trenches and lined them with sandbag walls. Other troops set up the perimeter's razor wire. Claymore mines and trip flares were put into place to prevent an insurgent from sneaking through to look the site over or deliver a bomb. Exterior lighting was set up even though the generators had not yet arrived. Only after the trenches were reinforced with sandbags and the wire in place were the companies allowed to set up tents inside the perimeter.

A platoon of MPs was due to arrive to handle base security. However, it would be Airborne troops who walked the perimeter while MPs managed all entry control points and specific classified locations, such as Army Intel and CID tents, a photo-lab, armory and supply tents, and the 4th Battalion's new headquarters tent. Here, the battalion's American Flag and the Afghan flag were posted. There was one large tent—jokingly referred to as Base Operations for Major Garnet and his men. Eventually, a series of large tents would be constructed to house the chow hall. Multiple outhouses were dug in several locations.

Chief was impressed; he had never experienced anything like this before, where different commands meshed together so well to accomplish the near impossible in such a short time. By the end of the day, when Taps was sounded by an MP with a bugle, more to impress the Taliban than anything else, Camp Camel Rider North was filled with over 1,000 military personnel. Revetments for the helicopters were to be built to protect the birds and the men working on them from enemy fire and shrapnel. With the experts finding the desert unsuitable for handling all but the smaller cargo birds, the big planes, such as the C-5A and C-141s, would have to wait until the grated runway was constructed. Plans were already drawn up in preparation for this. Engineers, operators, and their construction pieces were en route to get the project underway. Airlifts continued around the clock, with dozens of men dashing about with lighted wands to guide the helicopters in after dark.

One of the things not planned for was the area's dumpsite, so the construction people had to dig a massive hole for garbage. Bill ended up talking with the weather people before a site was chosen. He wanted to make sure the prevailing breezes didn't blow unsavory aromas over the camp.

Bill knew that it wouldn't be long before a new village popped up nearby as the Afghan people knew there would eventually be jobs available. People liked living close to a military installation to help protect them from the Taliban. Water would be a vital issue; a new pipeline was being discussed back at Command.

Since the grated runway hadn't been built yet, a long line of Chinooks and two newly assigned Sky-cranes airlifted 4th Battalion's armored vehicles. Bill saw plans for an artillery unit to be assigned with a battery of M-109s and possibly larger pieces. All this advanced planning was done in the event one of Afghanistan's neighbors kicked up a fuss.

4th Battalion's new TOC (Tactical Operations Center) was a large tent on the second line of the newly established tent city. It was positioned at the east end of a long line of canvas housing units. Bill had heard from a Supply sergeant that some of these tents were last used during the initial days in Kuwait for the first Iraqi War and had been stored since that time in England. Nights were turning chilly, and the troops slept fully clothed to stay warm. When winter hit, they would need cold weather gear as this area occasionally got snow. When the temperatures approached freezing, their Poncho Liners wouldn't help much, but they were better than nothing.

Mail hadn't arrived, and the men were still consuming MREs, hoping the new field kitchen would soon arrive. The Weather Station had been set up, and special balloons were launched twice a day. This was a forward combat base. Unlike Bagram, it wouldn't have a base/post exchange, a laundry, or eateries. This also meant that very few women were assigned to this place except for some nurses.

Trench foot was already a problem even though Bill made sure each of his soldiers had antiseptic foot cream and a canister of foot powder. He couldn't obtain enough of it from Supply, so he used Battalion funds to purchase it through the Bagram Post Exchange and had it flown out. There were sunburns and minor cases of sun blindness for failure to keep sunglasses or beer-bottle goggles on. This blindness could produce some nasty headaches.

4th Battalion Headquarters operated smoothly—a whole lot smoother than anyone expected. Patrols had not encountered the enemy but continued to stay vigilant. Sergeant Roman worked the late-night hours but often came in early to ensure the daytime troops were not messing things up. A new training range had been marked off to handle 20 shooters at a time, another one nearby for machine guns and a lot farther away, one for mortars. Stingers were brought out, but only used training pieces were fired. The weapon was simply too expensive to fire live for training purposes. As far as Bill knew, only a few of his men had ever actually fired a Stinger in combat. He knew the practice rounds failed to give them the actual effect of firing that weapon and hoped they would never have to use one. If they did, it meant an enemy with air power was attacking.

One of the things Bill liked about being a member of the 101st Airborne in a war zone was that these soldiers never seemed to catch the disease known as "Garrison Mentality". This was when a man became obsessed with his paperwork rather than the mission and fundamental soldiering. Security grew lax in those situations.

Airborne troops were always ready for the unexpected. From the chats Bill had with his men, he was impressed by how many wished they could stay and just finish this war and end the Taliban. Unless the U.S. and its allies started fighting this as a war, Bill could see American troops being sent into this land for another five to ten years. *Everyone said we stayed in Vietnam too long—10 years, and we're approaching 14 years here, with no end in sight. Someone's got to make some decision to either treat this place like we did in Korea or WWII or send us home. World War II only lasted four and a half years. But it did take a couple atom bombs to convince the Japanese to surrender. That wouldn't work here, as too many people had nuclear weapons.*

On the sixth day, new orders came down from Division. They were delivered by hand. The courier, an officer, flew out on a Blackhawk. Bill reviewed the orders and shook his head in dismay. He was being tasked to provide one of his companies to be flown by Chinooks to Afghanistan's northern border with Uzbekistan. A company of Army National Guard would arrive to cover their perimeter and area patrol duties. Unless told otherwise, Bill decided he would mix the troops from the guard unit among his own troops rather than have them handle a perimeter section on their own. This was met with mixed opinions from his two remaining company commanders, but his decision was final. He assigned B Company to handle the deployment north. Being Battalion Commander, Bill would have to remain behind which made him uncomfortable. He knew if he had chosen one of the other companies for this dangerous task, some would feel he was shielding his old company, and Bill could not have that. He also knew the Chief was the best man to lead this operation.

Bill looked the plan over several times. *Five Chinooks will be required to fly B Company to their destination. The flight would take just under five minutes, under optimal conditions. They can take along heavier automatic weapons. With all the moving they're going to be doing, they'll have to leave the mortars behind.*

Division wanted this unit to patrol the length of Uzbekistan's southern border, roughly 70 miles, and remain inside Afghanistan. They were under strict orders not to cross the border for any reason. They were to gain intelligence on local insurgents and observe any activity on this border that the satellites had not picked up. He glanced over at the helicopters on hand and was glad to see he had Captain Andy Salsby, and his flight of four Apaches still on standby. He would have them ready to go if B Company ran into trouble, plus Bagram could launch its alert aircraft to assist.

He walked out into the office area and told the RTO, a new sergeant he had trouble remembering the name of, and ordered him to locate Captain Salsby. "He's down where the Apaches are parked. Send a runner down; I need him up here as soon as possible. Then get me Division on the satellite phone—I need to talk with the duty officer."

Bill turned to go back into his office then remembered he had another need and advised the RTO, "Locate the Chief, over at B Company's area, and ask him to come here."

"Yes, sir."

When the Chief showed up, Bill led him outside and said, "I've got new orders—let's take a walk."

After hearing about his new assignment, Chief asked, "Sir, why are we patrolling Uzbekistan's border? Isn't this an assignment for the Afghan Army or even our own infantry? I know the order has already been given, but between you and me, this sure doesn't sound like an assignment for the Airborne to handle. Do you think the General suspects we're actually facing an imminent threat from this country?"

"Chief, I've just told you everything I know, but yes, I do have thoughts racing through my head. Apparently, someone in command is concerned, and that's why we were given this order. The company belongs to you now, but all those men belong to my battalion. I don't want them being used just to show someone that we're prepared—for whatever. But it's orders, and you've been in this man's army long enough to know we get assigned some shitty details. The General, I feel is the one who put this together, with our Colonel Rogers doing the planning. He knows that if push comes to shove, the Afghan Army couldn't handle this assignment. I imagine they want us up there to see if the Russians or Chinese are sending any patrols over that border. If so, you'll be up there to prove that theory.

One long hike and you get picked up and brought back here. It'll probably take you about seven to eight days, maybe a bit longer if you find anything. Those Apaches will be in the air the minute you call for support and fighters coming your way from Bagram. Make sure you have your colored panels, and I'll keep two of those birds on combat standby and a couple of Blackhawks if you have any wounded men. You have 20 hours to get your people ready for this op."

"Sir, we'll get it done!" Chief turned and hurried off to prepare his men.

Bill had not told Chief that a new highly classified report, marked for his eyes only, showed that some 30 Russian special operatives were said to be just across the Afghan border inside Uzbekistan. It was believed the Russians were training local mountain tribes to conduct raids deep into Afghanistan. It did not say whether or not these Russian operatives would be escorting tribesmen when they crossed that international border. Bill knew the Chief would love to bag some of those Russians if they were trespassing.

Bill was authorized to advise the Chief of this intelligence just prior to his departure. When, and if, these foreign patrols were observed, they could not engage them unless fired upon first. If a firefight did happen and any Russians were sighted or taken prisoner, they would be identified in code as 'Martians' when relaying information back to HQ, a word Russian or Chinese officers would not be using over the radio. It always struck Bill funny when Intel used such idiotic names for such things. But often, they worked.

If this report is right and the Russians are training these people, it might make sense for the Taliban to have moved north to meet with them. We've lost sight of them and have failed to find any in this immediate area. Supposedly this area was a stronghold; that's why we're here. But we haven't had a single sighting. Uzbekistan is close, and there hasn't been any border patrol to speak of. Our troops have avoided the northern border before now to keep the

Russians from growing concerned. Now, with us even closer, we may have kicked over the proverbial beehive. Chief might spot a Russian patrol, that'll really stir things up back at Division. I should be leading this; Chief's getting too old for this but I'm in command, and I'm stuck here! Damn it! Bill did not often use profanity; he was raised in a home where cuss words were for weak-minded people. His mouth was washed out with liquid soap on those occasions he slipped. However, being in a war zone, Bill was starting to slip and he did not want it to become a natural part of conversations. Kitty disliked it as she didn't want her children raised with such language.

The next day, Bill saw B Company off as they boarded Chinooks for the flight north. He had given Chief the new Intel in a quick briefing concerning possible Russian or Chinese involvement. The Chief only nodded. This told Bill that the Chief had already considered this. Saluting his men, Bill stood back and watched as his old company flew off, leaving their former company commander feeling like he had just said goodbye to an old and dear friend.

Except for patrols, the rest of the battalion kept busy with routine duties and maintaining a high alert on the perimeter positions. Bill stood by in operations, monitoring the radio as B Company was dropped off and disappeared into the low hills at the border. Within the hour, the Chief contacted Battalion via satellite phone to report they were moving across their assigned 70-mile stretch of border. Having nothing more to report, he signed off, then directed his men west, using old goat trails and narrow canyons to make their way. For the first two days of patrol, B Company did not lay eyes on a soul, their reports to Battalion were routine.

During the third day, the forward squad leader walked behind an EOD soldier on loan for this operation. A metal detector probed the ground in front of him at all times, searching for IEDs and other explosives. Every troop behind them walked lightly, knowing that the man might miss something, or the device might not have picked it up. The silence was crucial to survival in this unknown area, so the men refrained from talking, using only hand signals. During daytime, only the occasional mountain goat was sighted in the distance, but they kept alert for snakes and other desert critters that came with a sting or bite. The men were ready to find something—anything to break the tension.

At night, they huddled together over cold meals as no fires were allowed and went on a 50-50 watch. Some men reported hearing what they thought to be night birds out looking for a meal. With the onset of colder temperatures ahead of winter the wild mountain goats were growing thick coats of wool, and fewer desert critters were out and about. When the winds came up, the wind chill factors quickly approached zero. Several times the men had to seek shelter when the wind velocity became dangerous.

These men had learned to appreciate the mountains and stone foothills where it was much harder to leave a mine or set a trap. Down on the flats, 30 Taliban could conceal themselves in a hole or a dry riverbed, waiting to trap Americans. A sand-covered mat could cover a five-foot-deep hole, where a Taliban sniper could wait for hours in hopes the enemy walked by. As a result, the Americans had learned to tread carefully, always ready for the unpredictable. The seasoned men knew this and taught the lesson to the news guys.

Chief hoped they would encounter Russian advisors while on patrol preferably on the Afghanistan side. Temperatures plunged when the sun went down, and night fell. Chief could almost taste snow in the air—it was visible on the taller mountain. Chief hoped to be clear of this area before the snow came down to lower elevations.

During a break, Chief recalled reading the history of the Division's stand against the Germans during the Battle of the Bulge and Bastogne's siege. It was winter then too, and many good men died from frostbite. In World War II, very few people knew about hypothermia. A harsh winter storm prevented air cover from coming in to support the Americans in that historic battle. He didn't want that same thing to happen here, knowing his troops were not prepared for freezing temperatures, ice, and snow, and without air cover, this 70-mile patrol could end up being a death march.

Each night seemed colder than the last so with no fire for warmth when the sun went down, the men, when possible, snuggled together in an attempt to stay warm. By the fifth day, Chief began to feel he was getting too old for this. He was not getting much sleep.

Bill signed off after receiving his latest security check from B Company. Chief had reported movement in the west, but it ended up being a small caravan of Afghan people on the way to Kabul. "One of the local mountain tribes, taking the last run to get supplies before the winter snow sealed the passes up here... Over."

"Copy, did they say anything about Taliban or Russians moving about in their area? Over." Bill asked.

"Janke spoke with them for a bit, and we shared some of our rations with them to get them to talk. The old man in charge said there are Taliban in the area, but their force numbered less than 30. As for Russians, he wouldn't own up to it, but he looked nervous when I asked... Over."

"Copy, what's the weather like? Over."

"Getting damn cold here at night, expect snow any time, and we're not equipped for that. Unable to have fires due to security... Over."

"Copy, I've contacted Division about cold weather clothing, and they're working on it. I know that doesn't do you any good right now. How far did you make it today? Over."

"See if Division has any of those Alaska native scouts; they'd love it up here. Only made about eight miles today, rough going. About halfway; we've sustained half a dozen minor injuries from slippery rocks. Can't use the trail the caravan used because it goes up deeper into the hills and would put us too close to the border... Over."

"Roger on that, have your RTO check in every two hours. Good luck... Out."

Bill looked over at Roman, "Whoever thought this up ought to be up there with our men, freezing their butts off. Planners and Intel personnel should spend some time in the field before they come up with their big ideas. Make sure your relief wakes me up if shit hits the fan... Okay?"

"Will do, sir," Roman replied and watched as his concerned commander left to inspect perimeter positions.

Several men took turns scrubbing skivvies and fatigues and hung everything up on one of the half-a-dozen clotheslines made from parachute cord, comm cable, or razor wire which could rip it to shreds. During hours of darkness, parachute cord and comm cable lengths strung between tents could often make passing through this area a risky proposition. Within an hour of work, a soldier could be finished with laundry duties. Some, who had been wearing the same underwear for the last five days, simply discarded them into the burn barrel.

After completing his inspection, Bill called Division on the satellite phone to discuss B Company's weather problems. Like Bill, the Colonel was concerned about the cold and his men not being better prepared for it. The Colonel was quick to make a decision, "Advise them that if temps continue to drop, they are to discontinue the patrol and move back to the flats. We'll get them airlifted out and returned to your location. I'll advise the General of the problem, but until then, get them moving at daylight. Now, what about your area?"

"Colonel, I have two patrols out keeping an eye out for Taliban or ISIS units moving about. I suspect they're attempting to find a way past us, as we seem to have caught them by surprise with this operation. Otherwise, there is nothing new to report except the men could use some decent chow."

"I'll call up either McDonald's or Burger King and see if they deliver. Tell them to quit complaining, or I'll dig up some old World II K-rations for them to dine on. But let them know I'm proud of them. I'll see what I can do about putting a rush on a field kitchen. I actually expected it to be out there by now. How are your supplies?"

"Plenty of MREs, enough to last another eight to nine days, but could use some more water."

"I'll get you some more water trailers out there tomorrow. Make sure those pilots bring back the empty ones, or I'll start charging them a deposit fee. You might tell your men to start digging a well, give them something to do, it'll keep their minds off the chow. They might just hit one of those legendary underground rivers and save Uncle Sam a fortune constructing a water pipeline from here. We'll have to make it underground to keep the Taliban from blowing it up all the time."

"We'll get right on that, sir," Bill signed off and handed the phone back to Roman.

Roman took the phone and as he changed the battery asked, "Captain, why does knowing about these Russians change anything? We already know they're supplying the Taliban; we've taken a couple of them prisoner. Far as I know, it's been that way since Vietnam. They, and the Chinese, help one side, while we and our allies help the other bunch. It's nothing new."

Bill gave Roman his view, "This screwy mess goes way above my pay grade, but you're right, and it began before Vietnam. Started with Korea, with the Chinese helping the North Koreans, and then invading South Korea with over 800,000 Chinese troops. They thought General MacArthur was planning to invade China, so they invaded first, and for a while, it looked like we were about to lose South Korea. China's been doing it ever since and during World War II, they were our ally. Then the Communist Party took over, and China—well, the big question is, how long are we going to put up with this? Do we continue to turn a blind eye to what Russia and China are doing for the Taliban and ISIS? Seems to me we keep playing this same game repeatedly, letting out a little steam here and there just to keep from having a nuclear war. Our people and the locals here keep dying. Now we're having problems with Syria, and that's one place I do not want to go. From what I've read, the Syrians have no problem using chemical weapons, and at the moment, we're not equipped to handle that out here.

"Can you imagine trying to fight a battle in 100-degree heat while wearing those rubberized chemical suits? We'd die just from that. But being Airborne, we will continue to be the point of the spear and go where we're told."

"Captain, maybe you should pull the pin and look into politics; you'll have my vote."

"Sergeant Roman, that almost borders on sacrilege—perish the thought. I'd rather teach a class of first graders than enter into that quagmire—politics! Go wash your mouth out with soap!"

Roman laughed and updated his log adding Bill's contact with B Company and subsequent chat with the Colonel.

FIREFIGHT AT PRE-DAWN

2ND Lieutenant David Daniels, commanding B Company's 3rd Platoon called in over the radio with a hurried voice, reporting a Taliban patrol of about 20 or so insurgents. They had stumbled right into their scout patrol in a narrow valley, and shots were exchanged. He reported that two of his men had been wounded.

B Company's three-man point element had surprised them; the Taliban still had rifles slung over their shoulders. An enemy support squad moved in and pulled their men out. Daniels moved two squads up to higher ground, and their weapons fire forced the Taliban unit into a full retreat. Within minutes, the squads had decimated the fleeing enemy patrol. A search of the area revealed five dead and two severely wounded Taliban. Those two prisoners ended up dying from their wounds. Daniels requested a medivac for his two wounded men, both with crippling but non-life-threatening wounds. One man had taken a bullet to his upper left shoulder, and the other man took a bullet to his right leg.

Bill ordered the medivac flight and requested two of their assigned Apaches to escort the Blackhawk. It took a bit of time, but a squad of troops carried the wounded men down from the hills to meet the Black-hawk. Once the helicopter was in the air, the two Apaches, with Captain Salsby in command, and Lt. Daniels flying in the second bird, swept low over the hills and quickly discovered the fleeing Taliban. Snow clouds were rapidly moving in, and the Apaches could only make a single strafing run on the enemy. Mini-gun fire and rockets impacted all around the Taliban, and Captain Salsby knew they had caused numerous casual-ties among them. The quickly moving snowstorm forced the Apaches to break off, and they soon caught up with the Blackhawk. Captain Salsby advised Bill of their brief action and requested permission to escort the Blackhawk back to Bagram. This would give them a chance to refuel and rearm from Bagram's stockpiles and not make use of the limited supply on hand at Camel Rider North. Bill granted him permission and sent a runner to advise the two remaining Apache crews that they were now on combat standby.

Chief radioed in and advised Bill that it was starting to snow heavily, "Temps are already in the low 20s. Request permission to withdraw from these hills before we get snowed in... Over."

"Affirmative. I'll have Chinooks waiting for you at the foot of those hills... Over."

"Copy, standing by," Chief told his men to be prepared to move out and had his RTO contact the other patrols and advised them to fall back to the company.

Bill contacted Division on the satellite phone and advised the Colonel of the attack and the severe weather moving in. The Colonel added his support to Bill's decision to pull the unit out. "I've just been handed a new weather report; it looks like you should see snow in your area by tomorrow, with temps dropping down into the teens. I'll contact supply and order up extra winter gear and blankets for your people. Call me back if B Company has any other problems."

Chief clapped his hand on his RTO's shoulder and walked over to where Janke was cuddled up with a blanket. The First Platoon had dug down nearly two feet to provide adequate protection from possible enemy rockets and grenades. The cold ground had made for tough digging. Numerous times the men transformed their shovels into pick-axes to break ground.

"Looks like we're heading out of here as soon as everyone returns. Going back the quick way, we should make it to the desert within a couple of hours. Choppers are on the way, and they'll be waiting for us."

"Will be good to be warm again. My body does not like this mountain air." Janke responded.

"I know how you feel; I'm feeling a bit stove-up, myself."

Radio identification for the 4th Provisional Battalion was adjusted to include the new base. 4th Battalion headquarters originally Eagle Base was now officially known as Camel Rider North. Eagle One still referred to Lt. Colonel Rogers who remained at Bagram, and Bill kept his Eagle Two designation. Around camp, Camel Rider was simply known as "The FOB", or "Foxtrot Oscar Bravo" on the radio.

Chief, M-4 hanging at his side and helmet unfastened and tilted to the right side, frowned as snow drifted down to cover the surrounding hills. He hoped that wearing his helmet in such a relaxed manner gave his men reassurance that everything was all right, *no sweat, guys, all is good.*

"Chief, I've got Camel Rider on the radio; Eagle Two wants to talk with you," the RTO said as he handed the headset and microphone to the Chief.

"This is Eagle Four; go ahead Eagle Two...Over."

"Be advised, birds are in the air. Contact me when you hit the desert and provide your coordinates for pick up. Also, be sure to put out air panels with today's color, or you'll have a long walk back... Over."

"Eagle Four copies. Leaving now, estimate three to four hours to get out of these hills. Snow really coming down—will contact you when we hit desert... Over."

"Eagle Two copies... Over and Out!" Bill handed the radio back to Roman. "I'll be just outside if you need me." He walked out, hoping for a quiet moment to pray for his men's safety as they withdrew from the hills. He also prayed that this foul weather would hold off from hitting the flatlands. He knew the snow was coming too soon, but Bill wanted all his men back before winter came to Camel Rider North. He had been through one Afghan winter and was not looking forward to another. *We had to medivac out over a dozen men during that winter due to frostbite and another half a dozen to pneumonia. This might be desert country, but it's a high desert, and it gets damn cold here, and then the snow comes.*

Even with gloves on, Chief could feel his hands getting colder. He had frostbitten them during a Black Op mission to the northern border region in South Korea years before. The cold stung his ears and cheeks as snow began to fall and a slight breeze quickly became a stiff wind. It would a bitter cold hike down to the valley floor as the two scouts moved out to lead the procession. The lead squad fell in behind them followed quickly by the remainder of B Company. It was slow going because of the foul weather and slippery rocks.

A little over two hours later, Chief notified Camel Rider North that B Company was descending the last slope, gave his coordinates, and requested transport. Bill had Roman advise them that four Chinooks, with Apache escort, were close by. Though it was snowing lightly, the Chief advised Bill that it was still acceptable flying weather as long as the birds stayed below 500 feet. Chief knew that if this thick cloud cover got any lower, the men of B Company would have to continue hiking until there was a break in the weather.

TAKING FIRE!

Flying escort for the four Chinooks, 1st Lieutenant Andie Sharpe was 45 minutes north of Camel Rider when she started taking enemy fire from the ground. A string of rounds struck the chopper's fuselage. She banked her bird to the left and brought it up almost to the safety ceiling of 500 feet.

"Little Bird to Papa Bird, I've taken ground fire—probably from an AK-47—no injuries and no apparent damage to flight systems. We are staying with you... Over."

"Little Bird, continue on with those mother hens while I check to see where the visiting team is. You should be at the pick-up point in about 15 minutes or so. Be sure to look for panels before we send these hens in for pick-up... Over."

"Roger that, Papa Bird... Out!" Sharpe had already checked with her weapon's officer to ensure he was not hit and, for the tenth time in the last few minutes, checked over her control systems.

"Papa Bird to Mother Hens, recommend you climb to 500 feet. Little Bird has taken fire from below, I'm going to fall back and see if it was a lone scout or if we have other visitors to be concerned with. Catch up with you in a moment... Papa Bird out." Captain Salsby advised his own weapon's officer what he was doing and made a quick banking maneuver to the right while dropping to nearly 35 feet above ground. Though he expected ground fire, he didn't receive any.

The voice of the Major flying the lead Chinook came over the radio. "This is Mother Hen One, be advised I don't like that dark ceiling above us and will remain at 200 feet with my other hens. Remember, Papa Bird, I'm commanding this mission—not you... Out!"

"You idiot!" Salsby said aloud with the radio mic off and added a few profane words that made his weapon's officer smile. They had met this major for the first time only a couple of hours before and the four Apache crewmen had taken an immediate dislike to him. He was a newly promoted Chinook pilot, newly arrived from Germany, thought very highly of himself, and was quick to let others know it.

Unable to find the shooter, Captain Salsby returned to the Chinooks and assumed a tail-end Charlie position behind the 4th Chinook. He advised Lt. Daniels that he could not locate the shooter who had marked up Sharpes' bird. The lead Chinook landed 12 minutes later, directed down by one man waving his arms about. The Big Bird sank through one inch of fresh snow and five inches of sand. Once the Major brought the rotor speed down to idle, the Chinook's back door was opened, and a platoon of near-frozen troops rushed in.

The Platoon Commander advised the crew chief, "We're taking sniper fire; tell your pilot to get us airborne and advise those other birds to keep those rotors turning."

The crew chief advised the major, who suddenly jerked to his left as a single bullet pierced the window and entered the side of his seat, missing him by a mere inch. "Get those men loaded ASAP; we're taking fire! I've got to lift off—now!" He advised his crew to prepare for immediate take-off.

Thankfully, the men were aboard, but the pilot, in his rush to leave the area, lifted off and came dangerously close to clipping rotors with Captain Salsby, forcing the captain to take evasive action to avoid impact. "This is Papa Bird... Mother Hen One; you almost hit me! Climb to 500 feet and head to Camel Rider One; we will engage the enemy to cover your other hens!" *God, what a fool! he nearly killed us trying a fool maneuver like that!* "Get those birds in and out fast while we cover you— no one gets left behind. You copy me, Mother Hen One? Over." He didn't bother to wait for a reply but radioed the Chief, "Eagle Four, this is Papa Bird, can you see that shooter? Over."

"Negative, there's more than one—at least a couple of AK-47s on full auto. They must be in those rocks to our north, about 100-yards... Over."

Lt. Sharpe broke in, "Papa Bird, this is Little Bird; I can see three shooters to my north. We are engaging... Out!" She advised her weapons officer to prepare to engage. "Light 'em up; we need to keep those men safe."

"Copy," the weapons officer replied, and fired his mini-gun, then launched a single air-to-ground rocket from his left pod. Within seconds, the three shooters were silenced, and a cloud of dark smoke rose up from the ground.

"Be advised, Little Bird has taken out the target but will continue searching for others until hens are clear... Over."

"Good job, Little Bird—you go right, and I'll turn left and see if there's anyone else in the area. Keep low and move fast, you've already got a string of holes in your aircraft, and you do not need anymore... Out!"

B Company soldiers hustled aboard the three remaining Chinooks as the Chief remained outside the last bird until the last of his men dashed aboard. Janke already aboard, shoved the pistol that Bill had given him into his backpack. As he dropped into his jump seat, he asked one of the soldiers sitting beside him if he could share his canteen and took a large gulp to steady his nerves. He thought seriously of returning to the college campus and teaching again, preferring rowdy college students to facing the Taliban, and going on long, cold hikes in the mountains.

The two Apaches patrolled at different elevations and speeds while keeping an eye on one another. Meanwhile, the four Chinooks climbed to near 500 feet and quickly headed south with four loads of weary and relieved combat troops.

Flying lead, the Major glanced back at the bullet hole in his seat. *I'll need to get a photograph of that when we land, be something to show in the Officer Club back at Bagram.* As he scanned his control panel; his co-pilot's head exploded showering him with blood and body debris. There were large bullet holes high up in the side glass windows.

The co-pilot was killed by a Russian-made four-barrel, quad, .51 caliber machine gun, which the Taliban often carried atop a two-wheeled handcart. The weapon and the shooters had been camouflaged beneath snow-covered tarps and gone unnoticed until it opened fire. After firing the heavy machine gun, the Taliban noticed the Apaches preparing to dive on their position.

"Little Bird to Papa Bird, lead Mother Hen taking fire! I'm now engaging what appears to be a heavy caliber machine gun—have eyes on two figures—oh God! There are black plumes of smoke coming from the Chinook's forward engine compartment! I'm taking action now!"

"I'll be right behind you, Little Bird—give them hell!"

"I've got the Taliban weapon spotted—looks like a quad-51—must've been camouflaged when we flew by earlier."

"Take it out, Little Bird—I'll follow for a second run on that target."

Captain Salsby switched frequencies and contacted Camel Rider One and advised them that Mother Hen One had taken ground fire and was trailing black smoke. "Be advised we are now engaging the target. Get grounds crews ready for a burning bird with possible wounded on board... Out!"

Roman sent a runner for Bill and continued monitoring the radio.

Struggling to ignore his dead co-pilot and learning he had several wounded from the attack, the Major decided to abandon the landing at Camel Rider North and head straight for Bagram. He knew 4th Battalion had only a small field hospital and hoped his wounded bird would make the flight. The radio still functioned, so he notified the other pilots of his decision. "Mother Hens one, two, and three continue to the FOB: I'm heading for Bagram with wounded. I'll alert the tower we're in route with wounded. She seems to be handling, but the engine is heating up— be safe and get those men back... Out!" He switched frequencies, contacted Bagram, and advised them of his situation.

Busy with the Taliban, Salsby and Daniels overheard most of the Major's call to Bagram's Control Tower, "...taken enemy fire, northeast of Camel Rider North... My co-pilot is K-I-A! Some controls are jammed... I've got wounded on board and request multiple ambulances and fire department to respond as I'm coming in hot."

Salsby was amazed by how controlled the Major was, keeping his voice level and understandable. He was genuinely impressed with the man. Salsby changed to the Apache intercom system and contacted Sharpe. Once he confirmed she had heard the Major's transmission, he ordered, "Turn it around, Lieutenant and remember that Russian gun has a lot of distance. They were built primarily as anti-aircraft. They may also have support troops in the area. I want you to ride the sand waves and come in from the west. I suspect that big gun is three miles south-southwest of us. I'm going to stray to the east and make my run from the north to south-southeast. Let me hit them first, and you mop it up... Over."

As Sharpe came up, she spotted the wounded Chinook and warned the Major, "Mother Hen One, you're smoking heavily You may need to land before—" She stopped her gun run to do a quick fly-by and saw that the Chinook had multiple good-sized holes in both engine cowlings and the bird's body.

"You are on fire, Mother Hen One—I see flames! Take it down, Major —I repeat, I see flames—take it down!"

"Right... I copy you, Little Bird—my controls are no good, so I'm trying to stop the flow of fuel to the engines to effect an auto-rotate. Heading for the ground now!" The major yelled into his headset, "Prepare for crash landing—I repeat—prepare for crash landing—we're goin' to hit hard!"

"Where are you hit, Major?" The crew chief asked as he rushed forward.

"Not me—him!" The crew Chief saw what was left of the co-pilot and immediately upchucked.

The major yelled, "Grab ahold of something; we're goin' in!"

With a reputation to be a very survivable helicopter, the Chinook flew at a slow speed, rapidly descending, until it dropped suddenly from 40 feet. The dying bird swung nose first into a long sloping pile of sand and rocks. It hit hard and began to roll with everyone inside strapped down; loud screams and shouts came from the back as the bird settled.

The Major was held in place by his seat straps, his eyes closed as sand burst through the broken windshield, nearly burying him and his co-pilot. He shrieked violently, frightened he was about to be smothered by sand. Suddenly a severe pain pierced his back, he felt as if an icepick had been driven into his spine. Almost immediately, he lost consciousness, his hands still tightly grasped around his controls.

Several of the troops in back were tossed out of their restraints as the Chinook rolled down the embankment. Men were hurled into one another, crying out as the helicopter continued to slide. It collided with a rocky ledge and came to an abrupt stop. The two sets of rotors were broken off at different lengths. Nearly all the glass windows were broken out or cracked. The bird's portable bathroom's putrid smell began as feces and urine burst outward to hit several of the men.

The dizzy crew chief suspected the fuel tanks had ruptured, and fuel was probably flowing into the sand. This also meant a potential fire, and he needed to get everyone out before the bird exploded. Though his head hurt from knocking against the wall of the helicopter, he went to work clearing sand away from the major, "Major, I've got the side door open, but the back door is broken, and without electricity, it won't open!"

"What?"

"Sir, I tried to pry on it, but it's a no-go—can you move, Major?"

BACK WITH THE APACHES

"Papa Bird, that target has been destroyed—do you copy?"

"Good job, Little Bird! Now move south, and let's find that downed bird. They'll need cover fire until another Chinook can get out here to pick up the troops."

Captain Salsby contacted both Bagram and Camel Rider North and advised them of the downed Chinook. Bill sent several armed Black-hawks and the two remaining Apaches to the crash site. Another Chinook was on the way from Bagram, advised to airlift the wounded back to Bagram, while the Blackhawks would carry the others back to the 4th Battalion.

The first medic reached the pilot and saw he could do nothing for the co-pilot, he turned to the Major, "Where are you hurt, sir?"

"My legs—my back—guess I... I was showered with shrapnel from my terrible landing job. Can't feel much of anything below my waist, but my head feels like I cracked my skull! How are the men in the back doing?" He passed out.

WITH THE 4TH BATTALION

Bill briefed the two rifle squads from A Company's 2nd Platoon and the men climbed aboard the waiting Blackhawks. The birds proceeded to the location of the downed Chinook lying on its side. These two squads were to provide ground support for removing the wounded and the other members of B Company. Those who were unhurt or suffering only minor injuries would be returned to their company and checked over by medics. When the Blackhawks arrived on the scene, one of the door gunners said to his pilot-in-command, "She looks like a dead whale that's been washed ashore—makes me want to be a ground pounder again."

"You keep talking like that, Corporal, and I might make that happen —we've got wounded and dead down there, so show some respect—now hold on, we're landing."

When the squad arrived on scene, they found everyone alive had either walked out on their own, crawled, or were carried out. Only the dead and senior pilot remained, and special care was needed to remove him. The medic briefed the others that it looked as if the pilot might be paralyzed, and no one said another word about the rough landing. While one of the pilots stayed with each of the birds, the two squads worked to get wounded men ready for the arriving Chinook. Meanwhile, the Apaches continued to circle the area, keeping alert for possible shooters. With the smoke of the downed bird rising to meet the thickening clouds coming in from the north, Captain Salsby knew any Taliban within 10 miles would see the smoke and head this way.

Nothing else happened; the rescue was accomplished without any problems. One Chinook had gone on to Bagram with wounded, while the other Chinooks landed safely at Camel Rider North. The Blackhawks and the Apaches were returning. It was determined the dead Chinook could not be recovered due to structural damage and was later struck with two bombs from an F-15 Eagle out of Bagram. They didn't wish to leave anything usable for the Taliban. Between the bombs and the fuel remaining on board, the helicopter disappeared in a massive blast.

The operation to remove B Company was over, the 4th Battalion waited for their next assignment.

At Bagram, the injured Chinook pilot was treated and once stabilized, flown to Germany for a series of surgeries and later flown back to the states where he was retired on 100% disability. Word had it he was planning to enter politics in his home state.

THE RETURN OF B COMPANY

Chief Johnson contacted the hospital at Bagram to get an update on his wounded men. There were 11 men in the hospital and another five listed as KIA. B Company had taken heavy losses since arriving in Afghanistan only four months earlier. The Chief was concerned they were riding a spell of bad luck.

A month later, bad weather and heavy snow brought relative quiet to the upper desert region; Captain Salsby was finally granted permission to take his four birds north to patrol along the border with Uzbekistan under strict orders to remain five miles inside the Afghan border. On a clear winter morning, the four Apaches took off and headed north. Their assignment was to work with an Air Force RC-135 Intel bird out of Germany, flying at over 30,000 feet and out of Stinger range. The RC-135 worked with American Intel satellites, with both taking a constant flow of photos of Afghanistan. From these photos, the US military gained hard evidence of Russian involvement, which would be used by the US Ambassador to Afghanistan against the Russian Government. Several heavily armored Russian T-35 tanks were photographed inside the Afghan border, over 15 miles inside Afghanistan's northern province. These big tanks required a lot of technology. Because of this, the United States military believed the Taliban were probably not driving them. They were stamped with a red star, which told onlookers these were not from Uzbekistan or Afghan armies. Closer shots by costly cameras on the hog-nosed RC-135s showed numerous white men wearing Russia's current military arctic wear. When confronted, Russia refused to admit to making an illegal entrance or accidental venture into Afghanistan.

"Perhaps that unit simply got lost," the Russian Ambassador to Afghanistan said when challenged. "Happens all the time; you're making too much of this!" The photographs were leaked to the press and created an embarrassing moment for President Putin, who ordered the removal of the tank units.

While flying northern patrol, Captain Salsby and his pilots spotted three separate patrols, two of which had the support of those same tanks. Salsby was ordered not to attack. When he and his crews showed themselves, the patrols changed direction and returned to the northern border.

HEADING HOME TO AMERICA

The long winter was over, and 4th Battalion prepared to head for Bagram. Their twelve-month deployment was at an end. Camel Rider North was taken over by a regiment of Army Infantry, supported by heavy artillery.

By the end of the mission, the 4th Provisional Battalion, about to be decommissioned, had sustained 27 men killed in action and 98 wounded. One Distinguished Service Cross, nine Silver Stars, 14 Bronze Stars for Valor, 312 Commendations, and 98 Purple Hearts were awarded to men of this command. Multiple promotions had come through; the newly promoted Major Warrens prepared to return to the states. RTO Jimmy Olsen received a well-deserved Silver Star and promotion to Sergeant First Class. He had also been wounded and received his third Purple Heart. The Chief was awarded the Distinguished Service Cross for his gallant actions against the Taliban while commanding B Company during the ill-fated patrol on the northern border. He announced his retirement upon returning to the states and planned to remarry his ex-wife and live in Wyoming, but they would stay in touch with Bill and Kitty.

Following a much-needed leave with his family, Bill returned to his troops and continued their training. He now awaited his next deployment. From what he had experienced in Afghanistan, Bill knew this war was far from over and he wanted his soldiers prepared for the Afghanistan desert.

AMEN

AFTERWORD

I sincerely hope you have enjoyed this series so far, which has covered over 60 years in the history of our gallant soldiers. From Vietnam to the troubles with the VA and PTSD, and the long war in Afghanistan, our beloved country has been well-served by valiant troops from our Army, Air Force, Marines, Navy, and National Guard.

In the first book, Apache Snow, I selected the 101st Airborne Division because of its direct involvement in Vietnam. They fought one of the most historic battles of that 10-year war, "Operation Apache Snow" often remembered as "Hamburger Hill".

In the second book, "In Search of Honor," I tried to show the side of the wounded and disabled veterans inside a fictitious VA hospital in Los Angeles. I used a former member of the 101st to show the problems these men and women weather almost daily, and the effects of Post Traumatic Stress Disorder. I suffer from a small degree of PTSD, which, in my case, produced alcoholism and terrible nightmares. Only with the help of a loving wife, my family's support, and very importantly, my walk with the Lord Jesus Christ, I now live an exciting life here in rural Alaska. This is my 43rd year in the north country, and it's truly a beautiful and free land.

For this third book, "Sandbox Wars," I picked the Afghan War due to my sons and sons-in-law, who served in Iraq and Afghanistan. Thankfully, they all survived, but some have come home with PTSD. This story took place in 2014, and as of 2021, At the time I wrote this book, there were still troops in both Iraq and Afghanistan, with the war lasting twice as long as our involvement in Vietnam. I recall when many of our politicians shouted out back in 1973, "No more Vietnams!" promising it would never happen again. I decided to write a fourth book in this series covering the 2021 withdrawal of our forces in Afghanistan so look for Major Bill Warrens to return.

The goal of this series is to tell of the Christians who fought overseas or did battle back here in the states with PTSD and other disabilities. Many would fall away from God, while others would come to the Lord. There were too many men and women who never come back, and we miss them.

Sincerely,
William L. Casselman

ABOUT THE AUTHOR

William Casselman was raised in Southern California. He enlisted in the U.S. Air Force in 1971 to become a Law Enforcement Specialist/Military Working Dog Handler. He served the next ten years in the military and met his lovely wife, Mona Sue, at Eielson AFB, Alaska.

A Vietnam veteran, he left the service to become a police officer in Dillingham, Alaska, and spent the next twenty years in Alaskan police work. From patrolman to investigator, he has worked with four police departments and was the Public Safety Director for the City of Whittier during the tragic Exxon Oil Spill in Prince William Sound in 1989.

William, a 42-year Christian, retired as Senior Investigator for the State of Alaska gaming program. With 44 years in Alaska, he has six children and seventeen grandchildren, and great-grandchildren.

William and his wife, Mona Sue now live in rural Alaska.

Also by Alaska Dreams Publishing
Please visit www.alaskadp.com to see these titles:

By William Casselman:
Alaska Freedom Brigade | Rookie | Apache Snow | In Search of Honor | The Six Book Revelation Series | Legend of Silene | Blake's War

Titles by other ADP authors:
Inspiring Special Needs Stories | My Life In The Wilderness | All Over The Road | Ghost Cave Mountain | Inside the Circle | The Silver Horn of Robin Hood | Alaskan Troll Eggs | Through My Eyes | The Professional Ghost Investigator | The Adventures of Jason and Bo | Seeds Of The Pirate Rebels

The Alaska Off Grid Survival Series by Miles Martin:
Going Wild | Gone Wild | Still Wild | Beyond Wild | Back To Wild | Surviving Wild | Secretly Wild | Retiring Wild